IT STARTED WITH A KISS

LISA HOBMAN

Boldwood

This edition published in Great Britain in 2022 by Boldwood Books Ltd.

Cover Design by Alice Moore Design

Cover Photography: Shutterstock

A CIP catalogue record for this book is available from the British Library.

Paperback ISBN 978-1-80280-230-6

Large Print ISBN 978-1-80280-229-0

Hardback ISBN 978-1-80415-983-5

Ebook ISBN 978-1-80280-232-0

Kindle ISBN 978-1-80280-231-3

Audio CD ISBN 978-1-80280-224-5

MP3 CD ISBN 978-1-80280-225-2

Digital audio download ISBN 978-1-80280-228-3

Boldwood Books Ltd
23 Bowerdean Street
London SW6 3TN
www.boldwoodbooks.com

PROLOGUE
FIN

You know that feeling you get when you know everything in your life is just about to go belly up? Yeah? Well, I had it in bucket loads. The *really* stupid thing was, *if* I had listened to my gut and backed out before it got to that particular point, I wouldn't have been standing in the most embarrassing situation ever. A situation I didn't even *want* to be in.

But no.

Like the spineless moron I'd become, I stood there at the altar, waiting for her.

When it got to forty-five minutes after the time she *should*'ve arrived and no one had been able to contact her—not even her own family—I got it.

I'd been jilted.

1

FIN

Until recently, in all my twenty-seven years, I've always done the right thing. At least I've tried to. Finlay Hunter—the blue-eyed boy—both literally *and* figuratively speaking. Never putting a foot out of line but somehow, when it comes to my father, still never good enough.

Having grown up in a very wealthy family, the younger of two sons, I've strived to be the perfect prodigy. My brother was an overachiever and had already made my parents proud by qualifying as a GP and becoming a partner in his own surgery. It wasn't exactly what my parents wanted for him initially but as he saved people's lives they forgave him for not going into law. So, it was down to me to follow in my father's footsteps and continue the family business. Therefore, taking my degree in law had been part of *the plan*. Notice how I didn't say *my* plan? My degree had afforded me a great education and good friends, but not a choice of career. I would've been working for the family business in some capacity regardless. A serious case of nepotism.

A St Andrews University degree was seen by my family as a status symbol. '*The Royals study there, don't you know*? *If it's good enough for them...*' A famous phrase often repeated at me by my dad.

I worked my arse off for my qualifications, and it was no bloody picnic, but at the end of the day, to my father, it was simply a necessary piece of paper he could wave under the noses of his corporate cronies. Like I said, a status symbol.

My father, Campbell Hunter, is a senior partner in Hunter Drummond Law, based in the magnificent city of Edinburgh. A high-flyer, you might say, and since a very young age, I too was encouraged to do well, to prosper. My father doesn't suffer fools and ours was never really a relationship based on what you could call out and out love. I know he loves me.

Or at least I think he does. He just never shows it, not really. Never has. Dad is a great believer in keeping emotions in check. *'No one likes a cry-baby, Finlay,'* was another of his favourite phrases, and so I learned to keep my thoughts, feelings, and emotions to myself. It explains a lot.

Dad wasn't the kind of guy to play footy on a Sunday with my brother and me. We were both sent to boarding school, and when we were home for holidays, he was always working, so we spent our time with the housekeeper, Henrietta—or Hetty—as Callum and I called her. We didn't mind at the time because she was great fun. She had awesome taste in music and would smuggle CDs in for me of bands she thought I'd like. I can categorically say that my fantasies of being a rock star stemmed from Hetty.

You may be wondering what of my mother? Where do I start? Isobel Hunter was like a WAG; a footballer's wife of her day. In her teens, she'd been a fashion model with high society aspirations. She too was from a wealthy family, but it was her looks that propelled her forward. She's beautiful. Tall, with blonde hair and blue eyes, like my brother and me.

Once she married Dad, she gave up her modelling career and spent her time hosting dinner parties and adding to her ridiculous shoe collection. In all honesty, she was never cut out to be a mother, and regardless of how I tried to get her attention, I usually ended up feeling like an inconvenience. It's my guess that she would have remained childless if she had met anyone but my father. You see, he's of the old 'keep the family line going' generation, and I'm pretty sure the fact that he had male children was a bonus for him. Shame he never showed it. So in stepped Hetty. And I, for one, will be eternally grateful for her compassion and care.

My older brother, Callum, was the opinionated one. From an early age he rebelled, insisting he would choose his own path in life. He said that law looked boring and he couldn't imagine being a stuffed suit, shouting at other stuffed suits in a courtroom until the loudest suit won. Mind you, he'd argue black was white and up was down if he thought it would get a rise out of Dad, and there was always some feud going on between them. They were far too alike; two strong-willed alpha male characters vying for dominance over each other and neither willing to back down. It was due to *this* reason that I took it upon myself to be the *better* son. The compliant one. All I wanted was for Dad to be proud of me. But looking back, even when I graduated with a first, he didn't *tell* me he was proud of me. Instead, he bought me a new sports car and told me I was expected at the firm the following week to begin work.

That was over four years ago.

* * *

I suppose I should tell you about my fiancée. Or should I say *ex*-fiancée.

Elise Drummond is the daughter of Eoin Drummond, my father's partner at the law firm. She and I were kind of thrust together as teenagers. It was clear right at the start what our parents' intent was. She was sweet and pretty. Long dark hair, almost black, in fact, and bright green eyes. But she was quite thin. Now, I don't intend to 'thin shame' her by mentioning that. I just prefer women with curves in all the right places, if you get my meaning. Elise didn't have curves to speak of. But she was... well... nice enough.

When we were twenty, we started dating—another contrived setup by our respective parents. You'd think in 21st century Britain there would be no such thing as arranged marriage, but in a roundabout way, that's what we were being 'guided' into. We both silently acquiesced without protest, neither of us wanting to rock the proverbial boat. I grew fond of her if I'm honest, and for a long while, she was my best friend. I could talk to her about almost anything. I say *almost* because there were things I couldn't say to her because they'd no doubt get back to my dad, via hers. Things like the fact that I felt trapped, that it appeared my life was mapped out for me and I had no say. Deep down, I was sure she felt the same way, but neither of us broached the subject, and so life went on.

She too worked for the family firm, which left us with little to talk about apart from our respective cases at the office. And that was it. Our tastes in just about everything were completely different. I loved rock music, but she couldn't stand it. I loved art, but she preferred plain walls. She loved to travel, but I was a home body. They say opposites attract, but we were more 'opposites thrown together for the greater good'.

Only it wasn't *our* greater good.

We moved in together aged twenty-two, just after leaving uni. The vast apartment was in a stunning area of Edinburgh in an old Victorian building, and Elise chose all the furnishings. But, of course, between the four of them our parents paid for pretty much everything.

The only things I contributed to my new home were some photographs I'd bought from a little craft shop in the city. The photographer, simply known as S.A.M, had captured a totally different side of Edinburgh. He or she had made it look somehow ethereal with the light and the glow to the prints. I loved them. Elise wasn't keen, but I put them up anyway. I think we had got to the point of living on the path of least resistance, never mind just venturing down it.

Our relationship had been chaste up to moving in together, and rather embarrassingly, we were both virgins until then. In my defence, my upbringing and schooling hadn't allowed the allotted time for rebellion that most teens get. There were no wild, alcohol-fuelled parties, no one night stands, and no strip clubs. I guess I'd led a pretty sheltered life, but thankfully, so had Elise. Realistically speaking, we'd been promised to one another since before university. It had been a kind of unspoken agreement between our parents that just added to my feeling of being a puppet in someone else's theatre.

2

STAR

My dad's parents were Spanish but my dad was born in the US. My mom was born in Scotland, like her own parents, but they moved to the US when my mom was tiny for Grandpa Gordon's work. When my Grandma and Grandpa returned home to Scotland my newly married folks went to live there for six months, and I was born while they were there. My Grandpa called me his little Star and the name apparently stuck. I remember nothing at all of my brief time as a UK citizen as Mom and Dad moved back to the US soon after I came into the world. Why am I telling you this? Simply because it explains the origins of my fascination with all things Scottish.

I grew up in Fort Wayne, Indiana—Midwest USA —But after my grandpa Gordon passed away when I was eight we visited my grandma Agnes, aka Aggie, in Edinburgh to attend the funeral. Being there again, in the place I was born, did something to me. Something fundamental. And even back then at my tender age I decided I'd return again someday.

It wasn't that I hated my hometown or anything like that. It was simply that Scotland, Edinburgh in particular, had a kind of pull for me. We had this mystical fairy-tale connection you read about in books, and once it took hold it wouldn't let me go. I read every story I could find that was set in Scotland, from Walter Scott novels to the poems of Robert Burns. I learned all about the heartrending story of a little dog called Greyfriars's Bobby and how he had a monument by the cemetery he was known to stay by and guard the grave of his owner.

Of all the stories that gripped me, it was Muriel Spark's *The Prime of Miss Jean Brodie* that didn't let me go. Set in Edinburgh and with a strong-willed female at the heart of it, the book *sparked* something inside of me, and that was it. I was hooked. Edinburgh be-came even more dear to my heart as it jumped from the pages of the book in the full technicolour of my imagination. I had begun saving when I was ten years old, but in my teens, Miss Brodie captured my soul and determined my ultimate destination.

I had a small selection of good friends at school, but I wasn't what you could call one of the popular kids. I was the one who shopped at the thrift store by choice and liked to experiment with bizarre fashion. From a very young age, I decided I wanted to have my own identity. I didn't want to be a carbon copy of anyone else. I added my own personality to whatever I wore, and some kids at school either ignored me or made fun of me for not being 'normal'—but what's normal, right? And why strive to be anything other than your true self?

Only, for some bizarre reason, I seemed to be drawn to guys who were the total opposite of me, and those relationships always ended badly. My first real heartbreak came during my final semester. Sully was a handsome, ball-playing, popular guy who needed extra credit towards his football scholarship. Someone in the higher echelons of the school decided that *I* would be the perfect person to help him achieve that goal.

Without going into all the gory details—I mean, we all know how *Pretty in Pink* and *Some Kind of Wonderful* go, right? Let's just say I fell. Hard. And all the time I was tutoring Sully, he acted like he adored me too. But of course, once my usefulness had expired, I received a letter from him telling me we were from totally different worlds, and that while my quirkiness was sweet and endearing, it just didn't fit him and his future. He hoped I would find someone better suited to my 'style' and that now he was going off to college it would be best if we remembered the good times with fondness. He didn't even have the decency to speak to me face to face. Idiot. Suffice it to say, I was dropped from my place on Cloud Nine and hit the ground of reality with a huge resounding thud, my heart less than intact, and the ability to even consider trusting another guy was something I couldn't begin to comprehend.

While I was at college my need to return to Edinburgh grew. I studied art and became obsessed with the paintings of Scottish greats like Samuel Peploe, Henry Raeburn and the works of Charles Rennie Mackintosh. I loved the vibrant colours, the emotion-filled expressions of the subjects and the delicate designs, but mostly I loved how differently each artist had approached their chosen medium. My chosen medium was photography but I used elements and ideas from each of my favourite artists to guide my creativity.

When my time at college was coming to an end, with the blessing of my parents, I set the wheels in motion for my relocation to the UK. I renewed my passport and confirmed that my dual nationality would allow me to live in Edinburgh with my Grandma Aggie and to work. Then, after my parents and I had attended my graduation ceremony my mom and dad handed me an envelope that contained a plane ticket to Edinburgh, UK. I think I screamed with glee for a half hour solid. I just couldn't wait to get on that jet, head over the Atlantic and put Sully, heartbreak, and all that painful part of growing up way behind me.

I arrived in the UK around three years ago, aged twenty-two. It was my intention to take a year out before deciding what I wanted to do with the rest of my life, but when I discovered Edinburgh—I mean *really* discovered it—with its intricate stone architecture, peaceful cemeteries, and lofty castle, I decided I was home. I know that sounds crazy, but I just fell in love with the place, the people, the accents, and the atmosphere. You name it—I loved it. My grandma spoiled me rotten for the first year and a half I was here and I loved spending time with her. But as she got older I felt bad for being an extra burden. I managed to find work in a city centre coffee house and a room in a gorgeous apartment close to the town centre, and I moved out. But obviously I visited her every other day and spoke to her sometimes twice a day.

Back then, my camera accompanied me everywhere. You could say I was a little snap happy, but I've always been the same. And although I wasn't exactly rolling in cash or living in Edinburgh Castle, I had a roof and a wage, and that was enough for this uncomplicated, Midwestern girl. My parents were great about the whole thing. They're so supportive, know I can be trusted, and they always say that so long as I'm happy, and I stay in touch regularly, they don't mind what I'm doing. I really do miss them but we video call all the time and they've visited since I moved here. And of course they know the place so they totally get why I love it here so much.

The apartment in which I rented a room was really sweet. My roommate/landlord told me it was Victorian; it had high ceilings and lots of original features. I loved the fireplace, even though it only had pillar candles in it. The guy who owned it, *and* the coffee shop, was Alec McVey. He was just great; gay, and the *best* person to shop with. We had tons of fun, and he's still a great friend after all these years. The best. So, all in all, I landed on my feet and things were going really well for me.

The coffee house—very originally called *McVey's* —is in the main shopping area of the city, just off Princes Street. Every day, on my way there, I walked past the Scott monument with Sir Walter sitting there on his stone precipice. I'd usually say good morning to him and give him a salute, which got me some bizarre looks from people, but I didn't care. I got bizarre looks most days anyway. Let's just say I'm a... um... *colourful* character. I still love my brightly coloured *boho chic* clothing, and absolutely adore a thrift store, or rather *charity shop*. Add to this that my blonde hair spends very little time in its natural state and you'll get why some people balk at my appearance. But I'm an artist and I love to express myself through my appearance. I love to experiment with colour and have been known to have blue, red, and pink hair. Not all at once, though. Don't get me wrong, I'm colourful, not insane.

My average day started at eight, when I usually opened the shop while Alec stayed home with the admin for a while. Well, he used that excuse, but the truth was he hated mornings. My first customers of the day were the folks on their way to work, grabbing their caffeine fix on the go. But my favourite customer, Mr McYummy, usually called in at around eight twenty-five. He was so shy, which, of course, I found endearing. I had to remind myself I was there to serve him coffee, *not* drool and fawn all over him.

But boy, it was hard.

He was pretty much the opposite of me in every way. He was a tall, natural blonde and had the most *incredible* eyes I'd ever seen. I'm talking the brightest, most vivid blue. He worked out too. I could tell by the hang of his expensive suit. I guessed he was some high-flying executive on account of the briefcase he carried, but I had no clue where he worked. I kept thinking that one day I should stalk him to find out. But, of course, I didn't. Like I said, I'm *not* insane.

He always smiled at me, and when he did, my belly did this funny flip.

Okay, so here's how it usually went with him. I'll call him MMY (Mr McYummy).

Me: Good morning, sir. What can I get you today?

MMY: (Blushing and soft spoken) Um, good morning. Um… can I get a latte with skimmed milk to take out, please? (*Oh my God. I love his Scottish accent.*)

Me: Sure you can, sir. (I'd go off and start the coffee machine) It's a lovely/cold/horrible day out there today, huh? (Delete as applicable)

MMY: (Smiling briefly and blushing again) Yes, it really is lovely/cold/horrible.

Me: So, any exciting plans for this evening? (And no, I wasn't asking him out. It was just small talk.)

MMY: (Shaking his head and smiling again… drool) Oh, no. Not really. Working late again. (Rolling his eyes)

Me: (Handing his coffee over) Well, don't work too hard, huh? Here you go. Enjoy, and have a great day.

MMY: (Blushing again… so sweet) Th-thank you. You have a good day too.

Me: I'll try. (*But you've just made it a whole lot nicer*)

And then he'd walk out and I'd sigh dreamily. Okay, so it was no dramatic love scene from a Nicholas Sparks movie, but as you can see, I had no clue how to get him to talk. He just went beet red whenever I tried, and I'm not exactly hard to talk to. I gave him opportunities, but it was my guess that maybe I was a little too quirky for him to take notice.

So, much to the dismay of my heart and my ovaries, I just continued to watch him and swoon from afar.

I told my grandma about him on one of my many visits. 'Oh I do like a man in a suit.' She said dreamily. 'Your grandad used to wear one for his job when we met. I used to swoon whenever I saw him.'

'Aww Grandma, I bet you miss him, huh?'

'Oh hen, I do. When you've spent your life with someone, built a home, made a family and then they're gone... It's like... It's like part of you is missing.' Her eyes became glassy.

'I hope that I find someone to have that kind of love with some day.'

Grandma cupped my face in her wrinkled and

brown spotted hands. 'You will, hen, and I just know it'll be soon. I can feel it in my water.'

At that point I burst out laughing. 'Eeeuw! Grandma!'

She shrugged. 'It's just a turn of phrase.'

3

FIN

After plenty of encouragement from our parents, I proposed to Elise on her twenty-third birthday, almost four years ago now. We were in Paris, and as we sat there before the Eiffel Tower, eating pain au chocolat and drinking coffee from paper cups, I presented her with a cushion cut, diamond solitaire ring. Talk about cliché. But it seemed to make her happy, and so it all felt worth it. We agreed on a *very* long engagement, which eased my stress of being betrothed somewhat under duress. Although, our long engagement hadn't gone down too well with the parents. They were getting antsy about us setting the date. There had been several tense conversations between my parents and me where I was accused of stalling, and I was informed that Elise's parents were beginning to think I didn't *want* to marry their precious daughter. But like the dutiful son I was, I kept my feelings bottled up and my mouth shut. After all, me marrying the right girl would make Dad happy, wouldn't it? Hetty tried her best to encourage me to tell the truth. She insisted that marrying someone I didn't love was crazy, and that I deserved to be truly happy. Bless her.

I think the real cracks began to appear in our relationship when Elise was sent to London to assist our office in a temporary partnership with another firm connected to an international fraud case. She was gone for a month, and honestly, I enjoyed the time alone. I know that makes me sound like awful, but I felt *free* for a while. I could only presume Elise felt the same way.

Having the apartment to myself was great. I walked around in my undies. I sang along to my favourite music at the top of my voice, pretending to be on stage like I used to when I was a kid and Hetty was looking after me. I left the milk out on the counter top, didn't shave on weekends, and slept in until lunch time on Sundays. All the luxuries that living with an anal, music-hating, clean freak didn't afford me.

I began to wonder if perhaps I *was* better off alone.

* * *

It was the night before Elise was due home, and I was walking around the apartment, trying to ensure everything was tidy to *her* standards. I had done nothing but think about our situation, and I had come to the conclusion that Hetty was right. This marriage would be a step too far to please a man whose love I had not yet earned by any other means. Why would marrying my friend make a positive difference? After all, she was *just* my friend. We weren't in love. Our time apart had clarified that fact for me and I guessed it would be the same for her.

I was placing the last of my dirty plates into the dishwasher to ensure the place was spotless, when my phone rang with 'He Ain't Heavy, He's My Brother'. It was supposed to be ironic, as the weight gain of contentment already made itself known to Callum, and hearing his ringtone—knowing he was oblivious to my reasons for selecting it—usually brought a wry smile to my face. But this time when I picked up the call, I had a feeling in my gut that I couldn't explain.

'Fin?' There was a distinct edge of worry to his voice that made my hairs stand up. He had uttered one word, but the fact that it wasn't preceded by some rude name or a loud belch instantly told me something was amiss.

'Hi, Cal. What's up? Why so serious?' For a split second, I held my breath, waiting for the joke.

'Hi, kid. It's... it's Dad. He's had a heart attack.'

Oh, God. He's calling me kid. That's really not good. 'Is he... did he...?' I swallowed hard as my own heart began a futile attempt at an escape through my ribcage.

'He's not *dead*, no. But, it's pretty serious. I think you should get to the hospital as soon as you can.'

He gave me all the details I needed and I typed them, one-handed, into the memo pad on my phone.

When I arrived, Dad's room was silent, aside from bleeping machinery, and we all sat round his bed, watching him sleep in his drug-induced slumber. According to the consultant, the heart attack had

—thankfully—been mild, but of course, it didn't stop us from worrying.

My mother looked pale, and I realised I hadn't ever seen her looking her real age. Not until that occasion. She was usually fully made up, regardless of the time of day. Never a hair out of place.

Without even acknowledging me, my mother left the room to get coffee—I guessed it was at least her sixth cup judging by the empty cardboard receptacles beside her seat. Callum had left a while before to take his heavily pregnant wife home, and so when my father eventually awoke, I was alone with him. Campbell Hunter. My father, the force to be reckoned with. The man I had always tried in vain to please.

Should I tell him I won't be marrying Elise whilst he's in hospital? At least they'll be able to look after him if my news brings on another attack. Ugh... such macabre thoughts...

'Finlay? Finlay, is that you?'

My father's croaky voice dragged me from my thoughts, and I moved my chair closer. 'Yes, Dad. I'm here.'

He wearily glanced round his surroundings.

'Good… good. Where's your mother? And your brother?'

'Mum has just gone for coffee. It's quite late and I guess she wanted to stay awake. Callum's taken Tori home. She was exhausted. But we've all been here. Even Hetty and her husband Fred.'

He sighed. 'She's leaving, you know? Hetty, I mean. She's moving up to Arisaig to be closer to her sister. Thinks we don't need her any more. Pah!'

I smiled. 'Well, you don't really.'

His brow furrowed. 'Your mother's cooking is inedible, and mine's even worse. Lord only knows what we'll do for food.'

I couldn't help chuckling at his comment. 'I'm sure you'll manage.'

Dad reached for me with the arm that wasn't tied up to drips and gripped me weakly. 'Finlay. I need you to promise me something.'

Oh God… here it comes. 'Of course. What is it, Dad?'

He looked me straight in the eyes. 'That you'll set a date and marry Elise as soon as possible.'

My heart plummeted. *Oh, shit, shitty, shit.* 'Dad… I can't—'

'Pish tosh, Finlay. You *can* and you *must*. Promise me. I may not be around too much longer and I want to know that grandsons are at least on the horizon. That brother of yours is refusing to tell me the sex of his unborn child. Says he wants it to be a surprise, which leads me to believe it's probably a girl. But you know how antagonistic he can be towards me. If I thought it possible I'd believe he'd have a girl to spite me. But you... you Finlay... you could be the one to carry on the family name and business. So... promise me.'

Talk about a guilt trip. I took a deep breath, released myself from my father's feeble grip, and rubbed my hands over my face. 'Yes, Dad. I promise.'

4

STAR

'Are you going out with Mick the prick tonight, Twinkle?' Alec's voice called to me from the living room where he had papers spread all over the coffee table. I poured hot water into my peppermint tea and rolled my eyes. He had *never* liked my latest beau, and I doubted he ever would.

I met Mick at the bar where he works. It was one time when I was out with some friends and we got split up. I was sitting at the bar texting around trying to locate the gang when I was approached by some douche who presumed I was an easy lay. Mick came to my rescue and pretended to be my boyfriend until the asshole got the message and left. I was really grateful for what he did and so when he asked me out just as some of the group arrived, I said yes. That had been almost a year ago and things were going okay, I guess. There were no fireworks, but he was a decent enough guy. Our love life was nothing mind melting, but you know, it was okay.

Mick was skinny with spiky hair and tattoos—some of which a five-year-old could've done better—and he had hazel eyes. He was no Adonis, but he was cute in his own quirky way. I guess that's what attracted me to him, along with his chivalry.

I clipped the lid on my thermal mug and remembered Alec had asked me a question. 'No, Al. I wish you wouldn't call him that. Anyway, I think he has to work tonight. Why do you ask?'

Alec appeared in the doorway to the kitchen. 'I was going to suggest we grab a takeaway and have a movie night. Thought we could watch *Magic Mike XXL*.' I turned towards him and the grin on his face accompanied a cheeky sparkle in his eye.

I crumpled my brow and smirked. 'Aren't you sick of that movie? It came out years ago.'

He sighed and rolled his eyes. 'Honey I know a classic in the making when I see one.'

I couldn't help laughing. I was pretty sure he was the only person in the whole of Scotland, maybe even the world, who had that opinion. 'Okay. Sounds good to me. What time will you be in work today?'

He shrugged. 'Oh, probably around eleven. I have to go to the wholesalers for some more of those caramel wafers. We seem to have had a run on them this week.'

I cringed, not daring to admit that the 'run' had partly been thanks to me nibbling on them while I worked.

I walked through to where he sat, spectacles perched on the end of his nose so the vain guy wasn't *quite* wearing them. Why he couldn't just accept that his eyesight was beginning to worsen was lost on me.

I leaned down and kissed his cheek. 'Okay. See you later then. I'm outta here.' I left the apartment, singing to my latest Spotify playlist as I walked. You can't beat The Proclaimers to put you in a good mood for the day, and I found myself wondering if Mick would walk five hundred miles just to see me. Sadly, I doubted it.

It was a bright but chilly early April Wednesday, and the city I loved was buzzing to life as I walked along Princes Street, past the kilted piper who was gathering an early crowd of eager tourists snapping photos, to the coffee shop. All round me, shutters were being yanked up, lights were being flicked on, and each shop's music could just be heard over the sound of 'Rearrange' by Biffy Clyro which was now bouncing around my noggin.

I always arrived a little early, but I loved my job. There was something satisfying about being the first person through the door of the empty shop. The aroma of coffee delighted my senses and made my mouth water. Peppermint tea was always my first drink of the day, and in all honesty, I preferred the smell of the coffee to the taste. I loved the earthy, burnt aroma that made me think of hot climates and hotter, tanned men.

Why was I living in Scotland again?

Once the machines were switched on and ready to go, the point of sale sundries were topped up, and the music was playing, I stood behind the counter waiting for the first customer of the day. I should've known better. I always lost myself in a good song, and today was no different. Bouncing round behind the counter with my hands in the air like I just didn't care, I was busy singing along to 'Gigantic' by the Pixies when I turned and froze. I felt the heat of embarrassment rise in my cheeks as I looked into sparkling blue eyes filled with mirth.

Oh my God. Ground, swallow me whole right now. 'Oh… h-hey there. What can I get you?' I made a vain attempt to flatten my crazy morning hair and to *not* sound like I was on the verge of collapse.

Mr McYummy pulled his lips in, clearly stifling a grin. There he stood in a navy suit, navy shirt, and a bright blue tie that made his eyes pop. It was an odd combination in my opinion, but it somehow worked on him. Then again, a garbage sack with a dog leash tied round the middle would look good on *him*. He was clean-shaven, and all I could think was how good it would feel to run my tongue along his angular jaw. He was completely out of my league and not at all like the guys I was usually attracted to, but there was something about him that pulled me in like iron to a magnet.

A heart-melting smile spread across his face and I was gone… completely gone. 'Um… can I get a latte with skimmed milk to take out, please?'

Oh, man. That accent.

I smiled brightly. 'Sure you can.' I turned briefly to prepare the machine. 'So, any plans for the rest of your week?' I thought I knew the answer, but it was a great excuse to watch him blush and hear more of that delicious, deep voice.

A strange expression briefly crossed his features, and if I hadn't been looking closely I would have missed it, but it was rapidly replaced by an almost painful and evidently forced smile.

He clenched his jaw as his nostrils flared and he inhaled deeply. 'Actually, I do have plans.' It was cute that he seemed surprised by his own reply, and I immediately wondered what he meant. This was the most he had ever offered, and it was quite thrilling, but my mind went into overdrive.

Oh my God, this has the potential to be an actual conversation. Breathe, Star. Breathe. 'Oh, excellent. Anything exciting?'

He pulled his wallet from his inside pocket, and as he did, my gaze was drawn to his broad chest, but he spoke again and snapped me back from my fantasy. 'I suppose it is.' He didn't look convinced. 'I'm getting married tomorrow.'

Oh. Crappy. Crap.

My heart plummeted in my chest and I lost the ability to speak for a few moments. I was unsure of what to say. I was so bummed at what he'd said. Stupid, considering I had a boyfriend and had never actually had the courage to have a proper conversation with the guy until the day before his damned wedding.

Typical.

Once I'd recovered my off-kilter composure, I turned to him again with the biggest grin I could muster. 'Oh, that's great. Congratulations. Here's your coffee and a chocolate chip cookie on the house.' I handed the cup over with the cookie I'd wrapped in readiness as a way to hide my flustered state.

He smiled and looked me straight in the eyes, but paused for a moment and frowned with his eyes locked on mine. A shiver travelled down my spine, and I opened my mouth to speak, although I have no clue what I would've said even if my mouth had worked.

After what felt like an age—but was probably more like three seconds—he spoke again. 'Thanks very much. That's really kind. Have a great weekend.'

The look of confusion was nothing but a memory, and his eyes were once again clear and vibrant.

'Yeah, and you go have a great wedding!' I called after him, feeling like a complete douchebag.

He lifted his cup in a salute, turned, and walked out of the shop, leaving me a little shell shocked at both the intensity of his parting gaze and the news he'd imparted. Suddenly feeling a little emotional, I walked over to my iPod where it sat in its dock and flicked the next track along before the introduction had even ended. Listening to 'Hold Me While You Wait' by Lewis Capaldi would have broken my heart right then.

Later that night, Alec and I sat eating popcorn and watching hunky men remove their clothes to music, but all I could think about was the intensity of the locked gaze that Mr McYummy and I had shared. Add to that the strange but bold announcement he'd made and the odd look on his face when he'd made it, and I sincerely wished I'd got some clue as to what was going on in that head of his before he left the coffee shop.

'…don't you think, Twinkle?' Alec's voice ripped me from my reverie.

I turned my head towards him. 'Huh?'

'Where were you? I was just saying that Joe Manganiello has the best abs.'

I nodded. 'Oh, yeah, totally.'

'Mmm. I wonder what cologne he wears.' He sighed dreamily. Turning towards me, he scrunched his brow. 'Everything okay? You've been a bit quiet today. Did something happen at work?'

Yep. The guy I've been fantasising about for Lord knows how long is marrying someone else tomorrow. 'Um… no. No. Everything's fine. I think I'm just tired is all,' I lied.

He pulled his lips in as if he'd sucked on a lemon. 'Yeah, whatever you say, darlin'. You'll tell me when you're ready, I suppose.'

Alec knew me far too well. I could hide nothing from him. I feigned a yawn. 'I think I'm gonna crash, Al. I'm really tired. Do you mind?'

He rolled his eyes. 'I suppose not. I could think of

worse things than being abandoned in a room full of half-naked men.' He winked and I cringed.

I picked up a throw cushion and whacked him on the head with it. 'Seriously dude, you know it's only a movie right?'

I walked away as quick as I could, shaking my head and giggling at my best friend.

5

FIN

My father's voice rang out round the room. 'I can't believe you didn't treat her better, Finlay.' Don't get me wrong, I was glad he had recovered from his heart attack but it was clear nothing had changed. There had been no epiphany on his part.

After the non-ceremony, my darling brother Callum had hugged me and told me to stand my ground before he abandoned me to my fate and took Tori and their new baby, Charlotte, home. So there I sat, at my parents' kitchen table, being bombarded with accusations about my conduct when I hadn't actually done anything wrong. Elise had left *me* at the altar, yet there I was, head in hands, being shouted at. Bloody typical. Nothing I ever did was right in spite of trying *so damned hard* to be what they wanted me to be.

Unfortunately, he wasn't ready for giving up yet. 'If you'd set the blasted date earlier. If you'd shown some blessed commitment. What will people think?'

My mother wailed at his words and dramatically dabbed at her eyes with a lace hanky. 'Oh, how will I show my face in public? The shame of it all, Finlay. How could you?'

It was like shit-throwing tennis and I was the net. Dad piped up again. 'Honestly, Finlay, did you really think a girl like Elise would wait around forever? I think this is the worst thing you've *ever* done, and that's saying something.'

That was it.

My blood rushed through my veins and my heart hammered in my chest.

I snapped.

Slamming my hands down on the table, I stood to face my parents with gritted teeth. 'What the *hell* is that supposed to mean? I've worked my arse off trying to be the best son I could be. I stepped into the 'good son' role when it was clear Callum wouldn't let you walk over him. I've let you run my bloody life for twenty-seven years.' They stared at me wide-eyed as I let my feelings fly at full pelt and full volume. 'I've done *everything* you wanted me to do. I even agreed to marry someone I wasn't in love with for *you*! And this is what happens? You gang up on me when *I'm* the one who's been humiliated! *I'm* the one who was left at the damned altar! Not you! And all you care about is what people will say? Well, sod this shit. I've had enough! Do you hear me? ENOUGH!' And with that, I grabbed my keys and stormed out of the house, letting the large oak door slam behind me.

The door swung open again as I stomped away towards my car and my father's voice bellowed from where he stood on the threshold. 'Come back here this instant and apologise to your mother, Finlay Hunter!'

I ignored him and kept on walking.

Once I reached my car, I paused in the hope that they would somehow come to their senses, but of course, they didn't, so I opened the door and climbed in. After slamming the door perhaps a little too hard, I fumbled with the keys, dropping them into the foot well before retrieving them and putting them in the cup holder. I jammed my finger into the ignition button, very much aware of the tumult raging beneath my skin. This delay, unfortunately, meant my parents had the time to come out to the car, ready to hurl more crap my way. My mother was sobbing in that over-dramatic 1940's-movie-star way she had—she really should've been an actress—and my father's face was beetroot red. For a split second, I panicked that he may have another heart attack.

That is until my mother shouted at me, 'You have caused your father and me so much stress, Finlay. If your father has another heart attack, it will be on your head!'

Anger that she would take such a low blow mingled with the acid in my gut and my stomach twisted. I was ready to throw up, but thankfully I kept my composure, yanked the car into reverse, and sped away spitting up gravel on the circular driveway. Once I had screeched the car round, I sped off towards the main gates and didn't look back.

* * *

The day that followed my non-existent nuptials was a Friday and—unlike most Fridays—it came all too quickly, and I arrived at work as if nothing had happened. I could hear the whispers from staff and colleagues alike as I walked quickly to my office with my head held high. Their pitiful gazes made me feel nauseated all over again. Or it could've been the bottle of cheap red wine I'd consumed the night before. Once I was inside and the door was closed, I slumped onto the leather chair behind the desk and rested my aching head in my hands.

The intercom buzzed and I almost jumped out of my skin. 'Mr Hunter?'

'Um... yes, Morag?'

My secretary was understandably hesitant with her next words. 'I... I have Miss Drummond on the line for you.'

Elise? Shit! 'Oh, okay. Put her through.'

The line clicked and there was a silent pause. 'Fin? I somehow thought I'd find you at work.'

I huffed out a heavy, defeated breath. 'What do you want, Elise?'

Silence ensued for a few moments until she eventually spoke. 'I... I wanted to apologise. I know I did a terrible thing. But, let's face it; I only did what you wished *you* could do.'

Okay, so that's true. I shook my head. 'W-what do you mean by *that*?'

'Look, Fin, be honest with yourself. You didn't want to marry me really. We'd been pretty much forced into the whole situation. And if you look deep in your heart, you may love me, but you're not *in* love with me. And there's a huge difference. I know you must be angry and hurt, but I'm guessing that's down to the fact that I humiliated you, not that I broke your heart. Am I right?'

I let her words sink in for a moment. She was right. Of course she was. I'd known it all along, but admitting it aloud felt like some kind of betrayal of what we'd shared.

I sighed. 'I guess... I guess you're right.' Rubbing my hand over my face, I inhaled deeply. 'How did we let things get this far, Elise?'

She gave a faint laugh. 'I don't know. I really don't know. But I do know that great sex doesn't make for a long and happy marriage. I need more. So do you, Fin. We both deserve to be loved wholeheartedly by someone who adores us. Don't you agree?'

'I do.' My ironic choice of reply hung in the air for a long while and I listened to the sound of her breathing.

She cleared her throat. 'Look, I'm going to stay with my friend Serena for a while. I'll collect my belongings over the weekend.' She went silent again for a moment. 'I really don't want to lose you from my life, Fin. I hope you can forgive me. And maybe someday we could be friends again.' Her voice wavered and she sniffled. Suddenly I wished she was in my office so I could hug her. She was giving us both a major get out, and although I felt crappy—and humiliated as she had quite rightly pointed out—I was kind of relieved to know she felt the same way I did about us.

'Hey. Hey, don't cry, Elise. We'll be fine. I don't want to lose you either.' It was the truth. She'd been in my life so long that I couldn't imagine her not being around. The thought of it both scared and saddened me. She was my best friend, after all.

'Well... take care of yourself.' She went silent again and I could tell she had more to say. I knew her well. The airwaves between us were thick with unspoken words.

I sighed. 'Come on, out with it. What's up?'

She began sobbing down the line. 'Oh, God. Fin, I'm so, so sorry. I have to tell you something.'

I shook my head even though she couldn't see me. 'What? What is it?' *What the hell could be so bad? Oh, God. Please don't let her be pregnant. Please...*

She cleared her throat and I heard a deep inhale. 'I... I met someone else. I'm... I'm in love with him. Have been for a while now.'

Ah. 'I see. I see. Well... um... congratulations. I mean it, Elise. I want you to be happy. Sincerely I do.' A part of me ached inside with sadness and a twinge of envy.

'Really?' The sobs came harder, even though I'd pretty much just given her my blessing. 'Oh, Fin. You're so sweet.'

I couldn't help the laugh that escaped. 'Yes, so I've been told.'

She laughed too, and the heavy weight on my shoulders began to lift.

She sniffed again. 'Thanks for not hating me. I couldn't bear it if you hated me.'

'Of course I don't hate you. So, who is he?'

Elise went on to fill me in about Theodore Fitzsimmons. The lawyer from London who she'd fallen head over heels in love with so quickly. He sounded like a complete nerd in my opinion, but apparently he was good to Elise and had asked her to move in with him. It all seemed a bit quick to me, but she was evidently besotted. We ended our chat on friendly terms, but it felt like we'd never really been together.

A strange numbness settled over me.

For the next week, I concentrated solely on work. It was a place I could escape my parents as my dad was still taking things easy at home, which was *very* convenient for him as it meant staying out of my way. I made no contact with them at all after the verbal explosion that had occurred on the Thursday I was supposed to be married.

For some reason, I was under a tremendous

amount of pressure at work. It wasn't something that had bothered me before, but suddenly every case seemed to be filled with issues that needed extra work in order for them to come anywhere close to a conclusion. I had been going straight to work from the apartment that I had once shared with Elise— not even calling for my coffee as I guessed the pretty woman behind the counter would no doubt ask me how the wedding had gone, or she'd wonder why I wasn't on some exotic island having passionate sex with my new bride.

At around six, my best friend—and best man *as was*—Tom Fielding, art gallery manager extraordinaire—walked into my office without knocking. He plonked himself down on the edge of my desk and picked up my hole punch. Turning it round, he pressed it up and down, making it look like a mouth. 'Come on, Hunter. We're going to get you shit-faced.'

'Hello, Tom. I'm good thanks. Do come into my place of work and make yourself at home, won't you?'

He slammed the hole punch back on the desk. 'Sod off, you grumpy, sarcastic git. Just 'cause you got dumped at the altar, there's no need to take it out on me.'

Shocked at the callousness of his words, I looked up and found him grinning. *Prick.* I smiled in spite of myself. 'Bugger off.'

Tom threw his head back with a hearty laugh. 'Come on, mate. You're better off without her. Think of all the Edinburgh totty just waiting for you to pick them up.'

I raised my eyebrows. 'Oh, yeah. They're all falling over themselves to meet *me.*'

'Oh, pack it in with the 'woe is me' crap. You're a bloody good-looking bloke and you know it.'

I didn't know it. Well, not really. I looked after myself and spent an hour at the gym after work every day, and was known to take advantage of the gym in the apartment block on weekends too, so sure, I had a good physique. But I had been called a pretty boy by the guys I endured at school and then by some of the tossers I encountered at uni. So 'good-looking' wasn't really a phrase I generally associated with myself.

I heaved a sigh and let my shoulders sag. 'Look, Tom. I can't be arsed with going out. I've just got no energy for it. Work is manic and this whole thing with Elise... I'm drained.'

'Bullshit. It's Friday night. You were dumped a week ago. It's time to get on with your life. Come on. We're meeting the lads down at that dingy place just off Princes Street. It should be a laugh.'

I rolled my eyes, even more determined not to go. 'That ridiculous karaoke joint you've been going on about? What's it called? *Debasement*? The name says it all really. You must be joking. I'd rather cut my ears off with paper.'

He laughed, his shoulders shuddering in the process. 'Nutter. It's a play on words, you know? It's actually in *de basement* of *de old* bank. I think it's dead clever.'

Scrunching my brow and folding my arms like a sulking teenager, I informed him: 'Yeah, well I don't care how clever it is. And it could be on the sodding roof of Edinburgh Castle for all I care. The answer is *no*.'

It appeared my attempts to convince him to leave me to wallow fell on deaf ears and eventually he cajoled me into agreement. 'You know you want to. Think of how hilarious it'll be to stand there, pint in hand, and take the piss out of all the arses who think they can sing.'

It did sound like a laugh when he put it like that. Looking down at my work attire, I frowned. 'I'll have to go home and change, though.'

'Sod that, Hunter. No one will give a shit what you're dressed like. You'll be fine like that.' Ah, Tom. The articulate man of many words.

Most of them expletives.

Tom fannied about on his phone, checking his social media, whilst I finished off what I was working on and put my files away.

DeBasement was buzzing when we arrived, and the other guys were already a couple of drinks ahead of us. Tom insisted on a few shots to help us catch up, and by the fourth one, I was feeling a little light-headed. The club was one I'd never been in before. It was a karaoke bar with a difference. The music available consisted of many obscure rock and indie tunes, and the majority of the people getting up to sing didn't care that they were making fools of themselves. I think alcohol may have played its part.

I wasn't exactly scintillating company after the week I'd had, and I would rather have been at home drinking beer and watching rubbish on TV. But the more drunk I became, the more the lads insisted I got up to sing. Apparently to 'cheer me up'. Of course, I refused, preferring to watch everyone else strut their stuff in the limelight. I was in no frame of mind to laugh and joke, even in light of the relief I felt from Elise's admission.

I got increasingly pissed off as the guys badgered me. I was okay with drinking myself into a stupor and trying to stay in the background. That is until my so-called friend, Jake, asked if I'd made things up with my family. Why the hell bring *that* particular topic up and ruin my already crap night?

Jake had drunk far too much, and regardless of what I said, he wouldn't let it go. 'I just don't get it though, Fin. They're your *parents*. Surely they'll come around? Isn't it worth at least trying to sort it out? I'd give anything to still have mine around. You don't want to leave things like this and regret it, mate.'

I clenched my jaw and responded through gritted teeth, trying desperately not to lose my temper. 'You have no clue what went on, Jake. You've no idea how much I've tried with them. Can't you just drop it, eh?'

He shrugged his shoulders and held up his hands in surrender. I disappeared into my own head after that. Anger at the whole sorry situation churned anew in my stomach, along with the alcohol, leaving me with a bitter taste in my mouth and an even more bitter taint on my heart.

I'd never considered myself as having a duplicitous personality, but there I was stomping round a stage in a bloody karaoke club after telling my friends how ridiculous it was to see people up there and how there was *no way in hell* I'd be following suit *in* my suit.

I looked out over the blurry crowd as the bitterness of the lyrics seeped from my every pore. If only the man was here to listen. If only the father I had idolised and worshipped all my life could hear the way he made me feel. 'In the End' by Link Park was a great song choice and expressed my feelings better than I ever could using my own words.

After everything I'd done for him. After everything I'd given up so I could be the perfect son. Following in his footsteps even though I had no real passion for corporate law. Everything I ever did was to gain his approval, and it never happened. Regardless of how much of my life I handed over to him, nothing was ever good enough. And now I was being blamed for the fact that my fiancée had fallen in love with someone else on a business trip. A trip *he* had sent her on. It really took the biscuit, that's for sure.

Words flowed from my lips through my gritted teeth as I pictured his face on each of those staring up at me open-mouthed. Their actual faces were already hazy in the bright stage lights, making it easy for my alcohol-induced imagination to take over. I clipped the mic back in its stand and dragged it along the stage with one hand as I pointed at the multiple faces of my father in the crowd. It felt good. Cathartic somehow. He would despise the fact that his lawyer son was up there making a fool of himself.

But I didn't give a shit.

In fact, that tiny piece of knowledge made me enjoy it all the more. I leaned forward so I could see the real faces in the crowd. Real people watching me and dancing to the song *I* had chosen. It freaked me out, and I snapped myself into an upright position, dragged from my bizarre fantasy of telling him what I thought.

The song ended.

The place erupted.

I almost passed out.

I was dragged from the stage by my group of friends. I was slapped on the back and congratulated with such vigour that it took me completely by surprise. Their words registered in my brain but I felt like I was having some kind of out-of-body experience.

'Bloody hell, Hunter! What *was* that?!'

'You're a natural up there, buddy.'

'You've been holding out on us.'

'Abso-bloody-lutely amazing, mate.'

What the hell had I done?

My heart pounded in my chest so hard I felt it would tear right through the bones and skin that encased it. My mouth dried up and I stared. Just stared into the crowd of familiar faces grinning from ear to ear as they adulated me.

'You're some kind of Jekyll and Hyde character, Hunter. Shit!'

Jekyll and Hyde? Was that a good thing?

It sounded about right, though, considering the second personality that had descended as soon as the music had begun. As I stood there and looked to my right, a beautiful, familiar-looking girl with crazy pink hair walked by me almost in slow motion. The smoky, smudged make-up round her grey eyes made them stand out as they locked on mine. A smile slowly formed on her full lips just before she turned and carried on walking through the crowd.

Then she was gone.

Had I imagined her in my post-stage-debut haze?

Turning back to my friends, I fell back to earth with a crash as a drink was thrust into my hand. 'Here you go, mate. You look stunned! It's hilarious! It's like you were some kind of clone of yourself up there.'

Finally finding the words I needed, I shook my head. 'I know... I know. What the hell was I thinking?' I laughed at myself as I brushed a hand through my hair and gulped down the shot of clear liquid that burned as it made the journey to my stomach.

More compliments came forth from the guys. 'Hey, Hunter, you were astounding, mate. You should be in a band or something.'

'Yeah, eat your heart out *Britain's Got Talent*. Edinburgh's got Fin Hunter!'

They all laughed and the back slapping began again.

6

STAR

You know that song, 'It's My Party and I'll Cry if I Want To'? Yeah, well that was suddenly my anthem. Everything had changed in a matter of days and I had plenty to be depressed about. My twenty-fifth birthday came around without much of a fanfare, and that was all my own doing. You see, in light of the week's events, I was feeling homesick for the first time. For starters, my stupid-ass boyfriend, Mick, had given me the whole, 'It's not you it's me' speech —feel free to insert dorky voice—saying he needed his space, to be alone for a while and that we were moving too fast. *Prize asshole*. The shit-head dumped me *two days* before my birthday, but then I saw him out with some brunette from the bar where he worked. They were kissing in a shop doorway when I was on my way home from work. And from what I saw, there wasn't much 'space' between him and her double-Ds.

Then add to this that Mr McYummy was now married.

Married.

He would've been married a whole week by now and was probably off sunning himself on some tropical beach with his new, perfectly mani-pedied bride. I couldn't help myself, though. I still looked for him every morning, but of course, he didn't come by for his coffee. And—regardless of how stupid it was—I worried I would never see him again. Let's face it, just because he'd married the love of his life, didn't mean he'd stop needing his morning caffeine fix now, did it? Unless Mrs McYummy was in charge of that area of his life after the wedding.

Ugh! I *hated* her.

I hated a woman I had never met but who was good enough to capture the heart of that shy, handsome Scotsman. I hated the crazy sinking feeling in my gut when I thought of him with her. I hated the fact that he'd found someone and that no doubt she would be prim, well-spoken, and perfect. Of course, I didn't know any of this for sure. All I knew for definite was that *not* seeing him sucked and my mornings had got a little duller.

Okay, a *lot* duller.

On top of all this was the fact that I missed my parents terribly, meaning I didn't feel much like celebrating. Grandma had baked me a birthday cake and offered to cook me a birthday meal but she was really struggling with her legs and I didn't want to burden her more. I spent a few hours with her as she regaled me about her birthdays as a younger woman. She made everything sound so glamorous. Afterwards I decided I was going home to sulk and dwell on how unglamorous my life was.

Alec, of course, had other ideas. 'Come on, Twinkle. You're only twenty-five once, and you have to bloody forget about that wanker. He wore crap clothes and his hair was always a mess. You can do *so* much better.'

Okay, so he was right. Mick had never been long-term boyfriend material, but being dumped was never fun. Alec eventually convinced me that I needed to get out, and so I agreed to go to *DeBasement*. It was our usual drunken haunt in the city where we'd get up and sing a duet of 'Dead Ringer for Love'—Alec insisting, as always, that he sang the Cher parts—or some other old rock song that we could murder together. It never failed to make me laugh, even when I really didn't think I was in the mood.

It was Friday night, and I dressed in my long purple tie dye skirt with my clunky black boots, I topped off the ensemble with a black t-shirt that I had slashed the neck of, so it fell casually off one shoulder. My pink hair was left to dry in natural waves and then messed up a little with product. A glance in the mirror told me I appeared a little like an 80s Madonna crossed with Stevie Nicks, and a little Debbie Harry thrown in for good luck.

We made our way to the bar to meet up with some of our friends—Alec's on and off boyfriend, Gil, short for Gilbert, being one of them.

Alec opened the door for me like a real gentleman and I spotted the group immediately. Waving frantically, I dashed through the throngs of people and was enveloped in a group hug and treated to a very loud and raucous rendition of 'Happy Birthday' whilst hoisted up on the shoulders of two of my male friends, Slater and Conch—Bruce Conchola, in case you were thinking, *'Huh?'* His mom was from Texas and his dad was Glaswegian—go figure.

Anyway, I felt better already.

The drinks were flowing nicely, and Alec even ordered a bottle of champagne. I was more of a Jack and Coke kind of girl, but it was sweet of him to buy it so I helped drink it anyway. Well, it would've been rude not to. Conch and Mindy, his girlfriend, got up to sing Meatloaf's 'Paradise by the Dashboard Light' and the place erupted as they camped up their performance. Conch dabbed at his face with a white napkin—bits of the paper towel getting stuck to his forehead as he did so. It really was hilarious. But the thing I loved about the place was the eclectic music on offer. It wasn't your run of the mill Bette Midler, Whitney Houston and Abba kind of karaoke. You could literally sing anything you wanted—so long as it was rock or indie.

As the night wore on, we all got more and more drunk, and I was working my way up to my big duet with Alec when a guy walked onto the stage. His head was down so I couldn't see his face, but he looked completely out of place up there—in the club too, if the truth be told. Grey slacks, white shirt, short blonde hair and a tie that had been loosened half way down his chest. Most of the club's regular clientele donned black and were covered in tattoos. He took the mic from Pedro, the club owner and M.C. and stuck it in the stand, then rolled up his shirt sleeves just as the intro began to play.

I recognised it immediately. Now, I know you should never judge a book by its cover and all that, but to say I was shocked at the song choice would be a major understatement. He lifted the mic from its stand once again and began to sing but didn't lift his face to the crowd. His gravel-filled voice sent shivers down my spine. The guy could sing, that's for sure. A rarity in that place. But it was what happened next that had me almost passing out right there on the spot.

As the words fell from his lips and the song began to build, he slowly lifted his face and my mouth fell open. My eyes widened and my heart almost stuttered to a halt.

It was *him.*

It was *Mr McYummy*, the blonde bombshell from the coffee shop.

'Well, hellooooo there, handsome,' came Alec's voice from beside me.

I swivelled around to face him, opening and closing my mouth like a dying trout. 'It's... he's... I...'

Alec burst into fits of laughter and nudged me with his shoulder. 'Use your words, Star. Use your words.'

I stared aghast in the direction of the stage and at the gorgeous Scottish guy singing 'Numb' by Linkin Park.

Turning to Alec, I pointed towards the stage. 'I... I know him.'

Alec's eyes widened. 'Well, lucky you. Is he gay? Please say yes.'

I frowned and shook my head as my gaze trailed back to the stage and I realised I had no clue. He could've been marrying a guy, I suppose. 'I... I don't know.' But, deep down, I just knew he was straight. I think it was the way we had shared a moment on the day before his wedding. Something inside me knew he wasn't gay.

Alec bumped me again and almost knocked me

off my feet, I was so stunned. I glanced back to my best friend and pseudo big brother to find him standing, arms folded. 'You can't know him too well then, love.'

Ignoring Alec's bitchy comment, I switched my attention back to the stage once again. I watched as the beautiful, clean cut man stomped around the stage like he was meant to be there. Like he owned the damn place. The amount of venom and angst he injected into the angry lyrics made me shudder. It was like he was singing them *at* someone. Someone who had wronged him severely, and I pitied whomever it was.

He didn't quite look like himself up there.

But, oh my God, he was incredible.

Now, I know that up on a stage with bright lights shining on him, he was bound to look different, ethereal somehow, but his eyes looked a little sunken and... *sad*. But the rest of his demeanour screamed aggression—the clenched fist and gritted teeth along with the sneer on his lips—so either he was a great actor as well as an amazing singer, or he really *was* singing the lyrics to someone who'd hurt him badly.

Then it hit me. He was *here*. Mr McYummy was

on a stage in an Edinburgh nightclub. Not on some tropical island with his perfect new bride. Did this mean *she* was the one who'd wronged him? I hated the fact that my stomach fluttered at the prospect.

What the hell is wrong with me?

I could no longer form words, nor could I calm the thundering of my heart in my chest. He was... *amazing* There was no doubt in my mind that he belonged up there. His voice alone was panty-melting, but coupled with his electric blue eyes piercing through just about everyone in the audience—indiscriminate of gender—he had me ready to throw my underwear at him. He had the stage presence of a rock god. And I was in lust.

Head over heels in pure, unadulterated lust.

7

FIN

By the time I unlocked my apartment door, I felt as sick as a dog. I slammed the door and staggered my way to the bathroom, making it just in time to throw up the meagre contents of my stomach. What the hell had I been thinking? Seriously?

After I had splashed my face with cold water, I made my way to the bedroom. Elise's stuff was all gone. An eerie loneliness settled over the place, but thankfully, I was too drunk to really acknowledge it. If only I was so pissed that I couldn't remember the events of the night. Unfortunately, and much to my chagrin, I was not. The whole getting up to sing thing whirred round inside my head. Or maybe the spinning was alcohol induced. I don't know. All I *did* know was that I could remember what I'd done on that stage vividly.

Bollocks.

* * *

I awoke to a loud ringing sound, each and every piercing note drilling another hole into my already tender skull. I carefully opened my eyes and stared up at the ceiling. The noise registered in my hazy mind as the telephone.

Pulling myself to an upright position, I held my head as the room tilted and turned. I managed to clamber to my feet and looked down to discover I was still in yesterday's work clothes. My head was spinning so I took steady steps until I reached the living room where my phone screamed from its charging point.

Lifting it to my ear, I croaked. 'Hello?'

'Hunter, you're alive. How are you feeling, mate?' Tom's all too cheery voice annoyed me right away. Why wasn't *he* feeling like death?

I rubbed at my temples. 'Um... I feel like death on a stick. You?'

'I'm okay, pal. Didn't drink as much as you.' He laughed and I wished he was here so I could punch him.

'Great. Lucky you.' My response was filled with all the sarcasm my poorly head could muster.

His chuckle angered me further. 'Anyways, are you up for a bit of brekkie? Thought a nice plate of stodge might do the trick.'

The thought did nothing for my churning stomach. 'Um... nah. I think I'm going to get some work done, Tom. Thanks, though.'

'Oh, come on, Finlay. Live a little, pal. It's Saturday. Let's do breakfast and drink plenty of coffee and then if you *really* feel the need to work, you can do it later, okay?'

I didn't need much convincing, and although my stomach lurched again at the thought of food, I couldn't really be bothered working either. 'Yeah, okay. Give me half an hour and I'll meet you at The Edinburgh Larder, okay?'

'Great! See you there.' He hung up and I slumped onto the couch to rest my head in my hands.

A text pinged through and I lifted the phone once more.

Hey kiddo, how are things? Has Dad fired you yet? I wouldn't put it past the miserable old git. If I were you I would jump before I was pushed. I'm here if I can help. And remember, if that apartment gets too much you're always welcome to stay with us. It would be good to have someone else on the nappy changing rota. Love you. Cal.

My brother had a point. My father was nothing if not vindictive. I envied Callum for the way he could just switch off. He had the innate knack of letting my father's words wick away like water from a duck's back. Although Dad firing me wasn't something I was really expecting. Surely he wasn't that bad?

Once I'd showered, I felt a little more human, and grabbed the first clean clothes I set my hands on —dark jeans and a blue v-neck sweater. I pulled on my boots and stood in the centre of the vast space I had once shared with Elise. Callum was right, not only would I need to consider looking for a new job but I would need to move. The place was too big for me, and to be honest, I needed a fresh start. I needed to be somewhere that didn't reek of my father and his money and it was best I left before I was forced to do so.

Half an hour later, I walked into the Edinburgh Larder and spotted Tom perusing the menu. He looked up and waved as I made my way over to sit opposite him.

'Feeling any better?' he asked with a smirk.

I sneered. 'Sod off.'

His responding laugh caused his whole body to vibrate. 'I'll take that as a no then.' A young waitress came over, took our order, and quickly left us in peace. 'So... what happens now?'

I glanced at Tom to see the grin gone and concern etched on his face. The guy made fun of me constantly, but there was no doubt in my mind about how much he cared for me.

I rubbed my hands over my face as if doing so would bring some ideas forth. 'Honestly? I haven't got the slightest clue.'

'Are you looking to move out of that penthouse? It's a wee bit big for one, don't you think?'

I nodded as I stared at the tines of my fork. 'Funnily enough, I was thinking the same before I left there to meet you.'

The waitress arrived and placed our food and drinks down before smiling warmly and leaving us once again. Tom added sugar to his bucket of coffee. 'Have you spoken to your folks since the shit hit the fan?'

The mention of my parents made my stomach roil. 'Nah. Don't want to either. I'm tired of all the bull that goes along with being a Hunter. I wish I could change my sodding name.'

Tom threw his head back and guffawed. 'Oh, yeah. I can imagine it now. Like that time on *Friends* where Phoebe changed her name. Johnson McBudgysmuggler would suit you down to the ground.'

In spite of the fact that I felt like a bear had beaten me over the head and crapped in my mouth, I joined in his laughter.

* * *

Monday morning was dull and rainy. The dark clouds overhead matched my mood and the feeling of doom that hung over me. To make matters worse, I'd got up late, so I rushed round like a headless chicken, trying to get myself ready for work. Although, my father was due to be back and I really didn't feel like facing him—this made summoning up the energy even more challenging. We hadn't spoken since the day of the non-wedding and I felt sure he'd have more reasons to have a go at me.

Choosing a black power suit from my wardrobe—in the hope that I'd exude the confidence I was internally lacking—I dressed slowly, trying to delay the inevitable. Thoughts of a pink-haired girl sprang to mind as I fastened my tie. *Those eyes.* Where the hell did I know her from? Why was she so familiar to me? Why did I feel drawn to her? I remembered the slashed T-shirt she wore and the way it gracefully slipped from one shoulder, exposing her collarbone and slender neck. She wasn't the type of girl I was usually attracted to, but for some reason, the image of her walking slowly past, smiling, kept on flitting through my mind.

I shook my head. *Enough of that, Hunter. You've a father to stand up to.* I grabbed my overcoat, keys, phone, and briefcase before heading out of the door and down to the ground floor.

The doorman nodded and opened the main door for me. 'It's a cold one, Mr Hunter, sir.'

'Yeah, it looks that way, Mortimer. Thanks.' I gave a rigid smile and began the short walk to work just as the heavens opened. I'd forgotten to pick up my umbrella and considered heading back, but checking my watch, I realised I was already late.

Oh, great. More ammunition for my father to fire.

Once I reached my usual coffee house, I was soaked and freezing. Droplets of water slid from my hairline and down my nose, and the sky showed no sign of letting up its ice cold deluge. I stopped and peered in through the rain-covered window to discover there was a ridiculously long queue, and I debated whether to risk it and join the wait for the best coffee in Edinburgh. Could I justify being even later?

Suddenly, a flash of pink caught my eye from behind the counter and it hit me. *That* was where I knew the girl from. McVey's coffee shop. The realisation stopped me from joining the line of dripping wet customers, and I dashed off as quickly as I could before she saw me. Embarrassment at what she had witnessed at the karaoke bar caused my heart to leap, and made the thought of meeting her face to face once again something dreadful. *What the hell must she have thought of me?* And come to think of it, why did I care what she thought? She didn't know me. I didn't know her. We were only acquainted through our shared interest in coffee so what did it matter?

Thankfully, I'd seen fit in the past to ensure I had a set of towels at work. They were mainly for my post-workout shower in the days I deigned to go to the gym before work. Thanks to today's heavy downpour on my way to the office, I certainly needed one.

Once I'd dried off as much as I could, I sat behind my desk and stared at the pile of papers neatly stacked in order of importance. *Where to bloody start? Do I get the longer tasks done first or tackle the quicker ones?*

The intercom buzzed and my stomach flipped.

Taking a deep breath, I pressed the button. 'Yes, Morag?'

'Good morning, Mr Hunter. Your father wishes to see you in his office right away.'

Oh, God, he's on the ball this morning I see. No

chance to even get settled. 'Okay, thanks. I'll be right there.'

Once I had summoned up the courage and made a brief plan in my head of the retorts I might be able to use for whatever bullshit he accused me of this time, I made the short journey to the next floor up and approached my father's office. His secretary, Melissa, asked me to take a seat and so I plonked myself down and waited.

And waited.

And waited some more.

I felt like a school kid waiting to see the head teacher for a roasting. My knee bounced up and down, and I chewed on my nails. *This is ridiculous.*

And still I waited.

Oh sod this. I stood and walked over to stand at the secretary's desk once again. Speaking through gritted teeth I said, 'Melissa, can you tell my father I have work to be getting on with and that he should call me when he actually has the *time* to speak with me.'

Melissa's cheeks turned bright pink, and she opened and closed her mouth as if trying to work out how to protest at my request—which would no doubt land her in hot water.

Suddenly, the door to my father's office opened. 'Finlay. You may come in,' he said dismissively, without making eye contact.

When I glanced over at Melissa, her relief was almost palpable. I smiled at her and shook my head, but she dropped her gaze to her computer screen and carried on typing. I realised she must have been terrified of suffering my father's wrath just like everyone else.

Once inside the plush, mahogany and leather clad office that had been occupied by my tyrant of a father ever since I could remember, he closed the door. 'Take a seat, young man.'

Okay, so he has his patronising head on. Bang went any hopes of a civilised and adult-to-adult conversation. I watched as he walked round the desk and sat in his large, wing-backed leather chair, silently resting his elbows on the highly polished wood and steepling his fingers.

Unable to bear the silent treatment any longer, I interrupted whatever thoughts were bumbling around in his head. 'What did you want to see me about, Dad?'

He took a noisy, deep breath through his mouth and blew it out with force through flared nostrils. 'As you can imagine, Finlay, you upset your mother and me with the aggressive nature of your departure after the wedding.'

I rolled my eyes. 'There *was* no wedding.'

He huffed. 'And therein lays another issue. Your mother and I put a lot of time and effort into your relationship with Elise. Does that count for nothing?'

I couldn't help snorting. 'Do you not realise how *wrong* that whole sentence is?'

His brow furrowed. 'Meaning what, *exactly*?'

My heart rate picked up and my temples began to throb. I could sense my anger levels rising. 'Meaning that it was *my* relationship with Elise, and it was *me* who was getting married to her. Not you. Yet somehow you've turned the whole bloody thing around and made it look like *I'm* the guilty party.'

'Do you not see how your lack of insistence on setting a date caused a rift between the pair of you, Finlay?'

His persistent use of my full Christian name

rather than an affectionate term like 'son' made me seethe. It was more like a business meeting than a father-son chat. But then again, he chose to do this at our place of work.

My calm tone belied the turmoil under my skin. 'Dad. I will say this once more, and I will say it slowly so you understand this time. She. Did. Not. Want. To. Set. A. Date. And I will tell you why, shall I? It's down to the fact that *you* sent her to London where she met the man of her dreams. So don't keep turning this around on me. We never really loved each other. You and the Drummonds pushed us into a relationship that neither of us really wanted.'

He slammed his hand on the desk. 'Utter non-sense! She adored you! *You* ruined it!'

'No, Dad. She loved me as a *friend.* Nothing more. Looking back now, I realise we should have just stopped the whole charade before it went as far as me being jilted at the altar.'

'So that's the gratitude you show your parents, is it? You're not even prepared to fight for the woman you love?'

I felt the growl erupt from my body before I

heard it. Once it left my throat, it sounded alien to me. 'For the last time - I DON'T LOVE HER!'

The stubborn bastard wouldn't give up. 'I don't believe you. You can't be with someone for that long if you don't love them.'

I threw my hands up in the air in exasperation and laughed without humour. 'I don't care if you don't believe me. It's the truth.' There was no turning back. 'I've done *everything* I can to make you proud of me, Dad. I followed *your* dreams for my career, I got engaged to Elise, I moved into an apartment *you* chose. But I can't be that person now. I need to stand on my own two feet.'

My words fell on deaf ears. 'The embarrassment you've—'

'Are you even *listening* to me? Do you *ever* listen to me? I can't do this any more, Dad. I can't deal with hearing over and over what a failure I am because of this situation. I can't.'

My father stood slowly and leaned on his desk. 'Then you had better leave.'

'Fine! I'll take the rest of the day off and—'

He slammed his hands down again, and I almost jumped out of my skin. 'No! Finlay, you're fired.' And there it was. The sentence my brother had *almost* prepared me for but I had still, naïvely, believed wouldn't be uttered.

My heart stuttered in my chest and my eyebrows rose before scrunching. 'What? Y-you can't *fire* me. I've done nothing wrong! This is a personal matter, not a work issue.'

'You clearly feel that working for the family business is beneath you. You don't want to be a part of this family any more. Your actions of late have proved that. So you may leave. And you had better find somewhere to live too. I'm terminating the lease on your apartment.'

What the hell? My heart sank. 'I don't believe you. I *really* don't believe you.' I ran my hands through my short hair and rested them atop my head as I stared briefly up at the oak panelled ceiling.

The energy had been sapped along with the colour that I felt drain from my face, and the next time I spoke, all the fight had left my body.

Despite my attempt at strength, my lip trembled. 'All I ever wanted was for you to be proud of me, Dad. All I needed was your reassurance that I wasn't a complete disappointment. Do you know that when

I graduated from uni, all you said was, "*Here are your car keys. You start work at the firm on Monday.*" Were you aware of that?' My voice began to waver, and I hated myself for showing any kind of weakness in front of him. 'I just wanted you to love me, Dad. I just needed a little praise and some of your time. That's all. But I got *things*.' I clenched my jaw in a bid to fend off the emotion fighting for release. '*Things* instead of the love a son needs from his father. I worshipped you, Dad. I would've given *any*thing to have you love me back. But I guess when it really came down to it, I just wasn't good enough.'

I waited for him to speak. For him to tell me he loved me and that I wasn't a disappointment at all. For *one word* that would make me feel I hadn't just been disowned.

But he remained stoic.

And so with a heaviness in my heart that almost floored me, I gathered my remaining shred of dignity, turned, and left.

8

STAR

I was eager to know what had happened to Mr McYummy, but weeks had passed and we were heading full pelt towards summer. I hated that I hadn't seen him at all. He stopped calling into the coffee shop altogether—even though my hope of seeing him again had sparked anew with the events of my birthday night. Seeing him up on that stage had really affected me. I kept dragging Alec back to the club at every given opportunity, just in case there was a *slight* chance there would be a repeat performance.

But, of course, there wasn't.

In between pining for something that never was

and could never be, I had been spending my time wandering round the graveyards of Edinburgh with only the ghosts of lives past to keep me company. As crazy as it sounds, it was wonderful visiting forgotten resting places I had read about in one of my favourite books, and I could imagine being one of Miss Jean Brodie's girls, learning about the history of the great city I now called home. But I also gained a strange sense of peace knowing I was keeping the memories of the deceased alive—if only for myself—when the ancestors of most were clearly long gone. Most people consider graveyards to be sad or depressing places to visit, but not me. I found them fascinating and beautiful; filled with stories, either true or those of my own imagination.

Just over a month after my birthday, Alec and I met up with our friends at DeBasement once again, and I was on edge. Alec kept slapping my arm to get my attention when I was too busy scanning the room for blonde-haired, suit-wearing men. It was stupid. He wasn't going to be there, but it didn't stop me trawling the place every five seconds. An uneasy tension stiffened my spine and I couldn't shake off the feeling that things were awry.

Alec had far too many vodkas, as usual, and put his name down to sing a Bon Jovi hit. As he belted out a very camp version of 'Livin' on a Prayer' the rest of our group of friends sang along with him, completely out of tune, but my eyes were still busy searching the room. Alec's terrible rendition finished and he re-joined us to raucous applause from the alcohol-fuelled members of our crew.

I'd just about given up all hope of ever seeing the hunky blonde from my fantasies again when I heard the intro to 'Here I Go Again' by Whitesnake, and for some reason, my heart leapt and a cold shiver travelled down my spine. My gaze swivelled to the stage so quickly I almost gave myself whiplash. It was a real blast from the past but that wasn't the only reason I turned. I could sense him before I even saw him.

I widened my eyes and froze. I didn't dare move a muscle in case he turned out to be a figment of my imagination and disappeared into the ether. He gripped the mic where it stood in the stand and closed his eyes. His hair was messier than usual—and the clean-shaven man of a month ago was gone.

Stubble now graced his angular jaw, but this made him all the more delicious to me.

He wore a white T-shirt that sat tight across his pecs, a black leather jacket, and black jeans that had seen better days. He strutted around the stage, and my heart ached at his unique, emotion-filled delivery of the lyrics. It was usually an uplifting song about starting over but this was different. There was something very wrong. It was evident in his last performance too. My gut instinct was right. I was never surer of anything. His eyes were no longer bright, smiling, and sexy, but instead they were circled with dark shadows, and a line creased his forehead as he displayed the sentiment of the song in his body language.

I was mesmerised once again.

Alec nudged me. 'Hey, isn't that the guy you were drooling over on your birthday?'

I nodded slowly. 'Um... yeah. Yeah, it's him.'

He huffed and pursed his lips with disdain. 'He looks different. Could do with a haircut and a shave.'

Alec favoured cleaner cut men usually, although there had been some guys in his life who broke the mould. Personally, I thought Mr McYummy looked perfect. And my skipping heart was in agreement.

I remained completely focussed on Mr McYummy as the song came to a close. A shiver travelled down my spine as I let my assessing gaze trail the full length of his toned body. The aggression he had exuded last time had gone, and although the gravel in his voice had still been present, the arrogance had been replaced by a melancholy desolation. But regardless of his demeanour, he *still* owned that stage. I felt the urge to approach him but had no clue what I'd say. 'You were great', 'Wow, what a voice', 'You rock'. All far too lame and underwhelming considering the reaction he drew from the crowd.

I watched with concern as he walked, head down, over to a side table, and sat. His gaze remained fixed on the floor as applause and cheers continued to ring around the room. He appeared somehow oblivious, detached even; though it was clear the crowd had the same opinion as I did about his talent. I couldn't be sure if he was disbelieving of the reaction he had elicited, or if he was simply disinterested.

Alec leaned in so his mouth hovered by my ear. 'Go on. You know you want to go talk to him.'

I met Alec's wide eyed *you-know-I'm-right* stare and swallowed hard. 'What if he tells me to piss off? He looks so... *sad*.'

Alec shrugged. 'You've nothing to lose, Twinkle.'

He was right. I either pulled up my big girl panties and bit the proverbial bullet, or I would forever wonder 'What if?' And who knows how long it would be until I had this opportunity again. Or if the chance would arise at all.

Taking a deep, calming breath, I walked through the throngs of people dancing and waving their arms as the next performer belted out whatever the hell the song was supposed to be. It was out of key and sounded akin to nails down a chalkboard, so I tried my best to block it out of my mind and focus on the handsome blonde Adonis ahead of me.

When I arrived beside him, I was a nervous wreck. I had the whole sweating palms and thudding heart thing going on. I leaned in so he could hear me over the noise. 'Um... hi there. No coffee tonight, huh?' *Sheesh, Star. That really was dumb.*

He tilted his chin up to meet my gaze but his eyes were blank. 'Sorry, do I know you?'

Oh, shit. Smiling, I shook my head. 'No, not really. I used to serve you coffee every morning is all. But you stopped calling in.' I shrugged.

Acknowledgement spread across his handsome features. 'Oh, yeah. Pink hair. Crazy dancing. I remember.' His smile lit up his whole face and my heart melted.

Summoning up more courage, I leaned in again. 'So, where'd you go?'

His brow furrowed. 'Sorry?'

'For your honeymoon. Last I saw you, you were about to be married. Where'd you go for your honeymoon?'

He cringed and picked at the label on his beer bottle. 'Ah. There... um... there was no wedding, and ergo, no honeymoon.'

Oh, God. Hey, mouth, allow me to introduce you to my foot. 'Oh, shit. I'm so sorry.'

He waved his large hand around. 'Nah. It's fine.' The gesture caused the bottle contents to splash all over my top, and a look of horror spread across his face as he leapt to his feet. 'Oh, God! I'm sorry!' He reached out, and dragged his hand down the wet patch on my breast. His startled gaze lifted to mine and he pulled his lips in briefly before uttering, 'Oh, bollocks. That... that was an accident. I didn't mean to grope you. I'm so sorry. I'm so sorry.'

I stood stock still, just staring at him with my mouth open. I must have gone beet red, but thankfully, the club lights would have hidden the fact. Or at least I *hoped* they had. Suddenly he burst into fits of laughter. His whole body shook and he bent double. I couldn't help it. I joined in. His laugh was so deep, sexy, and kind of infectious. We stood there howling with laughter and getting some rather strange looks from the other patrons.

Once we had calmed down, he peered down to where I stood before him, still smiling. 'Jeez. I haven't laughed like that in too bloody long. Thank you.' He chewed on his lip for a moment, and I got the impression he had more to say, so I stayed silent. My instincts were correct, and he took a deep breath as he straightened his back. 'Look, do you fancy getting out of here?'

Tilting my head to one side, I narrowed my eyes. 'What did you have in mind?' *And don't think*

I'll be having sex with you, if that's what you're thinking.

He shrugged. 'Oh, I don't know. Maybe we could go somewhere a little quieter? My head's pounding.' How the hell did he make a headache sound sexy? Okay, so the Scottish accent helped...

I scrunched my brow in a moment's contemplation, my head telling me not to go because he was, to all intents and purposes, a complete stranger, but my heart was saying, *but he's so sweet and he's sad. He needs a friend.*

Clearly, the heart was in charge at that precise moment as the words, 'Sure. Why not?' fell from my lips before I could let my head intervene further. I gestured towards Alec's location. 'Just let me go and tell my roommate where I'm going. Um, *where* exactly should I tell him I'm going?'

He thumbed towards the exit. 'There's a small bar a few doors down. I think it's called the Jekyll and Hyde bar.'

Very apt.

I nodded. 'Oh, yeah. I know it. Cool place. Okay. Back in two minutes.'

I turned and fought through the crowd once

again to where Alec and the rest of my friends stood. I mulled over the irony of the bar's name and the apparent split personality of the guy I was going there with. He certainly had two sides to him that I'd seen. It would be interesting to find out more.

Alec raised his eyebrows at me as I made my way across to him. 'Any luck?'

I couldn't help the smile on my face. 'He's asked me to go for a drink at the Jekyll and Hyde. Says it's quieter there.'

He folded his arms defiantly across his chest. 'Oh, yeah. Does he think you're just going to jump into bed with him?'

I snorted in a very unladylike manner. 'What? No! We'll be in a pub, you dumbass.'

Still with a disbelieving expression, Alec insisted, 'You call me if he tries anything. You hear me, Twinkle?'

I rolled my eyes. 'Alec, I don't need a big brother. I'm an adult.'

He raised his eyebrows again. 'Really?'

I slapped his arm playfully. 'Eff off, Al.'

'Be good. And if you can't be good, use a condom.'

'Yes, Dad.' I saluted him before turning and making my way back to Mr McYummy. *I really need to ask his name...*

As I approached Mr McYummy again, he smiled at me and my stomach flipped. *You will not sleep with him. You will not sleep with him.* I repeated the mantra over and over in my head. Who was I trying to convince?

He stood and held his elbow out to me. 'Shall we?'

As I linked my arm through his, the butterflies took flight in my stomach, and I began to wonder what the hell I was doing. Just because he was handsome and had a sexy accent, didn't mean he was in any way sane. I assessed him once again, trying to ascertain if I could take him in a fight. The immediate answer that sprang to mind was *hell no.* He must have been around six two, and if his biceps and the thickness of his thighs were anything to go by, he was pretty damn toned under his clothes.

Nope. I'm doomed.

As we stepped outside the club, the cool evening air battered my overheated skin and I shivered.

'Hey you're freezing and you don't have a jacket. Here, have mine.' He began to pull it from his body.

How sweet. Still not sleeping with him. I held up my hand to halt him. 'Oh, that's okay. It's nice to finally cool down. It was way hot in there.'

'Yes, I suppose it was.' After a pause, he stopped and turned to me. 'I should introduce myself.'

I giggled and regretted it immediately. He'd think I was one of those silly girls who flick their hair and say oh em gee.

I nodded and smiled. 'We probably both should.'

He held out a long-fingered hand towards me. 'I'm Fin. Finlay Campbell Hunter.'

I took his hand in mine. 'I'm Star Anahi Mendoza. Nice to meet you... *officially.*'

We began walking and he turned to me with a smile. 'So, you're clearly not a local, what brings you to this fine city?'

I grinned. 'To cut a very long story short it was a love affair that began when I was eight but I was actually born here too.'

'Oh? So you have dual nationality, eh?'

'Sure do. I came to live with my grandma a few

years ago when I graduated college and I couldn't bring myself to leave.'

'So how did you end up with such an exotic sounding name? None of it's Scottish.'

I chewed my lip, trying not to grin like an idiot. 'Star because my grandpa called me his little star. Anahi and Mendoza because my pop is Spanish and had great dreams of me being some kind of leader I think.'

'Ah. I know what that's like.' His expression turned serious for a moment until he nudged me and stopped. 'Star, eh? It's a beautiful name. Hell, you've been serving me coffee for months now and I never even asked before. How rude am I?'

I waved my hand dismissively. 'Oh, that's okay.' We began walking again, and I felt drops of rain fall onto my bare arms. 'You always seemed quite shy and you were always on your way to work.'

When I tilted my face to look at him again, his expression was once more serious. 'Yeah.'

I cringed. 'Did I say something wrong?'

He shook his head and smiled. 'No, no. Nothing like that.'

I tried to lighten the mood again. 'So, where do you go every morning wearing those power suits?'

'Well, I *used* to go to Hunter-Drummond and Associates. It's a law firm.'

Edinburgh was as vibrant as ever. Revellers dashed from one bar to another to avoid the rain, and I was momentarily distracted watching people wearing far too little clothing trying not to get wet. We reached the Jekyll and Hyde as the rain began to fall in earnest.

Realising what he'd said, I tilted my head. 'You *used* to work at Hunter-Drummond?'

He wiped the rain from his forehead and slicked back his hair. 'Long story. Let's just say I'm currently between jobs.'

Whoops. Me and my big mouth. 'Ah. Okay. We don't have to talk about it.' I silently wondered if he was some relation to the Hunter in the firm's name, or if it was just a coincidence. I guessed the latter as he no longer appeared to work there. Surely he wouldn't have been fired by relatives? Unless he had done something *very* wrong.

Oh. Shit.

He glanced skyward for a moment, silently

watching the rain as it fell on his face. 'Look. I'm soaked. You're soaked. And I don't think I feel like drinking any more.'

Oh. Well done for screwing it up, Star. Bang goes getting to know him now. 'Okay. I understand.' I couldn't help the disappointment in my tone.

His luscious mouth turned up in a heart-melting smile. 'No, I don't think you do. My apartment is just round the corner. We could go grab a coffee… and a towel.'

Oh! 'Um… oh, I don't really think—'

He held up his hands and fixed me with a stern gaze. 'Look, I'm a lawyer. Well, *ex*-lawyer. I'm not an axe-wielding maniac, I swear. I promise I won't kill you.' He gave me a delicious half smile and my heart flipped.

I'm done for.

Before I had time to think things through, my mouth acted of its own accord once again. 'Okay.'

Shit. What am I doing?

His grin widened. 'Great. Come on then. I don't know about you, but I'm ready for a coffee. And you're absolutely drookit.' He slipped off his jacket and draped it round my shoulders.

I presumed he meant that I looked as cold and wet as I felt and we picked up our pace as we made it along the road. He came to a halt in front of a beautiful old Victorian stone building with bow windows, on a street I wasn't too familiar with. He jogged up the stairs and opened the door, but I stood, frozen to the spot.

Concern washed over his features as he gazed down at me where I hesitated. 'Look, I won't try anything, okay? I just want a coffee and your shop's closed.'

I threw caution to the wind, ignored my inner alarm bells, and jogged up the stairs to where he stood. 'If you murder me, I'll haunt you,' I told him, only half joking.

Once inside the building, we climbed one flight of stairs and arrived outside one of two doors on the floor. He unlocked the door to his apartment and stepped inside, holding the door so I could follow him in. It was a stunning place. High ceilings and tastefully decorated, if rather masculine, in grey, pale blue, and white, with a huge comfy-looking black leather couch in the centre of the room. The walls were devoid of artwork and I wondered if he'd actually finished moving in.

He threw the door keys on the dining table at one end of the living space and walked around, turning on some lamps. It was a smaller place than I imagined him living in, to be honest, and he must have read my mind.

Once he'd finished with the lights, he rested his hands on his hips. 'It's not as fancy as the place I used to live in but... well, I had to leave there pretty quickly and I didn't fancy living with my brother and his newborn.'

What the hell did he do that meant he had to leave his other place quickly? I widened my eyes and swallowed hard. 'H-how come? Did you run out of places to hide your victims?' Again, I was only half joking. Terrified I'd walked into some kind of trap, drawn in by his gorgeous exterior—it did happen after all, look at Ted Bundy—I began to back towards the door.

He laughed unabashedly. 'God, you look terrified. You actually *do* think I'm going to hurt you, don't you?'

I shook my head emphatically. 'D-don't be silly. I

just... I don't usually go home to apartments with men I've only just met.'

He smiled warmly and walked towards me. He came to a standstill around three feet away and held his hands out as if to show me he was unarmed. 'Look, there *is* a story to what happened. If you want to stay, I'll tell you all the sordid details. If it'll stop you looking like you're about to bolt, that is.' His husky deep voice made my heart pound. 'And I promise to keep my hands to myself.'

I almost whined, '*Awww,*' like a sulky teen, but managed to restrain myself. The thought of his hands on me appealed to me more than I cared to think about.

He gestured towards the large leather couch. 'Why don't you take a seat, and I'll go make a pot of coffee.'

My cheeks heated as I twisted my fingers together. 'Um... do you have decaf tea?'

He scrunched his brow and chuckled. 'Seriously? The girl who sells coffee doesn't even like it?'

'It's not that I don't like it, but if I drink coffee this late, I'll have bizarre dreams. If I get to sleep at all, that is.'

He shook his head in disbelief. 'Decaf Earl Grey it is, then.'

Curiosity got the better of me, and while he clattered around in the kitchen, which was through a door off the dining area, I tiptoed over to his old stacking stereo system, the likes of which my dad had at home, to check out the pile of vinyl and CDs beside it. In my opinion, you could tell a whole lot about a guy based on his music, and I loved that in the day of the iPod and Spotify, he still had LPs and compact discs.

I thumbed through an eclectic mix of bands feeling a little inferior for my love of all things 80s, especially Fleetwood Mac, Bon Jovi and Madonna. His taste ranged from Queen, Genesis and Rainbow, which I also loved and that took me back to my childhood and my dad's love of American rock, to bands I had barely heard like Soundgarden, Pearl Jam and A Perfect Circle. *Talk about intense taste.* He evidently had a thing for real guitars and solid sounds.

Impressive.

'Do you want to choose something to listen to?'

His voice made me jump and spin round to face him. 'I wasn't... I mean, I didn't mean to—'

He placed two steaming mugs on the oak coffee table in front of the couch. 'Really, it's fine. Choose something. The system is pretty ancient but it's still got amazing sound quality.'

I turned back to the stack of albums and tried to find something that wasn't exactly romantic. My head was telling me that the last thing I should be doing was getting cosy with him. My fingers landed on a Sisters of Mercy greatest hits compilation album. I removed the shiny disc from its case, hit the eject button on the CD player and slipped the CD into the drawer. Once I'd closed it and hit the random play button, I made my way over to where Fin stood, hands in pockets, with a wry smile on his face. My God, he was stunning. And I was losing my mind. I must have been. Why the hell else would I have been there?

'Great choice,' he said as I sat down opposite him in a leather tub chair. It was my head fighting my heart when I chose to sit so far away, and he frowned before sitting down too.

I took a sip of my tea from the mug Fin had

placed before me. 'So, you were going to tell me what happened.'

He huffed out a long breath and ran his fingers through his shaggy hair before looking me in the eyes once again. 'You're right. Okay. So, I suppose I should start at the beginning.'

Music played in the background like a movie soundtrack as he recounted the details of his loveless childhood, and my heart ached for him. So much pressure had been placed on him from such a young age. My stomach twisted as his blue eyes closed briefly and then opened again. He had evidently tried so hard to be the perfect son, but nothing he had done had been sufficient for him to win his parents' approval. How different his upbringing had been from mine. My parents weren't exactly poor, but I'd been nowhere near as privileged as Fin had materialistically.

But the one thing I *did* have in abundance was love.

Suddenly feeling that the distance between us was too great as he poured his heart out to me, I stood and silently walked to sit beside him.

His nostrils flared and he clenched his jaw before

speaking again. 'I guess… I guess it's time I stood on my own two feet now. Hence the new place and lack of job. I was forced into this situation, and I had to sell my car to fund this place for a while, but I'm hoping it'll be the making of me.' He tilted his face to meet my gaze and his eyes glistened in the lamplight. He held eye contact for a few moments before leaning towards me infinitesimally. I slipped my tongue over my lips in readiness, but he suddenly pulled away and shook his head. 'Oh, God. Listen to me rambling on like some wimp.'

'You're not a wimp, Fin. You've been treated awfully by parents who should've known better. I don't know you all that well, but no one deserves to have been ignored like that. No one deserves to have their life mapped out for them and to have no say in how it goes.'

He forced a laugh. 'Aww, come on. Don't feel sorry for me. I'm just being pathetic.'

Anger bubbled up from deep within me. 'No. No you're *not*. Don't think that. Honestly, you deserved so much more.' Without thinking, I reached my hand out to stroke his cheek, and he turned to face me once again. '*So* much more.'

My head was screaming at me to stop this immediately, but my heart wouldn't listen. It was beating so hard that I could hear my blood thumping in my ears. This time, when he leaned towards me, he didn't hesitate. He crushed his lips to mine with urgency and inhaled deeply as he slipped his hand into my hair. I gripped the front of his T-shirt as he tilted my head back and plundered my mouth with his tongue.

Every muscle below my waistline clenched with desire, and the groan that emanated from his throat vibrated down my chest where my heart raced at the passionate onslaught. What the *hell* was I doing? This wasn't me. I didn't behave like this. But regardless of my brain's protestations, my body betrayed all rational thought as I dove in, tongue first.

He pulled away, his chest rising and falling rapidly. 'Shit, I'm sorry, Star. I said I'd keep my hands to myself.'

My chest heaved too as I fought to pull air into my starved lungs. 'Y-you did promise that. But I guess it's a little late to worry now.'

His brow crumpled and he shook his head. 'What *is* it about you? I *never* open up to people. *Ever.*

But you... you draw me in, Star. Something deep inside me just can't hold back. Sh-should I hold back?'

Yes! Yes, you should. Get up and walk away, Star slutty-whore Mendoza! Get up now! Leave! Once again, my psyche screamed at me, and I was barely gripping onto my sanity as I walked on thin ice, but once again, the inner voice fell on deaf ears.

I shook my head. 'No. No, I don't want you to hold back.'

The song 'Temple of Love' registered in my foggy mind from the sound system. I loved that track, and it seemed to fit the intensity of whatever the hell was going on between me and Fin.

He searched my eyes for a moment before pulling me into his lap and reigniting the intense connection we had shared only moments before. I grasped at his clothing, unable to get close enough, and before I could protest, I was airborne and being carried from the living room down a corridor. With his mouth still latched onto mine, he raised his leg, kicked open a door behind me, and stumbled into the room. He flicked a switch and a bedside lamp illuminated the space just enough for me to quickly take in my surroundings.

Turning my attention to Fin, I watched as he swallowed hard. 'My God, you're beautiful.' His voice was a thick whisper, and his Scottish accent seemed stronger somehow. My cheeks heated so much I thought I was about to spontaneously combust. No one had *ever* looked at me like that, with such intensity and longing.

He gave a small, disbelieving smile and said, 'I've never wanted anyone like this before.' The sincerity in his gaze almost knocked the air from my lungs.

I felt exactly the same. I didn't understand myself or my behaviour but what I knew was I felt something intense for this gorgeous man who had opened his heart to me. This wasn't lust, it felt right. There was a real connection I was sure of it. I only hoped the connection didn't fade in the cold light of day.

9

———————

FIN

I awoke to a feeling of pins and needles in my left arm. When I turned my head in the direction of the numbing limb, I was greeted by a most beautiful sight. The alabaster skin of the girl I had only become acquainted with properly the night before.

Star Mendoza.

An intricate tattoo of vines and delicate flowers adorned her skin from her shoulder blade and weaved its way down her back to caress her ribcage. I had never really been into tattoos but these were so delicate, as if someone had painted a watercolour on her skin. As gently as possible, I freed my arm and she rolled onto her back but didn't wake. I propped myself up so I could see her face. The pale pink curls of her hair fanned out on the pillow beside me, and it was only when I looked closely that I spotted slim streaks of blonde showing through. For a few moments, I was mesmerised by her beauty and couldn't take my eyes off her. Her full lips were slightly parted in her slumber and I watched as they turned up briefly into the sweetest of smiles.

What the hell had I been thinking? I had *never done* the one night stand thing, but then again, I had been in a relationship with Elise since the dawn of bloody time. I didn't understand what had made me act so carelessly—so recklessly—the night I met Star. She was so sweet, and despite her quirky exterior, she wasn't the tough, experienced girl I had expected. There was something about her that drew me in. And like I said before, she wasn't the type of girl I usually found myself attracted to. But maybe that's because I didn't even know what I found attractive. I had been led for so long by my parents' wishes, that I had never really had a chance to explore what it was I wanted.

'Good morning.' She whispered and I felt my face warming.

I had been caught admiring her and for a split second embarrassment tugged at my insides. 'Sorry, I was just... um...' I cringed. 'I didn't mean to disturb you.'

She cleared her throat. 'It's fine. Actually, I probably should be going. It's a wonder Alec isn't blowing up my phone with calls and texts right now.'

I sat bolt upright and winced as anger spiked at my insides. 'Hang on. You've got a *boyfriend*? And you chose *now* to mention the fact?'

Great. Now I feel like a complete sleaze.

She laughed and sat up to face me. 'Take it easy. Alec is my roommate. Remember I mentioned my roommate last night? And anyway, I'm not *man* enough for him, if you get my meaning. You, however... well, he totally wanted you.'

My cheeks heated and I covered my eyes as I groaned. 'Ah, right. Sorry.'

'It's okay. You're not the first one to jump to the wrong conclusion. Alec's like a big brother, big sister, and best friend all rolled into one. He looks out for me and always has since I moved here. In fact, he owns the coffee shop *and* the apartment I share with him.'

Ugh. Now it all made sense. 'I see.' I turned and leaned to reach my boxers and jeans. With a struggle, I managed to pull them on without flashing my wares at Star, which was ridiculous considering the antics of the night before.

Once I was covered, I turned to face her. 'You don't have to rush off. Drop him a message to let him know you're fine and I'll go make coffee... um... *tea*? Feel free to grab a shower. Bathroom's just through that door.' I pointed to my en-suite.

She nodded and smiled. 'Okay. Thanks. I'll be out once I'm done.'

God, I loved her sexy American accent and the way her cheeks turned pink when our gazes connected.

I smiled and nodded like one of those bloody dashboard pets. I suddenly felt shy and unsure of myself. 'Great.'

I left the room sand the beautiful woman in my bed. I'd only taken four steps away from the door when I stopped. I wanted to go back and have a repeat of the night of passion we had shared. But I doubted she'd want the same. I guessed she might be filled with regret at waking to the blushing, bumbling, insecure idiot that was the antithesis of the alcohol-fuelled, yet confident man of the night before.

I turned to walk away again when I heard footsteps behind me. When I turned, the sight of her all cute and dishevelled from sleep took my breath away. Dressed in just the sheet from my bed, she leaned her head coyly against the doorframe and smiled.

I cleared my throat, afraid of what noise would come out when I tried to speak. 'Is everything okay?'

She chewed her lip for a moment. 'Um... yeah. But I was wondering...'

I swallowed hard and stepped towards her, I almost tripping over my own feet and was feeling like a total idiot. 'Wondering what?' I knew what I hoped she was going to say.

She paused and frowned for a second. 'Um... where are your fresh towels?'

Nope, that wasn't what I was expecting or hoping for

her to ask. Disappointment washed over me. 'Oh... yeah, sorry. They're in the drawers by the wardrobe. Help yourself.'

She blushed again. 'Thanks.' As she disappeared back into my room, I turned to walk away with a sense of defeat, but her voice stopped me. 'Fin?'

I could sense that she'd appeared again, and I turned my head to the side but didn't quite look at her. 'Yeah?'

Her voice was a breathy whisper. 'Join me?'

Thank you God.

What the hell was I playing at?

After placing a kiss on her nose, I stepped from the shower and wrapped a towel round my waist. 'I'll go and make us that drink now.'

It was clear that she could sense a change in me when she switched the water off, grabbed a towel, and covered herself quickly. She simply nodded and looked away. Taking that as my cue to leave, I grabbed another towel and rubbed it through my hair as I walked, collecting my clothes on the way out of the bathroom. I could almost hear my dad's voice in my head telling me I was a disgrace; that I had just proved his worst thoughts about me. *'She's the total antithesis of Elise, Finlay, what were you thinking?'* I shook my head to try and rid his scowling face from my imagination. What did his opinion matter anyway?

Once I had dressed and boiled the kettle, Star appeared, fully clothed again, in the kitchen doorway. I handed her a cup of tea and gulped down my coffee too quickly, burning the roof of my mouth. My eyes watered as I rubbed my tongue over the sore patch of skin.

I could feel her eyes on me, and when I looked up, she winced. 'Are you okay? That had to hurt.'

Heat rose in my face and I nodded. 'Yeah. That'll teach me for being too eager.'

She placed her mug down and smiled weakly. 'Look... I think I should go.'

Unsure of how to react, I focused on my coffee cup. *Ask for her number, you idiot. Say something. Anything! Don't you dare let your dad's ideals ruin this too! He's not even here!*

Scratching my head with my free hand, I simply replied, 'Yeah... yeah okay. Um, anyway thanks for...'

As soon as the words of gratitude fell from my mouth, I cringed and glanced up at her.

Her eyes widened and the flush of colour drained from her cheeks. 'For what? My services? Jeez. Way to let a girl down easy.' She followed this with a smile that didn't reach her eyes and then stopped making eye contact with me.

My heart leapt at what I had somehow inadvertently, and unintentionally, insinuated. I placed my mug down and turned to fully face her. I raised my hands in a defensive manner. 'No. It's not like that. I wasn't going to say... I mean, I didn't even think...'

She sighed and her lips turned up in another less than convincing show of positivity. 'It's fine. Guess I'll see you around. Or... or not. Whatever.' She shrugged and shook her head, and I closed my eyes as I lowered mine.

Say something for Pete's sake, Hunter, you arsehole.

Knowing I really wasn't in a fit state to start anything serious—a realisation that I should've reached the night before, I know—I lifted my chin once again. 'It was really great, Star. You seem like a really nice girl. I just... What happened last night wasn't... I shouldn't really... Oh, shit. What I mean is...' What *did* I mean? Did I actually even *know*? I doubted that very much. Why was I not asking for her number? Had my father wheedled his way into my brain so badly that I couldn't even contemplate a relationship with someone who didn't fit his idea of *appropriate*? Star and I had connected on many levels—not just the physical. But here I was, sabotaging any chance I had of this thing ever going any further.

I wasn't sure if the disappointment on her face was down to the fact that I was clearly blowing her off or down to the words I'd chosen. '*You seem like a really nice girl*' was kind of condescending, and she still made attempts to hide her ire. She was a better person than I, that one thing was certain.

Shaking her head she snorted a forced laugh. 'Oh my *God*. You'll be saying '*It's not you, it's me*' next. Or '*I'm not ready for a relationship*'.' Her mocking tone caused my insides to twinge with guilt. She rolled her eyes and kept the strained grin in place. 'Please stop, okay? Stop before it gets to that. We owe each other nothing. Okay, we had sex. *Twice*. And it was great. And FYI, *I* don't usually do that either. But you seemed sweet, and I liked you, and I thought we clicked. Guess I was wrong and it was just sex.' She shrugged. 'But I can live with that. I'm a big girl, Fin. See you around.'

Feeling more than a little ashamed, I dropped my gaze to the ring of coffee on the counter top as her footsteps carried her away from me, and I flinched as she slammed the door behind her.

10

STAR

An overwhelming sense of humiliation and hurt tugged at my insides and my eyes began to sting. *Don't cry, you moron. Don't you dare cry.* What an idiot I'd been. I really thought there was a chance he and I would see each other again. I wouldn't have slept with him so readily if I thought he would treat me like this. Clearly, my magnet for attracting douchebags was still in full force. I can't explain why it felt different with him but it just... *did*.

And the sex.

Oh. My. God.

I had *never* felt like that before. The way he took charge of my body and put my pleasure first was something I had never experienced. But I liked it. And I wanted more. What a shame he didn't feel the same. But then again, I'd probably appeared easy, sleeping with him right away, and so I couldn't blame him, really. I mean, what the hell did I expect?

I cringed as his words replayed in my mind. *'You seem like a nice girl.'* Patronising shithead. I'm a *woman*. And the speech I'd given him. Shit, he'd probably think he'd had a narrow escape from some promiscuous lunatic. Why in the hell did I have to say *'I thought we'd clicked'? Stupid ass.*

As I stomped the pavement away from his apartment, I heard footsteps behind me. It was early morning and my stomach lurched. Without looking back to confirm that I was being followed, I picked up my pace and almost broke into a run, but I heard Fin call out to me.

'Star! Star, wait!' His accent and the way my name dripped from his tongue melted my insides, and as much as I wanted to tell him to get lost, I stopped—against my better judgement—and turned to face him. He jogged up to me, panting. 'You... you left your phone.' He held the misplaced item out to me and I made a grab for it. 'Look... that... that didn't go quite how I'd planned. Aww, sod it... if the truth be told, I hadn't planned *anything*. I just, I'm a mess right now. You don't deserve to be dragged down with me. I meant what I said about you seeming nice and... I don't want to hurt you. If this goes any further, I just know I will.'

I snorted in that unladylike manner I'd apparently adopted. 'I'm an *adult*, Fin. You didn't take advantage of me. Your conscience should be clear. And I *am* a nice person. But I guess you'll just have to take my word on that.' I turned away and he grabbed my arm, swinging me back to face him again.

'Star, if I'd met you before, this would've been—'

I yanked my arm from his grip. 'Don't flatter yourself. I just felt sorry for you.' *Liar.* I plastered on a fake-ass, snide smile. 'I have a thing for a pair of sad blue eyes. Like I said, you can walk away with a clear conscience.' My voice betrayed me with a wobble and I looked away to avoid his penetrating gaze. I began to walk and willed him to follow. Willed him to prove me wrong—that he wasn't just another douchebag. Sadly, his feet stayed planted firmly where he had come to a stop and after what I'd just said I couldn't really blame him.

* * *

I unlocked the door to my apartment and closed it carefully behind me, trying not to alert Alec to my presence. I had no clue if he was even home.

'So... she finally returns.' I closed my eyes and dropped my head at the acidic tone of Alec's voice. He suddenly appeared in front of me. 'Where the hell have you been? I've been worried sick, you silly cow.' He pulled me into his arms and hugged me fiercely.

'I'm sorry, Al. I didn't mean to worry you.'

He pulled away and peered into my eyes. 'Worry me? It's a wonder I've any hair left. And I would *not* look good bald.'

I cringed. 'My phone died.' It was both an excuse and an explanation. But it was the truth. I'd realised it after Fin handed it back to me.

'Well, thank goodness it's just the bloody phone that's dead and not *you*. What the hell were you thinking? Where have you been? This is all so out of character for you.'

I rolled my eyes. 'Jeez, hold off with the Spanish Inquisition, *Dad*.' I did actually sound like an errant teenager, and my choice of words made Alec laugh.

'Come on, Twinkle. Spill it.' Alec's pet name for me had stuck ever since I met him and he decided he couldn't call me Star; apparently because it would make him sound too camp. After the length of time I'd known him, he'd become so in-tune with me and my emotions that it scared me sometimes.

'I... oh God... I ended up going back with the hunky blonde guy to his apartment.'

He folded his arms over his chest and pursed his lips. 'You slept with him, didn't you?'

I gasped. 'I don't know what you mean!'

He raised his manicured eyebrows. 'It was a one night stand, love. I know that look. Seen it many times on many friends faces. Don't kid a kidder.'

I exhaled a long breath and hoped the regret would leave with the air from my lungs. 'I didn't mean for it to happen, but he poured his heart out to me over some shit in his life and I just... I don't know... I felt for him.'

Alec's face crumpled. 'A pity shag? Really? Come on, Twinkle. That's not like you.'

I held up my hands defensively. 'No, no. It wasn't

like that. I really, *really* like the guy. I mean, what's not to like? He's drop dead gorgeous and he has that throaty Scottish accent thing going on. But he seemed different.'

'And this morning? Why are you not sticking around for round two?' I felt my cheeks heat and I closed my eyes. Alec whistled. 'Ooh, you al*ready* had round two! So now what? Are you seeing him again?'

I dropped my bag and placed my phone on the coffee table before slumping onto the couch. 'I don't think so. This morning... you know, *afterward*... he seemed to close down on me. He said, and I quote, "You seem like a nice girl."'

I heard Alec's sharp intake of breath and he covered his heart with his hand. 'Ouch.'

Nodding my head in agreement, I didn't need to speak. I rubbed my hands over my face and flopped back to gaze up at my best friend. 'What an idiot, huh?'

He came round and sat beside me, taking my hand in his. 'Not at all, darling. I think you just followed your desires and stepped out of your comfort zone for a while. Did you enjoy yourself?' My cheeks heated again as I was momentarily transported back to the passionate scene of the night before, and I pulled my lips in to try and stifle the grin threatening to give me away.

He nudged me with his shoulder. 'I'm guessing from the look in your eyes and the colour of your cheeks that it was good.'

Sadness washed over me. 'I've never experienced anything like it before.'

He grappled me into a hug and kissed the top of my head. 'Oh, that's shitty. So, so bloody shitty. If it'd been crap you could've just forgotten about him and moved on. Chalked it up to experience.'

'Not much chance of the forgetting part, but the moving on part is a given. I don't appear to have any choice.'

'He may see sense yet, Twinkle. Just wait and see.'

Filled with doubt, I shrugged. 'After the way I handled his brush off, I won't hold my breath.'

After squeezing me to him once again, Alec stood and walked towards the kitchen. 'Go take a shower, darling, and I'll make you some breakfast.'

I didn't bother to tell him that 'round two' had taken place *in* the shower and decided another one would do no harm. I could still smell Fin's woodsy shower gel on my skin, and it wasn't at all helping me to rid myself of the memories he had helped me create. With very little enthusiasm or energy, I pulled myself to my feet and made my way to the bathroom.

As I stared at my reflection in the bathroom cabinet mirror, I couldn't help but think I'd somehow changed. Not physically, that would be crazy. But something in me had shifted. Regardless of the fact that I had only just met him officially, Fin had affected me for a very long time and this had only made it worse. I wasn't too happy about the fact. It's like that situation where you dream of something for so long and then you get it, only to be greatly disappointed that it wasn't anywhere near as great as you expected. Except in my case, it was way better than I ever could have dreamed until it was over. And then it really *was* over. I would never have it again which was probably worse than never having it at all.

But I would have to just get over it.

11

FIN

Days passed by in a blur after my encounter with Star, and I couldn't seem to shake the feeling that I'd made a mistake of monolithic proportions in letting her walk out of my life like that. But what the hell did I have to offer her? After what had happened with my parents, the company, losing my job and losing the apartment, my head was a mess, and I couldn't figure out what the hell I wanted to do with my life, let alone involve someone else in my shit.

No one deserved to put up with me in such a crappy frame of mind—least of all someone as sweet as Star Mendoza. Just thinking of her name sent shivers down my back and conjured up images of her face and her porcelain, painted skin. It was like I'd tasted a drug for the first and last time all at once.

My body and soul craved her, but my head was having none of it—insisting on reminding me I was in no position to be starting a relationship until I got my shit together and made some decisions. And I also needed to grow the hell up and stop thinking about what my parents would think of her.

It. Didn't. Bloody. Matter!

But the problem was, once I *was* straightened out in my own head, there was very little chance she would give me the time of day. I couldn't blame her for that.

After a week of staying off the radar, I was bombarded by texts from Tom, wanting to know why I'd disappeared off the face of the earth. After he cajoled me for what seemed like hours, I agreed to meet him at the Jekyll and Hyde bar in the city.

I hadn't been shaving, and if I'm honest, I'd lost the wherewithal to even care about my appearance. I walked into the bar in my scruffy black jeans and an old Ramones T-shirt that was once black but had now faded to a dirty shade of grey.

Tom stood to greet me—rather uncharacteristically—with a manly bear hug, slapping my back a little too hard. 'Well, hello, Wild Man of Borneo. Have you brought my good friend Fin Hunter with you by any chance?' He glanced over my shoulder to emphasise his point.

I gave a snide raise of my lip. 'Very bloody funny. I need a drink.'

He held up a finger. 'Back in a sec.' He jogged through the early evening crowd to the bar and returned a few minutes later with a Jack and Coke. He plonked it down before me and sat down on the stool opposite. 'So. What's the story, pal? Where've you been?'

After taking a large gulp of the dark, amber liquid, I placed my glass back down and stared into its contents. 'Hiding in my own personal version of hell. Trying to avoid human contact. You know how it goes.'

He huffed out a long breath. 'Shit, mate. Are things really *that* bad?'

I glanced up to meet the concerned stare of my best friend. 'Worse. I just seem to make one mistake after another lately.'

He frowned. 'What do you mean? What's happened now?'

I inhaled deeply and closed my eyes for a second, only to open them again when an image of Star popped into my mind. 'I... I met someone.'

A big grin appeared on Tom's face. 'Oh yeah? What's she like?'

'She's beautiful and sweet and quirky. *The complete antithesis of Elise.*' My father's imagined words fell from my lips and my stomach leapt. 'Oh, and she has pink hair and this stunning ink on her back, like a painting. And her eyes...' Realising I was maybe talking too much, I let my words trail off as I waited for some snide comment from Tom—especially about the tattoos and pink hair.

Instead, he shook his head and smiled genuinely. 'Wow. That's bloody awesome, Fin. Good on you, mate.'

I shook my head as I took another gulp and swallowed. 'Nope. It's not in the slightest bit awesome because I totally messed it up, Tom.'

'I don't get you.'

I took another swig of my drink, buying a little more

time before I confirmed that I was, in fact, a giant imbecile. 'I asked her out for a drink one night when I was at the karaoke club. That night when you were busy and I went anyway. We… um… we ended up at my place and…' I waved my hand around, unable to finish the sentence.

'Oooohooo. So you got your jollies off, mate. Good on you. I still don't get the problem.' *Typical Tom.*

Dragging my hands roughly through my hair, I tugged at the roots, annoyed with myself all over again. 'I really liked her, Tom. But the next morning… after we'd… um… *again*, I kind of fobbed her off by saying something really lame about having too much shit going on in my life and that she seemed like a really nice girl—'

His eyes widened in horror. 'You didn't?' He'd just confirmed my worst fears in those three words. 'What did she say after she slapped you?'

Cheers for your support, mate. 'She didn't slap me, actually. But she pretty much told me to get stuffed. Can't blame her really.'

'Awww, mate. I get the feeling you regret that now?'

I shrugged. 'Yeah. I don't know, it sounds a bit

mental, but I felt... I don't know... *something*. Like a... like a connection or something. But that probably sounds insane. I don't know. I don't know what it's like to *choose* my own woman, for goodness sake. How the hell do *I* know what I'm talking about?'

Tom laughed, reached across the table, and punched me lightly on the arm. 'Fin, I think if you like someone and she makes you feel good then you've pretty much got your answer. When you're spouting off crap about making connections with her, take it from me, it sounds like it has the potential to *be* something. You just need to call her, mate. Take the plunge. What have you got to lose?'

Heat rose in my cheeks. 'That's the problem, though. I don't have her number.'

He raised his hands in the air in exasperation. 'Awww, you *idiot*! How could you not get her number? Do you know where she lives? Where she works?'

I knew where she worked but I wasn't sure if I could pluck up the courage to show up there. She would no doubt blow me off after the way I had treated her. 'I don't know where she lives but she works at McVey's Coffee House in the city.'

'Bingo! Just go and apologise. Ask her out on an official date. Sorted.' He clapped imaginary dust off his hands.

It *did* sound simple, and no doubt to Tom, it was. But he hadn't seen the look on her face as she had walked away from me. The hurt in her eyes in spite of her words. She had listened to my problems and given herself to me intimately, but I had acted like a total arse. Could a large enough portion of humble pie exist for one so bloody stupid?

Later on, when I arrived home to my empty apartment, a sense of melancholy descended over me once again, like a dark cloud unwilling to free me from its path. My phone rang and I eagerly answered it but instead of Star's voice I heard Hetty's. She had heard on the grapevine about my father's actions and was heartbroken on my behalf. Hearing the woman who had been like a mother to me sobbing, because of my actual father firing me, hurt so much I could hardly speak. My eyes stung and a lump formed in my throat.

'Hey, I'll be fine Hetty, I promise. You brought me up to be strong remember? Please don't worry.'

'After all the years I've known how hard hearted

that man is, I never thought I'd see the day when he let his pride rip him from his son. You don't deserve this, my love, you really don't. You deserve happiness. So much happiness.' I told her about Star, hoping that knowing I had met someone might lighten her worry but all that did was make me feel worse. I was lying to her. After all, I had mucked it up and Star and I weren't going anywhere.

Once the call was over the despondency I felt weighed me down even more. I had purposefully not told Hetty about losing my job because I knew how devastated she'd be. But hearing the pain in her voice had almost broken me.

I switched on my stereo and stuck in a Stone Sour CD and lay on my couch, thoughts whirring through my head of a pink-haired girl with the most beautiful brown eyes I had ever seen. If only I could go back and change how I'd reacted. It had all been so sudden and overwhelming. Having such strong feelings for a stranger wasn't normal, surely?

But she had clearly felt it too.

The next thing I knew, I was standing outside the coffee shop in a torrential downpour, looking in through the steamed up glass, watching Star smile brightly and make small talk with the customers in the shop. I rubbed on the pane to defog a space so I could see her more clearly. God, she really was stunning. Quirky yes. But beautiful all the same. Suddenly, she lifted her gaze and locked eyes with me. My heart leapt and I tried to raise my hand in a wave, but a look of disdain washed over her features and she shook her head with a sneer, her feelings for me evident in her closed-off body language. I tried to call out but my voice became trapped in my throat, and suddenly it was difficult to breathe. It was like someone had stolen the air from my lungs and I grasped at the window, trying in vain to catch her attention. Trying to scream her name.

But... nothing.

I awoke with a start to the irony of Stone Sour's 'Through Glass' playing in the background. Perhaps the lyrics had spoken to my conscience as I slept. I huffed and shook my head before rubbing my hands roughly over my sore eyes. The look on Star's face as I peered at her in my dream wouldn't leave my mind. How could I try to make amends now? I was pretty sure this was how she'd react. Perhaps the premonition had saved me from making an even bigger fool of myself?

12

STAR

The following Saturday, after my 'encounter' with Mr McYummy—who, for the record, I renamed Mr McAssface—took far too long to arrive. I had the day off which was on the insistence of Alec, who said I was souring the milk thanks to my newly acquired perma-scowl. I appreciated the fact that I would get to sleep in. Although, as usual, I was wide awake at seven a.m. just like always.

When I gave up trying to get back to sleep, I went into the kitchen and found a note from Alec.

Good morning, Twinkle Toes,
I've gone for a wee jog before opening up

the shop so I'll see you tonight. Text me later and tell me what you want for dinner and I'll grab something from the Chinese takeaway on my way back. I fancy something spicy but I'll go out on the pull another night 😉

Loves ya,

Al

I giggled and yawned simultaneously which made my ears pop. Try it. It's not easy. You're trying it, aren't you? Anyway, I made myself a peppermint tea and sank into the welcoming comfort of the ragged old couch that had seen better days. I put my feet up and carefully sipped the steaming liquid. The knock on the door that came next made me jump and I almost scalded myself. *Dumbass Alec no doubt forgot his keys... again.* I seriously worried about how forgetful he was becoming. After wiping the bottom of the mug on my fluffy robe, I placed it on the coffee table while cussing him under my breath.

As I unlocked the door, I shouted at him through it. 'I'm gonna get you one of those chains so you can keep the damn things around your neck.' I yanked the door open and gasped.

A wide-eyed look of horror greeted me. 'You're going to make me wear *what* on a chain around my neck? Should I be scared?' Fin stood there with a playfulness to his expression.

I fisted my hands on my hips, trying not to be amused. 'What are *you* doing here?'

He cringed as his cheeks flared bright red and he held out a huge bouquet of the sweetest smelling flowers. 'Well, I kind of made a rash decision to turn up on your doorstep in the hope that you'd forgive me. I was a complete arse. I know that now. And... I'd really like to take you out for breakfast. Like I should have after we... you know... *after*.'

I scowled and tilted my head as I defensively folded my arms over my chest. 'After you slept with me *twice* and then decided I wasn't good enough for you?'

His brow creased. 'Hey, I never said that. Nor did I think it. I'm not a snob, Star. I'm just an arse.'

I tried not to laugh, and pursed my lips before speaking with a stern expression and a sarcastic tone. 'Oh, well that's okay then.'

He rolled his eyes and then looked up at the ceiling. 'You're not going to make this easy for me, are you?'

'Make *what* easy? You made things perfectly clear—'

Before I could finish my snarky retort, he stepped forward, slipped his hand into my hair, and crushed his mouth to mine. At first, I shoved on his chest. *How dare he presume he can kiss me and make things okay?* But after a few seconds of fighting it, I gave into him. In truth, I *melted* into him. The fact that we were half in and half out of my doorway didn't bother me until I heard the voice of one of the neighbours.

'Good morning, Scarlet.' I jerked away from Fin's lips and flicked my head in the direction of the lecherous middle-aged man who had *never* gotten my name right. *Ever*.

'Oh... um... good morning, Sidney.' I couldn't be bothered to correct him yet again, and so I grabbed Fin's jacket and yanked him inside. I shoved him up against the wall, almost squishing the flowers he still clutched. Anger and lust bubbled up from deep within, in almost equal measures. 'What the hell are you *doing*? You treat me like crap then show up on my doorstep with flowers and some lame-ass apology and expect me to be okay with you *assaulting* me?'

He laughed and that irritated me even more. '*Assaulting* you? You kissed me back, *Scarlet.*' He sniggered and I wanted to slap the stupid expression from his handsome, gorgeous, face, with its luscious lips, and eyes as blue as the... *Oh, God. I've got it so, so bad.*

'That guy *never* gets my name right. And anyway... yeah... well... you...' I fumbled around in my kiss-fogged head, but couldn't find any more angry words to yell at him.

He smirked again and nodded. 'Yes, that's a very strong argument you're making there, Star. Ever thought about being a lawyer?' The sparkle in his eyes trapped me and I forgot why I was arguing with him.

A worrying thought crossed my mind and I narrowed my eyes. 'How did you find out where I live?'

'I did mention that I'm a former lawyer, didn't I?'

'That's not much of an explanation, *stalker* man.'

'Let's just say I wanted to find you so badly that I resorted to underhand tactics that included the misuse of my connections.' He pulled me against his firm chest and kissed me again. His tongue slipped into my mouth and caressed mine in a delicious, passionate dance. *Damn hunky Scotsman.* He pulled away and my eyelids fluttered open to find his gaze fixed on me. 'So... can I take you for breakfast now?' he whispered.

I narrowed my eyes suspiciously. 'Take me for *breakfast,* or *take me* for breakfast?'

He reached up and tapped his chin as he pursed his lips. 'Hmm. I'm not entirely sure what you're getting at, Star, but if that's an invite...' I slapped his arm and he chuckled. 'Look, I'm hungry. For *food.*'

The sigh that left me was supposed to sound like exasperation, but instead made me sound like some loved-up, swoony teenager. 'Gimme five minutes to change.'

13

___

FIN

I watched as Star disappeared through a door to my left and fought the urge to fist bump the air. She had agreed to go for breakfast. It was a start. I placed the bouquet of partly crushed flowers on the coffee table and glanced round the living room. The photo prints on her walls looked really familiar and I stepped further into the room to get a closer look.

Sure enough, the prints had the initials S.A.M in the corner, just the ones I owned and adored, and my excitement rose. Maybe this was *another* thing she and I had in common. We both liked the same photographer's work. How spooky was that? I made a mental note to chat to her about that. Next, I thumbed through her CD collection. It made me smile that she too had row upon row of discs in the days of playlists. My fingers landed upon a particular case and I pulled it out to examine it closer. My face stretched in a wide grin.

'Oh, you found my The Darkness CD.' I jumped and almost dropped the case. How had she sneaked up on me so quietly?

I turned to face her, holding the CD aloft, and we both spoke simultaneously. '*Sexiest band ever.*'

She burst out laughing, hands across her stomach. Her laugh was musical. Such a lovely sound. 'Wow. Who would've thought, huh?'

I couldn't help the wide smile that took over my face in response. She was truly fascinating, and I wanted to dig further. 'So, what's your favourite song of theirs?'

She pursed her lips and looked to the ceiling. 'Hmmm. That's a tough one. I guess it would be a tie between "I Believe in a Thing Called Love" and "Growing on Me".'

I nodded my agreement. My admiration for this sexy American was growing by the second. 'Wow. You've got great taste.'

'Oh, I know,' she answered playfully. 'So, where are you taking me for breakfast?'

I placed the CD back on the shelf. 'There's a little place on Rose Street I think you might like.'

Her responding smile was encouraging to say the least. 'I think I know the place you mean.' We walked towards the door and she grabbed a camera bag from the hall table.

I shoved my hands in my pockets and couldn't keep the inquisitive tone from my voice. 'You're taking your camera?'

She shrugged. 'It goes almost everywhere with me.'

Intriguing.

We left her apartment and I followed her down the stairs to the foyer. She'd pinned her hair up and my gaze was drawn to the delicate curve of her neck. She was such an enigma, and I loved that about her. I loved her individuality. Her spunk. But I loved the way she'd caved into me when I kissed her. Although I knew I had a long way to go to get her to completely forgive me, I felt like I was possibly on the right track.

We walked through the doors of Patisserie Valerie on Rose Street, and took a table by the window. After we had perused the menu, I ordered us eggs Florentine and a pot of breakfast tea.

Whilst we waited for our food to arrive, I decided to try again with the apology. 'Look, Star. I really am sorry about the way things ended last time. As soon as you walked away from me when I'd returned your phone, I felt awful. I just... I wanted to call into the coffee shop and apologise but I felt sure you'd tell me where to go.'

She folded her hands on the table before her and looked directly into my eyes. 'You would have been right.' A heavy sigh followed. 'I felt used, Fin. I don't *do* the one night stand thing, and after you and I slept together and it turned out to be just that, I realised I'd made a huge mistake. I'm not cut out for that kind of non-relationship.'

Shit. I really had done a number on her. 'I was the same. Believe it or not, I don't sleep around, Star. That wasn't me either. But... God, this is going to sound so bloody corny...' I let my head fall back and I closed my eyes for a moment.

'Go on. I happen to like corny.'

When I lowered my gaze to meet hers again, a

sweet smile played on her lips. For a moment, I forgot to speak. 'Oh, yeah... I was going to say that it didn't feel like a one night stand. It felt... *I* felt something more than that.' My face heated at the admission, and I worried she was going to laugh and tell me to get lost for being too full on.

Instead, her smile widened and her cheeks blushed pink. 'I thought that too,' she almost whispered. But then her sweet smile disappeared. 'Look, evidently we're both from completely different backgrounds and we lead totally different lives, Fin. Your family would no doubt reject me from what you've said about their feelings towards Elise, and I'm just not cut out to be a strait laced "normal" person. I just don't see—'

'Opposites attract,' I offered urgently, desperate not to lose the tenuous connection we had going on.

I was relieved when she smiled again. 'Apparently so.'

Leaning towards her, I took her hand in mine across the table. 'Can we maybe just see where this goes? Spend some time getting to know one another, perhaps?'

She silently stared at me for a few moments before nodding. 'I'd like that.'

Relief flooded my veins and my heart leapt. I was getting a second chance with my feisty American girl.

Well, she wasn't mine... *yet*.

Our food arrived and our conversation stopped for a short while whilst we tucked into our breakfast. After a few delicious mouthfuls of the creamy eggs and spinach, I figured there was no time like the present on the getting-to-know-Star front. 'So, the photographs on your wall. You like S.A.M too? Or do they belong to your flatmate?'

She paused for a moment, took a gulp of her tea and placed the cup back in its saucer. 'Oh, um, my flatmate mostly. Are... are you a fan?'

'Oh God, yes. The biggest. I bought my first piece a few years ago now and I'm always on the lookout for more but they're harder to find than rocking horse poop!' I laughed and shook my head. 'It's the way he captures light and shade and just gives everything this... oh, I don't know... kind of ethereal glow... if you know what I mean.'

She smiled and cocked her head to one side. 'What makes you think S.A.M is a man?'

Huh. What *did* make me think that? I huffed out a long breath as I pondered. 'I don't know. I guess I just presumed.'

She pulled her lips into her mouth and placed her cutlery down. Her gaze fell to her lap. 'I have it on very good authority that S.A.M is—in actual fact—*female*.'

Wow! She knows her! On a scale from one to a hundred of intrigue, I was at around a billion. 'Oh?'

She nodded slowly. 'She is. And I can confirm this... because... because I'm *her*.' She held her hands out to emphasise her point and her cheeks flushed cerise.

I sat there open-mouthed, just staring—gaping—at the beautiful, talented woman before me, and I think I fell in love at that very second.

14

STAR

I lifted my gaze to meet Fin's, only to find him staring at me with his mouth open. I wasn't sure what to make of it. I'd just admitted a *huge* secret to him. Something I just didn't tell people. Lord only knows why I felt it necessary to tell him *that* little snippet of information about me, but I'd felt compelled to tell someone. The only person who knew already, apart from my parents, was Alec. I'd never been one for bragging about my skills as a photographer. My friends just considered me 'snap happy' and I'd never bothered to correct their assumptions. But now someone knew. *This* someone knew. And I wished I could've sucked the words back in somehow.

The longer he stared at me, the worse I felt. I wiped my clammy palms on my jeans and waited for him to speak. When he didn't, I had to break the silence. 'I'm only kidding around.' I laughed, nervously brushing a stray hair out of my eyes.

He slowly shook his head from side to side. 'No. No, you're not kidding. *You're* S.A.M. You are, aren't you? Of course you are. Star Anahi Mendoza... *S.A.M.* Of course.'

Rolling my eyes, I rubbed my palms over my face. 'I should've kept my mouth shut.'

I watched his Adam's apple bob up and down and the open gawk was replaced by a wide grin. 'Bloody hell, you're amazing. Absolutely bloody amazing. Your pictures... honestly, nothing two dimensional has *ever* been able to make me feel such... such a range of emotions, Star. Oh, God. Now I sound like a groupie. Forgive me. I'm just... I'm blown away. I *love* your work.'

Tingles ran the length of my spine as I listened to him enthuse about *my* pictures. I'd never particularly felt proud of something before, but the way Fin spoke made me straighten my back a little more and hold my head up. 'Really?'

'The image of Edinburgh castle at night with the silhouette of the lovers. Wow... just...wow. I get goose-bumps whenever I stand in my living room looking at it.'

I scrunched my brow in confusion. 'I don't remember seeing it when I was there.'

'No. Most of my artwork was in boxes when I left my old apartment. I finished putting things on the wall this last week. Wow. I can't get my head around the fact that it's you. I *love* that it's you.' His voice trailed off and I met his penetrating gaze that told me there was more behind what he was saying.

Butterflies took flight in my stomach and hope flourished inside of me. 'Well, thank you. It's good to know my work is appreciated.'

'Do you ever do exhibitions or anything like that?' he asked, with obvious enthusiasm.

'Oh, no. I have my work in a few small outlets, but no. No plans to exhibit. I do it for myself mainly. Because I love producing images. And anyway, I don't think anyone would be interested.'

His responding wide-eyed stare of incredulity

shocked me. 'You're wrong. So wrong, Star. *I* love your photographs, and I can guarantee others would too. You should consider it. In fact...'

Narrowing my eyes again, I wondered what was going through his mind. 'In fact what?'

He waved a dismissive hand. 'Oh, nothing. Forget it. But I would love to see more of your work. If you'd like to show it to me.'

I couldn't help giggling like a teenager. 'Hmm, maybe I should invite you up to see my etchings.'

He laughed, throwing his head back, and I could've melted on the spot. That voice, that laugh, that smile.

Sheesh, I was *totally* done for.

15

FIN

After taking Star for breakfast, we went for a walk through the Princes Street Gardens, and she pointed out some of her favourite places to shoot. Every so often, she snapped a shot of a view that caught her eye, and on a couple of occasions, she snapped shots of me when I was supposedly focused elsewhere. She was absolutely fascinating. And when she spoke about her art, her face glowed, and her eyes danced with the passion she clearly felt, soul-deep, for her work.

I didn't want to make any more mistakes with her, and I decided I would ask her the question that had almost been burning my tongue off all morning.

'So... would you like to go for dinner with me sometime?'

She stopped and I followed suit, turning to face her. She pursed her lips and snapped a shot of me as I waited with a crumpled brow for her answer. 'I'm not sure if I've totally forgiven you yet.'

I stepped closer to her and stuck out my bottom lip. 'Pwetty pweez go on a date with me.'

She giggled and shook her head, taking another candid shot. 'Urgh! It's against my better judgement, but okay.'

My heart somersaulted in my chest. 'You're saying yes?'

She rolled her eyes and nodded. 'I'm saying yes.'

'Fantastic!' I fought the urge to hug her, deciding to be a gentleman instead. 'So, can I pick you up tonight? Say around eight?'

'Wow, you don't waste any time, huh?'

I laughed. 'Strike whilst the iron's hot, I say.'

'Okay. Eight tonight. Where are we going?'

'How about Café Andaluz?'

Nodding, she told me, 'Oh, I love tapas. It reminds me of my abuela. Sounds great.'

Confused by what she meant, I scrunched my brow. 'Abuela?'

She beamed. 'My grandma. My dad's mom. She's very traditionally Spanish hence *abuela*.'

'Ah! Sweet.' Excitement knotted my insides and I tried to stifle the ridiculous grin fighting to spread across my face. 'Great. Great. Okay. I'll see you at your place at eight then.'

She chewed her lip and stepped back. 'Uh-huh. Well... I should go. I need to pick up some stuff before I head home so...'

'Until tonight then.' I leaned and placed a gentle kiss on her cheek, and as I did, my senses were filled with that intoxicating scent of jasmine.

I paused maybe a little too long and she pulled away. 'Bye, Fin.'

'Bye, Star,' I breathed, like a swooning teenage boy.

* * *

As I made my way back to my apartment, I pulled my phone out and dialled Tom's number. He answered quickly, and before he could make some insulting quip like he usually did, I blurted out, 'Tom, I need to speak to you about something, mate. You'll never believe what's happened. Are you free?'

'Ooohkay. Siân's in at the gallery today, so yeah. What's up?'

'Can you be at mine in ten?'

After he confirmed he'd be there, I hung up and almost jogged back home as adrenaline and nervous excitement coursed through my veins. I had a way to make amends for my shitty behaviour to Star, and Tom was the right man to help me.

Once back at home, I paced the living room floor until Tom arrived. As soon as he knocked, I flung the door open, almost causing him to fall flat on his face.

He frowned and shook his head. 'What the hell has you all riled up, Hunter?'

'Come in. Sit down. Coffee?'

'I think you might have had too much of it judging by how on edge you are, mate. Cut to the chase, pal.' He plonked himself down on my leather couch and stretched his arms across the back.

I sat in the chair opposite. 'I've finally got S.A.M.'

He laughed heartily. 'Ah, don't worry, buddy. I'm

sure you can get ointment for it. Better get some quick before your dinky drops off, eh?'

'The photographer, you arse. You know the photographic prints I'm crazy about? The ones Elise hated? Well, I've found the artist behind them.'

He sat up straight and his eyes widened. 'No shit!' Tom knew how long I'd been trying to locate the artist, or any information, but even with all his contacts in the art world, he'd drawn a blank. 'So... who is he?'

'He is a *she*. And *she*'s called Star Mendoza.'

His brow crumpled. 'Wait... isn't she...? Didn't you...?'

I nodded emphatically. 'Yep. It's *her*.'

'Well, shag me sideways.' He ran his hands through his short brown hair.

I sniggered. 'I think I'll pass, mate.'

'You have to get her to agree to an exhibition, Fin. Would she do it?'

Spurred on by his enthusiasm but a little unsure, I shrugged. 'Honestly? I was hoping you'd say that, but I don't know. She doesn't strike me as the type of person to go in for the spotlight.' I continued to tramp across the carpet expelling as much nervous energy as I could.

'Well, I would've thought the same of *you* until I saw you on stage, Fin. We all have our secret passions. And isn't this the girl with pink hair? I'd say she was quite keen on attracting attention.'

That was a good point, actually, although she didn't come off as an exhibitionist which contradicted her appearance. 'I'm taking her to dinner tonight so I'll maybe put it out there.'

Tom chuckled. 'Oh, I don't know if she'd want to see it so soon again if it's about to drop off.' He broke into full-blown guffaws. 'Ask her about the exhibition too mate, eh? And don't get arrested, okay? Especially if you haven't got a cream for your *S.A.M* problem yet.'

I rolled my eyes. 'Seriously, you're an arse.'

He simply continued to laugh.

16

STAR

'Twinkle, you're going to wear a bloody trench in the floor at this rate.' Alec's voice dragged me back to earth from whatever fantasy world my mind had been briefly trapped in. I glanced over to where he sat on the couch with his glasses perched on the end of his nose, newspaper in hand.

'Are you sure you don't mind me abandoning you tonight?'

He shrugged. 'Didn't really want Chinese food anyway. Might go for a pizza at Marco's ristorante and drool over that Italian waiter instead. Now will you bloody sit down? You're making me dizzy.'

I sat as instructed. 'Do I look okay? I mean... he's

usually so well dressed in his designer suits and… well, I'm more shabby than chic.'

He peered at me over the top of the broadsheet. 'Oh please. You look bloody gorgeous. Sex on a stick.'

I shook my head. 'Need I remind you that you're gay?'

He placed down his reading material and waved a dismissive hand. 'Well, if I was straight, I'd pounce on you.'

I let out an exasperated sigh/growl. 'Alec! I don't want to be *pounced upon,* as you so delightfully put it. I just want to… I want to be *good enough.*'

Uh-oh.

His brow crumpled and he took his glasses off. 'What did you say, Star?' The look of incredulity told me I was in for a lecture. 'I don't *ever* want to hear you say you're not good enough for someone. Do you hear me, lady? You're intelligent, kind and bloody gorgeous, and if he doesn't think so then maybe *he's* gay. And if that turns out to be the case, pass him my number, okay?' He winked.

I couldn't help but laugh at his blatant attempt to steal my not-quite-boyfriend. Unable to settle, I stood and walked to my room once again. Standing before my full-length mirror, I examined my outfit. I had chosen a fitted tartan pencil skirt, with a black fitted shirt. My biker boots finished off the look and I had let my hair fall in natural pink and blonde waves round my shoulders. I was going for smart/casual, but with my individual personality slipped in for my own l comfort. The shirt was tight fitting and I wondered if it was too provocative. I was on the verge of changing when Alec appeared at my door.

'I'm heading out, babe. Will you be okay when Prince Charming arrives if you're alone?' My heart jumped so hard it almost escaped my throat and splattered on the carpet.

'Oh magooooosh.' I waved my hands like they were on fire. 'It's a date, Alec. An official date. Shiiit.'

'Breathe, darling'. You'll be absolutely fine. And one of these days I want to meet him and make sure *he's* good enough for *you,* not the other way around.'

Alec kissed my cheek and then disappeared, and I heard the door close as he left. My heart pounded in my chest and the butterflies were learning a *Stomp* routine in my stomach. Fin had been on my mind so much that I was beginning to get scared. I hadn't felt this way in... *forever*. And yes, I know the early part of a relationship is usually about passion and excitement, but what if I wanted more? And what if I was setting myself up for a fall with someone who was so different to me? How would I cope if it all went horribly wrong, considering the way he was already taking over my every waking thought? I inwardly chastised myself for over-thinking, as usual, and checked my appearance one last time.

Even though I was expecting it, the loud knocking that followed almost caused me to jump out of my skin. With shaking, clammy hands and jelly legs, I made my way to the door, inhaled a deep, calming breath, and opened it. Fin stood there in dark jeans, white T-shirt, and a black leather jacket. I trailed my gaze down the full length of his body and back up again, swallowing hard when our eyes met.

He smiled warmly. 'Wow, you look stunning.'

I touched my hair like women in the movies do when given a compliment, and immediately felt stupid. 'I... I was going to say the same about you.'

He pulled his bottom lip in at one side and tilted his lips up further. 'Shall we? It's a nice evening so I thought we could walk.'

I began to relax. 'Sure. Sounds good.'

We left my apartment block and began the walk into the city centre. I could see Fin glancing at me in my peripheral vision and it made my stomach flutter. His phone pinged in his pocket and he took it out, glanced at the screen and gave a light laugh before putting it away again.

I must have had a questioning look on my face as he said, 'Baby spam. My brother just sent the latest photo of his daughter dressed in a bumble bee outfit. Poor kid.' He laughed again.

'Do you see them often?'

He puffed out through inflated cheeks. 'Not as often as I'd like. They live outside the city and my brother is a GP with his own practice. He's always complaining there aren't enough hours in a day. I used to feel the same before I was between jobs.'

I detected a slight dip in mood and tried to lighten it. 'You'll be glad to know I left my camera at home for a change. No Fin spam this evening.' I nudged him.

He smiled then opened and closed his mouth a few times before finally speaking. 'On that subject... I have something to ask you.'

I turned and narrowed my eyes suspiciously. 'Hmm... sounds ominous.'

He fell silent and I wondered if he was going to ask me after all. Eventually, he took a deep breath and began. 'I have this friend. Tom Fielding. He manages an art gallery in the city centre. He... I... Look, I told him about you and he already knows how much of a fan I am. Anyway, he asked if you'd be interested in putting on an exhibition.'

I stopped in my tracks, horrified at the idea. 'No! No, I don't want to open myself up for all the crap that comes with being *known*. I'd rather just blend into the background, Fin. I don't want the limelight.' Panic set in, and what had been excitement turned sour.

He placed one hand on my upper arm and tilted my chin up with his finger so that I met his gaze. 'This from the girl with pink hair and tattoos?' Okay, so he had a point, but I didn't like it. He tenderly ran his thumb over the tip of my chin. 'Don't you realise how talented you are, Star? Tom knows your work through *my* love of it, and he knows good art when he sees it. I really think you could make something of this. It could be a fantastic career opportunity for you.'

I frowned and sighed, unwilling to think about the idea further. 'I like my career just fine. Photography is just a hobby.' I hoped that would be an end to it.

'But... I don't understand. I bought some of your work so you must be happy to sell it.'

He certainly was tenacious. And again, he had made a valid point. *How the hell do I explain?* 'That was a long time ago, and it was a mistake. Alec convinced me to sell a few of my pieces via a couple of little craft shops, but I felt... I *feel* really uncomfortable about it. I'm *not* an artist. It's something I do to relax and get through tough times. I... I can't think about changing that. You go down that road and things become a chore. I don't want that.'

He cupped my cheek and nodded as he leaned in and kissed the middle of my forehead. It was such a sweet gesture and it caught me off guard. My insides melted as he ran his nose along mine.

He smiled. 'Okay. I'll drop the subject. I wanted to do something nice for you, and I thought it would be something you'd like to consider. No bother though.' He let his hand fall away from my face but kept his gaze locked on mine. 'But... just for the record... and you may not like the fact, but you *are* an artist, Star. And a very good one at that.' And with that, the subject was, thankfully, closed.

We continued to walk, but my mind was whirring with worries and paranoid thoughts of my inferiority. Was he concerned about my lack of career? Was I simply not good enough for him whilst I worked in a coffee shop? Would an artist with a fancy-pants exhibition be more befitting of him? *Stop it, Star. Remember what Alec said.*

I gradually relaxed as we arrived at Café Andaluz and were escorted through the brightly tiled restaurant with its brass, punched lanterns and vividly coloured cushions to a cosy table in back. Fin pulled out my chair and we were handed menus by a handsome, olive skinned waiter who had a genuine Spanish accent and informed us that his name was Matias. After making our selections, Fin ordered a bottle of Rioja and our waiter left, returning moments later with the bottle for Fin to taste.

Once Matias was satisfied that we were happy he left us alone and I tentatively asked Fin, 'So... have you spoken to your dad at all?' I wasn't sure if my question was intrusive, but after how down he had been on the night I officially met him, I was concerned.

He took a long gulp of his wine and shook his head. 'I have no desire to contact him, to be honest. I think our relationship has finally hit rock bottom. I just don't see us getting past this.'

Poor guy. 'It must be hard for you. I can't imagine what it's like.'

Our food arrived and the waiter arranged it in front of us. The smell of spiced chicken and fresh bread infiltrated my senses and my mouth began to water in readiness for the feast.

Fin stayed quiet until we were alone once more before he spoke. 'Well, it seems you've always been close to your parents. They support you unconditionally. It's how it should be. I never really had that.' He shrugged, and the pain in his eyes made my heart ache for him.

Sadness washed over me as I watched him twisting his wine glass between his thumb and forefinger. I needed to lighten the mood. 'So, have you been singing lately?'

He laughed and shook his head before widening his eyes briefly and huffing the air from his lungs. 'No. No, I don't think I'll be doing that again any time soon.'

His reticence to perform surprised me, and I decided to dig deeper. 'Really? But you're so good. You should be in a band.'

His blue eyes sparkled in the dim lighting of the restaurant. 'Hmm. I'm not so sure about that.'

Okay, so he's happy to try and drag me kicking and screaming from my comfort zone, whilst his feet are firmly planted in his own, huh? Duly noted.

Our conversation was easy and light, and the food was sensational. So many different flavours to tantalise my taste buds and remind me of my grandmother's cooking. I didn't want to stop eating, but there came a point where I had visions of being wheeled home in a cart, and so I reluctantly placed down my fork.

I pushed my plate away and heaved a contented sigh. 'Well, I can't eat another mouthful.'

He patted his stomach. 'Me neither. Bloody good though, eh?'

I smiled, hoping my appreciation shone through. 'Delicious. Thank you.'

We sat in silence for a few moments, sipping the last of our second bottle of Rioja until Fin gestured to the waiter for the check. I excused myself and made my way to the ladies' room. Once I was finished washing my hands and touching up my lip gloss, I checked out my reflection. My cheeks were flushed, and for some reason, I was getting nervous again. But this was the end of the evening, so I would be going home, *right*?

'You will *not* sleep with him tonight. You *will not*,' I told my reflection. And then, '*Please* don't sleep with him tonight,' I finished off, more realistically, before making my way back to the waiting blonde dreamboat.

17

FIN

Walking through the city of Edinburgh at night was one of my favourite experiences. Being there with Star beside me made it so much more special. The place was alive with revellers and music. Even though it was past ten, there were people still making their way into town to start their night of fun. The castle was illuminated with colourful lights that cast rainbows over the stony surface, just like the print I had bought by S.A.M. Now known to be Star.

We'd shared a wonderful evening, and I wasn't ready for it to end. Reaching out, I tentatively took her hand, hoping she didn't pull away. When she laced her fingers with mine, a wide smile took over my face.

My mind whirred with what I could say to make the evening last longer. After taking a deep breath, I took the plunge. 'I'm not really ready to go home yet. How about you?' *Please say you want to stay out a little longer.*

She cringed and chewed on her lip briefly. 'Oh, I don't know. It's getting late.'

I didn't want to push the issue. I was still trying to regain her trust, after all. 'Okay. No bother. Shall I walk you home then?' I hoped I'd managed to hide my disappointment.

She nodded shyly. 'That'd be great, thanks.'

I couldn't help the sinking sensation deep inside as we walked, hand in hand, back towards Star's apartment. The last thing I wanted was to say goodnight so soon, but I was very much aware that I had to play it just right.

My phone began to vibrate in my pocket and my steps came to a halt.

Pulling my phone out of my jacket, I glanced at the screen. 'Would you mind if I answer this? I don't recognise the number, but ever since my dad had a heart attack, I always get a feeling of foreboding when my phone rings at night.' She nodded for me to go ahead and I hit the green button. 'Hello?'

'Hunter? Finlay Hunter?' asked a voice I didn't recognise.

'Who is this?'

The man chuckled. 'I'll take that as a yes. This is Alasdair McKendrick. You're a hard man to track down, Mr Hunter. You have a lot of friends protecting you, my boy.'

What the hell?

Alasdair McKendrick was my father's arch nemesis, and the main man at rival law firm McKendrick Law. Their feud went way back. Why the hell was *he* contacting *me*? And why so late at night?

Goosebumps prickled my skin. 'Why are you calling me?'

'I have a proposition for you, and I'd like to arrange to meet you. Face to face. Name the time and place and I will make sure I'm available.'

'I don't think there's anything you could possibly propose to me that I would be the slightest bit interested in.' My tone was terse and unforgiving. Although, I wasn't sure why. I'd never had any dealings with the man, and the only information I had ever garnered about him had come from the very biased source of my father.

'Come now, Finlay. Aren't you a tiny bit curious to hear what I have to say?'

'Not until I know *why* you want the meeting in the first place. There's no love lost between you and my father and I'm not sure *I* trust you either.'

He sighed and I noted a sense of disappointment. 'That's a wee bit unfair, don't you think? You don't know everything behind the issues your father and I have. Look, I have an urgent matter to be dealt with and I'm aware that you're currently between jobs which means you may be able to assist me. In fact, I can think of no one better qualified than you. As far as love being lost goes, I'm aware of the rift between you and your father. It's not my intention to exacerbate that situation at all. I simply need someone for an important issue and you come very highly recommended.'

Confusion and irritation increased in equal measure deep inside me with every passing second, and I scrunched my brow, regardless of the fact that he couldn't see me. 'Need someone for what exactly? And hang on, recommended by whom?'

'Someone we know mutually, but that's not important right now. What do you say?'

'I say why are *you* contacting me? Don't you have a team who does all your dirty work for you?'

'I *do* have a team, Mr Hunter. But I felt it best to converse with you directly on this occasion. Just come and meet with me. We can discuss the details then. Are you free tomorrow? Say eleven at The Balmoral?'

Curiosity got the better of me. But I wondered if I was about to become another dead feline as a result. 'Okay. Tomorrow at eleven. The Balmoral.' I hung up without saying goodbye.

Star stepped towards me with a look of concern on her face. 'That sounded intense.'

Still reeling from the call, I shook my head to dislodge the deep unease that had settled on me. 'Yes. Yes, very bizarre, in fact. That was someone from a rival law firm wanting to discuss *something* with me.'

Her eyes widened. 'Really? Wow. What are you going to do?'

I pursed my lips and exhaled loudly. 'I'm going to

meet him and see what he has to say for himself. Nothing to lose, I suppose.' I shrugged.

She nodded. 'Very true but... be careful, okay? Your dad's already pissed at you.'

I clenched my jaw as my stomach knotted with anger. 'My dad fired me, so quite frankly, he can sod off,' I snapped. She bit her lip and I felt shitty for taking my frustration out on her. Reaching out, I cupped her cheek and stepped closer. 'Hey, I'm sorry. You're the last one I should be taking out my anger on.'

Her responding smile was warm. 'It's okay. You're bound to be feeling a little stressed. All you can do is see what he says.'

Without another word, I bent and lowered my face to hers, gently brushing her lips with mine. The feel of her mouth yielding to me confirmed that I hadn't offended her with my outburst, and relief spread through my veins, warming my heart. She was special. I could feel it soul-deep, but it was too soon to tell her so. She'd think I was bat-shit crazy. But the awareness was there all the same. I would bide my time. Take it slow. I couldn't afford to scare her away.

We began walking hand in hand again, and much to my disappointment, we arrived at her home rather too soon. I glanced up at the door and then back at Star, where she stood before me.

'I'd invite you in but...'

'It's okay, Star. I totally understand. I have a long way to go to get you to trust me again.'

She gazed up at me with those beautiful big brown eyes of hers, and I tried hard to read her mind.

Her delicious mouth tilted up at the corners. 'I think you're doing well so far. Thank you for a lovely evening.'

Without thinking, I pulled her into my arms and pressed her against me. I found her mouth with my own and kissed her with all the urgency I was feeling. Her hands slipped up my arms until she grasped at the straggly strands of hair at my nape, kissing me back with just as much fervour. I was becoming addicted to the taste of her kiss. In fact, I was already there.

I wanted her. I wanted to stay the night and keep talking, keep kissing. But this wasn't just about sex. It was more. It was about being *with* her.

She pulled away, her breathing ragged and her eyes wide. 'I... I should go. If I don't, I'm going to invite you in and I really need to *not* do that. Not tonight.'

Smiling down at her, I was relieved I was affecting her the way she was affecting me. My heart pounded in my chest and I wondered if she knew what she was doing to me; how she was under my skin already.

'When can I see you again?' My voice sounded husky.

She smiled shyly again. 'Soon. Maybe we could meet in a few days? Wednesday maybe? We could go to DeBasement.' She tilted her head to the side.

The glint in her eyes was irresistible, and the words, 'Okay, sounds great,' fell from my mouth before I had really thought them through. *Oh, well. Too late to back out now.* 'Can I pick you up again? Say around eight?'

'That'd be great. Um... would you like my number just in case something comes up?'

'Oh, yes, good idea.' I bit the inside of my cheek in the hope it would halt my over-enthusiasm. I took my phone out and she reeled off her number for me.

I immediately texted her so my number would appear in her phone too.

'Thanks again, Fin, it's been lovely. I'll see you Wednesday.' She kissed my cheek then unlocked and opened her door.

'Goodnight, Star,' I said softly, just before she stepped inside.

Once her door was closed again, I set off back home, my thoughts flitting between the gorgeous girl I'd just left and the bizarre call from McKendrick. What the hell could he possibly want with me? To say I was intrigued would have been a major understatement. But I would find out soon enough.

I resolved to put thoughts of my father's enemy to the back of my mind in favour of the more desirable thoughts of Star Mendoza. My American girl. How could I have been so stupid when I almost lost her from my life? I was so bloody lucky she had been willing to give me a second chance. I would have to make sure not to mess it up this time.

18

FIN

I awoke at eight the following morning after dreaming about an intriguing, pink-haired American girl. I climbed out of bed, remembering I had a meeting to attend at eleven with Alasdair McKendrick. *What the hell could he possibly want from me?* Curiosity still niggled at the back of my mind as I turned on the shower and let the bathroom fill with steam before stepping under the cascade of muscle-melting hot water.

Once I was showered I stood before my bathroom mirror and assessed my less than clean-cut appearance. *Should I shave? Should I try to tame my shaggy hair?* I decided that I shouldn't. It's not like I was going for a job interview. So he needed my help, but I wasn't even sure I wanted to help him yet. I compromised by dressing smartly in my grey suit trousers and black shirt, and after burning the first lot of toast I put in, I sat down on the couch and flicked on the news. The opening story was about the first public appearance of the newest baby to be born into the royal family, funnily enough to an American woman and British man, but the next story had me almost choking on my breakfast.

There he stood, Campbell Hunter, my *dear* father, with a big cheesy grin on his face as he announced to the world that, 'Economic advancement had prevailed over sentimentality' for the major multi-million-Euro-wielding conglomerate who had just won the right to knock down a street of beautiful old cottages at Inveresk—where my brother lived and had his GP practice—in favour of a crass new shopping centre. It was a case I had worked on prior to my rapid extrication from my job, and I loathed myself for having any part in it. The proposed development had been a huge bone of contention between Callum and Dad, and had caused me and Callum to stop speaking for a while because he knew I too was against it and he was angry that I wouldn't speak up back then. I suddenly felt sick to my stomach. Callum had wholeheartedly supported the poor people who owned the cottages had fought tooth and nail with them against the compulsory purchase order, so they could hold on to their beloved homes —homes that, in some cases, had been in their families for generations—but clearly my father's powers had won out.

Again.

With a gut-wrenching determination, I grabbed my laptop and began to research McKendrick Law. The last thing I wanted was to jump out of the frying pan into the furnace. If I was going to meet McKendrick to discover what his proposal entailed then I had to be prepared. And knowledge *is* power, after all.

* * *

At eleven sharp, I was shown through the lavish lobby of the Balmoral Hotel in the city centre, and into a curved, white room with high ceilings, palm trees, and plush furnishings. I had been to dinner at the Balmoral before, but this particular room was new to me. Immediately I wanted to bring Star and made a mental note to book it.

Alasdair McKendrick stood as I approached. I knew of him already and had met him on a couple of official occasions, but not socially. He wore a slate grey suit, pale blue shirt, and a bold red, blue and green tartan tie.

'Finlay. Great to see you. Please have a seat.'

I shook his hand and took the comfy-looking chair opposite him. A dark wood table separated us, and regardless of his formal business attire, it felt a little like we were two friends simply meeting up for coffee and a chat—only in *very* sumptuous surroundings.

He looked relaxed and smiled warmly which, in spite of the fact that it probably should have, didn't make me uncomfortable. 'What would you like to drink? Are you hungry?'

'Just a coffee, thanks. I have plans for lunch,' I lied, figuring I needed a get out plan, just in case.

He called the waiter over and placed an order for a cafetiere and some petit fours. I scrunched my brow and he chuckled in response.

Leaning forward, he whispered conspiratorially, 'I'm not allowed to eat cake at home. My wife, Colette, is a fitness fanatic. It's all about the green tea and lentils.' He shivered and made a face which made me smile. Leaning back once again, he continued, 'Me, on the other hand, well, I have a sweet tooth and the petit fours here are to die for; especially the macaroons. Trust me, you'll love them.'

I smiled and shook my head. How could such a powerful man be so down to earth? He was *nothing* like my tyrant of a father. 'So... you wanted to make a proposition.' I folded my arms across my chest, very much aware of my defensive motion.

'My goodness, straight down to brass tacks, eh? You must get that from your father.'

I smiled briefly but without feeling any emotion attached to the expression. 'Well, I'm sure your time is precious, Mr McKendrick.'

He held up his hands. 'Please, call me Alasdair. And relax a little, will you? You're not up against a firing squad, you know.'

I heaved a frustrated sigh. 'Forgive me for my trepidation, but it's not often one's father's arch nemesis takes you out for coffee and mini cakes, *Alasdair*.' I stressed his name forcefully.

He laughed heartily. 'My, my. So, I'm Campbell's arch nemesis, am I? Well, I can assure you that was none of *my* doing.' The waiter arrived with a large silver tray adorned with coffee cups, coffee pot, and a selection of brightly coloured sweet things that looked far too good to eat. Once the waiter had gone, Alasdair continued. 'Do you know the facts behind the relationship between him and me?'

I shook my head. 'Can't say that I do. All I *do* know is that you're not to be trusted.'

He pursed his lips and nodded. 'I see. I see.' His brow furrowed and he briefly lowered and shook his head. 'Tell me... have you and your father reconciled?'

'No.' My answer was blunt and to the point, and I hoped the matter would be left alone.

He poured coffee into his cup and placed the pot down with the handle angled towards me so I could do the same.

After adding milk and munching thoughtfully on a miniature chocolate gateau, he dabbed at his mouth with a napkin. 'Finlay. I would like you to come and work for me.'

My jaw fell open and I just stared at the man. That was what you called a direct hit. Considering the hostile manner of my reaction towards him, it wasn't what I had expected.

After what felt like an age of me sitting there like a complete dumbstruck idiot, he rescued me. 'Look, I know this is a bit of a shock. But you are one of the best, Hunter. I *only* employ the best. In my humble opinion, you were wasted in your father's firm. Forever in his shadow, as it were. You should be *leading* on the big cases. Maybe you can take some time to think about it.'

'Has... has this got anything to do with you bearing a grudge against Campbell? Because I have enough shit going on with him as it is—'

He held up his hands. 'No. No, this has *nothing* to do with my relationship with your father, or lack thereof. I would have offered you the job whilst you were still employed by him but, well, I presumed your answer would have categorically been no at that point.'

Searching my brain for some kind of response, I

gulped down the hot coffee from my mug, scalding the skin on the roof of my mouth—evidently this was becoming a habit—and muttering expletives as I tried to place my cup down as gently as possible. 'I don't get it. Why me?'

He shrugged. 'Like I said, Finlay, I only employ the best.'

'But how do you even *know* about the standard of my work?'

'I have ways and means. I just want you to think about it. Will you do that?'

I inhaled a deep calming breath. 'Before I agree to even *think* about this, can you explain why Campbell hates you so much?'

He placed his dessert fork down and eyed me warily. 'What would be the point in that? He's your father, and anything I tell you will simply be dismissed as folly.'

'No. No, it won't. I feel it would help me to know... to understand.'

He heaved out a long breath through puffed cheeks. 'Well, to cut a very long, laborious story short... he stole my fiancée and proceeded to turn her against me by making up ridiculous rumours about me.'

My exhaled laugh was without humour. 'Seriously?'

A wistful expression came over his ageing features. 'Isobel and I were together first. I was deeply in love with her.'

What?! 'My mother was *your* fiancée?'

'She was, Finlay. And your father took her away from me.'

Things weren't adding up. 'But... So why does *he* hate *you*? Shouldn't it be the other way around?'

'The difference between your father and me is that I know when to let go. I saw how easily he charmed her. And yes, it broke my heart. But if she was taken with so little reluctance, she was never mine to begin with. The issue now is that your father is still looking over his shoulder, awaiting my revenge. I suppose when you treat people so despicably, you live in fear of reprisal.'

I raised my eyebrows. 'That would explain a lot. He *is* very paranoid.' I was speaking more to myself than to Alasdair.

He paused for a moment and disappeared into

his own thoughts. 'Do you know, Finlay, I will be honest with you. Now I think about it, perhaps on some subconscious level, my employing you *would* be a kind of revenge. Because it would be my intention that you *succeed*. And that would be something that would never have occurred for you, had you remained in your father's employ. But, as unlikely as this may sound, it was not my conscious intention to use you to seek revenge. My employees are treated with the utmost respect and that would be the same for you. We are a team. No one individual is placed under undue pressure. What I'm getting at, Mr Hunter, is that you would be treated fairly. Not used as a scapegoat for your father's misdemeanours.'

As I listened to Alasdair McKendrick speak, I began to see him in a whole new light. His honesty deserved the respect he had mentioned *I* would receive should I accept his offer. And, let's face it, the offer of employment couldn't have come at a better time.

I took a deep breath. 'Okay... I'm in.'

Alasdair's eyes widened. 'You don't want time to think it through? We haven't discussed pay... conditions and whatnot.'

I shrugged. 'Earning a wage is much better than earning nothing. And from the research I've done this morning on your firm, it appears you're an advocate for those who find it difficult to find good representation. To me, that speaks volumes about the kind of man you are, Alasdair. And I respect you for that.'

A wide smile spread across McKendrick's face, and he stood, holding his hand out towards me. 'Well... welcome aboard, son.'

His use of the word 'son' would otherwise have felt condescending, but coming from him, it warmed my heart. It was as if I had done something to make him proud, and the feeling was both alien and gratifying.

This felt right.

This felt good.

I just hoped my gut feeling wouldn't steer me wrong.

All I wanted to do was call Star and tell her the good news.

19

STAR

Hearing the excitement in Fin's voice did strange things to my insides. His enthusiasm was contagious. I listened patiently as he regaled me with the news of his new job, and all worries about him further aggravating his father faded into nothingness. Above all, I was touched he had made *me* the first one he called to share his great news with.

I waited for him to take a breath. 'So when do you start?'

'That's the great part, Star. I start next Monday. God knows what Daddy dearest'll think, but I don't really care to be honest. This job sounds like something I can really get my teeth into, and after seeing what my dad did to those poor people at Inveresk to-day, I can't think of a better way to stick two fingers up at him.'

I had seen the story on the news and seen briefly the type of man Campbell Hunter was. It was clear Fin was nothing like him, and that was a huge sense of relief. I couldn't help but laugh at his overzealous manner.

I'd never heard him so psyched, so enthused, and I liked it. 'I think we should celebrate.'

'Yeah? And how would we do that?' His voice dropped to a deep, husky whisper, and I could almost hear the cogs in his brain whirring over the airwaves. My insides turned to jelly at the mere thought of what he wasn't saying, but we both knew he was inferring.

Gather your wits, Star. Gather them right on up. 'I was thinking we could go singing.'

He huffed. 'Seriously? Wouldn't you rather go for a romantic meal somewhere and then back to my place, maybe?' My silence must have spoken volumes as he cleared his throat and carried on. 'Not that I mean anything other than we should spend a nice evening together, you understand. I know I'm still on your shit list and I don't blame you. I just—'

'Fin. Shut up. You're no longer on my shit list, okay? I just... I need to not rush into this. Let's just have a fun night out as friends, okay?'

'Yeah. Sounds great.' I could sense the disappointment in his voice, regardless of the words he had spoken, but I had to stick to my guns this time. Or at least, I had to try.

* * *

Wednesday rolled around, and as we had agreed, Fin arrived on my doorstep at eight sharp. I opened the door and swallowed hard when I took in his appearance. It was as if I was seeing him for the first time all over again. A fitted black T-shirt with *The Darkness* emblazoned on the front showcased the toned planes of his chest, and I trailed my eyes down towards his jeans. *Oh my God. I'm staring at his crotch!* I immediately snapped my eyes back up to his, which were now sparkling playfully. His dirty-blonde hair was getting shaggier, and he was looking less like a lawyer and more like a lead singer in a rock band which, obviously, made him even sexier. I was kinda glad he hadn't shaved off his beard. There was something just so damned... *manly* about him. Okay, so that's crazy talk seeing as he *is* a man and all, but wow... no man had ever filled me with such desire without even speaking a word.

'Hi. I was just in the neighbourhood and thought I'd stop by and, you know, see if you fancy going for a wee singalong? I know this great karaoke bar.' He had purposefully broadened his accent playfully, and as he winked, I fought the urge to giggle like a schoolgirl, and play with my hair, or throw myself into his arms.

Joining in on his little skit, I tilted my head to one side, putting on a little bit of a Southern Belle accent. 'Oh, I don't know. I do declare I'll have to check my diary. I may have other plans.'

He rubbed his chin and shook his head. 'Well, I can't say I'm surprised. Sexy girl like you with that accent. You must be fighting them off.'

I rolled my eyes and couldn't fight the giggle any longer. 'Oh, purlease... I'm from nowhere near the South. I'm a Midwestern gal and don't you forget it.

Come on, let's go before my head gets any bigger and we have to wheel my ego in a cart.'

He held out his elbow for me and I linked my arm through his.

'So...Wednesday is a happening night, is it?' he asked after we had walked in silence for a while.

'Oh, absolutely. All the sophisticated folks go to karaoke on a Wednesday. How did you not know this?'

He chuckled. 'Well, they do say you learn something new every day.'

'They sure do.' We walked along a while longer in silence, and every time I glanced at him in my peripheral vision, he was staring at me. I tucked my hair behind my ear, suddenly very self-conscious. 'What?'

He gave a small, nonchalant shrug. 'I was just admiring the view.'

'Well, Edinburgh is rather a beautiful city.' I chewed on my lip.

He shook his head, nudged me, and smiled in that lopsided way that made my heart do a dance. 'I was talking about *you* and you know it. God, you're so self-deprecating. It's endearing that you just don't get how gorgeous you are.'

I scrunched my brow. What the hell did I say to *that*? I figured it best to stay silent or change the subject. Luckily, we arrived at the door to the club and made our way inside. It was busy, which was a relief after I had insisted on going there. We grabbed a table and sat as someone murdered a really good song on stage.

Fin leaned in and spoke directly into my ear. 'So, are we doing a duet then?' Thankfully, he dragged my focus away from the guy on stage now everyone was booing him. Have you ever had that situation where your insides knot through embarrassment for someone else? Yeah, well that was me.

I opened my mouth and my response came out with a little too much passion. 'What? No way!'

He laughed. 'So you can't sing?'

'I choose *not* to sing. That's for the likes of those who *are* talented in that area, like you.'

He covered his heart with his hand and dramatically replied, 'Ah, the lady doth flatter me.'

'Nope. The lady doth not wanna get on that stage and make a total asseth hatteth of herself.'

Shaking his head and smiling, he stood and walked over to the bar without further response. As I watched him walk away, focusing my attention on his more than fine derriere, I had to remind myself I was taking things slow.

After a while I was beginning to think he had run out on me, and I was peering around the dimly lit bar, searching for him. Thankfully, I caught his gaze and his eyes locked on mine. Eventually he arrived back at the table and placed a bottle of beer down before me. He was grinning from ear to ear.

'What are you looking so pleased about?'

He chewed on his lip for a moment. 'Oh, I was... um... putting my name down to sing in a while.'

I was shocked he had chosen to do this when he was sober. The last time I had seen him sing he had been a little worse for wear, and so I was suddenly filled with admiration for the handsome, shy man.

Intrigued, I pried for more information. 'What song did you choose?' He simply tapped his nose and shook his head. *So, we're playing a guessing game, huh?* 'Oh, okay. I'll just wait and see then.'

'So how's life at the coffee shop these days?'

I snorted. 'Oh, God. You're not going to want to talk about the weather too, are you?'

His gaze dropped and he picked at the label on his beer bottle. 'Ugh, sorry. I'm not so great at small talk, I guess. I'm actually kind of shy, you know.'

Guilt needled at me and I reached over and squeezed his arm, hoping I hadn't just pushed the emerging conversationalist back into his cocoon. 'Hey, I'm sorry. Things are good. Although it was always more fun when my day started with a visit from my favourite blonde-haired, blue-eyed Scotsman.'

He lifted his gaze and a sweet, coy smile played on his lips. 'Would that be me, by any chance?'

I pulled a silly face. 'Um... duh! Of course it was you. I used to look forward to seeing you every morning. Well, that is until the day you told me you were getting married. You seemed a little different on that day. Changed somehow.'

He faked a shiver. 'Hmm. Well, now I know that kind of change is *not* good, I'll be sticking with my *usual* routine from Monday, so you can expect me at the *usual* time.'

I scrunched my brow. 'But... won't that mean you

take a detour each morning? McKendrick's building is way across the city.'

He reached out and took my hand. Shrugging, he looked directly into my eyes, searing me with his intense blue gaze. 'It'll be worth it.'

My insides disintegrated to mush.

20

FIN

I sat there feeling like a total numpty. I had just said the soppiest thing imaginable to the girl who had stolen my heart. Some crap about it being worth it to make a detour to go buy coffee from her on a morning when I started my new job the following Monday. I was on the verge of taking it all back and making some inane joke when a sweet smile slowly stretched across her kissable lips. I hesitated.

She squeezed my hand. 'Oh, Fin. That's probably the most romantic thing anyone has ever said to me.' *Seriously?* 'Just to know that you would even *suggest* it... I can't tell you how... ugh... words fail me.'

I heaved a relieved sigh. 'Thank goodness. I was

sure you were going to tell me I'm a pathetic wuss and you'd go off to vomit.'

She shook her head. If it hadn't been for the dim lighting, I felt sure I would have seen a pink tinge to her cheeks.

She laughed. 'Not at all. It's really sweet. But you don't have to do that. Cut all the way across town. I mean, I don't expect—'

'No, I *will* be calling. I've already made up my mind. *Every* day. Now, I don't want to be having to wheel your ego home in a cart again but... well, you do make the best coffee in Edinburgh. Even if you don't drink the stuff yourself.'

She fluttered her eyelashes dramatically. 'Well, now the gentleman doth flatter the lady.'

I chuckled at her response as she threw my own playfulness back at me. 'The gentleman doth speak the truth.' A gruff voice came over the P.A. system and announced it was my turn to sing.

Crap. What had I done? 'Ah. I think it's time for the gentleman to get on stage and maketh a titteth of himself.' I stood and gazed down at her mirth-filled eyes as she laughed. She had the best bloody laugh I'd ever heard.

I made my way to the stage, my heart pounding at my ribs, and my throat suddenly as arid as a desert floor. Would I even get *through* a song without alcohol? I wasn't sure at that point. The MC handed me a cordless mic and I took my place centre stage. The opening bars of David Bowie's 'Changes' began to play, and I swallowed, willing some moisture to appear from somewhere so that the notes would make it past my voice box. It was a song that had garnered new meaning lately. The lyrics, well my own interpretation of them at least, made me think of my life. Nervously, I peered out at the audience silhouetted by the bright lights boring into me from overhead. I knew where Star was seated but I couldn't make her out, which, I surmised, was probably a good thing. I may have walked off the stage and done a runner if I'd caught her gaze right then.

As the intro finished, I closed my eyes as the lyrics spilled from my lips almost of their own accord. I immediately relaxed and my grip on the mic loosened a little. Slowly, I opened my eyes and stared out at the crowd as the music vibrated through my bones, building, ready to carry me away. As if in some kind of trance, my feet moved and that was it... I was gone.

I had changed.

The stage persona had thrust his way to the front of my psyche, and I took charge of the stage like some rock star. It was amazing. Adrenaline coursed through my veins, as I let the emotion flow through me and out via my vocal chords. I could feel the smile on my face widening and a weight lifted from me. It had to be the best natural high I'd experienced. Well, after spending time with Star, that is. But my being up there was really down to her.

The crowd began to move and clap along, and although they were someone else's words, the lyrics really spoke to me, I felt them deeply. And Star had been instrumental in the transformation I was undergoing. I couldn't believe I had almost let this chance pass me by, just because she didn't fit the mould I had been trying to squeeze myself into for so long. Who the hell wants to be a carbon copy anyway? And who wants to spend their life trying to please someone who is inherently un-pleasable? I didn't *have* to be what they wanted. I didn't *have* to see things how they did. I was my own person. I was in charge of my own destiny. And if I played things right I would have my very own lucky Star. Thanks to her I had taken the first step to being the me I had wanted to be all along. I was stepping into the unknown but all I knew at that moment was that it was going to be so much better there.

21

STAR

Once again, I watched in awe as Fin's alter ego took up residence on the stage. He simply lit the place up. There was no doubt about it; the man could certainly sing and I loved the song choice. And seeing that transformation from shy sweet Fin to stage persona was like nothing on earth. Goosebumps covered my skin as I watched his mouth form every single word. It was as if he really believed every one of Bowie's lyrics as he belted out the song and strutted around the stage, commanding the audience like a natural born performer. My heart skipped a beat as I watched proudly. I knew he couldn't really see me; the lights were pretty darn bright up there.

But at one point, he seemed to look right at me, and a shiver tickled its way down my spine like he had physically touched me.

He. Was. Amazing.

The song ended and Fin stood there, head back, eyes closed, chest heaving and a serene smile on his gorgeous face. If there hadn't been such a large, loud audience, I would have been up there kissing the lips that had just imparted such powerful words as if they were his own. The crowd erupted, and the raucous noise was almost ear-splitting. They certainly appreciated him. There was no doubt about it. But as if waking from a trance, he dropped his face to the crowd and a look of alarm spread across his features. His eyes widened as whoops and cheers were shouted from every corner.

Lifting the mic to his mouth once more, he muttered, 'Th-thank you,' before sliding the mic in the stand and hurrying off. He didn't come back right away, and I worried again that he had taken off, considering the rabbit-in-headlights look on his face as he took the stairs down from the stage.

After around ten minutes, he plonked himself down beside me and heaved a huge sigh. 'Well, that was fun.' The words were what I expected, but the tone seemed rather sarcastic.

I turned to face him. 'You don't sound convinced.'

'I couldn't get back to you. People wouldn't let me by. Bloody women shoving phone numbers in my hand and guys I've never met before slapping me on the back. Bloody hell.' He shook his head. 'I'm only *me*. And this is only a karaoke club, not the bloody O2 Arena.'

'Well, yes. It was a little self-indulgent, to be honest,' I teased. 'I mean... anyone would think you *were* Bowie strutting around up there.'

He pouted sulkily. 'Hey, I take offence at that.'

I rolled my eyes and slapped his arm playfully. 'I'm kidding around, you jerk. You were amazing. There's no wonder people have that reaction to you. You look so... I don't know... *right* up there. All rock God-ish.'

His face scrunched. 'I... I don't *mean* to look like that. I just... it's like something takes over me.'

'Yeah. You're a regular Jekyll and Hyde, that's for sure.'

He looked thoughtful for a moment. 'Funnily enough, you're not the first to say that.'

'Come on. It's not an insult. Jeez, lighten up, Fin.'

'No, I mean it. I don't go up there to be all showy. I get some kind of rush. Like a release. But it's not an ego thing.'

'Every performer has an ego. Even if it's an *alter-ego*.' I snorted and regretted it immediately. A crease appeared between his brows and his shoulders sagged a little. I wished at that moment that my mouth had a rewind button.

He clenched his jaw. 'I'll show you I can be serious. Just you wait.' Before I could try and assure him I was actually complementing him, he stormed off once again, and I was worried he had just dumped me.

I was having a little trouble keeping up with the guy. He had disappeared more times than David Copperfield—the magician that is—and I was sitting there once again, waiting for his return. When he had left me *this* time, he had seemed to be on a mission to prove a point. What he failed to realise was that he had *nothing* to prove to me. Nothing at all.

I was already gone.

Sunk.

Hook line and sinker.

Done for. Get the picture?

On the stage, some pretty, black-haired girl was rocking out to a Paramore song and making a great job of it, but I couldn't relax. Where the hell had Fin gone? The girl received a loud applause but it came nowhere close to the reaction Fin had received. Music began to play once again; this time a mellow piano rang out around the room, and I guessed I would be watching another singer by myself.

It was getting ridiculous. I didn't even bother to look up at the stage. That is until a familiar voice began to sing about someone being watched from afar. Slowly I turned my head. The lights on the stage weren't as dazzling this time, and I gasped as my gaze locked with the blonde-haired, blue-eyed man I was falling for. I didn't recognise the song but he sang it with such intensity that tears stung my eyes.

This was Fin being *Fin*. This wasn't the strutting, pseudo rock god I'd observed on several previous occasions. This was the shy, vulnerable man I had met in my coffee shop, telling me he felt the same about me. Yes, it was happening fast, but I was helpless to stop myself, and judging by his song choice, he felt the same.

Wow.

He stood in the centre of the stage, holding onto the mic where it sat in the stand. The rest of the club ceased to exist. It was just Fin and me. Every so often, he closed his eyes, but then opened them again and locked his gaze on mine. My heart hammered in my chest and the intensity of what I felt for him in those moments terrified me, but what could I do? He had already stolen my heart.

It was a done deal.

I was transfixed as I absorbed the lyrics and the message he was sending me. There was no doubt in my mind that he intended me to hear them as *his* words. As the song ended, there was a silent pause and my heart leapt into my mouth. Remembering I was in a crowded club, I glanced around. Shit. Had the audience hated it? Then, one by one, people began banging their hands together. Soon whistles and cheers erupted around the room too, and I joined in the ovation. I didn't care that tears were now leaving damp trails down my face.

Fin humbly nodded and thanked the audience

before once again making his way to where I stood. My clapping slowed but the rest of the room continued to show their appreciation. He stepped slowly towards me with something akin to fear in his eyes.

Reaching out, he touched my cheek. 'Well, hopefully that was less of an ego display and you saw some of the real me up there.'

Without uttering a single word, I threw my arms round his neck and crushed my lips to his. The crowd's cheers gained fervour once again, and more whistles pierced the applause. His arms slipped round my waist and he pulled me into his body as he returned my passionate kiss.

I pulled away and gazed into his eyes that were now somehow darker. 'What was it? That song? It was eerily beautiful.'

He smiled. 'It was a song by a band called Aqualung. A little obscure but it seemed to fit. And it's called "Strange and Beautiful."'

I scrunched my brow. 'You think I'm strange?'

He laughed lightly. 'Not in the way you think. But the beautiful part goes without saying.'

I frowned but smiled simultaneously. 'Thank you then... I think.' I vowed to search the song on the web and read the lyrics for myself. 'Can we get out of here?' I asked breathlessly.

'Absolutely. Come on.' He grabbed my hand and turned, but his way was blocked by two *very* large, *very* intimidating men.

Oh, shit.

Fin protectively pushed me behind him, and I peeked out to see what the hell was going on. If they were going to start trouble, I needed to get a good look at their faces so I could be a witness when the cops arrived.

'Evening, gents. What can I do for you?' Fin's unwavering voice oozed confidence, even though I was a terrified, quaking mess behind him.

One of the men, tall... *very* tall *and* muscular, dressed all in black and with shaggy shoulder length hair, was the first to speak. 'We've been watching you for a while now.' *Huh? Oh, God. That does not sound good. Were they sent by his father? Would his father stoop so low?*

Fin tilted his head to one side and his grip on my arm at his back tightened. 'Have you now?'

'Aye. An' we think you're wasted.'

Drugs police? But we've only been drinking beer? Un-

less... oh, God. Someone spiked our drinks? I feel fine, though. I rifled around my head, trying to make sense of the situation. Maybe Fin was a drug addict and they'd been watching him. I mean, how well did I *really* know him? The urge to run came over me, along with a sense of impending doom.

'Oh? You do, eh?' Fin carried on in his firm and calm manner, giving nothing away.

I peeked around Fin's large frame once again. The other guy, the slightly shorter but no less terrifying one of the pair, had a beard and a shaved head, was the one to speak. 'Aye, that's right. A bloke with a voice like that shouldn't just be doing karaoke. He should be heading up a band.'

What the...?

Long-haired guy butted in again. 'And we just happen to be sans singer at the moment.'

I leaned my head on Fin's back and heaved a sigh of relief. *Sans singer? Seriously? Is this some kind of bad joke?*

Fin laughed, making his body vibrate and relax. I guess he was as relieved as I was. 'Are you kidding me? I thought you were going to beat me up or something.'

The two huge men burst into raucous laughter and I came out of hiding to witness not a beating, but a kind of bizarre male bonding as they all shook hands and laughed about Fin's—and my—error of judgement. Fin introduced himself and me to the guys, and draped his arm round my shoulder casually now he had relaxed.

'Thanks, guys, but I honestly think you've got the wrong impression of me. I'm... I'm a lawyer, and I'm definitely not good enough to sing with a band. I do the karaoke thing for a laugh. I just—'

'You're joking, aren't you? Have you *heard* yourself sing, pal? You're the dog's danglies.' The huge man's strong Scottish accent made me smile. I could listen to that accent all day.

I glanced up at Fin to see his face scrunched in disbelief. 'Nah. It's nice of you to say that, but honestly, I'm just not up to it.' He tried to push past them, pulling me along behind, but they were not letting him pass.

The other guy gestured wildly at Fin. 'Come on, come on, Fin. Just come and meet the rest of the crew, eh? We all agree you're the man for the job. You're amazing, seriously. And I think you may be a wee bit surprised at what you discover about us. Just come and meet everyone, eh?'

Fin turned to face me and pleaded at me with his eyes. I smiled widely and cupped his cheek with my hand. 'I'm sorry, Fin, but they're right. You have an amazing voice. But it's not just that. You've got stage presence. It's like you become someone else up there. You should go talk to them.'

His eyes widened for a moment. 'Really?'

'Really.'

'Right... so what kind of music do you play?'

Long haired guy—now known to be Nate—replied with a grin. 'It's usually classic rock, a bit of Whitesnake, a bit of Rainbow, Deep Purple, maybe the odd bit of Queen, Bowie and Fleetwood Mac thrown in for good measure. What do you think?'

A smile spread across Fin's face and he nodded. 'Okay then. I'd like to hear more.'

The men, Nate—the long-haired one who played lead guitar—and Billy the bass player—the bald one, took us to a table where other members of their band sat, along with their girlfriends. Nate went to order a round of drinks, and Fin sat beside Billy and pulled me into his lap.

'So, tell me more about this band of yours,' Fin said, after the introductions were made.

'Well, we play for fun. We all have day jobs and we don't take ourselves too seriously. The guy who was singing for us got fed up of playing. Can you believe it? Anyways, he went off to pursue his dream of opening a bloody deli in Kelso, and so we were left with Nate on vocals. Don't get me wrong, he's not bad but... well, we want him to be able to concentrate on lead guitar, and so we've been auditioning singers for around three months now.'

Nate returned with a tray full of drinks and handed them round. He gave me a bottle of beer and winked as he sat beside me. I felt my cheeks heat a little. I think I was still a little bit intimidated by the hulk of a guy.

'So, I take it none of the auditions have gone that well?' Fin said in response to Billy.

'Nah. But to be honest, we've had our eye on you,' Nate informed him.

Fin shook his head, gulped his beer, and glanced at me with a look of confusion. I shrugged. He turned back to Nate. 'I... I don't really get that.'

Nate and Billy exchanged glances before Nate

began the story. 'Okay, a wee while ago you were in here all dressed up like an accountant or something. You looked pissed sitting with your mates. But then you somehow ended up on stage, singing like a pro, man. It was like you'd been zapped by aliens or something. You know, given super powers or whatever. We were blown away. But you didn't seem in the right frame of mind to be approached back then so we bided our time.'

'Aye, and then we've seen you a couple more times up there today. You've got some kind of split personality type of thing going on; a real case of the Jekyll and Hyde's. Seriously, when you get up on that stage, you transform from this business suit wearing, serious, straight laced dude into a rock god. It's a freaky thing to watch. We all knew we wanted you for the band, but, well, it's not the kind of thing you say to a total stranger, is it? "Hey pal, you're a freak, wanna sing in our band? You'll fit right in."' Everyone round the table laughed again.

Another guy who had been introduced as Titch the drummer—which, let me tell you was totally ironic considering the fact he was *another* giant— joined the conversation. 'Look, Fin, we're not under any illusions that we're going to be rich and famous. But we love music and we know we've got potential. We just need the right guy up front once again so we can go out there and show folk what we're made of.'

'And you think I'm the one to help you do that?' Fin didn't sound convinced.

'We *know* you are, mate. If what we've seen you do up there on that stage...' He gestured to where a mousy-looking guy was singing 'Karma Police' by Radiohead. '...is what you're capable of in a karaoke club, then we can't wait to see what you do rocking out on a stage with a live band and original material.' The rest of the people round the table voiced their agreement with Titch.

Fin turned and gazed at me where I sat on his lap. His eyes were begging for me to say something. I stroked my finger down his cheek tenderly and smiled. 'I agree with these guys. I think you should go for it.'

His eyes widened. 'You do? Seriously?'

'Absolutely. They're right. You are an amazing performer, Fin. You just need somewhere to showcase your talent. You have nothing to lose.'

He chewed his lip for a moment and then

grinned. Turning back to the guys at the table, he held up his beer bottle. 'What the hell. I'm in.' Everyone at the table erupted into applause and cheers. Beer bottles were clinked, hands shaken, and backs slapped.

'So, what do you guys call this band of yours, anyway?'

Once again, the band members shared knowing glances. 'Now, that's the freaky part, mate. We're called *Mr Hyde.*'

The rest of the evening was spent getting to know the guys from Mr Hyde and making arrangements for them to meet up and rehearse. Numbers were swapped, many beers were consumed, and there were a lot of laughs. They were such a cool bunch, despite first impressions, and regardless of how patronising it may sound, I was so proud of Fin. I didn't mind sharing his attention for the evening.

My new man, the lead singer.

Because, let's face it, I couldn't resist him after he had sung especially for me, and I was going to give in. I was lying to myself if I thought otherwise. It somehow didn't matter that the situation was escalating like a runaway train going downhill. I just hoped there were no huge branches on the track...

Just thinking about him on stage did funny things to my insides and made me want a future with him. I *had* promised myself I wouldn't jump back into bed with him so soon, but after that song, things had shifted. My whole world had tilted on its axis and the realisation had hit me that *something* in my life suddenly had the potential to have a huge impact. He felt like 'the one', and regardless of how much I told myself not to rush, my heart wasn't listening. They say the heart wants what the heart wants, and my heart wanted to ignore my head and go full pelt, head first into the deep with this guy who seemed to have some kind of dual personality.

But that just made him all the more attractive and mysterious.

It turned out the name they had chosen for the band, Mr Hyde, hadn't been some kind of happy accident. Their band personae were their badass alter-egos. Nate, the lead guitarist, was an I.T. consultant by day, Billy was a Math teacher, and Titch—whose given name was David—was a property developer.

They all said they felt from the get go that Fin

was right for the band, simply by the way he had got on stage in his suit and rocked out like a completely different person. And if I had believed in fate, I would have agreed that perhaps it *had* been Kismet at work. In fact, the more I thought things through, the more I was beginning to believe...

* * *

After bidding the group of friends goodnight, Fin and I made our way outside. He took my hand and spun me round to face him. 'Hey, we didn't finish off the conversation we started earlier.'

I thought back to the moment he took me in his arms when he had finished serenading me with Aqualung's 'Strange and Beautiful'.

I felt my cheeks heat and was thankful we were outside in the dark of the Edinburgh night. 'Oh, yeah. We kind of got side-tracked, I suppose.'

He released my hand, and stepping towards me, he slipped his fingers into my hair and stroked my cheeks with his thumb. 'I know we said we'd take this slow... and I really want to respect your need to do that, and I do. I *really* do. But... I can't help the fact that I want you, Star. When we're apart, I can't stop thinking about you. I want to get this whole thing right, but I'm scared of messing up again, so please set the pace here. Tell me what you want... *please?*'

Gazing up into his hooded eyes, I saw such sincerity, need, and desire all mixed together, and my mind was made up. 'I want you too, Fin.'

We almost ran across the city in the direction of his apartment block, only sharing heat-filled glances and smiles. A promise-filled silence hung heavily in the air between us and I was sure passers-by could read what was on our minds. But I didn't care. Not even a little bit. I let him lead me, trying to keep up with his long-legged, determined strides.

He stopped abruptly at a crossing point, hit the button to cease the relentless evening traffic, and turned to me. 'Are we crazy? Are we going completely mental, Star? We've known each other for what... two minutes in the great scheme of things.'

My heart plummeted in my chest. 'We... I mean, I can go home—'

He stepped towards me and cupped my cheek in his huge hand. Dipping forward, he rested his forehead on mine, and I could see his jaw ticking under his skin. His warm breath made my face tingle. 'Oh God, no. Don't misunderstand me here. I have *no* intention of letting you go home. Not unless you want to. No, this... this between us. It's like nothing I've ever felt before. And it's terrifying the hell out of me. It's all so fast. But, at the same time, I don't want it to stop.'

Relief flooded through me. We were on the same page. 'Neither do I.'

The crossing began to beep to let us know it was safe to go, and Fin kissed my forehead before grasping my hand again so we could set off once more.

We arrived at the door of Fin's apartment, and he smiled warmly as he slipped the key into the lock, turned it, and moved aside so I could enter. Once I was standing in his living room, he appeared before me. Lifting his hand, he stroked his fingertips gently down my cheek. 'I want you so much, Star. So, so much. You're like no one I've ever met. I'm drawn to you. But I screwed things up before, and God knows I don't want to do that again.' A crease appeared between his brows and his internal conflict was almost palpable.

I stepped closer and smoothed my hands up his chest. 'Let's just forget what happened before, okay? I think you made it clear how you feel earlier. I think we may have passed the point of taking it slow, but... we can take *tonight* slow.'

He lowered his mouth to mine and inhaled deeply as his hands found my hair, and I gripped his jacket, tugging it from his broad shoulders. He removed his hands from my hair long enough to let the coat fall to the floor, but within a split second, he was pressed against me again. His heart pounded against my chest and my legs weakened at the intensity of the kiss. He pulled away from me once more and slipped his hand into mine, tugging slightly as he walked backward towards the bedroom.

22

FIN

You know how people joke about having an angel and a devil on their shoulders? The ones who have conflicting arguments about a person's decisions? Yeah, well that was usually me. It *had* been me the last time I had found myself in this position with Star. Thankfully, this time my angel and devil were on the same page for once.

I led her towards my bedroom, walking backwards so I didn't have to take my eyes off her. She was stunning. There was no other word for her. Every strand of her silky blonde and pink hair, every permanent mark of artwork on her skin; her curves, her eyes, her smile. *Everything.* I know they say fools rush in, but I wasn't going to dwell on that. I was overwhelmed by all these feelings and emotions that had never reared their heads before, and I couldn't think straight.

All I knew was that the way I felt right then and there bore no resemblance whatsoever to the way I'd felt for Elise. And I nearly *married* her. You hear all these things about love at first sight and such, but I was a total cynic about that kind of stuff. But *this* girl. My strange and beautiful Star had some kind of hold over me. And yes, it was scary, but nothing worth having ever follows the easy path, surely?

Since that first night she had infiltrated my every waking minute. All I could think about was being with this sexy, quirky woman who broke the mould of what I had been instilled with as my 'ideal'. She was like no one I had ever encountered. Now, I know my experience was limited, but there was no ignoring the reaction I'd had to her from the beginning. She was my *heart's* choice, and that was what mattered.

I was... *beguiled.*

Once inside my bedroom, I leaned towards her again and covered her mouth with my own. The taste of her and the feel of her heart beating against mine was an intoxicating combination; one that I definitely wanted more of.

When I woke the following morning and stretched out my arm to feel for Star, the bed was cold and my eyes sprang open. I was alone. *Oh no. Did she leave?* As my brain gained consciousness, I heard water running, and singing. I smiled at the sound and rolled onto my back, taking a quick glance at my clock. It was almost seven. I languidly extended my taut muscles and replayed the intensity of the night before. As I remembered the feel of her wrapped round me, a smile played on my lips. I closed my eyes briefly and imagined introducing her to Callum and Tori and the thought didn't terrify me. Perhaps I'd arrange a meet up. Tori was such a caring and accepting person anyway and my brother just wanted me to out of Dad's clutches and happy—two things I was more than on my way to achieving.

Climbing out of bed, I walked into my bathroom and was immediately cocooned in the steam billowing from the shower enclosure. Star was singing a medley of the songs from the previous night and I chuckled as she impersonated David Bowie. The singing stopped and her head poked round the shower screen.

'Good morning, Mr. Hunter. Care to join me?'

She didn't need to ask me twice.

At around eight, as we ate scrambled eggs on English muffins, I kept catching her watching me in my periphery. There was something on her mind.

I smirked and shook my head. 'Come on. Out with it, Mendoza.'

She scrunched her brow and her cheeks turned a sexy shade of rose. 'Out with what?'

'Oh, come on, Star. I may not have known you long but all the signs are there. You have something to say, so say it.'

She placed her fork down and pushed her plate away. 'I... I think I'm waiting for you to ask me to leave.' Her voice was a fragile whisper, and she momentarily let her head fall forward.

A wave of guilt mixed with dread washed over me and I swallowed. 'Really?' I placed my own cutlery down and pushed my chair away from the table.

What had I done to elicit such a negative reaction? 'Come here.' I patted my lap.

The pink in her cheeks grew brighter. 'What? Why?'

'Just come here,' I insisted, and thankfully the strong-willed woman acquiesced, walked round, and positioned herself in my lap. I tucked the curly strands of damp hair behind her ear. 'Star, whatever I've done to make you feel that way, I'm sorry. I don't want you to leave. Although I know you have to go to work soon, so I'll let you off for that. But I do want you here. I want to get to know you. All of you. I know we rushed into things the first time and I acted like a total idiot, but now I know what I want, and that's you, here with me. I want us to see where this is going because, I don't know about you, but I... I feel this could be something important. Do... do you?' I swallowed hard again, suddenly overcome with anxiety at what I was suggesting. In not so many words, I was telling her I wanted a serious relation-ship. I hadn't known her very long but I just... *knew*.

A sweet smile spread across her lips and she took my face between her palms. 'I really do, Fin. It feels right. Which—as you pointed out last night—is totally crazy considering the length of time we've known each other. But, every relationship has a beginning and I'm happy to see where this goes.'

On hearing her affirm her feelings about us, relief and excitement surged in my veins and I pulled her towards me so I could kiss her deeply.

And my God, I knew my heart could potentially be in serious danger. But I didn't care.

23

STAR

It was great to be home.

Not from Fin's. I hated leaving there. I mean from the coffee shop. Alec had badgered me for info all day long at work. He also had the audacity to tell me my ever present smile was beginning to look sinister. I couldn't help laughing out loud at that. Luckily, I knew he was only joking. Jeez, a girl couldn't win.

On more than one occasion, I found myself humming 'Strange and Beautiful' and realised I was drifting off into a dreamland where only Fin and I existed, wrapped round one another in his oversized bed.

Even after arriving home, making myself a peppermint tea, and sitting down on the couch to drink it, I was off in some fantasy world that almost caused me to scald myself. I caught the slipping mug just in time as my phone began to ring telling me there was a video call coming through from my folks in the States.

I tapped the screen. 'Hi!' I said a little too excitedly as my parents' smiling faces appeared.

'Hey, pumpkin. It's Mom and Dad. How's our little Star doing?'

I laughed. 'I know it's you. I can see you. And I'm hardly *little*, Dad. But... I'm good, actually.'

My mom narrowed her eyes. 'I know that tone of voice. Who is he?'

My God, how were parents so attuned with their kids when they lived so far away? 'I'm sure I have no idea what you're talking about, Mom.'

'Oh, come now, Star. I'm your mother. You can't fool me.'

She was so right. I sighed but did so with a huge grin on my face. 'He's gorgeous and his name is Fin. Oh, and did I mention he's a lawyer?'

My mom and dad shared a knowing look. My

mom pulled her lips in between her teeth and widened her eyes. It was hard to keep a straight face.

They both returned their attention to the camera. 'So, tell us about Fin. How long have you known him?'

'Oh, not long. But... well, I think this could *be* something. We just... we click. They say opposites attract, right? And I think that's us. He's all corporate suits and formality, and I'm all crazy clothes and pink hair.'

Mom's brow crumpled. 'He... he sounds very *serious*, honey. Are you sure he's right for you?' *Mom, ever the worrier.* Thankfully, I knew there was another side to his personality.

'Oh, Mom, you have no idea. He has an interesting hobby.'

My dad gasped. 'Oh, God. Tell me he's not into all that stuff you read about in those erotic novels. Not that I've read any, but... well, you *hear* things. And I know we're very open, honey, but I'm not sure I—'

My mom gasped and whacked his arm. 'Jerry, for goodness sake. Let the girl speak, will you? And how the hell is that the conclusion you drew?'

Dad's cheeks flushed as if he'd been caught with

his hand in the cookie jar and he rubbed his arm, even though I knew it wouldn't have really hurt him. 'I read something on the internet and there was a movie too. I just don't want her—'

I rolled my eyes. 'Mom! Dad! Stop! He's a *singer*. Okay? He sings. That's all. Jeez.'

I watched as both pairs of shoulders relaxed and their smiles returned. 'Oh, that's great, honey. What kind of music does he enjoy singing? Opera?'

I snorted, almost choking on the mouthful of tea I had just gulped. How the heck had they come up with that idea? Was it the mere fact he was a lawyer? Talk about judging. It surprised me as they weren't normally so quick to assume. 'Opera? Um... not exactly. He sings rock songs. Loud, gravelly rock songs. And his voice, ohmygod, it's enough to melt your p...' Suddenly remembering I was talking to my parents, I just about stopped the word *panties* from falling from my lips. '...heart. He melts my *heart* with his voice.'

'Awww, you seem smitten, kitten,' Dad replied, and it was my turn to breathe a sigh of relief.

'Yeah, Dad. I kind of am. It's all been very sudden but we're just seeing where it goes.'

'Well we're very happy for you, sweetie. You deserve someone wonderful.'

'Thanks, Mom. I think so too.'

The rest of the conversation centred on Grandma and if I was visiting her often enough, then what the family were doing back home, and what my old friends were up to. Alec walked in just as the call was coming to its usual emotional ending and I was feeling kind of homesick. But once I hung up, I was back to evading Alec's questions about my night with Fin. Alec was the master of distraction techniques, and he knew very well when I needed them to be used on me.

'So, was it better this time, Twinkle?' he called from the kitchen.

'I am *not* having this conversation with you,' I replied in a bright, sing-song voice.

'Oh, come on. We share *every*thing, you and I. Just tell me. Was it better knowing that he has feelings for you?'

Rolling my eyes for what felt like the hundredth time that day, I replied, 'Oh my God, is *nothing* sacred? *Yes*, okay? *Yes*, it was amazing. *He* is amazing. Happy now?'

Alec's head poked round the door into the living room. 'I knew it. You're falling for him.'

Bit late for that. I covered my face to hide the fact that I was blushing and grinning like a maniac. 'I think he's sweet. That's all I'm saying.'

Alec chuckled, and as I peered at him through my fingers, he made some dramatic gesture with his hand; a kind of *talk to the hand* thing. 'Yeah, whatevs. I know that bloody expression. Just... be careful, okay? He hurt you once before and I don't want to see you go through nasty stuff you don't deserve. Tell him I'll sort him out if he hurts you again.'

I lowered my hands from my face and was met with an expression of deep concern. I stood to face him and placed my hands on his arms. Looking him directly in the eyes, I boldly told him, 'I'm a big girl, Al. I'll be fine.'

Oh, please God let me be right for once.

'I sincerely hope so, Twinkle.' He leaned forward and kissed my forehead. 'Now come on, we've a date with Granny Aggie. I've brought her some of her favourite chocolate cupcakes from the café.'

I smiled and shook my head. 'You know how to get on her good side.'

He tapped my nose. 'Granny Aggie only has good sides.'

24

FIN

The weekend rolled around and I was getting 'Star withdrawal'. I hadn't seen her since our date on Wednesday, and although we'd video called and messaged each other in the few days since, I hadn't had my fill of her. I had hoped Saturday would make up for that but she had a prior arrangement with her Grandma. Thankfully, my brother called and invited me for dinner, complaining that he'd feared I'd dropped off the face of the earth. I apologised and accepted willingly, figuring I had so much to tell him —and it would be a good distraction from pining like a pathetic love-sick teen.

'So, how are you feeling about the stuff with Dad

now?' Callum asked as he poured me a glass of wine. It was early Saturday evening, and Tori, his wife, had cooked the most amazing lamb tagine. She was still breastfeeding Charlotte too but she wouldn't rest.

I took a deep breath, followed by a long swallow of my drink. 'I feel numb to be honest, Cal. Hurt that he could treat me like that, but numb at the same time.'

'Well, he was always a stubborn bastard. I don't see that changing any time soon. Why do you think Tori and I keep out of his way these days? She doesn't need it with us having Charlotte now. But to be honest, I suspected things would go this way.'

Callum's admission surprised me. 'What do you mean?'

'Well, you tried so hard to be what he wanted, Fin. And there was bound to come a day when you realised you had to live your life for *you*. The thing with Elise was never going to work. You two were forced together. It was tantamount to an arranged marriage. That shouldn't have happened. Not in this day and age. But you had to realise that for yourself. I couldn't help you there.'

I almost choked on my drink. 'But that's the

thing. *She* dumped *me*. I would've married her. That's how stupid I am. That's how important it was to me to please him. What does that say about me? The fact that I was prepared to marry someone I wasn't in love with just to make him happy. My God, what a pathetic arse I was.' Anger and resentment fought for priority and my skin prickled.

Callum reached across the table and grasped my forearm. 'Hey, you are *not* an arse. And there's nothing pathetic about wanting to make your dad proud. And believe me, brother, all this says more about him than it does you. And I think if Elise had turned up, you would have realised when the vicar got to the 'Has any one got any objections' bit. And if you hadn't, *I* would have said something at that point. Either way, you wouldn't have been marrying her; I can assure you of that.'

'Well, it's all a moot point now, anyway. And anyway, I have more news. I've been offered a job and I start on Monday.' I could hear the hesitance in my own voice.

Callum sat up straight and eyed me warily. 'Bloody hell. That's quick going, but great, obviously.

Sorry, go on. I'm guessing from your tone of voice that you're worried about telling me.'

I laughed. He was right in a way. 'I'll just come right out and say it. It's with McKendrick Law.'

Callum's eyebrows rose and he glanced at Tori who had just come back from her fifth trip to the loo. He nodded. 'Well, spank my arse and call me Mandy, my little brother has grown a pair.' A wide grin spread across his face. 'I'm proud of you, Fin. You have the potential to actually be recognised for your talents there.'

'Funny, McKendrick said the same thing.'

Callum rubbed his chin thoughtfully. 'From what I've heard outside of Dad's little bubble, Alasdair McKendrick is a decent bloke. Very family orientated.'

'Yes and on that note, have you heard the real reason Dad and McKendrick don't get along?'

Callum pursed his lips and narrowed his eyes. 'Can't say I have, why? Do you know something I don't?'

I nodded slowly. 'Our dear innocent father stole Mum from McKendrick. Not the other way round.'

Callum's eyes widened and he opened his mouth into an 'O'. 'Seriously?' I nodded again. 'Well the bloody old shit. Although I can't say I'm surprised. He tends to dig his heels in until he gets what he wants. Nasty piece of work. I know he's our dad but he's a bastard, isn't he?'

I tilted my head and grinned. 'You could say that.'

'Well, good luck, brother. Not that you'll need it. It's the right decision. And it'll piss Dad off no end. Another good reason to go for it.' He chuckled and held his hand out to me and I grasped it and shook hard as relief washed over me.

'I think it's wonderful too.' Tori returned from taking Charlotte up to her cot and walked over to me.

'Thank you Tori, I really appreciate this. I'm relieved you're both so accepting of my decision.' It almost felt that in losing a relationship with my father, I had gained a better one with my brother. A phoenix from the ashes, if you like.

'That's not all.' I stood between my brother and sister-in-law. 'I've kind of got a new hobby.'

'Please don't tell me it's skydiving. I think I may

cry. Post-partum emotions are great fun.' Tori laughed.

'No. I kind of accepted the gig as lead singer in a rock band.'

It was Callum's turn to almost choke on his drink. He coughed. 'Bloody hell! Seriously?'

'Yep. We start rehearsals next weekend. They saw me singing at that karaoke club, DeBasement, in the city and, well the rest is easy to suss, I guess.'

'Hells bells, Fin. I'm *so* impressed right now. This is bloody amazing. You're actually fulfilling a lifelong dream at last! Does Hetty know? If not you must tell her. And what have you done with shy, mousy Fin? Where's my brother? What have you done with him?' He laughed.

I shrugged and grinned again. 'What can I say? They think I'm awesome.'

'Well, you always could sing. I just never thought you'd have the guts to actually do something about it. That's bloody brilliant, Fin.' He grabbed me and hugged me hard.

I laughed as he slapped me on the back. 'God, I feel like this is some weird tell all chat show. I have other news too.'

'You won the lottery? 'Cause it sounds like you're having a winning streak, brother.'

My cheeks heated as I realised I'd saved the best news 'til last. 'Ha ha, it kind of feels like it, but not literally, no. I met someone.'

'This someone... is it a guy or a girl?' I smiled at my brother's question. Clearly, he was expecting it to be a day of admissions. 'Because you know we love you and it would make absolutely no difference to us.'

'I know that, Cal. *She* is a beautiful American girl called Star. And she's... she's just amazing.'

Callum clapped his hands together and laughed. 'Don't tell me you've fallen in love *for real*, Finlay Hunter?'

'Well, it's a bit early to say, but there are definite feelings. And I may be falling, yes.'

'Bloody hell! I'm cracking open that bottle of Glen Carragher. This is all cause for one mahoosive celebration. Good thing you've got a cab coming to take you home, eh?' And off he went to the cellar where the good liquor was stored.

* * *

After drinking too much whisky at my brother's house, I took a cab home, and the second I walked through the door, I decided to message Star.

F: Hey gorgeous. Have had a tell all sesh with my brother and his wife. All's good in the hood 😉

I hit send and then re-read my words. I clearly had whisky brain. If only there was a way to detract text messages. A reply came soon after.

S: Hey there, handsome. So glad all is good in the hood. You do know you're neither from 'the hood' nor American, right? 😉

She made me smile even when she wasn't with me. I instantly hit reply.

F: Imagine my embarrassment when I figured that out! Look I miss you. I mean really miss you. I know you're with your grandma tonight but maybe we can meet up after my first day?

I waited for her reply. And waited... and waited. After thirty minutes, I gave up hope of receiving another message and decided her battery must have died or she was having too much fun with her gran.

Figuring distraction techniques had worked earlier, I decided to choose my outfit for my first day at McKendrick Law—it surprisingly took me less than an hour. And it felt good to know I was prepared. A little drunk, but prepared all the same.

I selected my slate grey suit, white shirt, and silver and black tie, and it was all hanging on my wardrobe door ready. I'd decided I didn't want to wear black as I felt maybe that would give the impression either, a) that I was mourning, or b) that I was on some kind of power trip. Neither was the case.

I was feeling very positive.

I was making my way to the bedroom when there was a knock at the door. My heart rate increased, and I knew exactly whom I wanted to be standing at the other side.

After unlocking the door, I flung it open. There she stood in pink skirt that matched her hair, a black

T-shirt, and denim jacket. She looked good enough to eat.

She tilted her head to one side. 'I missed you too,' she breathed. And with that, I stepped over the threshold, scooped her up in my arms, and crushed my lips to hers.

25

STAR

I awoke on my back to find Fin wrapped round me once again. It was quickly becoming my favourite way to wake up. His left hand was hugging me to his side, his right arm created a halo round my head, whilst his left leg was entwined with both of mine. Each warm exhale that caressed my skin caused goosebumps to rise and a tingle to shiver its way down the length of my body. Turning my head ever so slightly, I watched him sleep for a few minutes. His blonde hair was sticking up at all angles, and the beard covering his angular jaw was no longer spiky but soft to the touch.

There was no other word for him right then than

delicious. I couldn't help but smile as I watched his eyelids flutter in REM sleep. He must have been dreaming as his arm twitched a little, and I stifled a giggle.

'It's creepy, you know?' he mumbled.

Huh? His voice startled me as his eyes were still closed. 'What's creepy?' I wasn't sure if he was talking in his sleep.

'Staring at someone when they're sleeping. It's creepy.' His Scottish accent and gruff morning voice melted my insides, and the smile that widened his lips turned me to total mush. I poked him in the ribs and his eyes opened abruptly. 'Hey, Mendoza. You're going to pay for that.' With one swift move, he had me pinned to the bed and was blowing raspberries on my neck.

I squirmed and fought whilst giggling like a teenager. 'Hunter, no! Stop it! I swear to God I'll pee in your bed! Please... stop!' Thankfully, the mention of pee on his high thread count sheets stopped his attack and he jumped off me as if I was on fire.

'Urgh! Go to the bathroom, woman! We'll have no incontinence here!' He shoved my naked butt, eliciting further giggles from me. I had to virtually hop to the bathroom as I laughed but, thankfully, I made it in time.

We shared a very lazy Sunday, eating toast in bed and getting crumbs everywhere you really didn't want them. We talked at length about our families and friends. I told him all about my Grandma and how she was eager to meet him, but then I backtracked, worried about scaring him off.

'I'd love to meet Aggie. She sounds awesome. I'd like you to meet my brother Callum and his wife Tori. Their baby, Charlotte, is bloody adorable of course.' The fact he had mentioned me meeting his family set butterflies stampeding inside of me.

He asked me a gazillion questions and listened intently as I rambled on about my love of photography, my hometown in the US, my eclectic music tastes. I felt like I must surely be boring him but from the way he drank in every word I guessed I was wrong on that score.

'What made you want to come to the UK in the first place?' he asked as he drew lazy circles on my naked back. I was laid beside him on my front, my head propped on my hand and my hair in a wild mess.

I sighed dreamily. 'Oh, I think I just fell in love with the place after reading books set in Edinburgh.'

'Let me guess, you read *The Prime of Miss Jean Brodie*?'

I felt my cheeks warming. 'You say that as if it's a bad thing. I *love* that book. It changed me.'

'Hey, no. It's not a bad thing at all. I haven't read it, a bit too girlie for me I think, but I know plenty that have.' He contorted his face as if he regretted his words. 'And Edinburgh is a wonderful city, but I'm rather biased, I suppose.'

I smiled. 'It really is. And you're allowed to be biased, Fin. It's your home, after all.'

'So, what appealed to you the most about it? Surely not the romantic ideal? Things can be very different in real life as I'm sure you've discovered.'

I pursed my lips as I contemplated the question. 'I think to begin with it *was* the romantic ideal. I knew I had visited as a child but I only have faint memories so the descriptions in the book definitely helped with the draw, that and my Grandma being here, but once I got here and visited some of the tourist attractions, that was it. I was completely head over heels; the architecture, the atmosphere, the people, the history.'

'Well, yeah. You don't have much of that to experience in the USA,' he teased.

I shoved his shoulder and he fell onto his back, laughing. I rose and gazed down at him where he lay, still shirtless and dishevelled in that delicious morning way.

'So, when did the pink hair and the tattoo happen?' he asked as he reached out to run his fingers through my hair.

'Hmm. I've always been encouraged to be my own person. My folks have instilled in me that it's better to be your real self than a fake version of someone else. The place I grew up in wasn't so bad, but some people weren't so open-minded. I used to buy clothes from the thrift store in town and chop them up, sew patches on and such. I always tried to be *me*. I didn't feel like a skirt and blouse type of girl.'

He laughed lightly. 'That's not particularly in keeping with Muriel Spark's novels.'

'No, but Jean Brodie encouraged her girls to be strong. To stand up for themselves. And that's what I took from the book. I had the start of my flower vine tattoo done in college and dyed my hair blue. Then after I'd been over here a while, I went with Alec when he got a tattoo and I got mine finished. It's kind of addictive.'

He traced his fingertips down her arm. 'It's not like other tattoos I've seen. It's delicate. So beautiful.'

'Thank you. I love it. And I love that it's not on show for everyone. Just me and... well you get the idea.'

His face changed a little and I could almost hear the cogs turning in his mind. Me and my big mouth. It wasn't like I'd been promiscuous but I really shouldn't have brought up the idea of former lovers in front of him. I waited with bated breath to see what he'd say. 'Why is this flower different? It's a rose but the others are more like cherry blossom.'

I relaxed a little when he didn't quiz me on my past relationships. 'Oh, yeah. That was done in memory of my abuela. My other grandma and my dad's mom. Her name was Rosa. She died when I was twelve and I miss her like crazy. We were very close too, just like me and Grandma Aggie. She used to tell me stories about how she met my grandpa just before the war.'

'A rose to remember Rosabel. That's really sweet, Star.' My eyes welled with tears as they always did when I remembered my abuela. He pulled himself up to face me. 'Hey, I'm sorry. I didn't mean to make you cry.'

I sniffled and wiped my eyes feeling a little foolish. 'Oh, gosh, no. Don't be sorry. I think the fact that I still cry over her just means that I still miss her. She had an amazing life, and I'm so glad I got to spend twelve years of my life getting to know her.'

'So... the *pink* hair?' He rapidly changed the subject, clearly wanting to continue his getting to know Star journey.

I giggled. 'Oh, I tend to change my hair colour around once a year. As I said earlier, the first colour I tried was blue. Last year it was purple. Pink is maybe a little too girly for me, but I'm sticking with it for now.'

He twirled a lock of my hair round his finger. 'I like it.'

'I'm glad,' I breathed, before lowering my face to kiss him once more.

26

FIN

Later, as we watched an old black and white movie, cuddled up on the sofa, she turned to me. 'So, you know lots about me, so I think it's only fair that you share too.'

I shrugged. 'I think you know everything. I seem to remember spilling my guts to you on our first proper meeting.'

'Okay. But I still have questions, though. For example, where did you get your passion for music? I don't mean to be rude but your parents don't seem the rock music kind.'

He laughed. 'Sadly your instincts are correct. But

therein lays a story. Our housekeeper, Hetty, was a real gem. She used to bring the best CDs in for me to listen to. She was quite the music connoisseur. I'm talking rock music from the seventies and eighties: Whitesnake, Deep Purple, Rainbow, to name only a few. When Dad was working, I used to put on the old Discman she gave me and jump round my room, miming to the songs as if I was on stage.' I laughed at the memory and how ridiculous I must have looked.

'Wow. Hetty had great taste, huh?'

I sighed and smiled as I thought about my dear friend. 'She sure did. I owe her a lot, actually.'

There was a long pause before Star spoke again. 'I... I don't mean to speak ill of your parents, but... well, Hetty sounds like she was more of a mom to you than your actual mother was.'

I sat silently, letting her words sink in. She was right. And that fact made me a little sad.

She turned to face me again, her brow was pulled in and she chewed the inside of her cheek. 'I'm sorry, Fin. I should keep my opinions to myself.'

I cupped her cheek in my palm. 'No, you're right. The more I look back on my childhood, the more I think I was an inconvenience to my mother. And my dad... well, let's just say nothing was ever good enough, and some things never change.' She covered my hand with her own where it sat on her cheek. I sensed a drop in mood once again and had to lighten things up. 'Oh, come on. Let's not get all melancholy, eh? I don't know about you, but I'm starving.'

We agreed that she would leave at around eight in the evening so I could do a little more research prior to my first day at McKendrick Law. Well, I say we *agreed*... Star *insisted*. I was more than happy to talk in between kissing for the rest of the night, but she quite rightly pointed out that one just does not turn up unprepared to the first day of one's new and important job. So, reluctantly, I acquiesced.

After we devoured a delivery of Chinese food and shared a bottle of wine, I called a cab to take Star home. The driver buzzed up and announced his arrival, and I walked her to the door.

I held both her hands in mine. 'I've had such a wonderful time. Thank you.'

'Me too. I'm so glad I made the rash decision to turn up on your doorstep last night.'

I smiled as she used my own words on me; the words I had uttered on the morning I turned up to ask for her forgiveness. 'Well, I think it was the best rash decision you ever made.' I kissed her nose.

'Why thank you, kind sir. I'm glad it worked to my advantage. So, are you excited about tomorrow?'

Excited wasn't a word I would have chosen to describe the prospect of starting all over again in a new job. 'Hmm. Nervous is more like it, I think. I hate the whole settling into new situations thing. I'm much happier just hiding in a corner.'

She laughed at me and shook her head. 'Says the guy who gets up on stage and rocks out to Bowie and Whitesnake. *And* the guy who has just agreed to front a rock band.'

I scrunched my face. She had a valid point. 'You got me there.'

She slipped her arms round my neck and tiptoed up to kiss me. Her lips touched mine lightly. 'Have a wonderful first day, and let me know how it goes, okay?'

'I sure will.'

She pulled away and I opened the door for her.

As I watched her go, my stomach knotted, and I wasn't sure if it was nerves about the job, or sadness at watching her leave.

* * *

And this is your office.' Alasdair waved his arm at the plush-looking space surrounded by glass walls. I wasn't expecting an office right away so it was a pleasant surprise. I stepped inside and glanced round the room. A sleek modern desk and chair sat against the window wall and was juxtaposed with the period features adorning the ceiling, but it somehow worked. The view from the window was stunning. A clear vista that took in some of my favourite architectural features of the city of Edinburgh.

'Thanks, Alasdair. This is great.' I could hear the enthusiasm in my own voice and cringed at my over-eagerness.

Alasdair smiled and patted me on the shoulder. 'This is what you *should* have had for a long while now, Finlay.'

'Look... call me Fin, okay? I feel like I'm getting in trouble when you use my full name.'

He laughed. 'Well, we don't want that, do we? Fin it is. I'll let you get sorted, and I'll get your new secretary to make you some coffee or tea, or whatever you'd like.'

'Actually, I'm good at the moment. I called at my girlfriend's coffee shop on the way here and had my caffeine fix.'

'Ah, I see. That's fine then. You just get settled in and she'll get you for the morning meeting.'

He turned and left me in my new surroundings. I pulled my phone from my pocket and dropped a quick text to Star. I'd only seen her briefly when I collected my coffee, and it hadn't been anywhere near long enough. I had it bad. There was no doubt about that.

F: Hey beautiful. Guess who has a luxurious new office.

After a few minutes, I got my much anticipated reply.

S: Hey yourself. Let me guess... ;-) You seem happy.

F: It's been a long time coming and I've only been here ten minutes but so far so good! Speak to you later. Miss you.

S: You're so sweet. Miss you too.

After the morning meeting, Alasdair called me into his office to go through some of the current cases that the firm was working on. He was big on environmental cases and I know it may sound a little cliché, but McKendrick Law seemed to be the good guys. They fought for the underdog; the folks who struggled to fight for themselves. I was shocked to discover how much pro bono work went on. And it was clear the passion that Alasdair had for his work *and* the respect he had for his employees.

Things finally felt right.

It was as if, for the first time in my life, someone was actually interested in *my* opinions. And that, for once, I was going to be a part of something *good*. I was going to be a part of something positive and fulfilling instead of being both my father's scapegoat *and* his yes man.

As I sat there letting the whole situation sink in I heard raised voices coming from down the corridor. Out of pure curiosity I opened the door to my office just a crack so I could listen to what was going on. That phrase *curiosity killed the cat* became a little too realistic at that precise moment.

'So you thought you'd poach him from his own family? Is that it? Can't find your own staff, eh, McKendrick? Do you know how pathetic that makes you appear?' My father's voice boomed and everyone in the corridor stood, glued to the spot, not daring to move and probably not willing to.

'Oh shit,' I whispered as I closed my eyes. I inhaled a long, shaking breath and stormed towards the direction of the shouting.

'Campbell, I can assure you this has nothing to do with our past disagreements,' Alasdair McKendrick was saying, hands raised and voice calm.

My father was standing in the middle of McKendrick's office, wielding his walking stick—a new acquisition since his heart attack. 'You and I both know what this is about, McKendrick. It's jealousy and bitterness! Can't deal with losing that's what it is. So you decide to use my own son to score points against me. Like I said, pathetic,' he spat with no little venom.

Alasdair rolled his eyes and then glanced at me. At this point my father spun round and became immediately aware of my presence.

'Ah, here he is. The traitorous son. Do you know how much you've hurt your mother, Finlay? Well of course you don't! You have abandoned your family to come and work for this charlatan.'

'Dad! You need to stop now.' I insisted, hoping he would remember how sick he had been and bugger off home. 'And you've got this whole thing wrong. It was my decision to work here because I want to do some good for once. Now calm down and think of your blood pressure, eh?'

'You'd like that wouldn't you? For me to drop dead. Well don't think you're getting a penny when I die. You and that idiot brother of yours don't deserve a red cent from me. After all we've done for you! This is how you repay us!'

My nostrils flared and my blood boiled beneath my skin but I calmly stepped forwards and with an even tone I told him, 'You gave me life, and for that I'm grateful but that's where it ends. I don't want your money if the truth be told. I don't need it. I'm my own man now and I make my own decisions. You've never been happy with anything I've done so, quite frankly this is the reaction I expected and is precisely why I have avoided coming home. Now, please leave so these good people can get on with their work.'

'Good people? That's a bloody joke! This man not only tried to steal my fiancée but now he's stealing my son!' He glanced around to ensure his audience were getting the full impact of his story.

Alasdair shook his head. 'For the record, Campbell, Isobel was *mine* first, remember? *You* did the stealing. But that's fine because now I have a good woman in my life, one that isn't so easily distracted by shiny and sparkly things. And as for your son, perhaps if you'd showed him any kind of love or encouragement over the years he's been on earth, you would still have him in your own employ. Now kindly leave before I have you removed.'

My father's face was beetroot red and his chest heaved. He waved his stick at me. 'You haven't heard the last of this Finlay,' he snarled through gritted teeth. 'Not whilst I have breath in my body.' And with his final words he stormed out of the office and headed for the elevator.

Alasdair turned to face me and a smile spread across his face. 'I see what you mean about the use of your full name. I don't know about you but I'd say you were definitely in trouble.' There was a pause before we both began to laugh.

* * *

My new secretary, Fiona, was a whirlwind. And a mind reader, so it would seem. It was as if she knew what I needed before I even voiced the request. Dressed smartly in a navy blue pin striped suit, and with her grey hair in a neat knot at the back of her head, she had the appearance of a school head-mistress. She was uber efficient and smiley, but not in a fake, annoying way. I got the feeling from our first day working together that things were going to run like a well-oiled machine.

At the end of my first day, Alasdair insisted on taking me for a drink across the way to a place called

The Voodoo Rooms. We claimed a curved booth opposite the bar and I took in the surroundings of the place I had never been to before. The ornate carved ceiling and padded seating gave it the feel of an exclusive gentleman's club.

'So, how are you feeling after your first day? In spite of your father's visit, that is.' Alasdair's direct and to the point question caught me off guard.

'Oh... great. Great. A little too easy though, if I'm honest.'

Alasdair assessed me for a moment as he took a long draw from the amber liquid in his glass. 'Too *easy*? What were you expecting? Walking over hot coals? Being thrown in at the deep end?'

I let out a long breath and pondered my words carefully. 'I don't mean the *cases* are easy. I'm not arrogant enough to feel that. I just mean settling in was easier than I expected. Everyone's been so respectful. Nice even.'

Alasdair's responding laugh was genuine. 'Well, I'll get them to throw rotten tomatoes and hurl abuse tomorrow then, if it makes you feel at home.'

His laughter was contagious. 'No, no. Don't get me wrong, it was *good* to be enveloped in such a positive atmosphere. I can't say it's something I'm used to.'

He frowned. 'What the hell were you subjected to at your father's firm?'

'Oh, you know, he made a point of there being absolutely *no* favouritism where I was concerned. In fact, I think he maybe went to the opposite extreme now I think about it. Nothing I ever did was good enough. And I don't just mean at work.' My mouth was running away with me, and the easy-going nature of my new boss made opening up far too easy.

Dammit. Too much information.

Alasdair clenched his jaw and he leaned towards me. 'Well, let me tell you now, Fin, you deserve to be treated with respect and to be acknowledged for your talent as a lawyer. I hope you believe me when I say that. I don't tell lies.'

I nodded and swirled my drink around in my glass, suddenly feeling a little embarrassed for sharing so much of myself with him. 'Thanks. That means a lot.' Why did I feel like I had been rescued on more than one occasion recently?

'Look, I know your family life has nothing to do with me, Fin. And I know that I was seen as the enemy for so long, but I just want you to know that how you were treated before, nothing ever being up to standard, your relationship with Elise… If you'd been *my* son, things would have been completely different. My daughter, Eleanor, runs a fashion boutique in the city.' His eyes softened with fondness. 'When she was growing up, all she ever wanted to be was a fashion designer. She'd sit for hours making dresses from scraps of fabric for her Barbie and Sindy dolls. Then she'd make me and her mother sit and watch her fashion shows. Bless her heart. She knew how to put an outfit together though, I'll give her that. She studied fashion at university for a while but then decided it wasn't for her so she dropped out.'

I gasped. In my family, failure wasn't an option. Dropping out wasn't an option, and choosing your own career path was *definitely* not an option. 'Oh. You must have been disappointed.'

He scrunched his brow and shook his head. 'Why would I be disappointed? She used her brain and made a decision that made her happy. She put a business plan together and went to the bank. She got a loan and opened up a vintage clothing boutique.

She *has* made a great success of fashion just like she wanted to. It just wasn't the route she initially expected to take. But she's *happy*, Fin. She's doing what she loves, and that's great as far as I'm concerned. *That's* what's important. Whatever she decided to do, I didn't care as long as it was right for her. That's what I'm trying to get you to understand. A parent should want their child's happiness above *anything* else. Success alone means nothing. This is why I feel it's so important for you to be with *my* firm. I think you could be fulfilled here.'

'I... I don't get why you're so concerned with my happiness. Anyone would think *you* were my father and not Campbell.' *Oh shit.* A cold sweat broke out on my forehead. 'You're not my father, are you? This isn't some kind of Luke Skywalker and Darth Vader situation, is it?'

Alasdair burst into laughter and held up his hands. 'No, no. I can assure you, Fin, I'm not your father. And I'm not trying to get you to join the dark side. Quite the opposite.' He shook his head, still laughing. 'I think I got the lines wrong there somewhere. That's not how it goes in the film at all.'

A wave of disappointment rushed through me. I

think every kid, at some point, goes through the whole 'Am I adopted?' thing, and Alasdair sounded like the kind of dad I would have liked growing up. I could have been a musician with a dad like him. If only we could sometimes choose our family as well as our friends.

27

STAR

Fin's nerves almost got the better of him, and it took all of my feminine wiles to get him to attend his first get together with Mr Hyde. I had *never* known someone so mercurial. One minute he was the shy, sweet guy who blushed when ordering coffee, and the next he was this amazingly sexy, confident singer with the stage presence of Freddy Mercury. In a strange way, it was nice that I got to see the sweet, tender side of him, but the stage persona of my very own Jekyll and Hyde was a *major* turn on. He brought a whole new, and positive, meaning to the word *duplicity*, that's for sure.

We made our way across the city to an old warehouse on the outskirts, and as we sat there in the back of the cab, Fin clung to my hand so tightly I was sure my fingers would drop off. I glanced sideways at him and my heart squeezed in my chest. He was chewing the thumbnail on his free hand, his knee bobbed up and down, and his jaw was ticking.

He was terrified.

I reached up and stroked my fingers along his fuzzy, bearded jawline, and he turned to me. In a heartbeat, he leaned in and slipped his free hand into my hair, and his mouth tenderly moved over mine in a sweet but heart-melting kiss. When he pulled away, he gazed into my eyes and a crease appeared in his brow.

'Thank you for coming with me. I don't think I could've faced it alone.'

I shook my head. 'You're going to be great.'

'But what if they realise I'm not actually that good, Star?'

Smiling warmly, I cupped his face. 'Fin, I believe in you and so do they. You are amazing. Please try to accept that.' Without speaking, he gave me a tight-lipped smile and pulled me possessively into his side.

I suddenly realised he and I had one very big thing in common. Neither of us truly believed in ourselves or our talent. The things he had said to me about my photography were exactly how I felt about his singing. It was like kismet. Even after such a short time, we each saw the best in one other. The realisation made my eyes sting a little. I was meant to meet this guy. At that moment, sitting there in the cab, I knew this for a fact. Regardless of my previous thoughts on such things, this felt like fate.

The rehearsal studio was like something from a movie set. I observed as the guys sitting in a circle, jamming. Fin's voice had its usual effect on me, and my body prickled with goosebumps. Every so often, he glanced over and winked at me. I decided that the photos I was going to take would only be taken when he wasn't aware—when he was lost in the music.

To say this was Mr Hyde's first practice with their new vocalist, things were going remarkably well, and the more I listened, the more impressed I became. My new shy, unassuming and kind of emotional man had found his Eden. There in the studio where he could just be ruled by the music, he let go and gave it his all.

As it was their first rehearsal, they stuck to covers they all knew and loved, and hearing the familiar songs delivered so emphatically by Fin made my heart soar. Nate began to play the intro to 'Need Your Love so Bad' by Peter Green's Fleetwood Mac on his guitar, and Fin closed his eyes. The softness of his voice took me by surprise as he began to sing lyrics that clearly resonated deep within him. They spoke of needing to feel loved.

The honesty of the lyrics was disarming, and my heart fluttered as I listened. He had been let down by those closest to him, people he had trusted, including his fiancée, and so there was no wonder he was reluctant to expose his heart again, but at the same time, he was saying he wanted to try. He showed a level of vulnerability in his deliverance of the song that made my eyes sting.

He opened his eyes and stared straight at me. Into me. Without thinking, I lifted the camera and began to shoot. I threw my original decision to only take incidental photos out of the window. I was mesmerised. Hypnotised by the emotions in his vivid blue eyes.

I was lost.

Captivated.

* * *

Once the rehearsal was done, Fin made his way over to me where I sat perched on a stool in the corner. The shy smile on his face was enough to make me spontaneously combust, and I shivered as he ran his hands up my bare arms and rested them on my shoulders.

He leaned in and placed a kiss on my forehead. 'So? What did you think?'

Think? Oh, hell no. I'm actually supposed to respond with something intelligent. How can I when I've turned to a gelatinous pile of mush? Come on, Star! Put brain into gear.

I gazed up into those pools of blue and finally found some words. 'You were amazing. You just... you gel. As a band, I mean. It... it just *works*.' My excitement grew as I enthused about the rehearsal. Every word filled with honesty. 'You're just so natural, Fin. You were *born* to be on stage with that voice. And those guys, wow. It all sounded phenomenal.'

His shy smile widened and became a full blown

grin. 'You really think it was that good? Or are you just biased?' He narrowed his eyes at me and tilted his head to one side.

'God, no. I mean, yes. Yes, I'm biased in a way, I guess. But honestly, you have such an effect on me when you sing.'

'Oh yeah?' He stepped closer and I widened my knees to allow him to slip his arms round me and rest his forehead on mine. 'What effect do I have on you?'

I glanced in the direction of the rest of the band and they were making kissy faces like dumb teenage boys.

I rolled my eyes and then focused my attention on Fin once again. 'Um, judging by what the guys are doing right now, I'm guessing this is not the place to have this conversation.'

Fin turned round and the rest of the band began whistling and pretending to pack up their gear. I couldn't help laughing at their feigned occupation. They were a great bunch of guys and, oh boy, were they talented. But they were typical *guys* when all was said and done.

Fin turned back to me, shook his head, and

kissed my cheek before whispering, 'Hold that thought, Miss Mendoza. You can show me later what I do to you. Come on, let's go. The sooner we get back to my place...' He pulled his bottom lip between his teeth and grinned. He took my hand and pulled me down from my seat and then led me out the door.

28

FIN

As Star and I walked out of the rehearsal studio, I was buzzing. It was the best high I'd had that didn't involve alcohol or sex. The cab ride over had been terrifying. I had felt nauseated and light-headed, but Star had calmed me simply by being there. Something about her grounded me. Even though she had considered us opposites to begin with, I now knew we had more in common than either of us first realised. Yes, there was an obvious and undeniable attraction, but there was so much more.

When I'd initially walked into the rehearsal studio, I'd immediately felt intimidated. Strange, considering I could stand up in a courtroom and defend someone with utmost confidence and come across as a very together, even arrogant, guy. But being there with the band was nothing like I expected. I was thinking church hall, pub function room. A professional rehearsal studio in a converted warehouse was *not* something I'd anticipated. Stupid really, when I knew the guys were adults and not some teenage wannabes being let out for a couple of hours by their parents. I really needed to increase my expectations.

Especially those I placed on myself.

I needed the fresh air, and so Star and I walked home across the city, taking in the atmosphere of the place as the Friday night revellers sang in drunken unison about some football team or other that allegedly wore the opposing team's mothers' underwear. We laughed as they walked past us, and one of them grabbed Star and spun her round, waltzing her across the precinct as his friends cheered him on. Luckily, there was no malice in them.

Once they were out of sight, I pulled Star into a darkened doorway and kissed her passionately, but she stiffened in my arms. I asked if I had done something wrong and she began to explain.

'My last boyfriend, Mick the prick, as Alec called

him... he dumped me just before my birthday because we were apparently moving too fast and he needed some alone time.'

'Ah. But the doorway?'

'Yeah, I'm getting to that. I was walking home one night after work, and I spotted him and one of the girls from the bar where he worked. They were making out in a shop doorway. It was pretty X-rated stuff from what I could see. It just proved to me that I have to be more careful who I trust, I guess.'

I smacked my head. 'Aww, no. And then I come along and drag you into a doorway. I'm sorry.'

She smiled, but it was fleeting. 'No, don't be. You didn't know any of that. It's fine.'

But her expression told me it wasn't fine at all. We began to walk again and I cringed and regretted my attempt at romance.

As we walked in silence, I could feel her eyes on me, and when I turned my head, she was chewing her lip, a distinct mask of worry on her face.

I stopped and pulled her into my arms. 'Hey, what's wrong?'

'I think I may have over-reacted about the doorway thing. I'm sorry.'

I smiled and shook my head. 'God, you're too sweet, you know that?'

Shyness replaced the anxiety on her face and she tilted her head to one side. 'Am I?'

'You are.' I leaned in and ran my nose down the length of hers, finishing the gesture with a tender kiss to her lips. She closed her eyes and sighed as I told her, 'Mmm, you taste sweet too.'

Her eyelids fluttered open and she gazed up at me. 'I love that Fleetwood Mac song you sang earlier.'

'It's a classic. Don't get me wrong I adore Stevie Nicks as much as everyone else but Peter Green had such soul to his voice.'

She almost whispered, 'Just like you.'

I was taken back by the compliment and felt my cheeks warming in spite of the chill to the evening air. I narrowed my eyes. 'Really?'

She giggled, a musical sound that did something to my insides. 'Are you fishing for compliments, Mr Hunter?'

'Maybe. I have an ego to inflate now you know,' I joked.

She smiled up at me and my heart melted. 'I'll

bear that in mind.'

I took her hand in mine again and we began to walk once more.

The rest of the journey back to my apartment was made in comfortable silence. We were both lost in thought, absorbing the weekend atmosphere of the city we called home with its buzzing restaurants and pounding basslines that made the pavements outside the clubs vibrate. Every so often, we shared knowing smiles and glances, and the anticipation of getting her alone almost made me break out into a run.

We reached my apartment block and she pulled me into the doorway and pulled me down so she could kiss me so passionately she stole my breath. *So, doorways are back on the table, hmm?* Once she pulled away again, I punched the security code into the exterior pad and she tugged me through the space created as the door automatically opened.

When I had unlocked my front door and we had walked in I turned to her. 'So, you had a good time tonight? I was worried you'd be bored sitting there watching us jam.

She slowly shook her head. 'I wasn't bored in the slightest. Your voice... it does things to me.'

She had my attention with that comment and I was intrigued. 'At the risk of sounding like I'm fishing again, what exactly does my voice do to you?'

She stepped closer. 'I get shivers. The edge to your voice makes me want you.'

'It does, eh? Tell me more.'

She pulled her full bottom lip into her mouth and let it slip out as I watched. My eyes fixed on the plump, pink flesh. Her breathing rate increased. 'My heart beats faster. I close my eyes and imagine your mouth next to my ear, your hot breath on my neck.' Of course I'd had those thoughts too.

I moved to her ear and whispered. 'Like this?'

'Uh-huh.'

'Anything else?'

'Passion. I hear passion in your voice and you sing the words like they mean something to you. It doesn't matter which song you're singing. I feel every emotion you express. Whether it's anger... or... or... lust.' Her voice wavered and her chest heaved. 'I think... I think you've found the *you* that you should've been all along.'

It was as if she'd read my mind. I felt the exact same way. She knew me. She could read me like no one else. The fact terrified and elated me simultaneously. Once again I was reminded that I almost let her go. She accepted me and both sides of my personality and I was so damned lucky. My heart beat faster and I knew that this was something real. Every thought I had about her—and there were many—reiterated the fact. My feelings were running away with me at speed, but if the truth be told she had intrigued me from the first time she handed me a coffee cup and gave me that disarming smile. But the deeper meaning had started when I had kissed her that first time.

Words rushed around my head and begged for escape from my lips, but what the hell would she think if I set them free? She'd no doubt think it was some clichéd expression of emotion attached to the desire I had for her. It was evident that I wanted her physically but this was so much more. And every moment spent with her told me the same thing. But the last thing I wanted was to fire benign and seemingly empty words at her. Not that they would actually *be* empty. The feelings I had for her were like nothing I had ever experienced before. But in all honesty, the words in my head just didn't seem enough. And so I lowered my face and kissed her again, only this time I was deliberately tender. Of course I wanted to take her to bed but I held back. I needed her to see that I wanted more. That I felt more. Only then would she really know what I had suspected for a while now.

I was in love.

29

STAR

The day that followed Fin's first rehearsal with Mr Hyde was bright and sunny. But to be honest, if it had been raining and cloudy, I truly wouldn't have cared. The intensity of the night we'd shared had affected me so much that, once again, I had that stupid grin on my face. I'd stayed over, and luckily I'd had the common sense to pack fresh underwear and clothes for work the next day.

I walked into the coffee shop to find Alec already there. I was humming 'Strange and Beautiful' again, and my boss/best friend rolled his eyes when I walked through to the back to take off my coat.

He followed me, and I knew he was about to start digging for information. 'Hmm, someone looks like the cat who got the cream. I hope he's treating you right. I hope he's not using you, that's all Twinkle.'

I rolled my eyes. 'Ugh! Alec, can't I just be happy without you being so negative?' I threw a dish towel at him. It's good it was the only thing in close proximity.

'Well, I'm just saying. You don't know him that well but you're spending every spare moment with him. It's all going too fast if you ask me. I'm just worried about you.'

I flared my nostrils and placed my hands firmly on my hips. 'Time is a moot point, Alec. He's respectful, kind, sweet and gorgeous. I'm an adult and my relationships are *my* business, Alec McVey, and I'd be happier if you'd stop poking your nose into my affairs.' He held his hands up in surrender but my good mood was ruined.

He picked up the dish towel that had landed on the floor and threw it onto the laundry pile. 'Like I said, I'm just worried about you, Twinkle, that's all. You trust so easily, darling.' He slowly walked towards me, hands aloft as if approaching a startled mare in a corral.

He was like a big brother to me, and I needed him. In spite of what I'd expressed only moments before, I was kind of glad he was around and that he had my back.

I sighed and softened a little. 'I know. And I do appreciate it, Al. I really do. But you've got it wrong about Fin. He's all the things I said and more. He makes me feel good and I love to spend time with him.'

He took another tentative step. 'I know, hon. It's just... it worries me how fast this is all happening after how he treated you before. I know I'm not responsible for you, but you're like family to me. If anything was to happen...'

I closed the remaining gap between us and slipped my arms round his waist. Resting my head on his chest, I told him: 'I'm grateful that you care so much, really I am. But I've got this, okay?'

His arms came around me and he squeezed me tight. 'I'll always look out for you, darlin'. You know that.'

The day was busy yet uneventful until around three in the afternoon when my cell phone rang. It was Fin's number, and a shiver of excitement passed through me.

'Hey.' My voice was breezy and a little breathy. This was the effect he had on me.

'Hey, your gorgeous self.' Oh my God, I loved his accent. 'I have news.'

'Oh? I hope it's good news.'

He chuckled and I could imagine the smile playing on his oh-so-kissable lips. 'Well, I think it's quite exciting.'

'Come on then. Don't keep me in suspense.'

'Na, I'd rather keep you in suspense.' His husky whisper made my muscles clench in anticipation.

'Fiiiiin,' I groaned.

'Okay, maybe I should just tell you now then, eh? Okay, so there's this rather posh charity ball thing in a couple of months. McKendrick Law attends every year. It's run by a children's cancer charity, and I really want to go. And...' He cleared his throat. 'I'd like you to go with me as my date. What do you think?'

Ugh. Events like that weren't really my kind of

thing, but I didn't want to let Fin down. The fact that I wouldn't know anyone there preyed on my mind, along with visions of being left with a table full of strangers whilst Fin went to mingle.

I realised I had been silent for a while and cleared my throat. 'Um... yeah. Yeah, sure.'

Fin sighed. 'Do I sense a bit of hesitation, Star? If you'd rather not go—'

I winced. 'No, I'll go. I'm just being silly. I'm just nervous. I don't usually get the chance to go to such things. And... I'm not sure my pink hair will really help me to fit in. Maybe I should dye—'

'You absolutely won't dye your hair! Don't change who you are for one night, Star. I've done enough of that in my time and I'll no be doing it any more.' There was a pause at his end before he continued. 'But, having said that, I don't want you to feel pressured into going. I just... I want to show you off.'

My heart skipped a beat when I heard those words and the sincerity in their delivery. I wanted so much to kiss him right then. 'You're so sweet.'

'When it comes to sweet, I think you win, hands down.'

'Don't you know that flattery will get you *everywhere*, Mr. Hunter?'

He chuckled. 'Well, I certainly hope so.' His deep voice sent a shiver of delight right through me, and I had to breathe deeply in through my nose to calm myself. 'Look, if you really don't want to go, that's fine. And it's a while away so I don't want to put pressure on you so soon.'

Why was I hesitating? This was Fin saying that he saw our relationship as meaningful; that he was looking beyond the next week and believing that perhaps we were going to last. Why else would he want to take me to such an important event?

I mentally pulled up my big girl panties. 'Fin, I'd honestly love to go with you. And besides, it gives me an opportunity to go shopping for a fancy outfit.' *Why the hell did I say that? I hate shopping.*

'Look, you're a beautiful woman, and I don't care what you wear. Don't feel you have to be all conservative. Just be *you*. It's you that I lo—I mean it's you that...'

My breath hitched and I covered my mouth. *He almost said he loved me. Oh shit, oh shit, oh shit.* It was too soon. *Much* too soon. But damn if I didn't feel it too.

'It's okay, Fin. I know what you mean. And I promise I *will* be myself. I think I'd struggle to be anyone else.'

'Good. Now when can I see you again?'

30

FIN

Just the thought of seeing Star all dressed up for the ball made my heart do somersaults in my chest. I couldn't wait to walk into that event with the most attractive woman in attendance.

We arranged to see each other a couple of nights later and go to DeBasement again, and I found myself counting the hours until I could see her.

When the day arrived, I was sitting at my desk, staring at the view of the vast city of Edinburgh, coffee cup in hand, having a break and fantasising about her when there was a knock on my door which yanked me from my daydream.

'Hi, Fin.' Alasdair's bright and breezy voice caught me off guard.

I spun round on my chair. 'Oh, hi, Alasdair. I was just... um—'

He held his hands up and laughed. 'Will you please stop panicking every time I walk into your office?'

I placed my cup down and huffed the air from my lungs through puffed cheeks. 'Sorry. Force of habit.'

He shook his head and rolled his eyes, smiling. 'I came in to ask if you and your lady friend would like to meet Colette and me for drinks next weekend. I thought perhaps... sorry, what's her name?' He cringed.

'Star,' I informed him with a cheesy grin. Good grief, if simply saying her name made me react that way it was definitely more than a fling.

'I thought perhaps Star may feel a little more comfortable knowing a couple more faces at the charity ball.'

This guy never ceased to amaze me. 'That's... that's really kind of you, Alasdair. Thank you. Where were you thinking of going? And when? We could meet you there.'

'Oh, I was thinking somewhere quite relaxed. Maybe just a bar in the centre? How about Deacon Brodie's on the Royal Mile? Say eight, a week on Friday? We can grab a bite to eat too if you're okay with that?'

'Sounds great. I'm seeing her tonight so I'll mention it then.'

'Great stuff.' He turned to leave. 'Oh, and Fin, I heard about the work you did on the Henderson case. The ideas you came up with really turned things around. It just shows you what a new perspective on a case can achieve. Well done, son.' And with that, he left.

I sat there, wide-eyed and with a knot of excitement in my stomach. Once again feeling that I had done Alasdair and the company proud made me feel on top of the world.

I could get used to this.

I knocked on Star's door on the evening of our next date, and when it opened, I was greeted by a stern-faced man. Confusion briefly washed over me until I remembered she mentioned her male roommate and best friend, and even though Star and I had been seeing each other a while now, I was yet to make his acquaintance.

I smiled warmly and held out my hand. 'You must be Alec. It's good to finally meet you.'

He seemed reluctant but shook my hand. 'Fin.' My name fell from his lips as though it tasted bad. 'You'd better come in.'

I frowned and nodded before stepping past him through the doorway and into the lounge area. It was a Victorian place like mine. Tastefully decorated in creams and browns with the original fireplace still intact. A wine coloured tapestry rug sat in front of it and huge pillar candles stood where a fire should be. The artwork covering the walls was a combination of renaissance era prints in ornate gold frames and the juxtaposition of Star's photographs of the castle and the Scott monument. There was a stunning one I had never seen before of the forth rail bridge silhouetted against a night sky as fireworks exploded in the distance. That one really took my breath away. I had never actually considered the old criss-crossed steel structure a thing of beauty but clearly Star had worked her magic once again. As I glanced round my unfamiliar surroundings I figured the coffee shop must have been doing well for Alec to afford something like this so close to the city.

I realised I hadn't spoken and turned to find Alec watching me. I cleared my throat. 'Is Star ready?'

'She won't be long. Have a seat.' He gestured to the couch and my stomach knotted, I was like a teenager meeting a date's father for the first time. My palms began to sweat and I wiped them down my jeans. I sat as instructed and peered up at him where he hovered over me.

Alec snickered. 'Do I make you nervous?'

I narrowed my eyes. *What a bizarre question to ask of another adult.* 'No, not nervous. I just feel a little hostility coming from you and I'm wondering why.' *Nothing like being honest.*

He folded his arms across his chest. 'Let's just say I didn't appreciate the way you treated my best friend after your first *date*. And it worries me that you're stickin' around, and if you're planning to do the same again.'

By first date, I knew he meant our almost one night stand, and it sort of explained why he was being so antsy. I nodded and smirked. 'Okay, so you're giving me the big brother talk?'

His frown deepened. 'I don't think it's funny. Star is a *very* special person. She has a heart of gold, and she deserves the best. She deserves to be respected and loved, Fin. Not tossed out like trash.'

I stood to face him, feeling that I needed to be on equal footing. 'Look, Alec. I know I messed up the first time around, okay? But, not that it's really any of your business...' I lowered my voice in the hope that the confession I was about to make was only heard by him. I wasn't ready to confess it in my own actual words to the object of my affections. 'But I think I'm falling for her. No... I *know* I am. She *is* special. You're right. And I feel like crap about how I reacted after our first encounter, but I've been going through a really difficult time lately. I won't bore you with the details but suffice it to say, I realised my mistake and I'm ready to do anything it takes to not hurt her again.'

Suddenly, he stepped towards me, and I flinched, ready to strike back, but instead he grappled me into a hug. 'I knew it. I bloody *knew* it.' He slapped my back and I stood there for a moment before returning the hug. He pulled away, and with his hands resting on my shoulders and sincerity in his eyes, he pleaded, 'Just don't break her heart, okay?'

I hoped my eyes held the sincerity I felt. 'I don't intend to.'

'What's going on here? Are you trying to steal my man, Alec McVey?' Star's beautiful voice was filled with humour.

Alec laughed and slapped me on the back, hard. 'No, Twinkle. Just warning him that if he hurts you, I'll open a large can of whoop ass on him.' He winked at me and I returned his friendly slap on the back with one of my own—maybe using a little too much force.

31

STAR

The strange atmosphere between Alec and Fin seemed to dissipate, and I was relieved to see them laughing and joking together as I pulled on my boots. When I was ready, Fin and I left the apartment under the watchful gaze of my best friend.

As we exited the building, Fin's voice broke the silence. 'Sheesh, he's pretty intense, eh?'

Dread washed over me and I stopped. 'Oh, God. What did he say to you? I knew he'd said something. Tell me.'

Fin stopped, turned to face me, and placed his hands on my upper arms. Smiling he told me, 'Nothing. It's fine. He just wants you to be happy and to not get hurt. I completely respect that.'

I lowered my head. 'He really did threaten you, didn't he?' I couldn't make eye contact with him. How embarrassing. I was going to kill Alec for this.

He tilted my chin up so I met his concerned gaze once more. 'Look, don't worry. I didn't take it seriously. He's a decent guy and he has your best interests at heart. I'm glad of the fact.'

'Ugh! He's so overbearing. He seems to think he's taking my dad's place or something. It's ridiculous, Fin.' I thankfully stopped short of stamping my foot like an errant teenager.

The sexy smile that spread across his lips made my stomach flip. He leaned in, slipped his hands into my hair, and kissed me. It was gentle at first but gained fervour, and I gripped at his leather jacket, doing my best to stifle the moan of pleasure bubbling up from within me.

When he pulled away, he locked his gaze on mine. 'Wow, you're hot when you're angry.'

I almost swooned on the spot. 'Angry? Was I angry? I don't remember.'

'Come on. Let's go watch people murder our favourite songs.' He grabbed my hand and pulled me along. I was relieved when my legs remembered how to function after that underwear-igniting kiss.

As we walked Fin blurted, 'How would you feel about meeting my boss and his wife prior to the ball?'

I was a little shocked. 'Oh... I... erm...'

'Alasdair is a top guy. He suggested we meet up so that you know someone else at the ball.'

'That's very sweet of him.'

'Like I said, he's a great guy. He suggested Deacon Brodie's.'

I was surprised by the choice of venue but re-lieved too. 'That sounds perfect.'

He put his arm round me and kissed the top of my head. 'Thank you.'

'For what?'

I felt him shrug. 'Just for being you.'

* * *

The club was buzzing when we arrived. Some older guy was on stage rocking out to Led Zeppelin's

'Whole Lotta Love' and the crowd loved him. He could've given Robert Plant a run for his money, no doubt. Fin still clutched my hand as he led me through the throng.

Suddenly he stopped and turned to me. He leaned in and spoke directly into my ear to make himself heard. 'Okay, please don't be angry, but I wanted to introduce you to my best buddy, Tom. Remember I told you about him? He's the guy who—'

I narrowed my eyes. 'Runs the gallery. Yeah, I remember.'

The annoyance must have been visible on my face as he cringed. 'Look, I really want you to believe how talented you are. And I figured I stepped out of *my* comfort zone with the whole singing thing with *your* help and so I thought—'

Irritation prickled at my skin. He had a *very* fair point. 'You thought you'd drag me kicking and screaming out of mine? Well, I'm just not ready. I'm sorry to let you down, Fin. I think maybe I should go.' I tried to turn away, intent on getting the hell out of Dodge.

How much of a hypocrite was I?

He gripped my shoulders. 'Star, please? He's my best mate and I want you to meet him anyway. You don't have to agree to anything you're not comfortable with.'

I sighed, feeling more than a little bit stupid. 'Fin, you've clearly got him here under false pretences, and I told you I didn't want exhibitions and notoriety. I trusted you to accept that.'

A pained, sorrowful look appeared on his handsome features and I felt shitty for my overreaction.

He dropped his arms from my body. 'Forget it. I'm really sorry. I just wanted to help you like you helped me. But the last thing I'd ever want to do is upset you, Star. You mean too much to me. Do you want me to walk you home?' The dejection in his eyes caused my insides to knot and I wanted to take back all of my negativity. I wanted to suck the words right back in and say that I would love to meet his best friend as I should have.

I softened, stepped towards him, and cupped his cheek. 'No, Fin. It's me who should be sorry. I'm being silly. I seem to make a habit of overreacting these days. Of course I don't want to go home. I want to be here with you. And... and I want to meet Tom.'

His eyes widened and he smiled. 'You do?' He pulled me into a hug. 'I promise I won't mention exhibits, or photography, or anything.'

He gripped my hand and squeezed it, and I followed him through the crowd once more until I was suddenly pulled around to his side.

'Hunter! You made it.' A handsome dark-haired guy pulled Fin into a man-hug and slapped his back. 'I thought you'd changed your mind. Oh, hey. You must be the girl who's stolen my best buddy's heart.'

He had smiley dark eyes. I guessed they were brown, but the club lights were kind of dim. He seemed sweet and was obviously one of those guys who didn't mind PDA as he pulled me into a hug and kissed the side of my head.

My cheeks heated as I glanced briefly at Fin. 'Um... hi. I'm guessing that makes you Tom.'

He grinned. 'It sure does. Hey, Hunter, go get your girl a drink, mate, and give us a chance to get to know each other, eh?'

Fin glanced at me and his face contorted in an *'are you sure you want me to leave you?'* kind of way, but I nodded. 'Jack and Coke please, Fin.'

He disappeared in the direction of the bar, and

Tom gestured for me to sit down at the table he had commandeered.

'So, Star. Fin tells me you are the elusive S.A.M? *Totally* fate that you met, if you ask me.'

I didn't ask you. 'Yeah, maybe.'

'Now, hows about you exhibiting in my gallery? You must have loads of fantastic pieces hidden away that deserve to be seen, and my gallery is the place to show them. What can I say to convince you?' He winked. Clearly, he was expecting me to jump at the chance to have an exhibition. Who wouldn't?

Me, apparently.

I shook my head as my cheeks flamed with embarrassment. 'Oh, no, that's okay. It's just a hobby is all. I don't exhibit.'

His eyes widened and he leaned towards me. 'Take it from someone who knows about this stuff, Star. Your work is *stunning*. Fin's been a fan for a while now, and I know for a fact that people would want to see it. Will you just think about it? An exhibition, I mean.'

Jeez, talk about a dog with a bone.

I shook my head and wished Fin would return. 'Look, I told Fin—'

He halted me with his hand. 'This has nothing to do with Fin. This is *me* asking as a gallery owner and art expert. Please can I exhibit your work? Just think about it.'

My stomach did somersaults at the thought of my photos coming in for criticism right before me, at least in the past I haven't been in the spotlight when my work was displayed in shops, but the look in Tom's eyes told me my worries were unfounded. He was confident it would be a success, even if I wasn't.

I swallowed the nervous knot in my throat. 'I'll think about it. But I'm promising nothing.'

He held up his hands. 'That's all I ask.'

Fin returned and placed a drink in front of me. He leaned over and kissed my head. 'So, did you two get to know each other better whilst I was gone, eh?'

Tom grinned at me. 'We're working on it, mate. We're working on it.'

After a while, a few more of Fin's friends arrived. They were a rowdy but great bunch. I particularly liked a girl called Siân. She worked with Tom at the gallery, and I got the feeling she had a bit of a crush on him. She hung on his every word, but once she'd had a few drinks, she told me he was a real womaniser. It explained why she appeared to only adore him from afar.

'He says he wants your work for the gallery. You gonna go for it?' Siân's strong Glaswegian accent didn't seem to fit her delicate features and pixie hair-cut. She looked so demure, but her accent was so thick, and I loved it.

I sighed and shook my head. 'Oh, I don't know. I don't think so. It's just not my scene. I'm not a showy person, you know?'

She raised her eyebrows. 'That coming from the girl with pink hair?'

I laughed as I heard Fin's words echoed in his friend's. 'Yeah, I know. It's hard to believe, but I'm kinda shy when it comes to my photos.'

She leaned towards me and conspiratorially glanced around. 'Look, Tom may be a skirt chaser but—and for God's sake don't tell him I said anything nice about him—he really knows his art. You should put your faith in yourself *and* Tom and give it a trial run at least. I've seen your work, and let me tell you, it's of a higher standard than most. You should be proud of it, not hiding it away and selfishly keeping it locked up.' She nudged me and I thought about what Fin had said about our respective comfort zones. Perhaps he was right. Perhaps meeting him *was* meant to draw me out of my shell—in more ways than one.

Taking a deep breath, I leaned over and slapped Tom's arm. He swung his head around and the glare in his eyes told me he was about to shout expletives.

Thankfully, he realised it was me, and he grinned. 'Hey, Starlet. What's up?'

Come on, Star. You can do this. 'I've been chatting to Siân. She's convinced me. I'll do it.'

Suddenly, he stood, picked me up and spun me round, and my stomach almost let go of its alcoholic contents. Once he had placed me down, he tugged on Fin's arm and told him the news.

Fin turned to me, cupped my face in his palms, and placed a luscious wet kiss on my lips. 'I'm so proud of you right now.' Before I could reply, he turned and walked away with purpose. I watched as he disappeared through the hordes of people dancing to someone's rendition of Kiss' 'I Was Made for Lovin' You'. He disappeared from sight, and I figured he had gone to buy another round of celebratory drinks.

I turned back to Tom, who was hugging Siân. She glanced over at me, and I couldn't help but smile at her face-splitting grin.

The audience cheered as the pseudo Paul Stanley left the stage, and I wondered absently who would be up next. A familiar gruff voice broke through my thoughts, and I spun towards the stage once more.

'This goes out to my shining Star.' A simple piano intro began, and a shiver travelled down my spine. The familiar lyrics to Hozier's 'Take Me to Church' began to fall easily from Fin's full lips. A lump formed in my throat, and once again, everyone else within the room disappeared, and my shy, reluctant rock god bravely locked his gaze on me and sang as if showing me that stepping out of his comfort zone was getting easier thanks to me.

Commanding the stage as he always did, the crowds of people stopped chatting amongst themselves and watched in awe, as did I. Something profoundly moving about the lyrics and the way he sang them to me made tears well in my eyes, and I observed in wonder as he once again told me his innermost feelings through song.

When the song was finished, Fin jumped from the stage and made a beeline for me, avoiding all of his well-wishers. Without speaking, he slipped his hands into my hair and crushed his mouth to mine in a kiss that took my breath—and my heart—away.

32

FIN

We arrived back at my place after a really fun evening. I was relieved Tom's enthusiasm over her art hadn't made Star run for the hills, and I was so excited at the prospect of seeing her work displayed for everyone to see. But all I had wanted to do from the moment I stepped off the stage was to bring her home and show her what she meant to me. How the hell I had fallen so quickly was beyond me, but I wasn't about to fight it any more.

Star glanced at her artwork where I had now arranged it in a variety of frames on the walls of my lounge. 'They do look nice framed, don't they?' There was a hint of surprise to her tone.

'Now do you believe me? People are going to love seeing them on display. You just wait and see.'

She chewed on her lip. 'Hmm... we'll see.' And with a dramatic change of subject she turned and tugged me down for a long lingering kiss.

* * *

Lit only by the moon shining through the window, we lay in each other's arms for a long while, just holding each other close until a loud rumble from my stomach made us both break out into giggles.

She pushed herself up and gazed down at me. 'I think maybe we should eat.'

I gazed up at her, her pink hair fell over her face and I tucked it behind her hair. I trailed my fingertips over her cheek.

I could've ravished her all over again but she was right. My empty belly was protesting and I need to sate it. I allowed myself a few more seconds of taking in the wondrous sight of her perfection above me.

She wrapped her arms around herself. 'You're staring, Hunter.'

I nodded slowly. 'I'm well aware of the fact. You're

much more beautiful than any photograph I've ever seen. Even your own, and that's saying something.'

The pink in her cheeks intensified and she slapped my arm playfully. 'I think hunger is affecting your eyesight. Go eat.' She slid off me and dashed to the bathroom.

I pulled on my boxers and T-shirt and went to find something... anything, edible in the kitchen. I was distinctly lacking in the grocery department and plumped for cheese on toast. I prepared the meagre meal whilst I heard the shower running and waited for Star to return.

We sat at the little kitchen table and munched away on our Welsh rarebit, silently contemplating... well, whatever.

* * *

Spending time with Star was by far one of my favourite things to do. Our weekends together consisted of long talks, walks through the city, talking about anything and everything, and passionate hours tangled together between the sheets.

Seeing the city through her eyes was awe-inspiring. Intriguing. She told me she wanted to take me to one of her favourite places, and as soon we had the opportunity, I was excited to discover this place she loved so much. Armed with her camera, she led me through the bustling city on a sunny Sunday morning. Distant church bells sounded, adding to the idyllic day in all its sunshine and glory. For a while, we walked without speaking, hand in hand, content in each other's silence down the Royal Mile towards the palace of Holyrood where it stood behind wrought iron gates in all its royal, neoclassical grandeur. The Royal Standard of the United Kingdom was flapping in the breeze from one of the turrets, indicating that her Royal Highness the Queen was in residence.

I watched Star in my peripheral vision. It was fascinating to see the expression of awe on her face as she revelled in the exquisite diversity and beauty of the city—the place I had called home, and taken for granted, for all of my life. Seeing her joy made me smile.

Since meeting Star and allowing her to show me the place through her eyes, I had started to look at Edinburgh in a whole new light. I no longer walked around with my eyes veiled, but instead I began to appreciate the myriad of architectural styles all around me, seeing something new along each and every well-trodden route. This also applied to the people that graced the city streets. The more I people-watched, the more I realised my fortune at finding Star—of us finding each other—out of all the endless possibilities surrounding us.

We continued to walk along, but it was clear there was purpose to her steps. She evidently had a destination in mind—somewhere she was leading me. We ambled to the bottom of the Royal Mile where the stark geometry of the new parliament building faced us; a jarring blot on the landscape in my opinion. From here, we turned left, cutting through to Calton Road, the crowds lessening as we moved away from the familiar tourist trails.

Eventually, we walked through wrought iron gates into Old Calton burial ground. Star released my hand and glanced around with a serene smile on her beautiful face.

I chuckled and shook my head. 'Well, it's official. You. Are. Weird.' I couldn't help thinking that of all the places to go with your new love, a graveyard seemed right up there as a location *not* to choose.

She shrugged. 'Hmm. I think I'd prefer interesting, quirky, or maybe even mysterious rather than weird.' There was mirth in her eyes.

'No, Mendoza, you can't sugar coat this. You're just plain weird.' I stepped towards her and slipped my arm round her waist before tenderly kissing her head. 'But I adore you for it.'

Star smiled up at me with a mischievous look glinting in her chocolate brown eyes.

'I love this place,' she mused. 'It's hauntingly beautiful, and an oasis of calm in such a busy city.'

I'd never really thought of a graveyard full of dead bodies as peaceful. But as I said, this was what she did. She made me see things through *her* eyes.

Although, I couldn't resist teasing her. 'Haunting, yes. Beautiful? Hmm, I'm not so sure about that.' I cast my assessing gaze over the multitude of headstones and mausoleums. She was right about it being an oasis. Even though we were in the heart of the city, it somehow felt like we were somewhere miles away. No road noise, no car fumes, no people. Well, none that were rushing around us, anyway.

She let out a wistful sigh. 'I love coming here. The atmosphere of the place changes throughout the day, and some of my best images have been captured here.' Enthusiasm radiated from her like sunlight, and I found myself caught up in the moment, appreciating the intricate stone carvings and the loving care that people clearly still took over the resting places of their loved ones.

I mentally went through the catalogue of Star's work that I had seen, but for the life of me, I couldn't remember seeing any pictures of this place.

When her gaze returned to mine, I linked my fingers with hers. 'It doesn't look familiar to me. I mean, I don't recall any of your work based round cemeteries and gravestones.'

Star released one of her hands and reached out from where we stood on a path that curved round the large open space.

She lightly ran a finger over the top of the nearest stone. 'Ah, well that's because they're a work in progress.' She pursed her lips and paused for a moment. 'I'm not really sure they'll suit everyone's tastes.'

She tugged at my hand and led me farther in

amongst the graves. 'I love the serenity here. The feeling of time standing still... the history.' She stopped and turned towards me. 'Have you never been here before?'

Being a native of Edinburgh from the start of my life, I could honestly say I had indeed never been there before. In fact, I was blissfully unaware of its existence.

I cringed, conscious of the fact that she was an interloper here and I wasn't. 'Erm, no this is definitely a first for me.' I laughed lightly. 'Can't say that visiting a graveyard was on my list of things to do *before* I die.' I pointed to our surroundings. 'Obviously, *when* I die, this is my go to place.'

She giggled, and my heart skipped at the wonderful sound.

We walked around for another hour or so, Star snapping away every so often when something caught her eye. I watched in awed silence as she tilted her head this way and that, trying to capture the image just right in her mind.

She read many of the stones, telling me: 'It's important to read the stones that look a little neglected. These were people too. Loved once. They should be remembered fondly, even when there's no one alive who's connected to them.' A look of melancholy graced her features as she spoke, and she stooped to pull some weeds away from one such stone.

I found myself clearing my throat, taken back by the emotion I experienced on listening to her reasons for taking her time to visit the less well-kept resting places. I vowed then and there to return to do just that.

Suddenly she stopped again, and her hand covered her mouth as she gasped. The stone before her was leaning and cracked. 'Oh wow, Fin. Look.'

I walked over to stand beside her and read aloud the wording on the stone. 'Forbes Hunter. Gone but not forgotten. 1889 to 1916. Loving son and brother.'

She placed a hand over her heart. 'He was only twenty-seven when he died. That's so sad.'

I took a deep breath, emotions knotting my stomach. *He could've been my ancestor.* 'I bet he died in World War One, looking at the dates.'

'Yeah, maybe. Gosh, Fin, that's the age you are now.'

I shook my head and re-read the wording on the stone. *Loving son and brother. That was me once.* It was clear that no one had tended to the grave in many years, apart from the caretakers at the cemetery. No evidence of flowers left by loved ones. But at some point, he had been loved and missed. My heart ached at the thought that I couldn't say the same about me as far as my parents were concerned. An overwhelming sense of loss tugged at me. What it must have been like to have been loved so dearly. A lump lodged in my throat, and I imagined my own grave looking the same way, but mine would be due to neglect.

Star grasped my hand and tugged me away from Forbes Hunter's final resting place. 'Come on. Let's go get some ice cream. I think we need it.' As we walked away, I glanced over my shoulder and found myself hoping the Forbes' family healed after his death.

We headed for the wrought iron gate once again, and I felt a sense of inner calm that I possibly wouldn't have felt had it not been for Star bringing me to this place. She truly was an enigma. This quirky, pink-haired American with a heart as big as the world.

33

FIN

Nate from the band called me at home a couple of days after my visit to the graveyard with Star. He announced that Mr Hyde had our first official bonafide gig. His call threw me for a loop and sent my brain into a tumultuous spin. Okay, the band rehearsals had been going great, but the thought of actually performing on stage with the band hadn't been a firm reality.

Until Nate's call.

'So, we've said yes to the show, pal. The guys are all psyched up and ready. And we know you're ready. You've knocked our bloody socks off, man. Anyway, extra rehearsals until the gig on Saturday if you're free. If not, we'll just go with the flow.'

My heart pounded in my chest. 'Y-yeah, sure. Sounds great. I... I can do extras.'

To say I had been given very little notice was an understatement. I was absolutely bloody terrified. Star insisted it was a good thing that I had less time to dwell on it and build it up into something scary and negative. She did her best to calm me and take my mind off things for the whole week, but the gig came round far too quickly after a run of solid rehearsals.

Star held my face in her palms and gazed up at me, oozing that tangible excitement I was growing to love. 'It's what you dreamed of all those years ago as a little kid, and it's finally happening, Fin. I'm so excited and so proud of you. You're going to be amazing, I just know it.'

I flared my nostrils as I locked my eyes on hers, wishing I was as confident in myself as she was. 'Yeah?'

She nodded slowly, a wide grin fixed on her gorgeous face. 'Oh yeah.'

I released myself from her grasp and began to pace up and down my living room. 'But... what if I forget the words or... or what if I get stage fright and just freeze up?'

She folded her arms defiantly and stepped into my path. 'Has that *ever* happened to you at rehearsals? Or when you've been singing at DeBasement, for that matter?'

I scrunched my brow as I thought about her question. 'Um... no. No, it hasn't.'

She opened her arms once again. 'See. No reason for it to happen at all then. Stop worrying. You're going to be brilliant.' She slipped her arms round my neck and tiptoed up to kiss me. And for a little while, at least, my fears melted away as I lost myself in her.

* * *

We arrived with the band at the Jekyll and Hyde bar in the centre of Edinburgh an hour before our gig was due to begin. The owners of the bar had been amazingly supportive in booking us for our first live gig, and I think the fact that we were named Mr Hyde endeared us to them.

Our set list for the gig was compiled of covers of our favourite songs. We *had* started to write some of our own material but decided as this was the first time we'd played to a live audience—that didn't only consist of our families and girlfriends—we'd save the original material for another time.

I stood in the poster-covered dressing room whilst the guys were tuning up and getting ready. The man reflected back at me from the mirror was someone I was slowly becoming accustomed to. I was surprised at how quickly my hair had grown, and after Alasdair had said there was no need for me to cut it for the office, that my work was what mattered, and Star had admitted that she loved my shaggy look, I'd stuck with it. My beard was trimmed, and I liked that I bore no resemblance to the Finlay Hunter of Hunter Drummond & Associates: all sharp designer suits and material items. I now looked like Fin Hunter, the guy who was daring to believe that dreams *did* come true, and that comfort zones were meant to be stepped out of every so often.

Before I knew it, the hands on the clock had reached ten p.m. and it was time for us to go on stage. My hands were shaking and my stomach was knotted. I had already downed a couple of glasses of Dutch courage, but my nerves were still jangling, and I felt sure I was going to either pass out or throw up.

Nate poked his head around the door. 'You right, pal? We're up.'

Oh, crap.

Just as I was about to step out of the tiny room, my phone began to ring. My father's number flashed on the screen. *Shit. Has something happened?* Panic and dread washed over me in equal measures, and I hit to accept the call.

'Hello?' My voice was hesitant.

My father's voice barked through the earpiece. 'Finlay. You really have gone stark raving mad, haven't you?' I pulled the phone away from my head as he continued. 'Tell me the rumours aren't true.'

I sighed heavily, partly through relief that the old bastard was still alive, and partly through frustration because the old bastard *was still alive*. Talk about a double-edged sword.

With flared nostrils, I replied, 'What rumours would they be?'

'That not only are you sleeping with the enemy, and by that I mean McKendrick, but now you've taken up with a bunch of morons and are having some kind of mid-life crisis by singing in a bloody poor excuse for a musical outfit.'

I clenched my jaw. *Could his timing have been any worse?* 'Ah, those rumours would be true then, yes. *All* of the above.'

His barrage began again in earnest. 'Are there no depths to which you won't sink to ruin the family name, Finlay? What makes you think these hair-brained schemes are a good idea? I mean, working for the man who almost ruined our family is a low blow. And I'm guessing it was a deliberate stab at your mother and me. And do you really think anyone wants to hear you caterwauling on a bloody stage? You're not a child any more, Finlay, so why are you acting like one? Prancing round on a stage like a little kid with a hairbrush. Honestly. I've never heard such utter preposterous nonsense. It's evident that you need help, young man. Serious help. You're not a bloody performing monkey, you know. Do you even care about your mother? What will people think? You've overstepped the mark this time, Finlay. You've really done it now. You've brought the word betrayal to a whole new level and given it an entirely new meaning. No doubt if I was to look up the word in a dictionary there would be your face plain for all to see! I want this damned nonsense to stop, do you hear me?'

His formal tone and ranting set the hairs on the back of my neck prickling in irritation. 'Quite frankly, Dad, I don't give a flying fuck what you think of me any more.' I hit end call and threw my phone at the wall where it bounced and fell to the floor in a heap of crumpled metal and fractured glass.

34

STAR

I sat clutching my glass of Jack and Coke in one hand and my camera in the other. I was determined not to miss a damn thing. But the drink was kind of a necessity, thanks to my state of nervousness. Fin had been in the dressing room for over half an hour and I had left him to gather his thoughts and prepare. My heart was in my mouth as I sat in the upstairs bar of the Jekyll and Hyde, waiting for Mr Hyde to begin their set.

I knew Fin would be amazing. There was no reason why he would suddenly fail, and I had every faith in him. I just wished he had the same faith in himself.

Titch came out and took his place behind the drums just as Siân and Tom arrived to my right. Tom put an arm round my shoulders, hugged me, and planted a kiss on the side of my head.

'How's he holding up?' he asked in a concerned tone.

'Pretty good, I think. Nervous, which is understandable, but I think he'll be fine.' I hoped I was right.

Tom sucked air in through his teeth. 'He sounded terrible when I rang him today. Totally freaked out.'

I shook my head in vehement protest. 'No, no. He's *fine*, Tom.' I think I was trying to convince myself more than Fin's best friend.

Siân nudged Tom and scowled at him before turning to me. 'We have a date to propose to you for the start of the exhibition.' She clapped her hands giddily, ignoring the look of worry on Tom's—and no doubt my—face.

I nodded and forced a smile. 'Oh... yeah. Yeah, great.' I tried to sound enthusiastic but failed miserably.

'Two months from tonight,' Tom confirmed, joining in Siân's enthusiasm.

I gasped and almost spilled my precious nerve-calming elixir. 'Wow, that's... that's very soon.'

Tom simply shrugged. 'Na. It's ages away. Loads of time. Don't panic. You two make a right bloody couple. Never known two people to be so unhappy slash terrified to have their dreams handed to them on a plate.' He chuckled and I rolled my eyes. He kind of had a point, I guess.

When I turned again, the rest of the band was on the stage and the lights had dimmed. A guy over by the mixing desk announced Mr Hyde, and the place erupted into raucous applause and whistles.

My shy, unassuming man stepped out into the spotlight. His gaze was fixed on the floor and his jaw was working so hard under his skin I could almost feel the grinding. The way his chest rose and fell told me he was on the verge of hyperventilating, and I longed to leap up there and just hold him, tell him he didn't have to do this if he really didn't want to. He had nothing to prove, despite his father's constant jibes and hints to the contrary.

It was so hard to comprehend the way he changed as soon as the music began. It was just like watching Dr Jekyll down the potion. Sure enough, the opening bars to Queen's 'Don't Stop me Now' kicked in, and the transformation took place. Fin gripped the mic, raised his head, and my heart almost stopped. The determination in his eyes verged on arrogance and he effervesced sex appeal that struck me like waves crashing over my body. As the song ramped up he dragged the mic from its stand, and strutted across the stage as Freddie Mercury's apt lyrics fell fiercely from his lips like he owned them.

Once again, he sang with such realism. Every word meant something to him. Every lyric filled with so much joy that I believed him.

Every. Single. Syllable.

He was singing about fulfilling a dream he'd had for so long and was finally living it. Okay so it was a club in Edinburgh not Wembley Arena but it may as well have been. Shivers travelled down my spine as I watched him. Utterly consumed. Beguiled even. And so damned proud.

I don't remember placing my drink down on the table, but before I could think, my camera was at my eye and I was snapping shots of him as he took command of the stage, and the audience were worshipping at his feet. It was the most natural thing for me to do as I watched him in his element.

Sweat dripped from the straggly strands of hair that fell onto his forehead, and he swiped his T-shirt from his body and wiped it round his face before tucking it into the waistband of his jeans. Most people would think he was doing it to draw attention to his sculpted body. But I knew different. It was simply a means to an end. He needed something to wipe his face on—it was as simple as that. He was the least showy showman I had *ever* witnessed. But that didn't make him any less mesmerising to watch. His inability to see himself how others saw him was both frustrating and endearing. And the people in the audience couldn't have been happier if they'd been on the front row of some private gig with a huge star. This is what he did to people.

What he did to me.

The entire show was amazing. The band was seamless. As the night wore on, Fin even began to speak to the audience in between songs, taking over from Nate who grinned widely as if he too saw the change in his frontman. My heart was full to bursting with love and pride.

My man, the rock star.

Alec and his on/off boyfriend Gil arrived and made their way across to me. The way they looked at each other told me things were distinctly on again. Alec handed me a Jack and Coke and turned his attention to the stage. 'Well hello rock god,' he said with a pout. 'I wonder if he needs anyone to wipe the sweat from his brow.'

I rolled my eyes. A terrible habit when in Alec's presence. 'You do remember you're not alone tonight,' I said pointedly.

Gil stepped forward and hugged me. 'Hey sweetie. Looking as gorgeous as ever. And take no notice of Al, he may pretend but he only has eyes for me.'

I smiled and wondered if it was true. They did make a lovely couple.

Another song ended and Fin stuck the mic back in its holster before stepping over and whispering something to Nate, who agreed with whatever was being suggested. Fin returned to centre stage as Nate passed around whatever Fin's message had been.

'You know, in life there are roads you travel because you *think* you should, and there are people you try to impress, even when they're the people who should love you unconditionally. I've been there. But no more. It stops right now. I say you do what you want to do. You do what makes you happy. You rise above it all and make your own plans. I dedicate this next song to every single person who has tried to be a square peg in a round hole. This is an oldie but a goldie... Bon Jovi's "It's My Life."'

A cheer erupted once more as the band began to play.

As always, I listened as he told the story of his experiences through song. I listened as he took a stand. The lyrics evidently resonated with him as he sang them with determination in his eyes and both hands gripping the mic in its stand. My stomach fluttered, but this time it wasn't butterflies or anxiety. This time it was a wonderful feeling of hope.

I was thankful for the fact that I'd remembered to bring along several memory cards for the camera as I eventually lost count of the number of images I shot. But I was excited to get home and load them onto the laptop and see what I'd captured.

Towards the end of the gig, the intro to our special song began to play, and Fin sauntered sexily over to the side of the stage where I had perched to get the best view. He crouched down so he was at eye level with me, his muscular chest glistening with sweat, and with a love-filled gaze, he sang 'Strange and Beautiful' as my insides clenched with need for him, and the last piece of my heart was lost to this mercurial man.

35

FIN

Regardless of how much I'd longed to be a singer when I was a kid, walking out on stage for real as an adult to front a band terrified me. Gone was all the bravado of performing to my reflection in the mirror. And after the barrage of insults flung at me during the ill-timed conversation with my dad, all I felt like doing was running for the highlands. But as I walked out there and the crowd erupted—a crowd that had come to see *my* band by *choice*—the unpleasant words of Campbell Hunter that had been rattling around my brain dissipated into the noise within the room and were replaced by the sound of whooping and cheering.

His words eventually meant nothing.

The first song was a great way to stick up two fingers to the man who had never believed in me. Never supported me in anything I wanted to do. And never told me he loved me in a direct sentence. He wasn't going to stop me. And as the intro began, my mask descended and I became the other version of myself. My own alter ego. It was the most bizarre feeling; almost indescribable. It was as if my body was possessed by the spirit of a *real* performer and I suddenly forgot I was shy as I let him take the reins.

It was hard to believe this was our first real gig. We just... *gelled*. The music flowed and we had fun playing up to the audience and to each other. Time flew by, and before I knew it, we were coming to the end of our set.

I added a song into the set at short notice and figured I'd get a strip torn off me later for mucking up the set list, but when I approached Nate on stage about singing 'It's My Life', he was enthusiastic about the choice. I said I'd explain later, but he told me there was no need, I'd just had to sing my heart out. And so I did. It was time to let go and move on. I knew there was a long way to go until I would be completely free of my anger, but I was prepared to try and *that* was progress.

Second to last, we played the song that had taken root in my heart along with the girl it reminded me of. And as I sang the words to her, Star's eyes sparkled up at me from where she sat, camera in hand. The look of pride I saw reflected back at me made my heart soar. Why should I care that my so-called father didn't care for my new hobby? The woman I was falling for thought it was great. In that moment, I realised that if I couldn't win my father's love then at least I had the support of the family I had chosen for myself. My friends. And as much as it hurt to know that no matter what I did, Campbell Hunter would never tell me he loved me, I knew I was surrounded by more love than I knew how to handle.

At the end of the set, the place erupted in applause and whistles. Two encores later, I managed to leave the stage and ruffle a fresh towel over my sweat-soaked, shaggy hair, as my T-shirt was soaked. The guys were buzzing, and I must admit, the feeling of adrenaline coursing through my veins was one of the best emotional highs I had ever experienced.

I'm sure you can guess what it came a close second to.

Once we were calmed and packed up, I began to make my way over to Star and Tom, but I was enveloped in a group hug by more of my friends who had turned up for the show. But the one person I wanted to see was Star. I glanced over to where she sat, still snapping shots of me, and smiled.

I thanked my well-wishers and made my way towards her again when I spotted my brother and sister-in-law. 'I didn't think you'd be able to make it!' I told Callum as I hugged him hard.

'And miss you sticking the proverbial two fingers up at Dad? Not a chance. I always knew you were good bro, but bloody hell, who knew you were *this* good?'

'We're so proud of you!' Tori said, eyes glistening with tears. 'I've never seen you as happy. You were amazing!'

'Thanks so much. That means the world to me. Hey, you must come and say hi to Star.' I turned to lead them to where my muse was sitting but I was stopped in my tracks by a woman I recognised from the TV. My heart jumped into my mouth as she held out a digital recorder.

'Hi Fin, I'm Lily Macrae from Scotland Today. I'm covering for my friend who edits Edinburgh Nights Magazine as a wee favour. Although I'm glad I accepted now. That was awesome. I'd like to ask you a few questions if you don't mind?'

'Thanks. And aye, I know who you are. Fire away.'

36

STAR

Watching Fin get the recognition he deserved was a beautiful sight. He was hugged and patted on the back more times than I could count. I observed the whole thing through my lens and shot as many frames as I could, making sure I captured as much of the night as possible. The change in him was so clear to me. His whole demeanour had altered since he stepped out into the audience, closing himself back inside his shy exterior shell and bowing his head as people rained compliments down on him, unable to acknowledge he was as good as they were telling him he was. His posture was a little more hunched, as if he was trying to become less conspicuous. That's the good thing with being an observer; nothing much passed by me.

Suddenly, he stopped paying attention to the crowd of well-wishers and glanced in my direction. The expression that appeared on his face was one of those heart melting half smiles that made my insides turn to mush.

It was meant just for me.

And I felt it right down to my core. To my soul. I lowered my camera to take in the sight of him with my own eyes. It was like he was the calm in the eye of the storm. I wanted him. Desperately. But I had to accept that he had a serious fan base that was un-willing to let him go just yet, and so I adored him from across the crowded room like some poor heroine in a romance novel. I watched as he hugged a man who looked a lot like him but slightly older. I guessed it was his brother, Callum and that the petite brunette with him was Tori. Butterflies took flight in my stomach. No doubt I was going to meet them very soon.

Fin turned with determination, but his attempts

to reach me were halted again when a familiar-looking woman with long dark wavy hair caught his attention. I watched as his eyes widened and he gawked at her. She held up a recording device and seemed to be interviewing him. Wow, he really was living the dream. After a few minutes he grinned at her as she shook his hand and left.

When he eventually reached me, his cheeks were flushed. I parted my thighs where I sat so he could step into the gap I'd created, and after kissing my cheek he gestured in the direction of the woman's retreating form.

'Did you see? Did you see who that was?' His eyes were wide like a kid on Christmas, and I couldn't help smiling.

I shook my head. 'She looked kinda familiar but—'

'It was Lily bloody Macrae, Star. I was just interviewed by Lily bloody Macrae.' He shook his head in bewilderment as it dawned on me who she was.

But I was confused. 'Isn't she the broadcaster from Scotland Today on TV?'

He nodded emphatically. 'Yes. Yes, it is her. And she interviewed me.'

His enthusiasm was sweet and endearing. 'Well... that's just great, Fin.' I hugged him tight.

He shrugged. 'Yeah. I mean, she was doing a favour for a friend, but...'

'Oh? What favour?'

'Her friend at Edinburgh Nights rag who reviews bands has broken his leg and so she came instead. How bloody awesome is that?'

I poked his arm playfully. 'Oh yeah? Should I be worried?'

He pulled me close and kissed me tenderly. 'A while ago, I would have said yes.' The wink that followed wasn't reassuring. 'But now I only have eyes for my pink-haired American lass.' Okay, so he redeemed himself. 'And anyway, she was wearing a huge engagement ring so some lucky bugger has snapped her up.'

The hurt that squeezed my insides must have showed all over my face as he ducked so his eyes were level with mine. 'Hey. I'm only messing, Star. You're all I think about now. You're the one I want. And I mean that in every sense.' His voice was husky, and I shivered as he lowered his mouth so it was almost touching mine. I suddenly forgot why I was annoyed as his hot breath teased my lips and the noise in the room no longer registered in my brain. My heart pounded as if trying to make its way towards his, and I closed my eyes, relishing the sensation of the anticipation of his kiss. At last, he brushed his lips over mine, and I sighed.

'Hey, you okay?' he whispered.

I nodded. 'I think your spell worked.'

He smiled as I hinted at the 'Strange and Beautiful' song lyrics. But I was already head over heels.

No spell needed.

He stroked his thumb over my cheek. 'That's good to hear.' I adored the way he rolled his 'r' and I closed my eyes to revel in his tender caress. I opened my eyes to find his vivid blues locked on me. 'Hey, I want you to meet my brother and his wife.' He turned quickly and pointed to the couple I had seen him with earlier. 'Cal, Tori, I'd like to introduce you to Star.'

'Tori immediately pulled me into a hug. 'It's so lovely to meet you. Fin talks about you all the time,' she told me enthusiastically.

'Yes he talks about you guys lots too. And baby Charlotte.'

'Tori's folks have the pleasure of our little bundle of joy this evening. I'm Callum. But call me Cal.' He held out his hand and I shook it.

'Great to meet you. So, what did you think of your brother's performance tonight?' I asked and eagerly awaited his response.

He grinned. 'Bloody amazing. A regular Jon Bon Jovi. Hetty would be so proud.'

I turned to Fin. 'Did you invite her?'

He nodded. 'I did. But she couldn't make it. She was so gutted.'

'I got lots of photos so I'll email them to her,' Tori told him. 'Although they won't be professional shots like yours,' she added with a flush to her cheeks.

'Do you guys want to come back and have coffee?' Fin asked.

Callum cringed. 'I'm so sorry, Fin but we have to get back to pick Charlotte up. Tori isn't ready for her to go for sleepovers yet.' He kissed his wife's head.

'It took all my willpower to leave her with my mum and dad,' Tori admitted.

'Understandable. Let's meet up again soon though huh?' I said with a bright smile.

'Deal. Now you make sure my brother can

squeeze his head through the door after all the ego polishing. Goodnight.' Callum hugged me and Tori followed suit, then they both hugged Fin and left.

Fin bent to whisper in my ear, 'I'm kind of glad they didn't come back for coffee. I want to take you home right now.'

My insides clenched at his unspoken intentions, but I frowned. 'B-but the other guys' girlfriends came over and mentioned a party they're having over at Nate's house. Don't you want to go?'

He shook his head slowly. 'I just need to get you alone.'

I pulled my bottom lip in between my teeth, trying not to grin like a complete idiot. 'Okay. I think it can be arranged.'

He crushed his mouth to mine and slipped one hand into my hair while the other snaked around my waist. I knew people could see our passionate exchange, but I didn't care.

It was just Fin and I that mattered.

* * *

After saying our goodbyes, the rest of the band headed off to celebrate more at Nate's house party, but Fin explained to them that he was ready for some alone time with me. They all poked fun at him and did the whole 'We know what you're gonna do' sing song bit. I was sure I was on the verge of spontaneous human combustion as the heat in my cheeks reached near volcanic levels.

Fin led me by the hand out of the club, and the welcome blast of chilled evening air caressed my burning cheeks.

He laced his fingers with mine. 'Are you sure you don't mind us just going back to your place?' he asked as we sauntered along Hanover Street, hand in hand.

I shook my head and smiled. 'Not at all. I was just surprised you didn't want to go celebrate such a successful night.'

He raised his eyebrows briefly. 'I *am* going to celebrate. Just not with loads of other people around.' His sexy half smile made me melt with the promise of what was to come.

'You really don't like being the centre of attention, do you?'

He pursed his lips and scrunched his nose. 'Nah. Not really my thing. Don't get me wrong, I love the buzz of being on stage and performing when I'm in the zone. But that buzz lifts pretty damn quick as soon as I leave the stage. I'm not the kind of person who'd handle all the shit that goes along with being well known. I'm happy to get up and do my bit and then return to being plain old *me* after.'

My heart screamed, *But Fin, there's absolutely nothing plain about you.* But I reined myself in before blurting it out and instead settled on, 'No chance of you going on Britain's Got Talent then, huh?'

His hearty laugh did funny things to every muscle below my waistline, and he squeezed my hand. 'Nope. Not a kitty in Hades' chance, sweetheart. But... I'd settle for being the centre of *your* attention instead.'

Oh. My. God. 'I think I could take delight in that scenario too.'

We walked along in silence for a while, until a thought crossed my mind and the words left my mouth before I could stop them. 'I bet your mom and dad would've been proud of you tonight.'

I glanced over at him and his handsome smile had been replaced with a scowl. He laughed derisively. 'Not likely. He rang me tonight, actually.'

I stopped in my tracks. 'Your dad *called*? *Tonight*? When? What did he say?'

His nostrils flared. 'Right before the gig. He said that it was a joke me getting up on a stage and that I was doing my best to ruin the family name. But apart from that, it was all sparkles and rainbows. Oh, and I smashed my bloody phone after.'

I stepped in front of him and cupped his face in my hands. 'Oh Fin, I'm so sorry.'

'Don't be. It's what I expect.'

'Is he like this with Callum too?'

He smiled. 'Yes and no. My brother is as strong-willed and stubborn as my dad. My brother became a GP so he's still doing something worthwhile even if it's not law. Although they didn't like Tori when he met her. She's not from a well to do family so she was beneath him in their opinion. That seems to have changed since Charlotte came along. Suddenly she's a wonderful mother and they couldn't be happier. It's all so false.'

'Don't they want you to be happy? Isn't that the main job of a parent, to ensure their children's happiness?'

He shrugged. 'You'd think so, eh? But with my folks it's all about status. What kind of car you drive, your parentage, your education, your job, your house.'

My heart sank. 'Oh god they're going to have a field day with me, then, huh?'

Fin stopped and turned to face me. 'Star, I don't care what they think. Not any more. You're the one I... care about. If they don't like that they swivel for all I care.'

His words were reassuring. But a dreadful thought popped into my head. 'They won't be at the charity ball will they?'

Fin took my hand. 'Don't worry. It's on a date they're usually out of the country in St Tropez so no, they probably won't be there.'

Relief flooded me. 'That's good. Although probably is still a little ambiguous.'

'Look, even if they were there I would avoid them so you'd still have nothing to worry about.'

'I don't get why he's like that with you.'

'Because I've decided to stand on my own two feet. He doesn't like it when he can't control things.'

I thought about my own mum and dad and my heart ached. Hearing how Fin's parents treated him made me miss my own tremendously. My lip began to tremble and my eyes stung with unshed tears.

'Hey, don't cry, Star. You've got nothing to worry about.'

'I'm sorry. No it's not that. I just... I wish they were different. I wish they were more like my mom and dad.'

'Me too.' He kissed the top of my head as tears escaped my eyes and dampened my cheeks chilling them.

A group of revellers across the street stopped and one of the men stepped forward. 'Hey, love! Is that guy bothering you?' His broad Scottish accent slurred as he called over to me.

I forced a smile. 'No. Everything's fine. Thank you though,' I called back with a shrug and a huge fake grin plastered on my face.

The guy didn't look convinced. 'Aye... all right

then. You take care, eh?' My would-be saviour waved as he began to walk on with his group of friends. He periodically glanced over his shoulder at us until he turned the corner onto Queen Street.

'I think maybe we should get home, eh?' Fin said with a sad smile. I feel like I've ruined the night with my family problems. I would understand if you just wanted me to walk you home, you know.'

I stared up at him and reached up to cup his cheek. 'You can't get rid of me that easily. And you didn't ruin things. We're not going to let him do that to us. Not tonight.'

He closed his eyes and let his head roll back. He rubbed his hands over his face and huffed a long sigh from his lungs before he lowered his gaze to meet mine once more. 'God, I'm so bloody lucky we found each other.'

My eyes began to well up again. 'Me too.'

He rested his forehead on mine. 'I can't believe I smashed my bloody phone. I really don't mean to let him get to me. But...' He closed his eyes. 'It hurts, Star. It hurts so much that he treats me like he does. All I wanted was a dad. Nothing more.'

My heart broke for the little boy inside of Fin

who only wanted his father's approval. 'I know, Fin. I know.'

* * *

Once we were inside my apartment, I closed and locked the door behind us. Alec had gone back to Gil's house after the gig and wouldn't be home until morning.

'What do you want to drink?' I asked Fin as I peered at him over my shoulder. He was standing in the doorway with his hands in his pockets, looking sheepish.

He cleared his throat. 'To be honest, I'm not really bothered for a drink. I'd... I'd rather go to bed.'

My pulse spiked, and I placed my keys down on the coffee table. 'Oh?'

He tentatively stepped towards me. 'Yeah. I've been thinking about being alone with you all night. But then I almost ruined everything.'

I tilted my head to the side. 'Well, it's a good thing I forgive you, huh?'

His brow furrowed and he fell silent for a few

moments as he just stared at me, or *into* me, I wasn't sure which.

'What the hell *is* this, Star?'

I shook my head, wondering what he was getting at. 'What do you mean?'

He stepped towards me again, and in three further paces, he was standing only inches from me. His vivid blue eyes remained steadfast, locked on mine. 'This. Between us. There's a pull. I've never experienced it before, and I don't know whether it's normal to feel so... *drawn* to someone. So *right* with someone you've known for a very short time.'

I slipped my hands up the length of his arms, and his came round my waist. I shrugged at his question. 'Honestly? I have no idea. This is all new to me too. And I have no clue what normal even is. Does the concept even exist? All I do know is that if we're both feeling it then it must be real, and that counts for something, right?'

With no further words, he took my mouth with his in a deep, toe-curling kiss, searing my soul and stealing the air from my lungs. Before I knew it, we were naked in bed, taking pleasure and giving it back in equal measure. Devouring each other. Feasting on each other. Silently expressing what I guessed we were both feeling, but maybe both thought it was too soon to say.

All thoughts of cruel fathers, TV presenters, bad intentions, and anger flew out through the window along with the sound of our muttered words and heavy breaths.

37

FIN

I awoke with a pounding head to find Star fast asleep in my arms. Despite my headache, I smiled as I watched her chest rise and fall with each silent breath. I would have loved to stay there with her forever. Just holding her, feeling her next to me, and taking in her beauty. Her warmth seeped into my own skin and settled somewhere round my heart. At that moment, I felt sorry for those who didn't believe in love at first sight, or falling fast for someone. I'd experienced it, and I say, don't knock it 'til you know the feeling.

The events of the night before both haunted and thrilled me. The words of disapproval from my father almost spoiled everything for me yet again. But I would be damned if I'd let him win this time. I allowed thoughts of him to dissipate and instead focused on the good memories—most of them involving Star. It was like our souls were already connected and we had been destined to meet, only it had to be the right time.

Her eyelids fluttered open, and she stretched like a satisfied cat after a bowl of cream. 'Mmm. Good morning, handsome.' God, I loved her sexy morning voice, and that bloody accent was enough to send me over the edge before she even touched me.

'Good morning yourself, beautiful. We have all day to spend together. What do you want to do?'

* * *

We chose to spend a lazy Sunday morning at Star's apartment following a call from Alec to say he was heading to Livingston with Gil for the day. Later, we sat munching on bacon rolls and planning for the evening. We were meeting my boss and his wife in the city to help Star feel more at ease when we attended the charity ball a couple of weeks hence.

Sitting on her bed with her wardrobe doors wide open and clothes strewn round the room, she stamped her foot like a petulant child. 'But what do I wear?' I pursed my lips, trying not to laugh, and failed, which earned me a playful slap to the arm. 'Finnn, this is serious. I've never met these people, and it's important that I make a good impression.'

I leaned forward and swiped a blob of ketchup from her lip before sucking it off my thumb. 'Just wear whatever you want to wear and be yourself. They'll love you. Stop worrying.' The fact that she seemed so hung up on what people thought was completely out of line with her appearance, and I wondered why.

She lowered her gaze. 'I just... I want to be... I want them to think I'm good enough for you.'

What? 'Star, why in hell would you think anything to the contrary?'

'Because you're a lawyer, and I make coffee. You're all normal looking, and I have pink hair and wouldn't know normal if it jumped up and bit me. You're intelligent, and I'm—'

Anger niggled at me. 'Whoa, hang on there. Okay, point one, I'm a lawyer because it's what I was *pushed* into, and it's all I know. Two, I love your pink hair, it makes you you. And three...' I inched closer to her on the bed and slipped my hand around to the nape of her neck. 'Qualifications don't mean you're intelligent. They mean you're good at answering questions at length within a time limit. You are the most intelligent, fun, caring, talented woman I've ever met, so don't go getting a bloody inferiority complex on me, okay? And anyway, Alasdair isn't at all like that. He's so cool, Star. He doesn't judge on appearance. Hell, he's fine with my beardy weirdness and shaggy, unlawyery hair, so he isn't going to care what colour yours is. I can't quite believe you're so eaten up about what people think.'

She chewed the inside of her cheek and folded her arms around herself protectively. 'I wasn't... I mean I never have been. Not until...'

My heart sank. 'Not until you met me?' She nodded. I placed my plate on the floor, and once my hands were free, I pulled her until she straddled my lap. 'You really have nothing to worry about. I don't know why you feel like this. If I've done something or... or said something to make you feel this way then I'm so sorry. But believe me when I say that I don't care what anyone thinks of *either* of us. As long as we're happy then that's all that counts, okay?'

Her lip trembled. 'I know. I just... I love being a part of your life and I want to make sure I don't give you any reason to make that change.' She lowered her head, unable to look in my eyes.

I sighed and cupped her face, forcing her to meet my gaze. 'I could say the very same thing.'

She smiled, but her eyes were still filled with sadness, so I pulled her down to kiss her in a way I hoped would express what I felt unable to say out loud in case I scared her away.

Suddenly an idea came to mind. Hopefully it would help her see that supposed status meant nothing to me. 'Let's go out this afternoon. There's someone I'd like you to meet.'

* * *

I gripped Star's hand as we entered Southern Cross Cafe, and a familiar pair of friendly eyes locked on mine. I glanced at Star and smiled before pulling her eagerly forward.

As soon as we arrived at the table, Hetty was on

her feet, pulling me down into her arms. For such a small person she could certainly squeeze hard, but she gave the best hugs ever.

'Fin. It's so good to see you, love.' Her emotion-filled voice tugged at my heart.

A lump formed in my throat almost trapping my voice, but I managed to choke out, 'And you too, Hetty. I've missed you.'

'Oh, my sweet boy. Let me look at you.' She held me at arm's length and trailed a parental, assessing gaze over me. 'My, you do look well. Rugged, but well, all the same.' Her smile widened as she spotted Star beside me. 'And who might this beautiful young lady be?'

I gently pulled Star forward. 'Hetty, I'd like you to meet my girlfriend, Star Mendoza. Star, this is the other important woman in my life, Hetty Mackenzie.'

Star held out her hand, but a sob broke free from Hetty, and she grappled Star into a hug. 'Oh, bless you both. How wonderful. How perfect.'

'Hi, Mrs Mackenzie. I've heard so much about you,' Star told her.

'Oh, please call me Hetty.' She glanced between

the two of us. 'I can see the look in his eyes when he talks about you. He's clearly smitten.'

Star's cheeks coloured, and she smiled over at me as she chewed her lip.

'I was so relieved to know you hadn't gone up to Arisaig yet. I wanted so much for you to meet Star.'

We sat down, and a waitress came to take our order. Once it was just the three of us again, I grinned like an idiot between the two most important women in my life.

Hetty patted Star's arm. 'I'm guessing you've met Callum and Tori and wee baby Charlotte?'

I contorted my face and narrowed my eyes. 'Actually no. Well only in passing. Cal keeps messaging me asking when we're free to meet up but we've both been so busy.'

Hetty tilted her head and shook it. 'Not too busy for me though?'

I leaned and took her hand briefly. 'I'm never too busy for you Hetty.'

Her cheeks pinked and she whacked at my hand. 'Och, away with you, you wee dafty.' She turned her attention to my girl. 'So, Star, tell me about yourself.'

She shrugged. 'Well, there's not much to tell, really.'

'Oh, come now. I doubt that very much. I mean, for starters you're an American lassie living thousands of miles from home. So, that alone tells me how brave you are.'

'Oh, I don't know about that.'

Hetty's alarmed gaze darted to mine, and I felt the need to explain. 'Star is quite... how can I say it? *Modest,* to say the least. Although she's the most talented photographer. In fact, you know the framed photos I loved so much?'

She rolled her eyes playfully. 'Oh, aye. How could I forget?'

I gripped Star's hand with an immense amount of pride. 'Well, this is the photographer. S.A.M. aka, Star Mendoza.'

Hetty gasped and covered her heart. 'Oh my goodness. Now there's a strìc de dhuais if I ever heard of it.'

Star's brow crumpled. I leaned over and kissed her cheek. 'It means a stroke of fate. It's Gaelic.'

'Mìorbhaileach,' Hetty continued with a warm smile.

'Yes, it is *wonderful,* Hetty. And if I didn't believe in fate before, I certainly do now.' I kept my gaze fixed on Star as I spoke the words, and her responding smile made my heart soar.

Tilting her head to one side, Hetty continued, 'So, Star, tell me more.'

* * *

When we left the café, hand in hand, a sense of relief and calm came over me. Star had captured Hetty's heart and vice versa. And just as I knew she would, Hetty instilled a sense of belonging and confidence in Star as only she could. There had been no words spoken on the matter, but it was evident in Star's smile and in her body language.

Mission accomplished.

38

STAR

After meeting Hetty I decided that I should return the favour. We stood outside my Grandma Aggie's little house on the outskirts of the city. Fin looked calm and collected which annoyed me because there was a war going on in my insides.

'Star my beautiful girl. I wasn't expecting to see you today. Is everything okay?' my grandma asked as she hugged me. She stepped aside and gestured for us to enter. As we sat on the flowery couch in the living room Grandma stayed in the doorway and eyed Fin with suspicion. 'And who is this handsome young man?'

'Grandma, I'd like you to meet Fin... Fin Hunter,

he's my... erm...' I glanced at Fin almost for permission even though he had introduced me as his girlfriend when we met Hetty. He nodded and smiled. 'Boyfriend.'

My grandma gasped and placed a hand on each of her cheeks. 'Well that's just lovely. Hello Fin Hunter.'

Fin stood again and awkwardly stepped closer to my grandma to shake her hand but she pulled him down to her four feet ten level and planted a kiss on his cheek. 'You may call me Aggie.'

Fin's cheeks flushed red and he grinned. 'Lovely to meet you Aggie. I can see where Star gets her beautiful smile from.'

My grandma glanced over at me. 'Oh he's a charmer this one. I think we'll keep him.' And with that she disappeared off to make tea.

'She's great,' Fin said with sincerity.

I nodded. 'I think so too. And the fact she let you call her Aggie... well, I'd say you more than meet with approval.'

He beamed and nodded his head. 'Initial family introductions... tick.' He made a tick in the air and relaxed into his seat and I almost burst with happiness.

* * *

Deacon Brodie's was hectic when we arrived, and I clutched Fin's hand as he pushed through the throngs of people already there. He lifted his other hand and waved in recognition of someone, and an older, handsome man waved back.

The man and his beautiful female companion stood as we approached the table where they were, and Fin was drawn into a hug.

'Good to see you, Fin. And you must be Star. It's wonderful to finally meet you. Fin has spoken very highly of you.' He shook my hand and kissed my cheek.

My skin heated and my nerves jangled. 'Likewise, Mr McKendrick.'

'Oh, no. Please call me Alasdair. It makes me sound so much younger.' He winked, and I decided I liked him. 'Fin, Star. I would like you to meet my better half, Colette.'

The stunning blonde woman leaned in and kissed me on both cheeks before giving the same greeting to Fin. 'I've heard so much about the pair of you that I feel I already know you,' Colette told us. I immediately warmed to her. She had the loveliest, friendly blue eyes that crinkled at the corners when she smiled. She was dressed in casual black trousers and a cream sweater that looked like cashmere. I suddenly felt very self-aware in my skinny jeans and off shoulder black top. As if knowing I needed reassurance, Fin squeezed my hand, and when I looked at him, he smiled down at me with a look of sheer adoration.

My heart leapt.

'Come, sit.' Alasdair gestured to the two empty seats.

'So, Star, Fin tells me you're from Indiana. Which part?'

'I'm from a town called Fort Wayne. Well, city, actually.'

'Oh, yes. I'm familiar with Fort Wayne. Great centre for art and culture. Colette and I travelled the USA just after we married. Fascinating place. Explains your artistic streak, maybe?'

Heat rose in my cheeks again as I realised Fin

had been telling his boss about my photography. I decided to try hard to be proud instead of shy for once. 'Yeah, my mom and dad used to love taking me to the museums and art galleries. There are so many of them back home.'

'So what brought you to Scotland?' Colette asked.

'My grandparents are from here and even though I visited as a child I couldn't remember much, if anything, so I decided I'd come and check the place out as an adult. To be honest, I arrived here and fell for the place. And now I don't want to leave because I have my grandma here and... well Fin too. And I feel so at home, you know?'

'Well, I'm sure Fin is delighted you stayed,' Alasdair said with a wink towards my companion.

I glanced at Fin, and he was beaming at me. 'I certainly am, Alasdair.' He ran his thumb tenderly over my knuckles. 'I don't know about you guys but I'm bloody starving. Shall I go grab some menus?'

Alasdair patted his forearm. 'Sounds like a good plan, son.' Fin stood to leave the table, and once he had gone, Alasdair's attention was back on me.

His smile was warm. 'So, you'll be accompanying Fin to the ball, I understand?'

I swallowed hard and nodded. 'Y-yes. Well, that's if I can find an evening dress that covers my tattoos.'

Alasdair frowned and glanced at Colette, who tilted her head to one side. 'Why on earth would you want to do that, dear?' she asked with a concerned gaze.

I sighed. 'Oh, well... I mean, I hardly fit in with... I mean you're all so...' I wasn't sure how to put my feelings into words without sounding dumb. I had never felt self-conscious about my ink, or my dress sense until I met Fin. He loved the way I looked, so that wasn't the reason, but I somehow felt inferior. The people in his circles were all smart, suit-wearing business types. But me? Well, I'm not the type of person who usually conforms. And that had always been fine. But suddenly my coffee shop job, my crazy coloured hair and my Japanese vine tattoo didn't feel very befitting of a lawyer's girlfriend.

Alasdair leaned forward and pinned me with his firm gaze. 'Look, Star, you are a beautiful and individual young woman, which is something to be embraced. Fin clearly adores you, so why do you feel it necessary to change? To cover up who you are?'

I closed my eyes, briefly trying to decide how to

word my response so I didn't sound feeble. 'I guess I've never really had to try and fit in with high flyers before, and I don't want to let Fin down. He mentioned that his parents may be at the ball, and the last thing I want to do is add to his problems there.'

Colette reached out and took my hand. 'Darling, why would you add to his problems? You are *you*. You change for no one. Least of all the Hunters.' The way she said Fin's family name with disdain spoke of an undercurrent of severe dislike. 'Fin is the only one of that family you should care about, and he's *crazy* about you. He hasn't batted an eyelid about taking you as his date because there's no reason for him to do so. To him, it's the most natural thing in the world. He adores you, so of course he wants you by his side. We want you there too.' Alasdair nodded emphatically in agreement with his wife. 'And your tattoos are beautiful. Please don't *ever* feel inferior because you choose not to be a sheep. Like Alasdair says, embrace your individuality, don't shy away from it.'

Alasdair chimed in, 'I'm with Colette. You have nothing to prove. And these *high flyers*, as you call them, are normal human beings, Star. They are in no way superior to you just because they wear suits and try criminals.'

Guilt washed over me at my reaction. 'I'm sorry. I didn't mean to offend you. I just—'

Alasdair waved his hands. 'No, no. You haven't offended us at all. We're simply trying to make you see that you have nothing to worry about. Nothing to fear. If Campbell and Isobel are there then you hold your head high like Fin will. Okay?'

Fin returned and placed four menus on the table. He sat beside me and glanced worriedly around at us. 'Is everything okay?'

I smiled as relief flooded me. 'Everything is wonderful, Fin.'

* * *

My feet were sore, but Alec was relentless in his determination to find the perfect dress for me to wear to the charity ball. I had found a pale blue long-sleeved dress in the first shop we visited. I tried it on and liked it. Well, *liked* may be exaggerating a little...

Although Alec voiced his opinion very loudly... as usual. 'Bloody hell, Twinkle. I wouldn't let my granny wear that frock and she's dead. Go remove it from your delectable curves before I have to use it to mop up my vomit.'

I rolled my eyes like the errant teenager I felt I was becoming. 'Don't sugar coat it, Al. Give it to me straight, huh?' With a huff, I returned to the fitting room. Truth be told, I was still hung up on having my tattoos on show, and all the dresses Alec showed me would expose more than a little bit of skin.

Once I replaced the 'granny frock' on its hanger, I skulked back out to Alec, who grasped my hand and pretty much dragged me out of the store and down Princes Street towards a side alley. We were surrounded by pretty boutiques with bay windows displaying items I would have to sell my left kidney to buy. We arrived outside one such shop and Alec stopped. When I lifted my gaze and saw the dresses in the window, a wave of panic almost floored me.

'There is no way in *hell* I can either *afford* anything in that store *or* fit into anything in there. Let's just go get me a dress from a regular store, Al. *Please*?'

He turned to face me and placed his hands on my shoulders. 'Twinkle, do you trust me?'

'Of course I do, but—'

He placed a finger over my lips. 'Ah dadadadadada. So, you trust me. That much we've established. Now for the next question. Well, it's not really a question... it's more of a statement.'

'Alec!' I mumbled around his finger.

'Okay. *I* am buying this dress. Call it your early Christmas gift. But I will take no protests. *You* are my family. And I won't take no for an answer. Besides, with what your boss pays you, there's no way you can afford anything but a carrier bag from this boutique.'

I cocked my head to the side. 'But *you* are the boss who pays me.'

He leaned forward and kissed my head. 'Yes, and I think you deserve a raise. Now come on.'

He pushed open the door and pulled me along beside him. Suddenly I felt like Julia Roberts' character in *Pretty Woman*. I was a fish out of water, and there was no doubt about that. The major difference in *this* story, however, was that the owner was wonderful. Very friendly and eager to help.

Between them, Alec and the owner, Cynthia, pulled out four dresses for me to try. They were all absolutely stunning. But I was way out of my depth. I much preferred my shredded jeans and off shoulder

T-shirts, while letting my dyed hair fall shaggily round my shoulders.

The final dress I tried was a floor-length, black strapless number with a boned bodice and crystals at the left hip. I had never worn anything like it. Ever. But as soon as Cynthia zipped me into it and turned me round to face the full-length mirror, I almost fainted. She had handed me a pair of black satin stiletto pumps and pulled my hair into a rough 'up-do'. For the first time in my life, I looked and felt sophisticated. Demure. Classy. Somehow, the dress made my tattoos look even more beautiful, and my eyes began to sting.

Cynthia clasped her hands in front of her face and sighed dreamily. 'I think we've found the dress, Star, my dear.'

I opened and closed my mouth a few times as if gasping for air. 'I... I... Sheesh, I have no words.'

She smiled at my reflection. 'Then we have *definitely* found the dress. Go show your friend.' She gestured excitedly at the curtain that led out to the shop floor.

I stepped through the curtain and felt like a

movie star as my feet landed on the red carpet of the boutique.

Alec gasped and his eyes widened. 'Well, slap me silly and call me straight.' His response made me giggle, and I dabbed at the salt water in the corners of my eyes.

I sniffed. 'You like it? Do you think Fin will like it, too?'

'Twinkle, if he doesn't want to rip that thing off you right away then he really is gay.'

'Great. But the price tag, Alec. It's... I can't let you—'

He made a clamping gesture with his hand. 'Shhht. What did I say to you? I'm not taking no for an answer.' Cynthia came out and stood beside me with a wide smile on her sweet face. 'Cinderella, you shall go to the ball. Cynth, we'll take the shoes and a little black clutch too.'

'Alec—' My attempt at a protest was met with an infamous *Alec scowl*. It was the warning expression that came just before he blew up and so I backed down and vowed to pay him back somehow. Someday.

39

STAR

Why is it that things we look forward to take an age to arrive, yet the things we're dreading or scared about seem to be here in the blink of an eye? In the previous days and weeks, I felt myself hurtling towards the night of the ball like a runaway train. Wishing I had some kind of time machine or at least a method to slow things down a little. But sadly, my wishes were all in vain and so there I was, all too soon, standing outside the doors to the charity ball venue. My heart tried desperately to vacate my body, and I fought to calm my breathing. This was *huge*. This was Fin and I at our first official function as a couple. It was all a little too soon, and I was terrified of making a fool of myself.

His parents might be there. *Oh, shit.* His colleagues, too. Alasdair had tried hard to reassure me in that soothing way he had about him that Fin and I belonged together, and that no amount of being looked down upon, by people who should know better, could spoil that fact.

I wished I believed him.

My heart was telling me he was right, but my head kept on chipping in with snide comments that took every step forward I had made and shoved them back to square one. I glanced down at my fitted, strapless black evening dress and wondered what people would think of me. It was a disconcerting frame of mind that had only affected me since I met Fin, and I didn't like it one bit.

Fin's eyes had nearly popped out when he saw me in the dress for the first time that evening. I was glad I had that effect on him, but standing there, about to step into the unknown, I wanted nothing more than to be at DeBasement wearing my ripped jeans and drinking a beer as Fin owned the stage. Colette had sent me some gorgeous make-up, and the glitter powder gave my tattoos a beautiful sheen, but regardless of how I looked on the outside, I was quaking on the inside.

Fin rested his hand at the small of my back, leaned in, and whispered, 'You look stunning, you know? You will no doubt be the most beautiful woman in the room.'

Shivers tingled from the base of my neck all the way down my spine but I still wanted to go home. I wondered if I clicked my heels together, would it have the desired effect.

He dragged me from my *Wizard of Oz* daydream by whispering, 'Come on, let's do this.'

I glanced down at my cleavage in the fitted bodice and wondered if maybe it was just a little too much. *Too late now, Mendoza.* My pink and blonde hair had been scraped into a chignon by the hairdresser recommended to me by Colette. I should have felt sophisticated, but instead, the ink adorning my body and my thick eye make-up screamed to everyone that I didn't belong there. I only had myself to blame, though. I had insisted upon staying true to myself in *some* way, just as Alasdair and Colette had said I should. Not that Fin would have wanted me to

change. He knew I wasn't about to completely transform myself for the event, charity or not. I was still
me, and it was *me* he wanted to be with. And it would
fine, so long as I kept repeating that as my mantra.

The double doors were opened, and I nervously
glanced round the vast ballroom. Monolithic ice
sculptures were placed round the edges of the space,
and circular tables draped in sumptuous heavy
jacquard fabric covered half the floor. There was a
stage at one end where a small orchestra played clas-
sical music, and several couples floated round the
dance floor already.

Gazing up, I spotted the hefty crystal chandeliers
that seemed to defy gravity. They lit the room with a
warm glow, sending shards of light this way and that
from their faceted surfaces. Men in tailored tuxedos
stood around chatting, while their female compan-
ions assessed each other's attire, smiling politely
every so often while their eyes told a whole different
story. The ball gowns were stunning. I couldn't even
begin to guess how much money was dancing round
the room disguised as taffeta and Swarovski crystal.

Fin gave my hand another reassuring squeeze as
Alasdair and Colette appeared before us. Colette

wore a deep purple floor-length dress with one shoulder strap that draped elegantly across the delicate bone structure of her shoulder. She was such a stunning woman; so kind and thoughtful too.

She pulled me into a warm hug. 'Star, my dear. You look wonderful.'

'Thanks, Colette. So do you.'

'My, my, Finlay. Your girl looks ravishing tonight.' Alasdair took my hand and kissed the back of it. His soft Scottish accent was welcoming and friendly as always, and I was so grateful for that.

Fin pulled me into his side possessively. 'Well, I certainly think so.' Suddenly, his mood changed. His nostrils flared as his gaze darted anxiously around the room. 'Is he... is *he* here?'

Alasdair grasped Fin's shoulder firmly. 'Not yet. Like I said to you before, don't worry. He can't hurt you any more.'

'No, but he can try. And it's *that* that worries me the most,' Fin said through gritted teeth.

Alasdair gave Fin a friendly slap on the back. 'It'll be fine. He may not even show, he may be sunning himself in St Tropez. Just enjoy your evening, and show off your beautiful girl, okay?' With that, he kissed me on the cheek and walked over to a group of smartly-attired lawyery types.

Fin smiled down at me and gripped my hand tightly. 'Come on, gorgeous. Let's go get some champagne.'

Champagne sounded like a great idea, and I was more than happy to partake of a glass—or several—to calm my nerves. The only problem was that they went down very easily, and I suddenly needed the bathroom. After telling Fin my predicament, he pointed me in the right direction, and I made my way there. Panic surged within me over how I would manage to pee with such a long, tight dress covering the essential parts of my body, but I was determined to be as fast as possible. And then I would be staying put at Fin's side for the rest of the night and limiting my liquid intake.

Suddenly someone stepped into my path, and I almost jumped out of my skin. 'So, you're the one, are you?' The man's gravelly, deep voice startled me and stopped me in my tracks.

'I don't think there's any mistaking her, is there dear?' his companion said snidely.

I was face to face with none other than Campbell and Isobel Hunter.

I scowled at the man and shook my head. 'Excuse me?'

He oozed animosity, and I cringed inwardly as he stepped forward. 'He changed, you know? Virtually as soon as he met *you*. He changed. And not for the better.'

'Everything he held dear went straight out of the window. He abandoned us, and all because of you.' Isobel said 'you' as if the word made her sick to her stomach.

Oh, shit. Oh, shitty shit. 'I'm sorry, but I have no clue what—'

Campbell took another step closer and blocked the entrance to the ladies' room. 'He ruined the only solid relationship he'd ever had. All because of you. *She* was more befitting his social standing.' He laughed derisively. 'Who the hell do you think you are, anyway? I'll tell you who you are, shall I? An ugly little trollop with badly scribbled tattoos, and a shitty little job serving meagre coffee to those of higher standing, that's what *you* are. You're the maid. The help. What the hell does he see in you?'

'Frankly I can't believe he's stooping so low,' Isobel added with venom.

'Mark my words young lady, I know my son and he *will* see you for what you are, a gold digging harpy. Sadly he's already out of my will thanks to you, so you won't be getting a penny. Might as well duck out now, eh?'

My eyes began to sting, but I bit my lip. I wasn't going to let these poor excuses for parents see they had upset me, and had just pointed out *all* the things that made me feel inferior and unworthy of Fin, while adding painful insults for good measure.

I raised my chin and sneered. 'I think you'll find, if you do your research properly, that Fin met me *after* the issues arose with you and his fiancée. And being of, how did you put it, social standing, doesn't make you a decent person, does it? I think you are both evidence of that fact. Now, I'm going to the bathroom, so unless you would like me to call security, I suggest you get out of my way and allow me to pass.'

Campbell's lip curled and he stepped aside. 'Think about what I said. If you remove yourself from his life I may consider reinstating his inheritance. You'd be well advised to do the right thing.'

Without dignifying his request with a response, I bashed into the door and let it slam behind me. Once inside, I let out a long, shaking breath and closed myself in a cubicle. Once behind a locked door, the tears began in earnest. My make-up was ruined without a doubt, and my heart was back to vying for freedom from my chest.

The bastard. The absolute bastard. How dare he look down on me like that?

40

STAR

When I left the bathroom, I did so with a cautious glance left and right. Thankfully, Fin's parents were nowhere to be seen. I had managed to rescue my make-up for the most part, but my eyes were puffy, and I wished I could just walk out and go home.

Suddenly, Fin appeared and was walking towards me. 'Hey, there you are. Everything okay?' He frowned as he got closer. 'You look... you're pale. Have you been crying?'

My lip began to tremble once again, and I fought back the tears. 'Oh, no. I'm fine. I somehow managed to get something in my eye. I think it might have been an eyelash. Anyway, it hurt like a mother, and I had to get it out. Oh, the joys of mascara,' I joked, unable to look him in the eyes for more than a few seconds.

His assessing, concerned gaze told me he didn't buy it. There was no wonder. Acting was never my strong suit. 'Come on, Star. You forget how well I can read you. What really happened? Did one of the stuck-up bitches say something to you?'

I sighed deeply, afraid of sounding like a tattle tale. 'Your parents happened, Fin. Well your dad mostly. But it's okay. I handled it. Kind of.'

Fin clenched his jaw. 'The bastard. I'll—'

'No, no you'll do nothing, okay? I know you have my back without you going to make a scene. Let's just enjoy the night... or at least get through it. Okay? Promise me?' His frown and ticking jaw belied his inner turmoil but he forced a smile.

He stepped towards me and enveloped me in his arms. 'No, Star. He can't do things like that and get away—'

'Please, Fin. For me. The last thing I want is to get in the middle of this. I don't want to make a bad situation worse. Please, just drop it, please?'

He clenched his jaw and glanced around, clearly

scanning the room for the Hunters. Then he nodded stiffly. 'Okay. Whatever you say. But if he says anything else I'll punch him, I swear. He doesn't get to treat you like shit, Star. No one does. I will *always* have your back.' He gripped my hand. 'Now, come on. Let's go and have a dance.'

Relief flooded my veins momentarily, but only until the thought of his father and his cronies sniggering at me attempting to be 'normal' on the dance floor entered my head.

I pushed myself away from him. 'Oh, I don't really feel like it. I think I'll—'

'Oh, no you don't. Come on, you. I need to show you off.'

I rolled my eyes as he dragged me along behind him to where a crowd of people were dancing to Dean Martin's 'I've Grown Accustomed to Her Face'. He pulled me into his arms and with one hand at the small of my back and the other clutching my hand, he swept me round the dance floor. A wide, handsome smile graced his angular features, and my heart melted as I gazed up at him. In a short period of time this man had somehow become the centre of my universe. It simultaneously scared and excited me, and I feared for my poor heart.

As the song ended and a rumble of applause traversed the room, he caressed my cheek and bent to kiss me gently on the lips. 'I think I love you, Star Mendoza. In fact I know I do.'

My breath caught. He had said the words I'd been feeling but dared not utter in case it was too soon. It probably *was* too soon. *Much* too soon, but I felt it too. My heart soared, and I suddenly felt like I was floating.

He loves me.

Gazing into his cerulean eyes, I allowed my own feelings to take flight as words. 'I think I love you too, Fin Hunter. In fact, I know I do too.'

He closed his eyes briefly and shook his head. When he opened them again, his gaze was filled with desire. 'Oh, God. I want to take to you home and show you how much I love you. I wonder if we could escape without anyone noticing. What are the odds, do you think?'

I giggled like a teenager and glanced around surreptitiously. 'Oh, I think Alasdair would notice. He's heading our way.'

'Fin. There you are. I'd like to introduce you to Malcolm McClintock. He's the managing director of Clarke Estates. Remember I mentioned their involvement with the Inveresk cottages?'

'Oh, yeah. I remember.' Fin nodded. He glanced down at me. 'Would you mind?'

Fear spiked within me at the thought of being left alone. I didn't wish to experience another encounter with Campbell Hunter. 'Can I come with you?'

He smiled warmly. 'Can't bear to be away from me, eh?'

Heat rose in my cheeks. 'Something like that.'

He held out his hand. 'Come on then.'

As we walked through the ballroom I swore I could feel eyes boring into my back. I nervously glanced round but couldn't see the Hunters. It didn't mean they weren't there though.

Colette was standing with a man I presumed to be Malcolm McClintock and after Alasdair had made the introductions Colette linked her arm with mine. 'Come on, let's go and find some more champers, eh?'

I glanced up at Fin but he was already deep in

conversation. Colette could obviously sense my hesitation. 'Let me guess, you've spotted the Hunters?'

I nodded and swallowed as I fought threatening tears once again. 'I've more than spotted them.'

Colette frowned and pulled me close as she led me away. 'Have they said something to you?'

'You could say that.'

She stopped and turned to me. 'Star, whatever they said to you, which looking at your expression and the tears in your eyes was undoubtedly cruel; please do not take it to heart. They are the bitterest people I've ever had the displeasure to meet. And whatever they have said speaks volumes about the type of people they are. What hypocrites to be in attendance at a charity event when they don't have a charitable bone to share between them. You are worth ten of each of them, and don't you forget it.'

Her support was appreciated and so sweet, but it didn't stop me looking over my shoulder. If they had intended to spoil my night and to make me feel even more like a fish out of water, they had succeeded with aplomb. But I plastered a fake smile on my face and linked my arm through Colette's again.

'Come on, let's go find that champers. I think the key here is not to let those bleepers grind me down.' I wished I felt the conviction that my delivery suggested.

41

FIN

Malcolm McClintock was a force to be reckoned with. He'd recently been pipped to the post by a rival on the purchase of the row of cottages at Inveresk that my father had helped to acquire for a large conglomerate. The company was hell bent on knocking the old buildings down and constructing a muckle shopping centre that no one wanted nor needed. Like my brother Callum who lived and worked in the wee village, McClintock wasn't happy about it in the slightest.

'The thing is, Hunter, people have their roots in those homes. Their family trees are established there. I can't allow the cottages to be demolished as if they mean nothing. Hundreds of years of family history will be lost. A part of our country's culture will be lost. Those buildings aren't just bricks and mortar. This is... well, it's sacrilege, that's what it is.' The man's face turned beet red, and I feared for his heart. He was a portly man, to say the least, and his passion for the row of cottages was palpable. 'My own family has history there. This whole ridiculous situation sickens and angers me, Hunter.'

'Of course. I completely understand your anger at the situation, Mr McClintock, but there is little chance of us getting the decision overturned at this late stage.'

McClintock wagged a fat finger in my face. 'Now, look here. I came to *your* firm because you are the best. Don't you bloody let me down. I'll not live if those cottages are demolished. It will *break* me. You have my life in your hands, Hunter. McKendrick.' The man nodded, turned, and walked away, heading for the bar.

Alasdair heaved a heavy sigh. 'You see, that is one very passionate man. He truly believes in his cause,' he told me as he watched the man leave our company. 'I suggest we get our thinking caps on, Fin. And fast.'

At that, my boss left too. Star had returned clutching a glass of champagne and I glanced down at her. Her eyes were focused on something, and she nervously chewed on her lip.

Never a good sign.

I heard an emotion-filled voice coming from behind me. 'Finlay, darling.'

The reason for Star's demeanour became clear. I turned and came face to face with Isobel Hunter. 'Mum.' She wore a demure blue gown, and her skin was paler than usual. She looked... *ill*.

She leaned in and kissed my cheek. 'Oh, I've missed you so much, Finlay. We both have. Why haven't you been in touch?' *Stupid question, and God, if there was an Oscar for most melodramatic mother...*

I gritted my teeth. 'You know very well why I haven't been in touch.'

'Oh, come now, Finlay. Blood is thicker than water, dear. You would do well to remember that.' She trailed her disapproving gaze over Star and turned up her nose.

I slipped my arm round Star but said nothing.

'Have you heard from Elise... your *fiancée*?'

Anger bubbled up inside me, and I fought to calm the storm that was beginning to rage beneath my skin. 'No, Mother, and you know very well that Elise is no longer my fiancée. She's moved on and so have I.'

Ignoring me completely, she continued, 'Oh, Finlay. Why must you make such rash decisions, dear? There are so many eligible young ladies out there just like Elise. You could find someone more of your standing. Is it really fair to let this... this girl believe you're going to be together long term when you and I both know that's not who you are.'

Star gasped and I swallowed hard. 'How *dare* you judge and make assumptions when you don't even know Star?'

My mother turned her nose up. 'You see? Case in point. Her name is Star. I'm not judging darling, I'm sure she's a very pleasant girl but I feel you're being cruel to her by leading her on.' She turned to Star. 'I'm trying to do you a favour dear.'

I clenched my jaw and tried to breathe calmly and slow my heartrate. 'I think we'll be leaving now.' I turned and pulled Star along behind me.

'Leave him, Isobel. He no longer cares about his family,' my father bellowed. 'It saddens me that you've turned your back on us, Finlay. You've made your position quite clear. And to think I was hoping we could come to some arrangement over the Inveresk cottages. But you've clearly made your decision and chosen your place.'

I spun round to face my father. 'What do you mean by that? I didn't turn my back on you, it was *you* who turned your back on *me*. And the cottages are nothing to do with you now. You won, remember?'

There was something that looked like sadness in his eyes, and for a split second, I felt for him.

He sighed and stepped towards me. 'Look, I know what a big win it would be for McKendrick Law to overturn the demolition decision. I *had* been thinking about assisting you in making that happen. It's time to make amends for many past wrongs. Or so I thought...'

My heart began to pound as the distraught faces of the poor Inveresk villagers sprang to mind. 'Why would you do that?'

He reached out and gripped my shoulder. 'Let's

just say it would be good to have you back in the fold, son.'

The word *son* fell from his lips for the first time *ever*, and I was dumbfounded. Stunned. My mouth opened and closed like a dying goldfish, and I stood there, just staring at him.

'But, let's face it, son...' There it was again, *that* word. 'You can do much better than a scruffy, pink haired coffee server.' His belligerent remarks slipped from his mouth with such ease and without a single thought for the woman standing beside me. I couldn't get over his audacity. But he wasn't done. 'If you really are determined not to reconcile with Elise, we can introduce you to someone else. Someone Scottish and more suited to your status as a Hunter. Think of the future, Finlay. Your mother and I love you dearly, and we just want the best for you. I'm... I'm sorry I didn't tell you that sooner, son.'

Love? Did he just profess to love me too? Shit. Is this happening?

He placed both hands on my shoulders and looked directly into my eyes. I was suddenly so over-come with emotion at the sincerity reflected at me that his words were no longer registering in my brain. No other words were getting through except the ones where he said he loved me. It had been a long time coming, and now it had happened, I was shell-shocked.

He squeezed me gently. 'She's not right for you, Finlay. Don't you see that? Your mother and I could help you find the right girl. *We*'re the ones who matter. Us. Your family. *We* are the ones who love you. If you love us, Finlay, just say the words and all this can be forgotten. We'll be a family again. We'll move past this nonsense; All the silly ideas about singing and working for my rival; the rebellious streak that led you to being with the utterly wrong woman. We can put it down to experience and move forward with all that in the past. *All* the bad decisions. You'd be back in my will and you'd get the inheritance that's rightfully yours. Just say you still love us Finlay. We love you and want you back in our lives. Can *you* find the words to put it all behind us?'

I'd had champagne, yes but here he was, *my father*, telling me he loved me and wanted what was best for me. I had waited my *whole life* to hear those words. Yet I couldn't react right away. His words were rattling around my head but it took a while for them to sink in. I wondered if they were true or just a ploy to get his way again. Why couldn't I speak? Why couldn't I tell him to stick it? Why couldn't I tell him that I was in love with Star? That I didn't care about inheritance or the family business, nor did I care about a so-called family who couldn't accept the woman I loved. But I couldn't form a sentence; such was the shock of the whole situation.

'Say you love us, Finlay, that's all it will take to make this all right again,' my mother pleaded.

My heart beat so hard at my ribs and I swallowed, trying to dislodge the ball of pain and emotion in my throat. 'Of course I... I love you.' It was more a statement of the obvious. I loved them but didn't have to like them or what they stood for. I shook my head, a little blindsided by everything when I heard a sob, and Star yanked herself free from me and ran. In my trance like stupor, I watched her go.

What just happened?

42

STAR

I pulled the stupid high-heeled shoes from my feet and began to sprint. The evening air was cold in spite of it being June, and it chilled my hot skin as I ran. The drizzle in the air soaked through my clothes but I didn't care. I just had to get away.

Fin had more or less just agreed to let me go so he could be a pawn in his father's game all over again. All he'd had to do was tell his father he loved him and I would be forgotten. I had almost thrown up when I'd heard him say the words. I knew he loved his parents in spite of their ridiculous manipulation. They were his parents. But oh how it hurt the way his father had used the words 'I love you' like a weapon of mass destruction. And Fin had been the one with his finger on the button. As easily and quickly as that, I had been cast aside.

My vision was blurred by not only the rain that was falling much heavier now, but the relentless tears streaming down my face. I stopped briefly to wipe my eyes on the hem of my dress and then began to run again. Once I reached a place that was far enough away from the Balmoral that I could be sure no one would have followed me, I stopped and pulled out my cell phone. With shaking hands, I hit the speed dial for my best friend in the hope that he would answer quickly.

Thankfully, he did. 'Twinkle, sweetie. How's the big night going? What are you doing ringing me? Shouldn't you be dancing and drinking champers?'

I could hear someone in the background murdering an old Bon Jovi track and knew he was at De-Basement.

I tried to calm my breathing. 'Alec,' I sobbed. 'Alec, I need you. It was... it was awful. I feel such an idiot. It's over. We're over.'

'Shit. Where are you? I'm coming to get you.'

I sniffled and swiped at the moisture round my eyes. 'Princes Street. By the Scott monument.'

'Okay. Stay out of sight. It's bloody busy in town tonight, and you don't need drunken yobs trying to help you. I'll get there as soon as I can.'

He hung up, and I walked to the top of the Scott Monument steps in the shadows of the arches where I could avoid being seen by the revellers of the city.

Fin's wide-eyed stare tortured me over and over. Why didn't he tell his dad he loved *me*? Why didn't he say he wasn't prepared to let *me* go regardless of how much money he threw at him? Regardless of the bribe about the cottages? Regardless of the long overdue profession of love? He told me he *loved* me so why couldn't he tell them he wasn't going to abandon me for them that way? How could he let them talk about me like that and just give in? He had agreed to their terms simply by saying those three words to the man who had belittled and hurt him over and over. And just like that, I was betrayed. My heart shattered into a million pieces as I curled my knees up to my chest and rested my head down, letting the salt-water flow freely all over the beautiful, expensive fabric of my dress.

The harshness of the words uttered by Fin's parents stabbed at my insides, and I almost threw up. How could someone think so lowly of a person they didn't know? How could they think so poorly of someone who made their son happy? Why couldn't they at least give me a chance? And why hadn't he asked them that?

My cell phone vibrated, and I lifted my head to peer at the screen. Fin's smiling face gazed up at me beneath his caller ID, but I hit the end call button. Several seconds later, it buzzed again. Once again, I rejected the call. How could I speak to him now? After he stood there and let his parents speak about me like I was scum. After he had accepted the vilest ultimatum. *'If you love us, Finlay, just say the words and all this can be forgotten. We'll be a family again. We'll move past this nonsense; all the silly ideas about singing and working for my rival; the rebellious streak that led you to being with the utterly wrong woman.'* His father's words and Fin's response rattled around my brain and twisted at my insides. No. It was over. I had to get used to it. I clearly wasn't important enough to him. And to answer his call to listen to some lame ass apology and him wishing me well for the future would finish me off. I didn't need to hear him say it. I didn't need to hear him ask for forgiveness for letting me go. I wasn't going to forgive the betrayal. I should never have given him a chance after the first time he hurt me so this was all on me. I was stupid and blinded by love. But I wouldn't let him drive the final blow home. I had to at least try to keep some dignity intact.

For the next ten minutes, my phone kept on ringing, and I kept on hanging up in the hope that he would get the message eventually. I stopped looking at the screen when it lit up. It hurt too much to see his smile; the smile that lit up his face and was so filled with love. Or so I'd thought. Maybe I really was just a way to get back at the Hunters. Who was I kidding? There was no maybe about it.

After around twenty minutes, I heard a familiar voice through the hammering rain. 'Star? Star is that you?' My heart leapt, and I scrambled to my feet and stepped out from my hiding place. Alec scooped me up in his arms and held me tight. It felt good to be surrounded in his warmth, and I shivered.

He slipped off his jacket and wrapped it round my shoulders. 'Come on. Let's get you home.'

We walked to the nearest taxi rank, and Alec flagged down a cab. He opened the door for me, and I clambered in. A kind of numbness had set in. I closed my eyes as Alec pulled me into his chest. He smelled of fresh linen, and I was thankful that it was nothing like how Fin smelled. I didn't need reminding of him. Not when things were so painfully raw.

The look of disdain on his mom's face flashed through my mind and I clenched my eyes tight, hoping to rid myself of the image. But it was simply replaced with an echo of his father's words. *'You can do much better than a scruffy, pink haired coffee server.'* Each time the words replayed, a wave of nausea washed over me and I covered my mouth.

We finally pulled up outside our apartment block, and Alec paid the driver. As if I was some drunken idiot, Alec helped me from the car and up the stairs to our door. I stood there staring blankly as he unlocked it and then walked through to the living room and slumped onto the couch.

Alec disappeared into the kitchen and returned with a tumbler of amber coloured liquid. He handed it to me, and I held it between my hands as I stared into the glass. I caught the strong smell in my nostrils. Brandy.

He crouched before me. 'What happened, Star? I've never seen you like this. Come on, sweetheart. Tell me. You're worrying me.'

I closed my eyes. 'Not tonight. Please don't ask me to tell you tonight. All I want to do is take a bath and sleep. I can't go through it again now.' My voice was unrecognisable as my own.

He tucked a stray strand of hair behind my ear. 'Okay, darlin'. Whenever you're ready.'

I took a gulp of the brandy, and it burned my throat as it made its way to my empty stomach. We didn't even make it to the meal, and the champagne had just made me dizzy.

I handed the glass back to Alec and slowly made my way to my bedroom. Once inside with the door closed, I collapsed onto my bed and began to sob once more.

I awoke; face down on my bed, still in the damp, black evening gown. *So much for having a bath.* I could hear raised voices coming from the living room and recognised them immediately.

'Just let me talk to her, Alec. I need to explain. She got it wrong. It wasn't how it looked.'

'Fin, please just go home, okay? You look like shit, and I think you need to sleep. Just go. She doesn't want to see you.'

'How the hell do *you* know, eh? She needs to hear *my* side!' His accent strengthened, and my heart ached on hearing the pain in his voice.

'I'm not letting you in, so you may as well just go home.' Alec's tone was filled with anger, although it sounded like he was trying hard to control it.

I heard a slam on the wall. 'Please, Alec. I'm begging you. Just let me speak to her.'

'Watch where you're punching, arsehole. I'm getting pissed off with you now. This is the last time I will say this. Bugger off home. I. Am. Not. Letting. You. In.' His determined staccato speech showed just how much his temper had increased. Alec didn't get angry easily, and the times I had witnessed it, it hadn't been pretty.

'Star, sweetheart, if you can hear me, please know that I'm sorry. I didn't mean for things to end that way. I meant what I said to you. Please forgive me!'

His words tore at my heart and I wanted to go to him. Although, deep down I knew that if he couldn't set his parents straight about me at the ball when the verbal daggers were flying then we had no future. Seeing him now would only prolong the inevitable.

The door slammed and I almost jumped out of my skin. I realised tears were leaving damp trails down my cheeks, and I dragged myself from the bed. I peeled myself out of the beautiful dress and dropped it the floor where it pooled in a black puddle of fabric. The sexy boned corset and hold-up stockings were next to go. A pained sob left my throat as I removed them, and a deep sadness washed over me. The underwear was meant as a surprise for Fin, for when we got back to his place after the ball. I had chosen them especially, but he would never get to see them.

Not after his betrayal. Because that's what his admission of love to his father after the ultimatum had felt like.

When I caught sight of my face in the mirror, I almost laughed. But only almost. My black eye make-up was running down my face and turning me into a very poor Alice Cooper tribute. My hair was in wild disarray, with strands sticking out of the previously lovely style, and the parts of my eyes that weren't black were red-rimmed and puffy.

I took some comfort from the fact that Alec had told Fin he looked like shit.

He deserved to.

I didn't.

43

———————

STAR

July was whizzing by ridiculously fast and summer was in full swing; although in Edinburgh that could mean four seasons in a day. The flowers were blooming in Prices Street gardens and tourists were appearing in the city in droves. I took refuge in Calton Hill cemetery when I needed time to myself, but even there I was worried I might bump into Fin. I'd managed to avoid him for the weeks after the ball. Even Tom had stopped acting as a messenger when he saw how hurt I was. We had spent time together working on the exhibition at his gallery and things were getting so real. He had gained Fin's permission to use the images I took of him and for that I was grateful. Tom said he'd taken no convincing at all and that he wished me every success, that he looked broken. But hearing that sent my emotions into turmoil. Every time I carried out a task connected to the exhibition I was reminded that it was all thanks to Fin that I was even doing it.

My grandma had tried her best to comfort me and I had cried on her several times. I was so grateful that I had her as I missed my mom and dad more than words could express. My video calls to them had been short. The last thing I wanted was to worry them. Although my most recent call was longer. Thanks to Grandma.

'Why didn't you tell us what had happened honey?' my mom asked, a crease of worry between her brows. 'We shouldn't have had to hear it from your grandma.'

I sighed deeply. 'I'm so sorry. I've just been so busy getting ready for the exhibition that I forgot to mention it.'

My father gave me a knowing look. 'Star, be honest, we're your parents. You didn't say anything because you didn't want to worry us, that's the real reason isn't it?'

Busted. My lip trembled and I nodded. 'You just feel so far away right now and it hurts,' I told them with a wavering voice. 'I'm not sure I can stay here.'

'Oh sweetie, this has been your dream for so long. And now you have the exhibition. Don't let Fin's mistakes become yours. We're going to try and make it over for the opening. See how you feel then huh? But don't make any rash decisions.'

I agreed and changed the subject. I didn't want to think about Fin any more. So I bombarded them with questions about the neighbours, the neighbourhood and anything else I could think of until we ended the call.

The opening night of my début exhibition was going well. I was astounded at the feedback I'd been getting for my work, and I was so glad I had stepped out of my comfort zone. But the Fin-shaped hole in my heart was still aching. The fact that I didn't fit into his world had initially made me more determined to make a go of things. In spite of my initial desire to run, I'm no quitter. Clearly, the same couldn't be said for him. I was hoping my photography could help take my mind off my sadness at losing him. It had always helped in the past when I'd been down. I could quite easily lose myself in a spectacular view for hours.

The gallery walls were adorned with some of the most exquisite works of art I had ever seen, and it still amazed me that *my* work—photographs *I* had taken—were being viewed as just as influential and important. The images I had taken of Fin's on-stage persona were some of my best work. The fact that he was so damned attractive probably helped.

The duplicity of his character had always fascinated me. The way he changed when he stepped out into that spotlight and dominated the stage like he owned the place amazed me beyond belief. The growl to his voice and the passion in his eyes made me believe every single word he sang. Even lyrics written by others were believable as his own. And some of the songs he chose to perform made me feel like I was on an emotional rollercoaster. Angst, loathing, adoration, pain. You name it, he expressed it beautifully.

The photos on display at my exhibition showed

each side of his character, and it was so clear to me which song he had been performing just by looking into the azure eyes staring out at me from the canvases.

'We're so proud of you Estrellita,' my dad said as he slipped his arm round my shoulder.

'You must get your creative streak from your grandad. He was really good with his hands.' Grandma Aggie told me with a wink.

I felt my cheeks flush and I whispered, 'Grandma, behave yourself.'

She feigned innocence and with a glint in her eyes she replied, 'I meant sketching, I don't know what you thought I meant.'

'He certainly is a handsome man,' my mom said as she stared at the blue eyes staring out from the canvas before us. 'But looks aren't everything.'

My dad scowled at her. 'Oh really?'

She playfully whacked his arm. 'Oh honey, you know I think you're a dreamboat.'

'Miss Mendoza?' The deep, masculine, American-accented voice pulled my attention away from my cute parents.

Frowning, I turned to face whoever had distracted me. 'Yes?'

The tall, handsome man of around mid-fifties, with salt and pepper grey hair, held out his hand. 'Marshall Davies. I'm the director of The Napier Gallery in New York. I have to say, I'm very impressed with your photographs.'

I felt heat rise in my cheeks. I just couldn't get used to all the compliments. 'Oh. Thank you.'

'Tell me, is it true that you've had no formal training?'

'Nope, it's all natural,' my dad interjected. 'My Estrellita is just a naturally talented artist. The best I've seen.'

I felt a flush of heat rise from my chest to my cheeks as I glowered at my father. I cleared my throat. 'No formal training, that's correct. It's all me. Y-you can probably tell.' My stutter and nervous laugh told of the imposter syndrome I was fighting yet again. Still. Fin's words echoed in my mind. *You are the most intelligent, fun, caring, talented woman I've ever met, so don't go getting a bloody inferiority complex on me, okay?'*

My mom leaned in and whispered, 'We'll leave

you to it honey.' She squeezed my shoulder and the three of them wandered across the room.

'Quite the contrary, Miss Mendoza. I find it startling that someone could have such a natural eye for composition. I especially like the shots of the singer. Is he a friend of yours? I'll bet he'll be getting a lot of attention following on from the exhibition. Modelling contracts, perhaps.' He raised his eyebrows and I forced a smile. In all honesty, I had no clue what was going on with Fin any more. In the weeks that had passed since the ball, the calls and messages via Tom had gotten less and less until, I'm guessing, he'd decided to give up. I hadn't received a call in almost five days, and although my heart hurt at the fact, I knew it was for the best.

'He's... um... he's someone I used to know.' I dropped my gaze to the floor as my eyes began to sting.

'Ah.' His tone told me he understood what I wasn't saying. 'Well, they say that the most creative people draw from heartache. Look, I don't want to keep you as I'm sure you'll be getting many more offers like mine.'

I pulled my gaze up from the floor to meet the

man's smiling eyes again. Confused at his choice of words, I shook my head. 'Offers?'

'Miss Mendoza, I'll cut to the chase. I want your work for my gallery. In fact, I would like to bring *you* out there to work for a while. I know you were born in the USA, and I feel that back home, you and your obvious talents would be appreciated *so* much more. I'm willing to pay you an advance. And to find and fund you a place to stay until you're established. Now, I know this is a lot to take in, but I had to get in first with my offer. Name your price. Whatever it takes, Miss Mendoza. I want you and your work in New York. And I want you to produce more of it. I will do whatever it takes to facilitate that.'

I swallowed hard as my heart tried to escape through my ribcage. He wanted *my* work? *Shit!* I opened my mouth and tried to speak, but no sound would come. This was an amazing opportunity for me. But...

Words, Star. Use your words. 'I... um... I...' I shook my head to try and rid myself of the fog that had descended to rob me of all cognisant thought processing.

Marshall smiled warmly and patted my shoulder.

'It's okay. Take some time to think things through. I'll be in Edinburgh for the next couple of days. If you decide to take me up on my offer then just give me a call. I'm staying at the Balmoral Hotel in the city. Here's my card.'

I took the card from him and stared at it, as if answers would miraculously appear there for me. When they didn't, I shook my head. 'S-sorry, I'm just a little... Th-thank you, Mr Davies.'

'Please, call me Marshall. And if it's okay by you, I'll call you Star?'

I bobbed my head, feeling like one of those dumb nodding dogs that old ladies have in their cars. 'Uh-huh. Sure.'

He smiled, patted my shoulder once more, and walked away. Before I could process what had just happened, I was grabbed from behind and swivelled around.

Alec was standing there with my mom, dad and grandma. 'Who was the silver fox, Twinkle?'

I rolled my eyes and made an un-ladylike noise. 'Urggh. Some dude from a swank gallery in New York. He wants to *hire* me and give me a place to live or something. I don't know... I made a complete fool out of myself.'

All of their eyes widened in shock, and Alec dragged me through a large oak door into an empty hallway, the others followed. 'You've been snapped up by a New York gallery? Oh, my gee, Twinks! That's amazing!' He pulled me into his arms and swung me round.

'Honey that's incredible!' my mom exclaimed.

'Amazing!' My dad agreed.

'I knew something like this would happen,' my grandma said with a hint of sadness.

I laughed humourlessly. 'Guys, I can't... I can't *go*.'

Alec scowled at me and grabbed me by the arms. 'What the hell are you talking about? Of *course* you can go. This is an amaz—'

'Zing opportunity. Yeah, I know that, Al, but...' I dropped my gaze to the floor that had apparently fascinated me earlier too.

He huffed and stepped back, folding his arms defiantly over his chest and glanced at my family before demanding. 'Is this about Fin Hunter?'

Once again, I did my dumb impersonation of the nodding dog as my bottom lip trembled.

Suddenly I was engulfed in a group hug.

Alec insisted, albeit softly, 'Twinkle, you need to let him go, darling. He's let *you* go. You need to move on with your life, and maybe this is the way forward, eh?'

My dad tilted my chin up with his finger. 'I think Alec is right, cariño.' I gazed up into the compassion-filled eyes of my father and thought about how lucky I was to have him.

The tears that had been threatening only moments before spilled over. 'I *can't* forget him, Dad. I know I should. But I...I just *can't*.'

He didn't speak again. Instead, he pulled me into his arms and held me.

44

———————

FIN

I watched from a distance, not wanting to be seen, but with a heart so full of the pride I felt for her that I was sure I'd burst. She almost floated round the room in the black and grey, tie-dyed, flowing dress that fitted her personality so well. She looked every bit the classy, gracious host. The artist. My God, and she thought *she* didn't fit into my world. *I'd* thought she didn't fit into my world at first. *Crazy.* She *was* my world. How could I have been so stupid?

Seeing images of myself adorning the walls made me feel a little too conspicuous. I was sure I'd be spotted, and so I kept to the side-lines and watched my girl - my *former* girl - as she chatted to eager attendees, her arms gesturing wildly as they did when she was enthusiastic. Seeing her in her element warmed my heart. But even though her beautiful smile was fixed in place, I could tell her heart wasn't feeling it. *I* was responsible for that. I felt like crap, but what could I do now? There was no way she'd take me back. No way she would accept any kind of apology from me after how I'd treated her.

When she had run out of the ball that night, I had been so confused. But then, when I realised what my father had done—how he had shocked me with his admission of love for me— I realised I had inadvertently appeared to be agreeing to let Star go. How could I have been so damned stupid? How could I have let him manipulate me again? He'd known exactly how to twist the knife and I'd fallen for it, hook, line and sinker. Stupid idiot!

I'd left so many voicemails apologising for my stupidity that I'd lost count. Hell, I'd even typed up letters. Although I hadn't posted them through her door, as I'd remembered about that arsehole in America who'd dumped her that way. Either she had deleted the voice messages before listening to them or she had listened and deleted them anyway.

Whichever it was, my calls had been unreturned and my appearances at her apartment and the coffee shop had been met with threats of police intervention for stalking by Alec.

And so in true stalker fashion, I turned up at the gallery, hiding in the shadows. The urge to go to her. To talk to her. Hell, just to be *close* enough to catch the scent of her perfume was almost overwhelming. She stopped at the back of the gallery with Aggie and the people I guessed were her parents. Pride emanated from their beaming smiles and I was so glad she had parents like that. I had cut mine off after the ball. I told them I needed space and that they couldn't manipulate me any more but it was too late. I'd lost the one person I didn't want space from.

I watched Star sip her champagne as her eyes flitted nervously over the crowd of people who were all in awe of her work. Was she looking for me? The stone pillar before me shielded me well as I tried my damnedest to pluck up the courage to go and congratulate her. To say how proud I was to have known her, and to have called her my friend. To tell her how stupid I was and that I hadn't intended for things to happen how they did; that I'd been caught off guard.

But I wasn't supposed to be there, so my words would remain as prisoners, along with my heart. I watched her with a group of friends and family. She laughed and threw her head back, and my mind was suddenly flooded with memories of her laughing with me; of her chocolate brown gaze fixed on my every word as I sang. Of how I loved her then. The feeling of her beneath me as I worshipped her body was almost tangible, and I closed my eyes, inhaling a deep and calming breath.

Resting my head on the cool stone for a moment, I realised I *had* to do it. I *had* to talk to her. It was now or never. Even if it was only to tell her how proud I was. It had been far too long since I'd heard her voice. With my resolve set firm, I opened my eyes again and lifted my gaze in her direction once more. A tall guy with silvery black hair was standing beside her. *Dammit.* I watched with interest as the man smiled at *my* Star. She peered up at him, open-mouthed and with a crease between her brows. What was he saying to her? She looked shocked, in-credulous even, at whatever it was. I hoped he was being kind. Not harming her with his words as my parents had done. She didn't deserve that. Her parents and friends slipped away but the man continued to talk and I could sense my opportunity to speak to her slipping away. I had to make a decision whether to go and interrupt, and I had to be quick. My stomach twisted, and anxiety reached my heart, making it hammer almost in time with the music playing over the sound system.

I clenched my jaw as I continued to watch the stranger with my girl. An air of self-importance oozed from him, and I was jealous. Who *was* he? And what was he saying to her that had her so mesmerised? A waiter passed me by, and I placed my empty glass on his tray. My nostrils flared and my fists clenched.

Come on, Hunter. It's now or never.

'I think you should go, Fin.' Alec's voice startled me, and I swung my head to meet his piercing eyes.

Speaking through my clenched jaw, I told him, 'I'm staying put, Alec. I've *got* to talk to her. She needs to know—'

'She needs to *forget*, Fin. Don't be cruel. You made it clear she doesn't fit into your world. Now leave her alone, okay? Do her that one small grace.'

His eyes pleaded with me, but there was no malice there. What I saw was pity.

I pulled my lips in between my teeth and bit down hard. I told myself that my eyes were watering because I'd almost drawn blood, but deep down I knew it was because he was telling me something I didn't want to hear.

He placed a hand on my shoulder. 'She's come this far, Fin. If you go and talk to her now, she'll be back to square one. Don't do that to her. If you care for her at all, you'll walk away. I love that girl like a sister. I can't watch you break her heart all over again. Please, Fin. Just *leave*.'

He was right. I closed my eyes for a moment again and tried to get a handle on my emotions. I *hated* that he was right. Absolutely hated it.

Once I had opened my eyes and met his determined gaze again, I nodded. 'Okay. You're right. But will you at least tell her I asked you to pass on a message? Just... tell her that... *this* is wonderful.' I gestured around the room. 'That she's done an amazing job and that her photographs are stunning. Tell her I'm so sorry I hurt her. It kills me to know I did that, and I regret it more than she can ever know. She didn't deserve to be treated so callously.' My eyes stung, and I cleared my throat before I continued. 'Tell her I wish her all the success in the world, Alec. I wish her every bit of happiness that I couldn't give her. She deserves this. And... and I didn't deserve her.' My voice broke, and with a heaviness in my heart, I turned and walked away.

I knew there was absolutely no chance he would pass the message on. But at least I'd told him.

At least *he* knew how I felt about her.

That would have to do.

45

STAR

I fell back to reality with a bump on the day following the exhibition. The coffee shop had been busy on and off, but my concentration levels were worse than normal. Alec was in the shop for once, and he had ordered me to grab an iced tea and go take a break. I took my cup out to one of the bistro tables on the precinct just outside the door and sat there in a daze. Thankfully the sun was shining and I watched people stroll by with their bags and brief-cases, going about their usual routines, and there I was with the words of Marshall Davies, Napier Gallery director, rolling around inside my head.

'Whatever it takes... I want your work for my gallery... name your price...'

I was in a world of my own when I felt the table dip. I looked up and inhaled sharply.

'Hello, Star.' The way Isobel Hunter said my name in that well-to-do, husky voice of hers spoke clearly of the utter disdain she felt for my very existence.

I straightened my back. 'Mrs Hunter. Why are you here?'

A sly smile barely crept across her perfectly botoxed features. 'Oh, I think you know.'

I sighed deeply and shook my head, hoping my exasperation was evident. 'No. I'm sure I don't.' I forced a fake smile, unwilling to let her know her presence bothered me.

She cocked her head to one side. 'I'm here to talk to you about New York.'

'I... I don't know what you mean.' So much for her not bothering me.

'Oh, come now, Star. Don't pretend to be as dumb as all that. I know all about Marshall's offer.'

I ignored her insult, but an unpleasant shiver traversed my spine. 'You? You set that up?'

She laughed, and the mirthless sound recalled to my mind a villain from the movies. 'Oh, absolutely not. Why would I do anything good for the woman who stole my son?'

Why indeed. 'Then how... why?'

'I know Marshall Davies. I had no idea he was in the city until I bumped into him at the Balmoral last night. We had drinks, and he happened to mention a talented young female photographer he was trying to contract. When he said your name, I couldn't believe my luck.'

I bristled at her words. The fact that Marshall had any connection to that witch made me think more than twice about accepting his business proposal.

I sneered at her. 'So, I would be working with a friend of yours?' I couldn't help the scrunching of my nose as if a bad smell had appeared beneath it.

'Oh good heavens no. Marshall is more... how should I put it? More of a business associate. You would be insane not to take him up on his offer, Star.'

I pushed myself away from the table and began

to stand. 'Well, thank you for your concern, but I can make up my own mind.'

She reached out and grabbed my wrist. 'Think about this, Star. It really is the opportunity of a lifetime. You get to move on with your life and do something you love.'

I snorted and yanked my arm free. 'Meaning I'm out of the way of your son.'

She smiled again. 'There have to be some perks.' Her smile disappeared and she stood to face me. 'Look, Star, I don't dislike you, as such. I'm sure you're very sweet in your own, quirky little way. But I think Fin needs someone who understands his position in the family. His life. His reputation. If you're gone, I think he could reconcile with his father and move on with his life in a direction befitting him. With someone befitting him.'

My eyes began to sting. 'My God. How many insults can you indirectly insert into one goddamn monologue?' I placed both hands on the table and leaned towards her. 'Isobel, I loved your son. I was in love with him. I didn't care if he had pots of cash or not a single cent. All I cared about was him. His happiness. But he didn't think we could be together, so I think you're safe. It seems you're more bothered about appearances than your son's happiness and what he wants. And believe me when I tell you he has no desire to be back at the family firm. No amount of cajoling on your part will change that.' My voice wavered. 'My break is over. I have to go.' I turned and began to walk away.

'He never really loved you, Star.' I stopped and turned my head to glare at her as she continued. 'He may have thought he did, but it was all an illusion. You were something different. The novelty would have worn off sooner rather than later. Do yourself a favour and save yourself the heartache. Take the opportunity in New York. It's the right thing to do. For both of you.' For a split second, I thought I saw compassion in her eyes, but as if she sensed my awareness, the mask dropped again.

Turning away once more, I stormed back inside the coffee shop. Alec was cleaning down the main machine when I stomped past him and into the back room. My eyes were blurry with unshed tears, and I knew he would follow.

Sure enough, he appeared in the doorway seconds after me. 'Who was that? Why are you so pissed off? Are you crying?'

My chest heaved as I fought the threatening tears of anger that were ready to overflow. 'That was Isobel Hunter.' Alec's expression said who? 'Fin's witch of a mother.'

His nostrils flared. 'What did that bitch want?'

'To encourage me to take the New York job offer.' I laughed derisively. 'She thinks if I'm gone, Fin will reconcile with his father and he'll meet some lawyery, wifey type who's befitting of him, and they'll have little befitting babies, and they'll all live happily ever after in a house that's befitting of them all.' A sob escaped my chest, and I crumpled onto a chair beside the small table in the back room.

Alec dropped to a crouching position before me. 'Hey. Hey, Twinkle,' he said softly, but I continued to sob. 'Star Mendoza, look at me right now!' I jerked my head up at his harsh tone and he cupped my face in his huge palm. 'Star, you are the most beautiful, kind-hearted, thoughtful woman I have ever met. If I wasn't as gay as a teapot, I'd be asking you out. If she thinks you're not good enough for her son, that's her problem. You're more than good enough. But you need to move on now. Just like I told him at the gal—'

I widened my eyes and my heart leapt. 'What?'

He shook his head and stood quickly. 'Nothing. But remember you're—'

'Wait, no. Back up. What were you going to say?'

He plopped back onto the chair opposite me and ran his hands through his hair. 'He was at the gallery. On your opening night.'

I exhaled rapidly as I said, 'What?'

'He was going to come and speak to you but... I advised him against it.'

I clenched my fists and spoke through gritted teeth. 'You did what?'

Holding his hands up in surrender, he tried to explain his reasoning. 'Look, Star, it was for the best. All he does is break your heart, love. I can't watch him do that to you again. Not for a third time. You deserve better. Don't you agree?'

The bottom suddenly plummeted from my whole world. 'And... he just... he walked away?' Tears overflowed from my eyes, and I wrapped my arms round myself.

Alec nodded, his eyes now filled with sadness as

he reached out towards me, and unable to touch me, rested his hand on the table. 'I think he knows it was for the best too, darling.'

It hurt like hell, but he was right. If Fin had wanted me, he would've fought for me when his parents attacked me, and he would've ignored Alec's advice and come to me anyway.

So that was it.

We were definitely over.

It was time to move on, after all, and New York was a good way to do that.

46

FIN

After walking away from the opening night of Star's exhibition, I was plagued with dreams about her. She was all I could think about. I was enjoying the work at McKendrick Law, but over the past few weeks, my mind was everywhere except on my work. I should have been concentrating on the Inveresk case, seeing as my father had hinted at a possible loophole to get the case overturned. But it was something I couldn't bring myself to do. For starters, I would have had to figure out the loophole myself. There was no way I could, or would even want to, ask him for help after the way he spoke to Star at the charity ball. His treatment of her was totally unacceptable, and I would never forgive him for that. I lost her that night because of him, and I was unsure how I would ever win her back. *If* I could win her back.

The guys from Mr Hyde and I had begun writing our own songs, and we'd been booked for a few more gigs on the back of our first one in the city, thanks to Lily Macrae, the TV presenter and journalist, and her rave review. The only problem was that Star's face appeared every time I closed my eyes, and every song I had penned in the weeks since I'd last seen her echoed the melancholy that tugged at me deep inside.

After several attempts to make her listen to me, I'd had to admit defeat and give things time. I'd talked it through with Alasdair, with Tom and Siân, and also with the band. They'd all said the same thing. Allowing the dust to settle would give her a chance to think it all through. Maybe that would result in her giving me a chance to explain. I certainly hoped it would.

Although things changed dramatically in a very short space of time.

It was the first Saturday in August, and I was getting ready to play with the guys at Bannerman's underneath South Bridge. It was a great club with a fantastic atmosphere, and the rest of the band was excited about playing there. My heart wasn't in it, but it was a night when we would be showcasing some of our original material in amongst the covers we loved.

I was showered and ready. The nerves were jangling, and my heart ached at the fact that my favourite supporter was no longer in my life. I could have done with her calming presence and loving words of encouragement.

As I was about to leave, I noticed an envelope on my doormat. It was late in the afternoon, so I figured it had been delivered by hand. I scrunched my brow and opened it quickly in case it was something important. The envelope was typed, and when I pulled out the folded pages, they were too.

I began to read and my heart almost stuttered to a halt...

Dear Fin,

How do I start this letter and explain all the changes that have happened in my life recently? It's been a rollercoaster. The exhibition was a great success, but I'm sure you heard all about that from Tom.

On the night of the exhibition, I was presented with an offer I simply can't refuse. A gallery in New York wants to exhibit my work. It's a huge opportunity for me, and so I'm sure you can understand my eagerness to accept it.

Knowing you was fun, and I cared for you. But when all is said and done, it wasn't love. It was just a passing phase. A way to pass the time and enjoy myself. After giving it lots of thought—and in my honest opinion—I now believe your parents were right. I'm just not right for you. You need to be with someone who fits you. Someone who understands your lifestyle in a way I never will.

By the time you read this, I will be on my way to New York to start over, and to see where life takes me. I suggest you do the same.

I wish you well.

All the best,

Star

I flopped onto the couch and scrunched the pages into a ball. Tears needled my eyes. It was over, and there was no turning back. The letter was so cold and without any expression of emotion. That just wasn't like her. That wasn't the Star I knew. The fact that she had written a damned letter in the first place was a low blow, especially considering the way she had been hurt by Sully the Sasquatch back in the US. Clearly the success of her exhibition had changed her, which was in itself a huge shock. Did I know her at all?

And New York? Why the hell would she want to go there when she loved Edinburgh so much? Any dim hopes of reconciliation were snuffed out, and anger bubbled up inside me. Why had she never been willing to listen to my explanation? If she had, she would have known that after the charity ball debacle, I told my parents to sod off out of my life for good. That they had no clue how happy she made me, and that I didn't care what they thought. That she was the one I loved and wanted to spend my life with. She would also have known that the reason I had been so dumbfounded was because my father had expressed love for me for the first time in almost twenty-eight years. It was enough to knock me off my feet and scramble my brain for a few moments. But only until it sank in that they were playing a cruel game.

But I'd never had that chance, and so I had to resign myself to the fact that whatever I felt hadn't been mutual. She had returned to the US, and no matter how much I loved her, I had to let her go.

As I stared at the crumpled pages of the letter, my mind drifted back to the last time I spoke to Isobel and Campbell Hunter.

Campbell's eyes followed Star's retreating form. 'Quite the little drama queen, isn't she, your plaything?'

I gritted my teeth and stepped towards him with clenched fists. 'Don't you ever speak of my girlfriend that way again. She is the woman I love, and quite frankly, if you don't like her, that's just tough shit. I'm in love with her, and she makes me happy. After all these years of waiting for your approval, I think all these sudden expressions of love are a little bit too late, don't you? The reason you've decided you suddenly 'love' me is because I've finally grown a pair of balls and stood up to you. I've found someone I want to be with and something I want to do with my life. And you didn't get to choose it. So you can both leave me alone. Keep me out of your will. Please, go ahead and do it. I want nothing from you. Because nothing is what I'm used to. You're both living in la la land if you think for one second that I would ever come back and work for you. And as for you disowning me, no need. Because as of this moment, I consider myself an orphan.'

I turned and went to find McKendrick to tell him I was leaving. To tell him I had to go find my heart, as Star had left with it firmly in her grasp, and that I had been a total idiot to let her walk out of the place without me.

Bannerman's was already heaving when we arrived. Nate pulled me to one side once the guys had set up. A look of concern clouded his eyes.

'You're not yourself, mate. What's happened? Have you spoken to Star?'

I laughed without feeling the slightest hint of humour. 'Had a letter from her. Talk about a cold-hearted bitch.'

His eyes widened. 'Why? What did it say?'

'That she's realised she's not right for me, and

she's received a better offer. She's…' I swallowed the ball of anger and emotion that had begun to restrict my throat. 'She's gone, Nate. She's left for New York.' My voice broke, and I internally berated myself for it.

He gripped my shoulder. 'Bloody hell, Fin. I'm so sorry mate. That's terrible.'

'Yeah, you could say that. I really thought she'd listen. That she'd let me explain. But, well, it's over. She's moving on, and I guess I need to do the same.'

47

STAR

Early on an August morning I stood in a crowded Edinburgh airport, and I clung to Alec and my grandma like they were my lifelines. In a way, they were. They were the only things I had left in Scotland. And even though I would miss them both so very much I was no longer attached to the city I once loved. Thanks to Finlay Hunter, my heart was broken, and the only way to heal was to start over.

New York was as good a place as any.

Marshall Davies had organised an apartment for me on the Upper East Side. Quite a prestigious location, from what I'd heard. The photos of the second-floor apartment looked wonderful, and I should have been so excited. Marshall and I had been in regular contact since I had accepted his offer.

Alec had been instrumental in encouraging me to accept the opportunity of a lifetime. He cupped my face in his hands. 'If you don't like it, Twinkle, you will always have a home with me or Aggie, you know that, and you can come back *any* time. But you'll never know if you don't at least try.'

His eyes had glistened with tears as he fought to keep his emotions in check, but I loved him for being so positive about the whole thing. I was having so many doubts about my abilities that I appreciated him believing in me enough for both of us.

As my flight was called, I hugged Alec and my grandma tightly. 'I'm going to miss you both so much.' A sob escaped me and tears over-spilled my clenched eyes.

Alec gripped me back just as tightly. 'We'll keep in touch. There's Facetime and email and WhatsApp. It'll be like we're not really apart. You'll see.' But his voice sounded strangled, as if he was struggling just as much as I was. He mumbled into my hair, 'If Fin gets in touch, what should I say?'

I pulled away and gazed up at him. 'He won't be in touch. I can guarantee it.'

'My sweet girl. You go and show them what you're made of,' Grandma said smiling up at me. 'And don't forget to call me on my Alexis will you? Alec has shown me how to use it. And it's even named after a character in my favourite TV show.' She grinned and then her smile disappeared as she took my hand . 'I'm so very proud of you, and your grandad would be too. Now you take care, okay?' She swiped at the tears cascading down her face. I didn't have the heart to tell her the little unit Alec had bought her wasn't actually called Alexis, nor was it named after the Joan Collins character in Dynasty.

I reluctantly made my way towards departures and waved to my best friend and my grandma. They had their arms round each other and I could that Alec was trying his best to console her. A ball of emotion and fear knotted my stomach.

This was it.

My life was about to change dramatically. Again. The one saving grace in it all was the fact that I would at least be on the same continent as my parents again. The flight from Indiana would take just over an hour and a half, and they had already booked to come see me. But the thought of starting over terrified me. I knew no one in the Big Apple. I had never even visited there. I feared how impersonal it might be after the friendliness of Edinburgh.

But I *had* to go.

* * *

Around five hours later, with just over an hour left of the flight, I reached into my bag and pulled out the white envelope that had appeared on my doormat only a few days earlier. The contents still hurt. Every time I read the words, my stomach flipped and churned. But somehow, re-reading it re-iterated the fact that I had made the right decision in leaving Edinburgh.

Dearest Star,

I hear your exhibition went well and I'm very happy for you. You are incredibly talented and after seeing the newspaper reviews, I'm glad you received the praise you deserve. I understand you were offered a long-term exhibition in New York's Napier Gallery. You must be so very happy. I wanted to drop you a line and wish you well.

It's a shame things didn't work out between us. But when you think about it, we were never truly meant to be. I want you to know I understand why you wouldn't speak to me after the charity ball, but you have to know my parents were only looking out for me. The fact that they love me warms my heart, and I'm so grateful to have them in my life once again. And I think I maybe have you to thank for that.

Things have been difficult, and I'm so sorry you were dragged into the middle of my mistakes but I now realise that many of my decisions were real errors in judgement. I had no right to use you the way I did, and again, I can only apologise. I've had the opportunity to discuss everything with my parents and they've forgiven me, I just hope you can too someday. I'll be taking back my position within the family firm too. My rightful place.

I sincerely wish you the very best in all

your New York endeavours and hope that you
meet someone who can love you as much as
you deserve. I'm sorry I couldn't.
All the best for the future,
Fin

I folded the paper with shaking hands and stuffed it back in the envelope as my heart broke all over again. I hated that he had written a letter, but I suppose my unwillingness to talk to him had forced his hand. The letter was so matter of fact. So final. *I wish you all the very best in your New York endeavours.* Jeez, what was it, a job rejection? He may as well have said, 'we sincerely hope you find gainful employment very soon'. If this was the real Fin Hunter then I'd had a lucky escape.

Okay, so that was a lie.

I still loved him, and it hurt like hell fire to know it was over. Every single lie he'd told me came back to haunt me. He'd never loved me. I'd been some kind of fun distraction while he rebelled against his parents and found himself.

Clearly, the duplicitous personality wasn't just connected to his love of music. I felt humiliated. Like he was laughing at me. Poor Star, the silly American barista girl with the crush on the high-flying lawyer who was way out of her league.

God, how pathetic.

The plane eventually began its descent into JFK, and the lights in the cabin dimmed. Tears trailed in streaks down my face as I gazed out over the twinkling lights of my new home.

Home.

That word was never farther from the way I felt than right then.

48

———————

FIN

I sat staring out of my office window at the multitude of architectural styles of the city. The leaves were turning brown, orange and gold, the colours of Autumn, but then again it was September. Star had been gone from the UK for around a month. But even though she had left my country, she most certainly never left my heart or my mind. And as difficult as it was to admit it to myself, I knew I'd been a coward. I should have spoken to her. *Made* her listen to me.

The folks of Edinburgh carried on with their everyday lives in the city below, and I envied every single one of them who could focus on normal things. Obviously, I'm not omnipotent, and I had no idea how many of those people down there were suffering something similar to my fate, but I would've gladly traded places with any one of them. At least a new pain would have been something different.

My intercom buzzed, dragging me from my pity party for one, and I hit the buzzer. 'Yes, Fiona?'

'Finlay, Miss Drummond is here to see you.'

'Great. Thanks, Fiona. Please send her in.'

I stood and walked round my desk, ready to hug my ex-fiancée Elise when she walked through the door. She looked lovely. Very fresh-faced, and it was good to see. Before she could say a word, I pulled her into my arms.

'Whoa! Is someone happy to see me?' She giggled and hugged me back.

'I sure am, Elise.'

She patted my back and pulled away to kiss my cheek. 'Still no news?' The concern in her expression knotted my stomach, and I shook my head, unable to say the answer out loud. 'She'll come around, Fin. I just know she will.'

I closed my eyes and sighed. 'I honestly don't think so, Elise. I think it's really over.'

'Let's go for lunch, eh? We can talk.'

I nodded my agreement and grabbed my jacket. Fiona gave me a pitiful smile as we left the building. It was sweet that everyone was being so understanding, but in all honesty, I was sick of them all walking on eggshells around me. Relationships ended all the time. Why mine was the hot topic, I'd never know. Reconnecting with Elise again had been inadvertent. We'd bumped into each other while she was out in the city creating her wedding gift register. We'd gone for coffee and I had ended up pouring my heart out to her about Star. She'd been so supportive and it felt good to have her back in my life again. She had always been a good friend even if we were never meant to be more than that.

As we walked along Princes Street amongst the hustle and bustle of the lunchtime rush, I remembered the times Star and I had walked the same street late at night. We'd held hands and chatted easily as we watched the passing trams and taxi cabs. But today, regardless of the number of people around me on the street, I had never felt so damn lonely.

Elise stopped at the end of one of the side streets

and pulled my arm. We quickly arrived on Rose Street, and she tugged me into a small café where there was one table free.

She gestured to a chair. 'Sit. I'll get you a coffee.'

Too miserable to argue about who was paying, I did as she had ordered and sat at the table by the window. A girl with pink hair passed by outside, and my heart leapt. Just as she was level with me, she glanced at me through the glass. Of course, it wasn't Star. She was thousands of miles away in New York.

The clunk of a coffee cup being placed before me pulled me back to Elise, and I smiled warmly at her. 'Thanks for this, Elise.'

She shrugged. 'It's just coffee.'

'You know what I mean. You being here for me. I appreciate it.'

She responded with a sad smile. 'I know you do. And what are friends for if not when we're in need of a hug and chat, eh?'

'Doesn't it feel weird? You know, you coming up from London, leaving your boyfriend behind for the weekend just so you can console your dickhead of an ex?'

She shrugged nonchalantly. 'Rand happens to be

a very understanding man. And he knows how important you are to me.'

I fell silent for a while, lost in my thoughts once again. 'What the hell am I going to do, Elise?'

She huffed and tilted her head to one side. 'Well, the way I see it, you have two options. One, you forget about her and move on. You have lots of groupies vying for your attention now you're a local rock god.'

I scrunched my face, irked by her description of my hobby. 'And two?'

'Two, you get your arse on a plane and fly out to New York to tell her she made a mistake by leaving. That you love her to pieces and can't live without her.'

I closed my eyes and let my head roll back. 'But work... the band...' She nipped the skin of my forearm and I cried out whilst glaring at her. 'Ow! What was that for?'

'Because, Fin Hunter, you're an idiot. You don't even want to be a bloody lawyer. You never have. And the band has no gigs for a month whilst Nate and his wife go to Australia. You told me all this, remember? So, what the hell are you waiting for? Why are you making excuses?' Of course, she was right, and I hated her for it. But only briefly.

I held up my hands. 'Okay, okay. You've got a point. But... what if she tells me to sod off?'

Leaning across the table and clutching my hand, she gazed at me with heartfelt sincerity. 'You won't know if you don't try. And if she *does* tell you to sod off then have a few days to get everything out of your system in the Big Apple and come home with a clear head.'

God, she made it sound so easy. So why was my gut telling me it wouldn't be?

* * *

Alasdair steepled his fingers and rested his chin on them. 'I think Elise is right, Fin. But I also think you need to be careful. From what you said, her parting letter was very cold. Perhaps she *has* moved on. I just don't want you going all the way out there to get hurt, son.'

'I know and I appreciate that, Da—oh shit.' My hands covered my mouth. 'Sorry. I mean Alasdair. Shit. That just slipped out.' I held my hands up in some form of surrender as my cheeks almost spontaneously combusted with embarrassment.

Alasdair's eyes were fixed on mine, his eyebrows raised. A low chuckle erupted from his chest and his cheeks also coloured. 'That's okay. I *did* call you son. I think you can be forgiven. Not that there's anything to forgive. I'm glad you feel able to talk to me as a friend as well as an employer. And... well, I do look on you as a son of sorts.'

His words touched my heart, but I had to remain on task. 'So tell me honestly. Do you think I'd be making a colossal mistake going out there?'

He shook his head. 'No, no. I think it's a good idea. Perhaps this way your questions will be answered one way or another, and you'll be able to move on either with or without Star in your life. But at least you'll know. There's a lot to be said for closure.'

'And are you happy with me taking the two weeks off? I mean, I may be back sooner but—'

'Fin, it's absolutely fine. Go get some flights booked and get some bloody food, will you? You're looking very pale and gaunt lately. Colette would have my guts for garters if she thought for a second I hadn't at least *tried* to make you eat something.'

I grinned wide as my heart thudded in my chest at the prospect of the journey I was about to embark upon. 'I promise I'll eat tonight.'

'Good. Now bugger off and get some work done. You're slacking.' He winked and I laughed for the first time in what seemed like months. I knew he was only jesting considering I had worked late every single night since I received Star's letter. It was better to be occupied and too busy to think than to sit at home wallowing in whisky and self-pity.

49

STAR

Standing in The Napier Gallery in New York surrounded by walls adorned with my own work never got any less surreal. So far, the exhibition had attracted lots of attention in its month-long run to date, and I'd sold several of the larger pieces. The one that hurt the most was the original enlargement of the Edinburgh Castle shot that Fin had loved so much. Seeing that leave to go to its new home had left me in the back office in floods of tears. Marshall, the gallery director, had been concerned, but I'd managed to convince him that letting any of my pieces go would be emotional. Thankfully, he'd bought my lame ass excuse, although he must have thought I was a total flake.

I was relieved that the shot of the Forbes Hunter gravestone that Fin and I had visited together was still hanging in the gallery. After the research I had done it seemed the man had been a distantly connected ancestor of Fin's and it would feel wrong to let that go to someone who didn't understand its sentimental value. I vowed that if it didn't sell within the next week, I was going to request that it be marked as 'not for sale'. Each time I thought about the times Fin and I had walked through the Old Calton Burial Ground, a deep sadness washed over me. The fractured stonework resembled the state of my heart, but the memory of the day I took the photo was one I treasured. It was a day I'd been able to show Fin the side of Edinburgh that *I* loved. But I wondered if any of the experiences we had shared had meant anything to him.

They had certainly left their imprint on my heart.

* * *

New York was an astounding city. Everything was on such a grand scale compared to my hometown in the USA *and* to Edinburgh. The volume of traffic and the general cacophony of noise that greeted me when I was out walking around the bustling streets was almost at deafening proportions. In many ways, it resembled the TV shows I'd seen. Yellow cabs and subway vents, food carts, and doormen standing proudly outside the more exclusive hotels. It was a melting pot of faiths and languages, but it made me realise how much I missed the Scottish accents of Edinburgh. I missed them so much that my heart skipped whenever I heard one.

I'd had plenty of opportunities to go around the city with my camera. In fact, it accompanied me everywhere. But I didn't want to capture the usual tourist sights. While I appreciated the value of the Statue of Liberty, the Empire State Building, and Times Square, I wanted to photograph the *real* people. Just everyday folks going about their normal lives.

I'd been chatting to an old guy called Carlos, who worked a hot dog stand on the corner of East 8th and University Place. I'd got some beautiful shots of his friendly, gap-toothed grin as he served his faithful, regular customers. Instead of me paying him in some way for allowing me to take his picture, he had insisted on giving me free hot dogs the three times I had been to see him, telling me I was too darn skinny. I'd bought him a Yankees baseball cap as a thank you. The old one he wore looked real tired, and his face had lit up when I presented the new one I had bought for him. He had immediately pulled it on and posed for another photograph.

I'd shot some great images of performers in Central Park, who were playing very alternative music considering the crowd that gathered. They were a group of younger guys, maybe in their late teens. A guitarist, a singer, a violinist, and a guy playing a single drum but somehow making it sound like a full kit. I sat on the grass, munching on a dog from Carlos' stand and listening, head back, eyes closed, facing towards the sun. Suddenly, the opening bars of 'Strange and Beautiful' caught my attention and I gasped. I opened my eyes, my gaze darting around the area as my heart thudded at my ribs.

Is Fin here? Please let Fin be here. What would I say if he was?

As the singer began to deliver the very words that Fin had used to steal my heart, I clambered to my feet and began to walk back towards my plush Upper East Side apartment. It was a good thing I had grown familiar with the city as my vision was blurred with tears. My appetite ebbed away, and I dumped the hot dog in the nearest garbage can as I swiped at the damp trails on my cheeks. Of course he wasn't there. He would *never* be there. His letter had made it patently clear how he felt about me. And I could never forgive him for the things he had said. Even if he came and apologised.

Which he wouldn't.

I had to give up and move on. Jeez, how many times had I had that conversation with myself? I was like a damn broken record.

Zara from the gallery had asked me to go out for drinks after work on several occasions, but I had always avoided it. I wasn't ready to socialise. But my reaction to hearing *that* song made me realise I was living in the past.

Next time she asked, I would force myself to go.

50

FIN

I had always hated flying. Not so much because of the fear—although I admit that did play a *wee* part—but more because of the hours of time it afforded me in my own head. Thinking was such a dangerous pastime. I should've been using the time wisely to plan what I would say to Star once I was face to face with her again, but alas, my brain chose to torture me with conjured mental images of her slamming the door in my face. It was a very real possibility. One I hoped beyond hope wouldn't come to fruition.

I stuck my ear-buds in and listened to the track list I had created especially for the flight. The problem was that every single song reminded me of

Star. It hadn't been my intention to do this, but regardless of that fact, every time I hit skip I was greeted with something that struck a chord inside me.

I decided to watch a movie. I had heard great things about The Goldfinch so I figured I'd give it a go. The cinematography was amazing, the acting was great too but I just couldn't focus.

Eventually, I gave up and tried to sleep instead.

The plane landed in JFK and I was off there as fast as my feet would carry me, and as fast as the throngs of people with the same idea would allow. It was almost midnight, and the late October temperature felt subzero. I just wanted to crash. My stomach protested its emptiness, but eating was the last thing on my mind. I figured the sooner I got to sleep, the sooner I could go to the gallery and tell Star how I felt.

After going through customs and grabbing my bag from baggage claim, I made my way outside into the chilly New York night air and hailed a yellow cab.

One pulled up right away, and I clambered inside. 'Hi. Plaza Hotel, please. But can you go via the Napier gallery. I don't need to stop I... I just want to see it.'

'Sure thing, boss,' came the gruff voice with the strong Bronx accent. I smiled to myself about the fact that I had walked into a cliché of my own imagining.

We darted through the brightly lit streets of New York City, and I watched the myriad shops and businesses whizzing by. I wondered why I had never visited in all the time Elise and I were together. It was the kind of place she would have loved. As we passed the Napier Gallery, my heart jumped into my throat. The thought that I was passing by the place where Star spent much of her time filled me with a variety of emotions. Pride, fear, regret but most of all *hope*. I had to cling on to that.

It was all I had left.

The cab eventually drew up to the curb outside the stunning, multi-storey Plaza Hotel building, where it glowed like a beacon on Fifth Avenue. A beacon provided to me by a very insistent Alasdair, who assured me it was Colette's treat, not his. As I glanced up at the structure, I could see the hue of many room lights where the occupants had left their drapes ajar. Knowing I would soon be in one of the plush rooms made me relax a little. I paid the driver and grabbed my bag.

Once I had checked in and been shown to my room, I dropped my bag on the floor at the end of the bed and stripped out of my clothes. I gave myself no time to check out the luxurious suite. I needed to wash the grime of the day from my skin before bed.

Standing underneath the powerful jets of hot water and cocooned in a blanket of steam, I closed my eyes and relaxed. A sense of relief that I was at least in the same city as the woman I loved washed over me, and my anxiety began to leave my body and run down the drain with the water.

* * *

Sleep didn't come readily, and by the time I decided to get out of bed, I had to make peace with the notion that I wouldn't look great for my first meeting with Star in months. Although, maybe seeing the evidence of my lack of sleep would make her realise I was seriously missing her.

I hoped so.

I ordered bacon, eggs, and fresh orange juice to be delivered to my room, and when it arrived, I sat at the small table by the window and almost vacuumed the food off the plate. My appetite was back. The sharp, refreshing tang of citrus awoke my taste buds, meaning I thoroughly enjoyed devouring the rest of the food on my plate.

I was refuelled and ready to go. A kaleidoscope of butterflies had taken flight inside me, and my palms were slick with sweat, but I made my way down in the elevator and left my luxurious surroundings, stepping out onto the hectic streets of New York City. The kindly doorman dressed in a long coat and a top hat hailed a cab for me, and I clambered in, almost losing my balance. I had never been so bloody nervous. Walking out on stage to perform was a walk in the park compared to how I felt right then.

The cab pulled up outside the Napier Gallery, and I paid the driver before climbing out onto the crowded sidewalk. The skyscrapers surrounding the roads afforded a little shelter from the biting wind, but my teeth were still chattering.

I glanced up at the stark, modern exterior of the building that housed everything that meant something in my life, and I inhaled a deep, shaking breath.

This was it.

My heart hammered in my chest, and I suddenly saw stars dancing before my eyes. Panic began to mount, and I swallowed hard. I realised nothing was going to calm me. I just had to bite the bullet.

I pushed through the door and was greeted by a pretty, petite brunette in a sharp skirt suit. 'Good morning, sir. Welcome to the Napier Gallery, New York. Is there anything I can help you with?'

Her scripted patter came out in a formulaic rush, and I smiled, trying to gather my thoughts. 'Erm...yes. Yes, I was hoping to speak with Star Mendoza, please.'

'Miss Mendoza isn't in the gallery today. She's taking a well-earned break.'

Aww, dammit. 'Ah, okay. Is there a way I can find her? Or contact her?'

The woman narrowed her eyes suspiciously. 'And who might you be?'

'My name is Fin Hunter. I'm a... erm... a friend.'

Her eyes widened and she opened and closed her

mouth several times as her cheeks coloured pink. 'Oh. *You're* Fin Hunter.'

I frowned and nodded. 'That's what I said.'

'I really don't know if I should give you her address. She's a friend as well as a colleague, and I don't... She's trying to get over you.'

I crumpled my brow. 'Trying? What if I don't want her to get over me? What if I want her to know how I feel and that I've travelled all this way to tell her I love her?'

She visibly melted. 'Well, when you put it like that, I guess... Maybe I should call her first and check it's okay for you to go to her apartment. I really don't think—'

I held up my hands. 'Look, I know it's probably not company policy and all that, but the way things were left between us is just so unfinished. I need to see her. I have to tell her.'

The woman closed her eyes for a moment, clearly toying with the idea of giving me Star's address, but her eyes jolted open as someone walked in through the gallery doors.

'Oh, shit.' As the brunette's eyes widened, I spun

round to see why she had reacted in that way, and my breath caught.

'Fin?' The colour drained from Star's face and she leaned on the wall as if to steady herself.

The brunette interjected. 'Star. I was just about to call you.'

Star shook her head and kept her eyes focused on me. 'It's... it's okay, Zara. I know him. This is Fin.' Her words came out in a breathy whisper and her eyelids fluttered.

'Yeah, he said who he was. I didn't want to give him your address in case you didn't want to see him.'

Star moved her focus onto Zara and her eyes filled with panic, but I stood there like a moron whilst they talked about me as if I wasn't even in the room. Anger and pain began to surface from deep within me as it dawned on me. She wasn't happy to see me, so perhaps the letter *had* been intended as a final goodbye after all. Maybe I should have stayed in Edinburgh.

I stepped into her line of sight to interrupt the dialogue between the two women. 'Star, can we go somewhere to talk? Please?'

Her attention snapped back to me again and she

nodded before turning and walking back out through the door. I didn't bother to thank Zara. Instead, I followed Star out into the street.

'Star! Slow down!' I called after her as she strode away from me.

She stopped and turned to face me. Her eyes burned with rage. 'What the *hell* are you doing here, Fin?'

I came to a halt before her. 'I had to see you. I had to tell you—'

'I think you told me enough, don't you?'

Hang on. It's me who should be pissed off here. That letter had all but finished me off. And she's angry? 'I couldn't leave things how they were, Star. I had to come here to see if—'

'To see if you'd hurt me enough? Or maybe to see if I can actually survive without you maybe? Yeah, well you have, and I can, so you can go home now.' She turned and began to pick up speed once more.

What the f—? 'Star, please. I just want to talk.' I jogged until I was level with her.

'Oh, so now you want to talk? Writing not good enough any more, huh?'

Confusion clouded my mind. She was the one

into letter writing. I'd never favoured it as a way of communication. 'Writing's okay for some things, yes. But not for this.'

She stopped again and turned to face me. Her eyes were red and tears trailed down her cheeks. 'Fin, please leave. It's over. Okay? We didn't work. I get it. I wish you and your folks all the best in your newly re-established relationship. I'm glad you worked it out and you got your damn job back in the family firm, okay? I have to admit to being very surprised at that part but...' *Huh?* She held her hand up and a cab stopped. She quickly opened the door and climbed in. 'I wish you all well, Fin. I really do.' And with her parting words, the cab whisked her away.

'Star! What do you mean? Star!'

51

STAR

I closed the door to my apartment, leaned against it, and slid down until I hit the floor with my ass. What the hell was he thinking? Why would he come here? To rub salt in my wounds? Was he some sick kind of monster that got pleasure out of hurting his ex-girl-friends?

Bastard.

I'd been doing okay. Well, maybe okay was pushing it a little. Maybe a little too optimistic, but I'd been getting by. And then he had to show up in New York and knock me back to square one. Why? I just didn't get it.

I leaned my head on my knees and sobbed. My

heart ached with a kind of homesickness I had never experienced before. And the awful fact was that I wasn't homesick for my parents' home. I was homesick for Edinburgh. I missed my grandma and Alec. I missed the fun times at DeBasement. I missed the Scott Monument, the castle, the trams, Princes Street Gardens. I missed every little thing about it.

After everything Fin said in his letter, and after he worked things out with his folks, why would he show up here? Why was he willing to go against their wishes so soon? Was he missing the rebellious streak he discovered in his temporary relationship with me? Was he bored with the money and prestige again already? The question rolled around in my mind. But the fact was, I wasn't willing to be an exciting distraction for him again. I deserved someone who loved me for me. But then again, what if he'd realised he'd made a mistake in losing me? This whole thing was driving me insane. And tough shit. He had lost me. Nothing could change how small and insignificant he had made me feel simply by telling his father he loved him too. That simple phrase, whilst it should have meant something wonderful, actually meant I had been easily cast aside and it was shitty that Fin had found a conscience after hurting me so much, but that was his problem. And that damn letter, urgh! I couldn't afford to let hope spring to life inside me. How could I trust him again, even if he had realised it was me he wanted after all?

My head began to throb, and I had the urge to call Alec. It would be seven o'clock in Edinburgh, and Alec would no doubt be in the shower or out for a run. But on the off chance I would catch him, I dragged myself up from the floor and grabbed my cell.

'Twinkle! How are you, babes?' Seeing Alec's smiling face was my undoing once again, and I began to sob uncontrollably.

52

FIN

Home.

Not where I had hoped nor expected to be so soon after my trip to New York.

Sadly, it had turned out that Star had no intention of listening to me. I had visited the gallery over the few days that followed but she was either out or pretended to be so, making Zara pass on the news. After a week I had admitted defeat and returned to Edinburgh, complete with my broken heart. The callous letter she'd sent really had marked the end.

So much time had passed, and I was still walking around in a dumbstruck trance. Another Sunday rolled around, and I decided to get some much-needed fresh November air. After walking absent-mindedly for what seemed like hours, I found myself in Calton Old Burial Ground. I glanced around in a bewildered daze, unable to remember how I'd ended up there of all places, and the first flurry of a snow shower began to dance about me. It wasn't going to last, but I smiled as I imagined Star standing there with me, head back, tongue out, allowing snowflakes to settle and melt on her tongue. She'd told me she loved Edinburgh in the winter.

For me, everywhere was a little duller. A little less vibrant. Star brightened everything. Brought everything to life. Her colourful character and happy nature had, for a short time, made everything seem wonderful.

She had changed me. I had temporarily become a happier, more colourful, more adventurous person. The newest feature to my skin had been a part of the memory I had of what true happiness felt like.

But the absence of her from my life now had turned a once multi-hued palette into monotonous grey and brown.

* * *

After my trip, I had cut short my so-called vacation, figuring that work was what I needed. Hetty had been in constant contact, checking on me and my mental state. At least she cared. My brother and Tori kept insisting on having me round for dinner. Charlotte was a delight and watching my niece change as she grew was wonderful. But I knew what they were doing. They were on some kind of 'keep Fin sane' watch. And since my return, Alasdair had made regular appearances in my office under the guise that he needed information on some case or other. I knew he too was checking up on me and my emotional state. It was great knowing he cared. It was more than my father had bothered to do. And the offer of assistance with the Inveresk cottages had turned out to be a pile of bullshit. Alasdair had informed me on my first day back that he had been considering the case in detail, and it was tightly sealed and free of any supposed loophole. My father had blatantly lied to me in the hope that he could steal me back from McKendrick. No doubt with a view to fire me once again if I returned to the family company. His way of teaching me a valuable lesson.

My mother had made several attempts to contact

me, but I refused to give her any response. I had resolved with myself the fact that my parents were toxic. And as awful as it was to admit that about one's own flesh and blood, it was the truth. I couldn't understand her tenacity, however. But the calls continued, and I continued to ignore them.

Luckily, Alasdair had thrown me right in at the deep end with another small fish takes on big fish case, and I was chin deep in files and research. I had a cold cup of coffee on my desk and a half-eaten BLT that Fiona had insisted on getting for me.

The intercom on my desk buzzed, and I reached out to hit the button. 'Yes, Fiona?'

'I'm so sorry, Fin. I couldn't stop her. She said it was vital that she saw you and—'

My office door burst open and in stalked my mother.

She stood there, a picture of manicured perfection, as she demanded, 'Finlay, why are you ignoring my calls?'

I scowled at her. 'Come in, why don't you, Mother dear?'

'Answer me, Finlay. You were brought up with more respect than to ignore your mother.'

I leaned back in my chair and regarded her with disdain. 'But we all know respect must be earned, *Mother.*' Using the word 'Mum' felt way too forgiving.

She stepped forward and sat down in the leather chair facing my desk. 'Stop being so obnoxious, Finlay. Now, tell me why you won't speak to me.'

I sighed and rubbed my hands over my face. I wasn't in the mood for Isobel Hunter drama. 'Seriously? You really need to ask me that after what you did to me and Star?'

She blanched and her eyes widened. 'How did you find out?'

I scrunched my brow. 'What do you mean *how did I find out*? I was present at the time, for God's sake. I was there when you and Dad made her feel about two inches tall at the charity event, remember?'

She heaved a sigh. 'Oh. Oh, *that.* Oh, yes, well, water under the bridge and all that.' She reached into her oversized designer handbag and pulled out her compact, flicked it open, and peered at her reflection.

Confusion washed over me anew. 'Hang on. What did you mean when you asked how I found out? Found out about *what*?'

She snapped the compact shut and pursed her lips. 'Oh, come on, Finlay. It isn't all about you, darling. Have you considered what this whole situation is doing to your poor father? He's been ill, you know.'

'Whoa. No, you're not changing the subject, Mother. What did you mean?'

A fake sob escaped her throat and she reached into her bag again to pull out a hanky. 'Just know that we want what's best for you. And anything that's happened has been because we have your best interests at heart and we *love* you.' She dabbed at her non-existent tears.

My heart began to thud in my chest, and I clenched my jaw. 'I'll ask you once more, and I expect an honest answer. For once in your life, Mother, do something selfless, please. What did you do?'

The calmness in her voice was a total contrast to the anxiety and anger building rapidly inside of me. She waved her hanky. 'Oh, nothing. It was just a letter.'

My stomach clenched. 'What letter?'

She smiled as if remembering a happy incident. 'Well, two letters actually. One to each of you. Just to make sure you both made the right decision.'

'What. Letters. Mother?'

Her lip began to tremble in that Oscar-winning actress manner again. 'One to Star to let her know you were back in your rightful place with the family firm, and one to you to let you know Star was moving on.'

I slammed my fists on the desk, and she almost jumped out of her skin. 'You bitch!' I stood and slammed my fists down again, the thud vibrating through the wood. 'You evil bitch! You're supposed to be my family. Where the hell is your maternal instinct? You're supposed to care about me!'

She stood and wrung her hands in front of her. 'I *do* care, Finlay. I just wanted what was right for you. And *she* wasn't right for you. I mean, come on. Pink hair and those ghastly tattoos? What kind of impression did it give to—'

'That's just it. I don't give a crap about anyone else's thoughts on my relationship with Star, Mother. I loved her. I *love* her. And you... you ruined it with your lies. You've made her think I don't love her!' I shouted at the top of my voice. My lungs began to burn as I fought to pull air in. My heart wanted out of the whole sorry mess, and it was almost breaking free of my ribs.

Alasdair and Fiona appeared in the doorway. 'What the hell are you doing here, Isobel?' Alasdair demanded.

I jabbed a finger in her direction. 'It was *her*. *She* wrote the letter pretending it was from Star. And she wrote one to Star, too. It was *her*.' I glowered at the woman who'd given birth to me as Alasdair gaped at her too, disbelief plastered on his ageing features.

Alasdair stepped aside and gestured at the gap he had created. 'To think I used to love you, Isobel. To think I was willing to marry you all those years ago. Thank goodness Campbell Hunter stole you away. I can't imagine being married to someone so despicable. You and Campbell deserve each other. Now, I think you should leave before I have you removed.'

She pleaded at me with watering eyes. 'You may not believe me, Finlay, but we *do* love you. We just want to put the family first as a unit. Your relationship with that... that...' She closed her eyes briefly, allowing tears to spill down her perfectly made-up cheeks. 'With *Star* made a mockery of us all and everything we have built.'

I inhaled a wavering, unsettled breath. 'There is a saying about judging books by their covers, Mother. But let me tell you that if it was a choice between someone manicured and 'perfect' on the outside but as ugly as you on the inside, I would choose someone like Star every damn time. But do you know what? I think she's the most beautiful, kind and intelligent woman I have ever met. And I love her with every ounce of my being. Now, I think Alasdair is right. You should leave. And please don't bother to contact me again. As far as I'm concerned, the only mother I ever really had was Hetty. And as for a father, I never had one. And that's fine with me.'

She sobbed dramatically as I slumped into my chair, spent from my verbal onslaught. Without saying another word, she stormed out of the office and out of my life.

For good.

53

FIN

I sat across from Alec in the empty coffee shop. It was after closing time, and I was still nursing the same latte he had given me an hour before.

Alec huffed out a long breath. 'I just can't believe a mother could be so damn cruel, Fin. I mean... *why*?'

I shrugged, just as disbelieving as he was. 'Beats me. I... I don't know what to do. I can't just get on a plane again and expect Star to be happy to see me just because it turned out the letter wasn't even from me. Let's face it, she still thinks I betrayed her at the charity event. And that part *is* my fault. Because that's exactly how it looked to her.'

'Yes, she does still think that. But if you explain. If you tell her what happened after she'd gone.'

I shook my head. 'I tried that before. I left voice-mails. I sent text messages. I turned up at your apartment, if you remember? I don't think it'll make a difference. I ruined it all, Alec.' My throat tightened and a stinging sensation needled at my eyes. 'Next time you speak to her, could you just tell her I never stopped loving her? She'll listen if the message comes from you. Just tell her I'm so sorry I hurt her. And that I know my mother's letters were meant to cause damage, but the last thing I ever wanted was for Star to be hurt. Or for her to be dragged into the hell that is my stupid family. Could you tell her that for me? Please?' I swiped away a trail of moisture that had begun to make its way down my face.

Alec reached across the table and squeezed my forearm. 'I still think you could get her back, Fin. She still loves you. You don't get over a love that deep so easily.'

I shrugged and laughed without an ounce of humour. '*Loved* me. Past tense. I think I just need to let her go. Let her be happy. And if that means she moves on then so be it. She deserves to be happy, Alec.' My voice broke and my lip trembled.

What a fool.

Alec patted my arm. 'Well, of course I'll tell her. But you could always contact her yourself.'

I shook my head again. 'I can't. After everything that's happened, I just can't. I want to. Believe me, I do. But, to be honest, I see now that she deserves so much better.' I pushed my chair away from the table and placed my cup down. 'I should go. We're rehearsing tonight. Got a gig tomorrow.'

He stood too. 'Oh, right. Great. Where?'

'We're playing Sneaky Pete's in the city.'

He patted my back. 'Okay, well I might bring some of the guys down.'

'Great. See you there maybe. And... thanks for not telling me to sod off, eh?'

He smiled sadly. The pity in his eyes almost pushed me over the edge again, and I fought my emotions to keep them in check.

* * *

I wrote to Hetty and told her everything. All the sordid details of my mother and father's betrayal. How they had treated me like a commodity. Like something with as little soul as themselves. I told Hetty she was the closest thing to a mother I'd ever had—that I loved her and wished she had been my birth mother instead of the callous, bloody-minded, self-centred monster who had brought me into the world and then tossed me aside.

It had been a cathartic letter to write, but the resulting phone call from Hetty had almost broken my heart. She had sobbed down the phone line and told me she loved me dearly. That she was so proud of the man I had become and that I had finally taken a stand. She said she had wanted to leave their employ for so long, but she couldn't bear the thought of leaving me and Callum there. She knew my brother was made of tougher stuff as a kid, she said, and that watching my eyes fill with disappointment every time my father belittled one of my achievements made her stand fast in a job she hated. She told me she would one day show up at a gig to surprise me, and I loved her so much for that, even though I guessed she never would.

She had apologised over and over for things that hadn't been her fault, and I had spent time telling her that all she had ever done was help me. That if it hadn't been for her, I would never have picked up a hairbrush to sing into, never mind a real mic. That I owed her so much. All the words I should have said a long time ago. But at least I said them. Better late than never, I suppose.

The band had been awesome since I got back from New York. They were good mates, offering an ear if I needed it or to get sloshed if I needed that more.

Sneaky Pete's didn't look like much from the outside. It certainly didn't look like one of Edinburgh's most popular live music venues. In fact, it resembled an abandoned shop by day, and most people would, no doubt, walk right by it without a second glance. Close to a beautiful stone archway on Cowgate and some of the most incredible architecture Edinburgh had to offer, it was the most unassuming venue ever. And that's exactly why I loved it.

On the night of our gig, I arrived at the venue along with the rest of Mr Hyde at around ten o'clock. The club was due to open at eleven, so we had a good hour to get set up. Our original material was coming along nicely, and we were excited to be sharing it at the newest venue in our portfolio.

We carried the gear into the club and set up like the well-organised team we'd become. Music was a huge part of my life, and it was a great distraction. I knew that once I was up on that stage and my alter ego took over, I could forget about all the rubbish that had happened in my life and just become a whole other person. Fin the 'rock god'. The thought made me smile and shake my head. It was what Star had called me. *Fin the rock god*. Who would ever have thought that the clean cut, pretty-boy, reluctant law student would one day be a shaggy-haired, bearded guy who stomped around a stage every weekend, screeching out rock and indie songs at the top of his lungs? Certainly not me.

I was standing inside the small venue and admiring the graffiti style artwork on the walls as a sense of pride washed over me when I recalled Hetty's words. I was there to sing. With a live band.

And it was thanks to Hetty and Star that I had taken the steps to become who I was in that moment. Two important women who had no idea how much they had affected me. I loved them both so much for it.

* * *

Midnight. The club was buzzing, and my anxiety had ratcheted up ten notches. I was pacing up and down at the back of the club while the other guys laughed and joked with their wives and girlfriends. Thankfully, I was too terrified to be filled with envy as I chewed on my nails and watched them enjoying the company of the women in their lives.

Time ticked by all too slowly and much too fast simultaneously. I ducked into the men's room to check my appearance. My faded old grey jeans that were ripped at the knee were just too comfy to throw out. They were a far cry from the Hugo Boss suit I wore for the office. The Sonic Idols T-shirt I wore was my favourite, even though it had shrunk a little thanks to user error with the washing machine. It was tight but, thankfully, not cropped.

The door was flung open and Nate poked his head round. 'Hey, pal. We're up.'

'Be right there.' The door closed again, and I was left with nothing but the thudding coming from the club and my heart.

I stepped out into the throngs of people in the club and pushed through the crowd in what felt like slow motion, making my way to the stage. I jumped up as Titch hit his sticks together and the intro to 'Sweet Child o' Mine' kicked in. Nate bounced round the stage as he strummed his guitar to the track made famous by Guns n Roses in the late 1980s.

My mask descended, and once more I became Fin Hunter the lead singer of Mr Hyde.

The crowd jumped up and down in time with the beat, and I strutted about the stage, letting myself go. My inhibitions melted away along with every worry that had plagued me in the last couple of months. But as I stared out at the audience of people dancing and flailing wildly, I was hit with a pang of sadness. Star loved this song. And I had lost her.

Dragging myself from the edge of a pit of melancholy before I fell into the abyss, I began to dance around like Axl Rose as I sang. The crowd loved it. And for a short while, so did I.

* * *

I stooped to gulp from my glass of water and swipe the T-shirt from my body. A raucous cheer erupted round the room, and I chuckled at the reaction. I decided I needed to start bringing a towel on stage so I could stay fully clothed up there. I wiped the shirt round my damp face, and for a laugh, I threw the sweat-sodden item out into the crowd of women who had gathered at the front of the stage. They went wild, and when I turned to glance at the band, some of them were bent double, laughing hysterically. Nate was shaking his head with a huge grin on his face.

I turned back to the crowd and took a deep breath. 'This next one has a special place in my heart. I won't bore you with the gory details, but let's just say my life has been pretty messed up this year. But thanks to these guys, I think I'm back on track.' I gestured to the band and the crowd cheered. 'This next song reminds of an American girl who stole my heart.' I paused as images of that beautiful American girl sprang into my mind, and a twinge of sadness tugged at me. 'It's funny how you can live in a place your whole life and not even *see* it. I mean *really* see it. But this special person helped me to see this city in a whole new light, and I've a new-found love and respect for it. So I want to dedicate this to her and thank her for encouraging me to be the man I am to-day.' Taking a deep breath, I closed my eyes and shouted, 'For you, Star! Because wherever you may be in this world today, I know your heart will always be in Edinburgh. Snow Patrol's 'Take Back the City'!'

Once more, the crowd cheered, and as the song started, the bouncing began again in earnest. The energy in the room lifted me and carried me away somewhere entirely different. For a few minutes, I was playing the O2 Arena instead of a little back-street venue in Edinburgh. And as I sang and heard the audience's loud voices joining with mine, a grin spread across my face.

I scanned the crowd of happy, smiling faces, and everything clicked into place. This was me. This was who I was. As I peered out beyond the spotlight, I caught sight of a shock of the most vivid red hair. I held the mic out to the people dancing at the front, but my eyes didn't leave that one woman, dancing with her arms in the air. I couldn't see her face, thanks to the huge burly bloke in front of her. Her hair was shoulder length and choppy, but I would have known those tattoos anywhere.

The guy stepped sideways, and my heart almost stuttered to a halt. Her face lifted with perfect timing, and her gaze connected with mine. A stunning smile stretched her ruby red lips as she began to walk towards me.

54

STAR

As I stood there in the crowded club, my mind drifted back to the conversation I'd had the day before, when Alec had called to fill me in on the whole letter debacle.

'So, she sent one to Fin too? Pretending it was from me?'

'Yep. Told him to move on because you were.'

I gasped. 'The bitch. Why would she do that to me? She doesn't even know me. And to her own son?'

He snorted. 'I know. Just what I thought. Fin was destroyed, Star. Completely.'

My heart sank. 'Is he... is he okay?'

Alec sighed. 'I think he'll be fine eventually. But it'll take time. He's lost so much, Twinkle.'

I pursed my lips briefly. 'Alec McVey, are you sympathising with my ex?'

There was a silent pause. 'I know that as your best friend it's not exactly right for me to side with him, but, yeah. I felt so bad for him. He loves you so much.'

I huffed. 'Yeah? Well, he should've spoken up when his bastard of a father asked him to dump me at the charity event.'

'But he did, Star. He'd been dumbstruck for a moment after his father had used the 'L' word for the first ever time. But once he'd snapped out of that, he gave them hell. You just didn't stick around to see it.'

'Oh.' My heart plummeted in my chest and my stomach rolled.

And now I was back in Edinburgh. Hoping and praying he would take me back.

I was dragged back from the past when Fin's voice rang out across the room and tugged at my heart. He told the audience he'd had a rough time lately, but that he was taking his life back. Suddenly my name rang out across the room, falling from his lips like an oath.

My view was restricted by a chunky guy in front of me, which I was relieved about. I wasn't ready for Fin to see me. But seeing him up on stage again was like some kind of miracle happening before my eyes. The song he had chosen was perfect, and it told me every single thing I needed to know. From that second, I wanted to be with him so desperately my chest hurt. I'd missed him so much.

When Alec had called and explained the situation with the letters, I had initially decided I wouldn't contact Fin. Too much had happened; too much water under that metaphorical bridge. But deep down, I think I knew I was just delaying the inevitable. He was all I could think about. He filled my every waking thought and was centre stage of every dream. And discovering he *had* defended me and tried to come after me when I bolted from the charity event where his parents had insulted me just made me angry with myself.

If I'd just given him a chance to explain. Why hadn't I done that and saved us both the heartache?

When he turned to take a swig of his water and

removed his T-shirt, I got the shock of my life. The huge, intricate tattoo of stars and Celtic markings on his back along with the words 'Stric de dhuais' was just beautiful. *A stroke of fate.* The words Hetty had used for mine and Fin's meeting. The colours danced under the lights in the venue, and a lump of emotion lodged itself in my throat. He had done that for *me*—this man who vowed never to have a tattoo on account of the pain. I smiled through the tears fogging my eyes. I wanted to run to him. Throw my arms round him and kiss him until we were both breathless.

Suddenly, the huge dude in front of me moved, and Fin's eyes locked on mine like a homing device. As if drawn by some unseen force, I walked towards him as he sang about an eternal kiss. A smile spread across his face, and my insides knotted as tears over spilled my eyes. Wow, he looked amazing. All bare-chested, shaggy haired, bearded, and sexy.

And that tattoo.

Oh. My. God.

Fin stuck the mic back in its stand and nodded to Nate, who took over on vocals, and then he jumped down from the stage and the crowd parted like the red sea, and he was Moses. My heart thundered in my chest, and I was grinning like a goof in spite of my tears, but I didn't care.

He stopped only inches from me as most of the crowd around us carried on dancing. 'You're... you're *here*,' he said disbelievingly.

I swiped at the damp trails on my face. 'I am. If you... if you still want me.'

He shook his head. '*If* I still want you?'

I nodded, and the fear that he might say no suddenly hit me. My stomach dropped. After all, he hadn't closed the remaining gap between us. He hadn't touched me, even though my fingers were itching to reach out and caress the skin of his chest. But still he stood there, his chest heaving and glistening with sweat.

'I like your hair.' He reached out and took a strand between his fingers. 'Red suits you.'

'Th-thanks. I like your tattoo.'

Finally, he stepped closer. 'It's for you.'

I could feel the heat radiating from his body, and I swallowed. 'It is?'

It was his turn to nod now. A smile tilted up his

mouth at one side. 'I'm glad you like it. Strìc de dhuais. Do you remember?'

'Oh, Fin. How could I forget?'

The fact that the music had stopped and the whole room was now staring at us began to register in my brain, but my eyes were transfixed on the blue irises of the man before me.

I reached out a tentative hand and touched his firm chest. 'I love it. In fact... I... I love *you*, Fin.'

Suddenly, he scooped me up into his arms and my feet left the floor. His lips crashed into mine, and my hands found the strands of his sweat-soaked hair. The familiar taste of his kiss melted my insides.

I was home.

Home with Fin where I belonged, and where I would remain. For as long he wanted me.

Strìc de dhuais.

EPILOGUE
FIVE YEARS LATER...

The summer sun beat down on us as we took the familiar path through Calton Old Burial Ground, the little blonde-haired boy skipping before us as I held his mother's hand.

She gazed up at me and sighed. 'What a beautiful day.'

I nodded my agreement. 'It sure is, sweetheart.'

She inhaled a long breath and let it go again with a big smile on her face. 'I love this city so much.'

I chuckled. 'Aye, I kind of guessed you did.'

'Mummy, Daddy, look!'

We both willingly skipped over to where our boy stood pointing at the cracked and leaning stone.

'What is it, son?' I asked as I ruffled his mop of blonde curls.

'Look there. Fa oh ra ba eh sa. That's like *my* name!'

Star crouched down beside him. 'That *is* like your name, baby. Remember I told you about when Daddy and I used to come visit here before you were born? The gentleman named on this stone is Forbes Hunter too, one of daddy's ancestors.'

His little brow crumpled. 'What's a hansettor?'

I crouched down at his left side and gave my beautiful wife a warm smile before ruffling our son's mop of hair. 'It's someone from my family who lived a long, long time ago. You were named after him. So people could remember.'

'I like my name,' he said with a smile. 'Can we go get ice cream now?'

I stood and lifted Forbes onto my shoulders. 'Worm flavour? Oh, I think we should do that right now, son. What do you think, Mummy?' I asked as I winked at her.

Forbes made a noise expressing his disgust at my suggestion.

Star stroked my arm and took our little boy's

hand where he sat perched above us. 'Only if I can have mint choc chip instead.'

Forbes giggled. 'You always have *that* taste, Mummy. All the time.'

She beamed up at our son. 'That's because it's my favourite, and worms are too slimy.'

'Just one scoop though Forbes, remember we're going to Charlotte's birthday party later. Your baby cousin Joshua is walking now so you'll need your wits about you.' I laughed as I imagined Joshua, Charlotte and Forbes running round Callum's garden and Callum cringing when they got too close to his newly planted borders.

'Remind me when we've been for ice cream that I need to call in to see Alec. He and Gil are taking my grandma out for dinner tonight and they're going to tell her they're getting married. She'll be so happy I want them to take a photo of her face when they tell her.'

We left the graveyard and began to walk back into the city, counting the paving stones, red cars, and trees as we went. As we approached the Balmoral Hotel, an older couple was walking down the steps. He wore a suit and she was perfectly manicured. His gaze settled on me and his eyes widened as he gripped his companion's arm. She lifted her face and her gaze followed his. Her hand came up to cover her mouth and she reached out for him to steady herself.

My heart twinged for a split second until I tilted my face up to look at my little boy where he sat giggling and singing along to a nursery rhyme with his beautiful mother, and we kept on walking by.

'Finlay?' A wavering voice came from over my shoulder. I stopped briefly and turned to face the couple on the steps of the stunning old building. But I didn't speak. Familiar blue eyes filled with regret pleaded with me, and I smiled knowingly. But not out of love. Out of pity. Those two people, my parents, had missed out on so much. Especially the new life that my wife and I had created.

I turned back to continue walking, and Star gripped my hand tightly. 'Are you okay, honey?'

I bent to kiss her cheek and reassured her, 'I'm wonderful, thanks, sweetheart.'

Forbes tapped my head. 'Who were that old mister and lady, Daddy? They looked weally sad.'

I lifted him down from my shoulders and held

him close to me as I kissed his head. 'Oh, they were just some people I used to know a long time ago, son. Now, come on. Let's go get that worm-flavoured ice cream.'

He scrunched his cute little button nose. 'Euugh! No, Daddy. I want tocolit and rapsaberry.'

I rolled my eyes playfully. 'Oh, *okay* then. I *suppose* so.'

Forbes giggled and his laughter reached in and warmed my heart. With one hand holding my son, I linked my free hand with my wife's, kissed the side of her head and whispered, 'I love you so much, Star Hunter.'

'And I love you too, Fin Hunter.'

A voice from between us chimed in, 'And I love you both!'

MORE FROM LISA HOBMAN

We hope you enjoyed reading *It Started with a Kiss*. If you did, please leave a review.

If you'd like to gift a copy, this book is also available as an ebook, digital audio download and audiobook CD.

Sign up to Lisa Hobman's mailing list for news, competitions and updates on future books.

https://bit.ly/LisaHobmanNewsletter

Dreaming Under An Island Skye, another uplifting and feel-good read from Lisa Hobman, is available to order now.

Dreaming
under an
Island Skye
Lisa Hobman
You can take your
memories anywhere

ABOUT THE AUTHOR

Lisa Hobman has written many brilliantly reviewed women's fiction titles - the first of which was short-listed by the RNA for their debut novel award. In 2012 Lisa relocated her family from Yorkshire to a village in Scotland and this beautiful backdrop now inspires her uplifting and romantic stories.

Visit Lisa's website: http://www.lisajhobman.com

Follow Lisa on social media:

facebook.com/LisaJHobmanAuthor

twitter.com/@LisaJHobmanAuthor

instagram.com/lisahobmanauthor

ABOUT BOLDWOOD BOOKS

Boldwood Books is a fiction publishing company seeking out the best stories from around the world.

Find out more at www.boldwoodbooks.com

Sign up to the Book and Tonic newsletter for news, offers and competitions from Boldwood Books!

http://www.bit.ly/bookandtonic

We'd love to hear from you, follow us on social media:

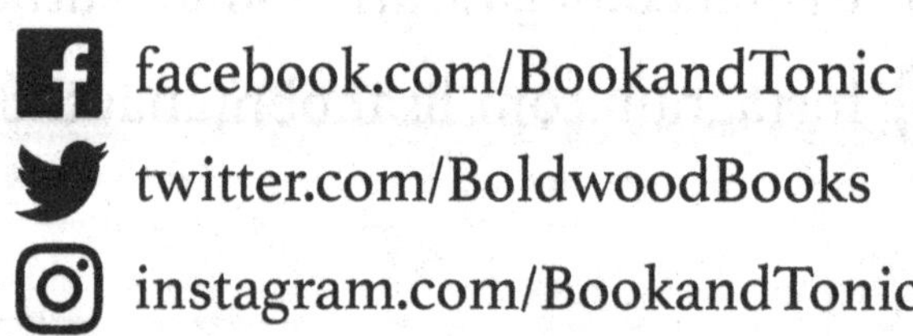

facebook.com/BookandTonic

twitter.com/BoldwoodBooks

instagram.com/BookandTonic